DELICIOUS SURRENDER

"You must be a devil," Meg whispered. "You've made me forget everything but you."

A light touched his eyes, and Kalib grinned. "You'd laugh if I told you my reason for hunting treasure. It's very similar to your reason for building railroads."

"Tell me," she teased. "I need a laugh."

Kalib shook his head solemnly. "No, Maggie, my love. I know what you need and, right now, it isn't laughter."

As she closed her eyes in surrender, he claimed her lips, arousing her fully with sensual kisses. She had no idea why she stood so still, unprotesting, under his wanton ministrations. But she did know one thing for certain: she could no more have stopped Kalib from making love to her than she could have stopped the moon from rising . . . and she had no desire to stop either one. . . .

ZEBRA'S GOT THE ROMANCE
TO SET YOUR HEART AFIRE!

RAGING DESIRE (2242, $3.75)
by Colleen Faulkner

A wealthy gentleman and officer in General Washington's army, Devon Marsh wasn't meant for the likes of Cassie O'Flynn, an immigrant bond servant. But from the moment their lips first met, Cassie knew she could love no other . . . even if it meant marching into the flames of war to make him hers!

TEXAS TWILIGHT (2241, $3.75)
by Vivian Vaughan

When handsome Trace Garrett stepped onto the porch of the Santa Clara ranch, he wove a rapturous spell around Clara Ehler's heart. Though Clara planned to sell the spread and move back East, Trace was determined to keep her on the wild Western frontier where she belonged — to share with him the glory and the splendor of the passion-filled TEXAS TWILIGHT.

RENEGADE HEART (2244, $3.75)
by Marjorie Price

Strong-willed Hannah Hatch resented her imprisonment by Captain Jake Farnsworth, even after the daring Yankee had rescued her from bloodthirsty marauders. And though Jake's rock-hard physique made Hannah tremble with desire, the spirited beauty was nevertheless resolved to exploit her femininity to the fullest and gain her independence from the virile bluecoat.

LOVING CHALLENGE (2243, $3.75)
by Carol King

When the notorious Captain Dominic Warbrooke burst into Laurette Harker's eighteenth birthday ball, the accomplished beauty challenged the arrogant scoundrel to a duel. But when the captain named her innocence as his stakes, Laurette was terrified she'd not only lose the fight, but her heart as well!

Available wherever paperbacks are sold, or order direct from the Publisher. Send cover price plus 50¢ per copy for mailing and handling to Zebra Books, Dept. 2610, 475 Park Avenue South, New York, N.Y. 10016. Residents of New York, New Jersey and Pennsylvania must include sales tax. DO NOT SEND CASH.

SWEET TEXAS NIGHTS
Vivian Vaughan

ZEBRA BOOKS are published by

Kensington Publishing Corp.
475 Park Avenue South
New York, NY 10016

ZEBRA BOOKS
KENSINGTON PUBLISHING CORP.

ZEBRA BOOKS

are published by

Kensington Publishing Corp.
475 Park Avenue South
New York, NY 10016

First printing: March, 1989

Printed in the United States of America

This Book is Dedicated,
With
Love and Devotion,
To the People in My Hometown

The Indians called it Summer Valley.
J. Frank Dobie called us "Coronado's Children."
In my four Zebra Books, I have called it Silver Creek.

We Call Ourselves
The Free State of Menard

But to see her was to love her,
Love but her, and love for ever.
Had we never lov'd sae kindly,
Had we never lov'd sae blindly,
Never met—or never parted—
We had ne'er been broken-hearted.

From "Ae Fond Kiss"
Robert Burns

Chapter One

Silver Creek, Texas
October 23, 1889

Exasperation brewed in the pit of her stomach as Meg Britton pulled on her robe and hurried across the parlor of the spacious suite she shared with her father, Rube, on the upper floor of the Hotel O'Keefe.

"I'm coming . . . I'm coming," she called in answer to the persistent rattling of the door. It's Rube, she thought angrily, drunk again. Why don't I ever learn not to trust him?

Turning the key in the lock, she jerked the door open, ready to lay into him, as he so often accused her of doing these days, only to find herself face to face with Grady Thornton, Rube's assistant chief engineer.

"Uncle Grady," she whispered. Her exasperation quickly developed into a heightening sense of anxiety. Standing aside, she motioned the assistant chief engineer into her parlor. She'd known Grady Thornton since, in his words, she was knee-high to a railroad tie, and of all the men Rube had ever worked with, Uncle Grady was the only one who understood his problem with Demon Rum. Or Rye. Or Redeye. Or whatever happened to be Di's latest concoction at the Diamond-Stacker Palace Saloon in the current edition of Hell on Wheels. In spite of Di, however, Meg and Uncle Grady usually managed to keep

9

Rube in line.

Or had, she thought ruefully, until four years ago when Uncle Grady took a job on the Great Northern up in Montana. About that time, Rube had sent Meg back East to school, and he'd promptly lost his job with the Santa Fe Railroad.

Meg clenched her straight white teeth. But she was back now, educated and ready to take care of him again.

And Grady was back.

And Di. . . .

Anxiety boiled inside Meg, spreading fear and disappointment like Dr. Townsend's Wizard Oil through her veins, along with something else—something very close to despair, she now realized.

"What's happened, Uncle Grady? Where's Rube?"

The lumbering, gray-headed man twirled his cap in his hamlike hands, looking for all the world like an ox out of the woods in this elegant hotel suite. "I was hoping to find him here." He avoided her eyes.

Softhearted Uncle Grady. She sighed, wondering for the umpteenth time how he'd ever found himself in the rough-and-tumble business of building railroads. "And I hoped he was at the end of track with you. He hasn't been back to Silver Creek for almost a week."

"He *was* at camp," Grady told her, then shook his head. "Haven't seen him, though, since early morning two days back. We've got a little problem needs his attention."

Meg laughed, but the sound was bitter, like the stench of last night's whiskey. "Likely a lot of things on this railroad need the attention of the chief engineer." Tears welled in her eyes, and she quickly squenched her lids against them. No sense crying over Rube Britton at this late date. If she started, she'd never have reason to quit. "I made a big mistake, trying to straighten him out again. It's a losing battle, Uncle Grady."

The older man patted her arm sympathetically. "Don't you go getting worked up, missy. We've trod this road before, and we'll like as not travel it again. But we need Rube to set the railroad clear into Silver Creek by the

10

deadline those danged politicians laid on us. Reckon I'll go look in on Hell on Wheels."

Meg straightened her shoulders. Uncle Grady was right. The railroad *must* be finished on time. And to accomplish that, they had to keep Rube off the juice. But Uncle Grady had never been able to straighten out his old friend by himself.

"I'll go," Meg said. "Tell me what the problem is."

Grady stared at her with his soft gray eyes, and she knew he understood the situation as well as she did. "Some danged fool prospector fired on the graders when they reached the Silver Creek River crossing yesterday. Won't let 'em budge an inch in his direction without firing rounds of buckshot at them."

Meg squinted, thoughtful. "The right of ways have all been secured . . . ?" she muttered, half in thought, half in question.

"Sure have, missy. Rube and me went over the paper work together. But paper don't go far in stopping buckshot."

"We'll see about that," Meg vowed. "The law's the law. And since it's on our side, your prospector will have to relent or go to jail. I might just take the sheriff with me."

"Missy," Grady objected, "don't be riding out there yourself. That man's plumb dangerous. Rube'll know how to handle the situation—he's good at those things—once we get him dried out."

With a halfhearted grin, Meg placed her hand on Uncle Grady's shoulder. "Once we get him dried out," she repeated. "I know you have other work to do, so you go on ahead. I'll meet you at the Diamond-Stacker."

After Grady Thornton left her suite, Meg dressed quickly, steeled by the knowledge that he was right—they had sobered Rube up on more occasions than she cared to recall, and likely they'd do it a few more times before the one hundred eighty-one miles of railroad between Summer Valley and Silver Creek were completed. Luckily, she'd grown up with railroad building. Wasn't that why she had returned? To keep Rube on the job?

11

Throwing aside her batiste and lace morning robe, Meg surveyed her wardrobe, while fury mounted within her. Fury at the present situation Rube had thrown her into, fury at the past.

Especially the immediate past, she thought, examining her wardrobe full of new clothes. For graduation three months earlier, Rube had sent her five hundred dollars, along with instructions to buy herself a fancy, "working girl's" wardrobe. At the time she'd been overjoyed, never mind the fact she hadn't for a moment intended to carry out his other instructions: to take the position she had been offered as a language instructor at the proper girls' school, until "the right gentleman came to call."

The four years she had been away from him had been the most miserable of her life, something she had difficulty understanding, given the fact that her whole life had been spent drying Rube out from one drunk after another. She should have been relieved to get away from the headaches of keeping him sober and on the job. But all she thought about the entire four years was Rube. Was he eating all right? Was he sleeping enough? Was he working? Was he sober?

She knew her fears should have been assuaged by the checks for her education, which arrived regularly, always on time and for more than ample sums. But they weren't. She missed him. She longed to be back with him. After the excitement of the world of railroad building, boarding school was dreadfully boring.

She sighed. It was more than that. At school no one knew Rube Britton. Everyone had fathers, and each girl thought hers more important than any other.

Even though she kept it to herself, Meg knew different. Her pride swelled with the knowledge that her father was the best railroader in the entire country. Why, she couldn't count the number of times she had heard higher railroad officials—all except that damnable general manager Leslie "Rattlesnake" Hayden, of course—exclaim that with Rube Britton in charge, any railroad could be built, anywhere, no matter how short the time.

12

With long, slender fingers, she pushed her near waist-length chestnut hair back from her face and sighed again. What these officials didn't know, of course, was that keeping him on the job required a prize-winning performance itself.

Grabbing her mahogany wool grenadine riding habit from its hanger, she searched the bureau drawer for a matching linen collar and cuff set, then pursed her lips and took out two sets, one to wear today and another to take along in her tapestry satchel with extra changes of clothing. When one started out after Rube Britton, one never knew how long the journey would be, nor where the road would lead.

Incredulously, she recognized the thrill of excitement stir inside her stomach. Stretching on her stockings, she adjusted her riding corset and pulled on her trousers, fitting the cloth stirrups beneath her insteps, before she stepped into polished mahogany boots. Could it be, she wondered, that she was as addicted to this outrageous lifestyle as Rube was to his cups?

She bent at the waist, brushed her chestnut hair to a lustrous sheen. Then, with rat in place, she quickly and expertly swept her mass of silky hair into a fashionable pompadour. Absently plucking loose hair and tangles from her brush, she stuffed them through the hole in the lid of the porcelain hair receiver on her bureau. Rats didn't last forever, she thought idly. Soon she would have enough loose hair to send back East to have another one made.

Looking up, she saw for the first time her deep scowl reflected in the looking glass, and she grimaced. He wouldn't do it to her. He absolutely wouldn't, she vowed. Rube Britton was not going to turn her into a shrew. He'd sent her to school to prepare her to be a lady, and damn him if she wasn't going to turn out to be one! Even if he did prefer the company of soiled doves like Di, Queen of the Diamond-Stacker Palace Saloon.

Sustained somewhat by kindling anger, she buttoned on her swag skirt and the tightly fitted basque with prim

13

collar and cuffs attached, then snatched up her gloves and riding crop. It wasn't until she stepped into the saddle of a rented sorrel horse that she recalled she had hurried away from the hotel without so much as a cup of coffee—or her hat and veil.

"I'm headed to see my father at the end of the track," she told the ancient hostler. "I may keep this horse a week or more."

Then, as she guided the mare into the filtered sunlight of the hazy fall morning, the slight figure of Ellsworth Fredericks, editor of the *Silver Creek Sun*, scurried toward her.

"Where're you headed, Miss Britton?" the editor asked in his rather high-pitched voice. "Is there trouble at the end of track? I saw Assistant Chief Thornton arrive and take off again like a rocket on the Fourth of July. What's up?"

Meg inhaled a slow breath to steady her quickly rising sense of indignation. Ellsworth Fredericks had been a nuisance, at best, since her arrival in Silver Creek three weeks earlier. Always nosing around, never trying to see the positive things going on with the railroad, he looked only for something sordid. Even Rube Britton—especially Rube Britton, she corrected herself—didn't need such haggling.

"Trouble, Mr. Fredericks?" As she spoke, Meg fixed him with the coldest stare she could conjure from the depths of her moiling stomach. "Whatever gave you such a . . ." *No, Margaret Marie Britton*, she cautioned herself, *do not call the local editor foolish. Nor stupid.* Her lips curved in a cold smile. ". . . such a false notion? I'm merely riding out to spend a few days with my overworked father. Good day."

Even though she had never traveled this country before, the ride to Hell on Wheels would be simple, Meg told herself. All she need do was follow the survey markers. Simple. The survey had been completed for the entire one hundred eighty-one miles of this spur from Summer

14

Valley west to Silver Creek before she arrived. Drawing a deep draft of early fall air into her lungs, she spurred her mount.

Before she arrived. She sighed, thinking back on her arrival, not in Silver Creek, but two months earlier, in Austin, where she had returned unannounced—unexpected and unwanted, too, judging by the cool reception she received from Rube and Di.

What a stir her arrival had caused. Rube was drunk. Down and out, really. And Di was *caring* for him—if feeding him drinks by the barrel could be called caring for a man with a problem the size of Rube Britton's. Of course, there wasn't much work building railroads, these days.

This was election year in Texas, and the political controversy centered on corruption in the railroad business. Texas had not built a single mile of track in all of 1889, until some smart politician got the brilliant idea to set a spur from Summer Valley to Silver Creek.

One hundred eighty-one and fifteen-hundredths miles, to be exact. Not many railroad miles for a state where the record was in the thousands. That it was political, they all knew.

Yet, it was exactly what the doctor ordered, as far as Meg was concerned. A gift from Heaven, dropped straight into their collective lap. A chance for Rube to get back to work . . . back into life . . . to reclaim his reputation of bygone days.

Of course, Rube wanted no part of it. But Meg insisted. Meg dried him out, cleaned him up—with Di's help, she now admitted grudgingly to herself—and Meg prevailed.

Meg applied for the contracts. She even sent wires to reassemble the crews. Then she moved them all to head of line—Summer Valley, Texas.

Uncle Grady returned, unconvinced at first, but after she talked to him, he, too, agreed it was worth a try.

Scotty McCaa put his surveying crews into the field immediately, while Portis Flannery dragged his Irish tracklayers out of the bars in Summer Valley where they awaited word on who would be awarded the contracts. Jerry Sullivan gathered his bridge monkeys. The construction train was outfitted, and contracts were let for livestock to feed the various crews.

A couple of things worried Meg. The foremost, at least until they all got into the field, had been General Manager Leslie Hayden. She'd had to work overtime to convince him Rube could and *would* do the job. When they left Austin, Hayden still had a tight-lipped "hide and wait" attitude, waiting and watching, Meg knew, for Rube to slip.

But Rube had surprised everyone. Meg guided her mount absently in and around the clumps of mesquite grass and prickly pear. Once he got a grip on himself, once the contracts were awarded, Rube had taken control as though the whole affair had been his own idea. Like in the old days, she mused. Like in the *best* of the old days.

Some of his directives didn't set too well with her, she admitted. Especially his insistence that she move to the end of line, Silver Creek, so she could coordinate the town's part of the bargain from the hotel there.

She went along with it, because Rube promised to stay in the hotel with her, and because she recognized that someone was needed in Silver Creek: the depot and loading and holding pens had to be completed on land the community provided. And most important of all, the citizens of Silver Creek must be kept constantly aware of their bond obligation to the railroad. Without the periodic payments the community was obligated under contract to make, the workers could not be paid, the supplies would not be forthcoming, and the entire operation would fall flat on its—Rube's—face.

And now this. It appeared the good old days were returning, full steam ahead.

Feeling its heat penetrate her piled-up hair, Meg suddenly realized the sun had burned away the early morning haze. She longed for her forgotten hat and veil. Crossing a stream, she topped a small rise, where she sat

16

her mount beneath a large mesquite tree and mopped her face with a handkerchief taken from her sleeve. Now, Rube had done it again.

With a start, her thoughts returned to the present. *Now*, she thought, clamping her teeth over her bottom lip in a completely new line of thought, now, she'd done it herself. Where were those dratted survey stakes?

She scanned the area. The rise where she sat was by no means the highest point around, but she could see a good distance. And nowhere in sight. . . .

Nowhere in this vast, empty land did she see even one survey stake. She swallowed. Not one.

The enormous emptiness spread around her endlessly, and she berated herself aloud. Why couldn't she keep her mind on the business at hand? Turning the mare with a jerk of the reins, she retraced her steps, her eyes trained on the ground beneath her horse's hooves. Finally, her persistence was rewarded. Across the stream, she found a stake.

One stake. Turning back toward the direction where she supposed the numerous dirty tents of Hell on Wheels to be, she searched the area rock by rock. Urging her mount forward, she held the reins tightly in her leather-clad, now damp hands, studying the ground below her and ahead of her at an orderly pace.

Then she saw the river, and she sighed with relief. The Silver Creek River. Surely, she could find her way, now. Hell on Wheels had been moved only this week to its new location, ten miles east of the Silver Creek River. The crews would be even closer. She strained to hear the ring of maul on spike.

Suddenly her eyes widened in terror, as she recalled her conversation with Uncle Grady earlier this morning, and along with it, the sole reason she had set out to ride through this desolate wilderness all alone.

The prospector. He'd fired on the grading crew as they approached the river. She swallowed. The Silver Creek River.

17

Her shoulder blades tensed involuntarily. Carefully, she swiveled in the saddle to survey the country. Her ears fairly prickled in expectation of a gunshot. What was it they said? Would she hear the shot first? Or feel it?

When neither of the above transpired, Meg gingerly urged the sorrel horse forward, toward the river. After a few more moments, during which none of her gravest fears were realized, she relaxed a bit and began to look for a place to cross the river. There must be a shallow place nearby.

The country around her could be termed rolling, she supposed. Grass-covered rises, slight enough to allow almost uninterrupted vision, stretched around her, tapering to the river, then continued in an undulating motion that mimicked the swaying yellow grass beneath her. North, a couple of hundred yards to her left, a higher range of hills ran perpendicular to the water, with cliffs dropping off sharply, as though scooped out by some giant hand to allow passage of the Silver Creek River.

Nudging the sorrel down a slope and around a slight bend, she studied the river in front of her and behind, searching for a shallow crossing, which appeared as though on command, just around the bend. Balking at entering the gravel-bottomed stream, however, her horse put up such a fuss to drink that Meg dismounted, and with reins held firmly in her gloved hands, she let the mare drink. Then she knelt on the gravel bank herself, drew off a glove, and attempted to quench her own thirst with a palmful of cool water. About all she accomplished was to wet her lips and the few strands of loose hair flying about her face.

Rising, she dusted her skirts, adjusted her basque, and drew a deep breath, thoughts of the prospector nudging the back of her mind.

Vying for her attention, though, were fierce mental denouncements of the survey crew. She clearly recalled Scotty McCaa's telling Rube he had set the line the full distance. But she had seen no stakes for half a mile or

18

better. Instead of crossing the river, she remounted and rode north along the bank, searching for signs of the survey.

Finally, she stopped and studied the terrain. They wouldn't lay the railroad on ground so low it would be swept away by floods. She knew that much. They would choose a sturdy embankment to support the trestle for the bridge.

Sweeping her hair back from her face, she held it there with her hand a moment, studying the situation. That long range of hills appeared, to her mind at least, to be the best place in the area for a trestle bridge. Could she have ridden this far afield merely by not paying attention?

With a heel to its flank, she urged the sorrel to a lope, feeling more foolish by the minute. The stakes were probably there, she told herself, right where Scotty's crew set them. She'd just ridden astray.

Suddenly dust kicked up well in front of her mount. Her horse shied and reared on his hind legs. The report of a rifle shattered the silence. By the time she managed to bring the sorrel under control, she felt so weak she feared she might very well slide off the saddle.

Grasping the saddlehorn, she forced herself to look in the direction from which the shot had come.

A lone rider sat his horse a good fifty feet in front of her. The range of hills loomed behind him. She swallowed, but her throat was so dry she felt like she hadn't had a drink of water in a week. She ran her tongue around her mouth, between her gums and lips, thinking . . . thinking . . . thinking.

This man must be the prospector, she reasoned, even though she had never envisioned a treasure hunter riding a fine bay horse. And why did he sit so deathly still? Her tensed muscles trembled. *Don't even think the word deathly*, she admonished herself furiously.

Her brain spun. Since she was here, she should . . .

Her backbone drooped forward like a coiled rope, but she resisted. Forceably straightening her shoulders, she used all her strength to hold them in place. She was here; he was here; she must talk to him. Perhaps, she could solve the problem before she even saw Rube. Time was, after all, very short. The entire railroad had to be finished and dedicated within the next two and a half months.

But this man had fired on the crew, her brain recanted, and at her. She studied him carefully, desperately trying to keep her eyes steady and her head from shaking. Loose hair whispered about her eyes in the breeze, and she bit her lip to keep her anxieties inside.

He hadn't killed . . . nor even injured . . . anyone. Uncle Grady said he fired *at* the crew; he didn't hit anyone.

She nudged the sorrel forward with trembling knees, step by slow step. Her hands felt welded to the saddlehorn. What would Rube say? she thought. He'd taught her never to hold the saddlehorn—a tenderfoot clung to a saddlehorn.

The man sat his horse without moving a muscle, his rifle held casually across his lap. Only his ramrod-straight stature bespoke his threatening intentions.

Her eyes never wavered from his as she approached him slowly. But when she was no closer than twenty yards away, he raised his rifle and motioned her to halt.

"That's far enough, ma'am," he called. "You must have lost your way." He nodded his head toward Silver Creek. "Town's about ten miles thataway."

"I'm not going to Silver Creek," Meg answered tentatively, trying to keep her voice steady.

"Well, you're not coming this way, either," the man replied, after a pause to reflect. "This is private property. You're tres . . ."

"It certainly is private property," Meg answered, anger fueling her fears. "It belongs to the railroad, and you're the one who is trespassing."

The man shrugged, but his rifle remained steady. "You must have ridden astray," he answered. "Now get moving. We've work to do here."

Meg inhaled a deep breath, for courage, she thought. Of

course, she'd ridden astray. But not that far astray. The railroad survey was somewhere in this very area, and since she was here, facing the prospector . . .

"I have not lost my way, sir," she told him. "I have come purposely to speak with the prospector who fired upon our railroad crew. Are you he?"

The man frowned beneath his floppy broad-brimmed hat. He considered her silently a moment before answering. "I work for the prospector," he said. "I'll relay your message, but I must tell you again, you're trespassing, and you are not welcome here. State your business, and be gone."

"My business is with the prospector," Meg insisted, feeling her blood stir inside her veins. The fact that this man wasn't who she thought him to be both relieved and further angered her. She'd often seen Rube thwarted by obstinate property owners who refused to deal directly with him. No wonder he'd been driven to drink!

"I will speak only with the prospector," she repeated. "And I will not leave until I do. Even if he is so weak a man that he hides behind someone else's gun."

The man facing her winced at her disparaging remarks, and she thought she saw a hint of humor, even though his face was covered with a thick mass of unruly brown hair. "What you think, ma'am, is your own affair, but the man you wish to speak with is busy. I'm perfectly capable of relaying your message."

"I am sure you are," Meg began, thinking that their camp must lie behind him, beyond the ridge of hills. If she could manage . . . As she spoke, she urged her mount forward with, thankfully, steady knees. "However, sir, time is short. I have neither the patience nor the inclination to deal with second fiddles." Meg fixed him with an icy stare, and at the same moment shoved her heels into the flanks of the sorrel.

The horseman was surprisingly quick. In one fluid motion he spurred his horse across her path and reached for her reins.

"What's the problem, Tobin?"

The voice was so loud and deep it sounded like thunder. Meg jerked in her saddle as its impact reverberated through her taut muscles. Instantly, she looked toward the source of the sound, and the very sight of the hairy giant who stood straddle-legged atop the hill froze her blood in her veins.

She started to speak, but could find no semblance of a voice left in her body. Her mouth was open, she sensed it, but for a moment, all she could do was stare transfixed in terror.

The prospector.

Kalib had just left their camp to search the cave one more time in confirmation of the new evidence they turned up when he heard the shot. Thinking the railroaders had returned, he smiled. Tobin would take care of them.

Sure enough, he heard voices, Tobin's call to halt, and . . . he stopped to listen, well hidden on the opposite side of the ridge of hills.

A woman's lilting, musical voice—no matter that it was raised in anger. How long had it been since he'd so much as heard a woman speak? Turning, he advanced toward the hillside, keeping behind cover.

Then he glimpsed her, sitting primly erect astride her horse, all decked out in proper riding habit with white collar and cuffs, no less.

His pulse quickened at the sight of her, regardless of the fact that he abhorred prim and proper ladies, the kind he would be destined to spend the remainder of his life with, if his dear mother had her way.

Even from a distance, he could see that this lady, for all her propriety, was nothing short of an enchantress. Chestnut hair flying about her oval-shaped face . . . whoever heard of a lady going bareheaded, without so much as a parasol for protection against the sun's blistering rays?

And she definitely had spunk. He chuckled. Wasn't she giving old Tobin a tongue-lashing? Then she looked toward the hill and saw him.

22

Their eyes held across the distance. The once limitless space suddenly shrank to include only the two of them and the mere fifty yards or so separating them, one from the other.

Kalib stepped forward. A warning voice within called him back, but he waved it aside. He would only say hello, see what the problem was, get a look at her up close. She wouldn't recognize him, not in a million years in the disguise he'd grown. . . .

He ran a hand clumsily through his unkempt black hair, fingered his unruly beard. Why hadn't he combed his hair, trimmed his beard, washed his face?

"Get on back over the hill," Tobin called, but Kalib never broke his stride. Her skin reminded him of his grandmother's cameo pin, smooth and delicate, pink tinted from the sun. . . .

"Go back to camp," Tobin insisted. "I'll handle this."

With difficulty, as though he feared she might disappear before he returned to her, Kalib drew his eyes away from the apparition in the valley and gave his friend and defender a reassuring look.

"I can manage, Tobin. You run on back. . . ."

"You don't know what you're saying," Tobin insisted. "She's with the railroad."

Kalib shrugged. "So, I'll hear her out." He stared hard at Tobin. "She isn't even armed, for God's sake. Go ahead, leave it to me."

Tobin stared at first one, then the other. "We agreed. . . ." he began harshly. "You were to stay out. . . ."

"I said, leave it to me." With that Kalib returned his full attention to Meg, listening with half an ear to Tobin's horse clatter over the rocky valley and up the hill. He'd stay close, Kalib knew, within sight. But that was far enough away that he would have this beautiful creature's full attention . . . and she would have his. He cocked an eyebrow. "To what do I owe this unexpected visit?"

Meg had stared at him from the time she first saw him standing on the hill, seeing first only his outward, frightening appearance—his tumbled-up state, as if he'd never seen sight of a razor or a bar of soap; his size—the closer he came the larger he appeared. But he walked with a natural grace, and even the loose cotton garments he wore could not conceal a quality of refinement in his movements. And his eyes . . .

His eyes, though brown instead of black, were nevertheless almost as dark as his ebony hair, and as he drew closer and spoke, they glowed, showering her with a warmth that had nothing to do with the sun pouring down on her head.

Suddenly she knew she was in the presence of a man very used to turning heads and stopping spinning universes. *But to see him was to love him,* her mind thought crazily, paraphrasing a line from her favorite of all Robert Burns's poems.

Blinking, she grappled with her wayward brain. Somehow she had lost sight of where she was and why she was there, and she had to scramble to find the right emotions from the multitude bombarding her senses.

Incredibly, her fear had vanished completely, a fact that both surprised and infuriated her. She gritted her teeth, allowing her anger to build naturally within her quivering body. Finally, she slid purposefully to the ground and challenged him with fists on hips.

"Don't flatter yourself," she said. "This is not a social call. I'm here on behalf of the railroad. I demand an explanation for your firing upon our graders."

Kalib stroked his bearded chin and studied her quizzically with tilted head. "On behalf of the railroad?" he asked, nodding seriously, while a taunting smile gleamed in his eyes. "And just what might your position with the railroad be?" Suddenly, his eyes widened, parodying surprise. "Don't tell me . . . you're a gandy-dancer!"

Meg glared at him. Then, as the absurdity of his suggestion hit home—the idea of her imitating the brawny Irish tracklayers' dancelike movements for driving steel spikes into the track with their heavy steel mauls—she laughed in spite of herself.

24

His eyes softened. Quickly, he gave her a thorough, and alarmingly improper, inspection. His answering laugh resounded through her suddenly quivering nerve endings, and she stiffened.

If she were to solve Rube's problem, she told herself emphatically, she must present her case in a dignified, businesslike manner, never mind the fact that this oaf likely didn't know the meaning of either word.

Squaring her shoulders, she raised her chin and offered him her hand. "I'm Margaret Britton," she answered in clipped tones. "My father is chief engineer of the spur being built through this area, and I've come for an explanation of your actions against our graders."

Kalib took her hand, and the instant her flesh touched his she regretted not replacing her glove after her unsuccessful attempt to drink from the river. Her elbow tensed and a flush sped up her neck at the very idea he might have noticed the tremor she felt at his touch.

Squeezing his hand around hers to thwart her attempt to withdraw from the handshake, Kalib stared at her and unconsciously wetted his lips with the tip of his tongue.

Her backbone seemed suddenly turned to jelly; her legs sagged above her knee-high boots. Her eyelids attempted to close, and she furiously fought to gain control.

However could she be expected to deal with such a man? Standing so close, not two feet separating them, he loomed head and shoulders above her—she swallowed—and she was no slouch herself at five foot six in her stocking feet.

He was so covered with hair, she couldn't even see him well—only his penetrating eyes—his black eyebrows, tilted at a taunting angle, and his lips. . . .

Full, chiseled, moist now from his tongue. . . .

"Maggie Britton," he boomed in the thundering voice that had been her first introduction to this dreadful man. Forewarned, she thought dismally, wishing she had been able to hold on to her fear of him.

He loosened her hand, but she barely had time to give silent thanks before she realized that he retained the reins to her horse and was now proceeding to tie the animal to a low branch of a nearby mesquite tree.

"Margaret," she corrected, to his back, then added fiercely, "*Miss* Britton, to you."

When he turned, his smile had broadened into a huge, devilish grin, exposing glistening, perfectly formed white teeth, and suddenly she wondered what he really looked like. Was the rest of him—she swallowed again—the rest of his *face* as perfect as the few exposed parts?

"Miss," he mused, returning to her with slow, infuriatingly arrogant steps. "How fortunate. How very, very fortunate."

"The business at hand, Mr. . . . ." She stopped abruptly, wondering, quite without her own approval to do so, what his name was. "The bus . . ."

"You can call me Kalib," he said, knowing Tobin would be furious with him, absolutely furious, that he dared give his name to anyone.

Meg gritted her teeth and stared at him through narrowed eyes. How dare he put their relationship on such a personal, first-name, basis? "The business, sir," she resumed. "If you will please tell me your grievance with the railroad, and give me your assurance that you will honor our right of way. . . ."

"Now, Maggie, how can I do that, when it's the railroad who isn't honoring *my* rights?"

Meg inhaled, started to object to his use of that dreadful name, then decided to ignore him—as best she could. "The railroad has secured the necessary rights of way for the entire spur," she told him. "The survey has been completed, and we have clearly marked our two hundred feet. All you have to do is leave the graders alone so they can prepare the bed." A second thought struck her, which she added. "We're working on a very tight schedule, so the bridge monkeys will begin the trestles shortly. They will not bother you, and you are not to bother them. You may go about your business . . . looking for gold or treasure or whatever it is you do out here, without interfering

26

with us."

While she spoke, Kalib stood, fists on hips, watching her so intently that she finally had to look away in order to retain any sort of control over the situation.

He grinned and took the opportunity to study her openly from head to foot. She was indeed the most beautiful woman he had come across in some time. No, he corrected himself, running his tongue around his dry lips once again, Maggie Britton was the most beautiful and spirited woman he had ever seen—in all his thirty-five years. He pursed his lips. Something deep inside told him that her kind happened along only once in a lifetime . . . and then, only if a man were truly under the watchful eye of Providence.

Still thinking along those lines, Kalib cleared his throat. "Who sent you out here, Maggie?" Even her name was magical, he thought, grinning as fire spit from her green eyes when he spoke it—emerald green, more magnificent even than his grandmother's prized emerald ring.

"My father is Rube Britton." She paused to let the name penetrate his thick skull. When it didn't, she sighed. She was indeed dealing with a backwoodsman. "Rube Britton is chief engineer of this railroad," she repeated. "He's the best railroader in the entire . . ."

"Then why did he send a girl to do his work?"

Her eyes flared, and he felt the fire from their green depths penetrate his lonely soul. Lonely soul? He scowled. He wasn't lonely. He hadn't known it, anyhow, until this moment.

"I can see I'm wasting my time trying to reason with you," Meg stormed. "The sheriff will be out with eviction papers."

Reality suddenly struck Kalib, and he moved with the speed of a panther, grabbing her arm and jerking her toward him. "Like hell, he will." He practically shouted in her face. Pulling her around, he pointed to the range of hills directly behind them. "That's where your damned surveyors put their stakes, and I pulled them up. That hill

27

belongs to me."

She jerked to free her arm from his grasp. "It certainly does not," she retorted. "It belongs to the railroad. You will not get away with this. I promise you, you won't." She clamped her teeth tightly together to stop her trembling voice. "The new governor of Texas is going to dedicate this railroad two weeks after he takes office in January. It has to be finished by then, and it will be. Some . . . some . . . some ne'er-do-well like you is not going to stop my father from building this railroad."

Kalib bristled at her words, then he grinned. At this point, he definitely resembled a ne'er-do-well, along with a passel of other unsavory things. But regardless of what she called him, Maggie Britton was as attracted to him as he was to her. She might deny the fact, but she hadn't been very successful at hiding it. And he had no intention of letting her get away from him.

Neither did he intend to stand by and let her expose him to the sheriff . . . nor to anyone else in these parts.

"Certificates of right of way have been known to be wrong," he ventured.

She glared at him.

He shrugged. "Why don't you contact the land office in Austin. They'll tell you who holds title to this land."

Still she stared at him.

"You can't run me off my own land, Maggie."

Enraged, she found her voice. "I can do anything," she said, "anything it takes to get this railroad built on time. I may not like it, but I can do whatever has to be done. And I will."

She turned on her heel and strode toward the mesquite tree where he had tied her horse. Before she took two steps, however, Kalib grabbed her by the arm and swung her around.

As she turned, her eyes met and locked with his in an instant frozen somewhere in time and space. Later, it would seem like an eternity. Later, she would realize that her eyes had sought his . . . by choice. Had she merely looked along her own line of vision, she would have stared somewhere in the neighborhood of the top buttonhole on his coarse brown vest.

But in that one magical moment, no thoughts interrupted the intense fusion of their two separate, yet united, wills. Her senses drugged by some very real, yet totally unfamiliar sensation, she felt herself pulled to him, as though she were on the end of a rope, which he ever so gradually drew forward hand over hand, until at last their lips met, and time resumed its normal hell-bent-for-leather pace.

Kalib's heart beat wildly as he slowly pulled her to him, conscious only of her face, her searching green eyes, her rosy parted lips. When, lowering his head, he at last covered her lips with his, it was with a combined sense of culmination and beginnings all rolled into one.

Her timid response became eager beneath his caressing kiss, fueling the fire inside him with increasingly urgent desires. Releasing his grasp, he circled her with his arms and drew her close, groaning with the pleasurable feel of her very womanly body next to his.

His lips touched hers, and Meg's heart throbbed painfully against her corset, as though in an effort to free her to experience to the fullest this, her very first, kiss. And it was as different from what she had expected as peppermint candy was from sparkling champagne. His lips were soft, moist, and warm against her own, and as they moved over hers in caressing, plucking motions, her whole body became infused with a fiery, liquid heat, pulsating in exotic rhythms.

His fingers slid beneath her piled-up, silky hair; his hand spread against the back of her head, holding her face closer to his own.

She nuzzled her face in the soft nest of his beard, overcome by uninhibited yearnings. She felt his tongue trace the outline of her lips. Then she opened them to him, gasping at the new and fervid sensations radiating along her nerve endings as he explored the inner reaches of her mouth.

At her gasp, he pulled her tighter against him and molded her body to his with a sweep of his hand up and down her back. Her sweetness intoxicated him as wine had never done, her shyness, her eagerness, her innocence, her boldness. . . .

Drawing back, he gazed into her face through a haze of passion, then kissed each eye in turn, her nose, and, moving down her chin, her . . .

When he took his lips from hers, Meg moved her face toward him, silently beseeching him not to stop. She looked into his eyes, so full of begging and desire. She felt his lips on her eyes, her nose, her chin. . . . Her body reacted quite on its own to the animal passion in his eyes: her breasts ached with shameful, unfamiliar sensations, and this same feeling of urgent longing throbbed inside her abdomen . . . and lower, frighteningly lower. . . .

She stumbled backwards out of his embrace, frightened now, not of him, but of herself, of what was happening inside her body and mind. She rocked on her heels, and he grasped her shoulders. Flinching, she stepped back another step, two steps, held to him only by their unbroken gaze.

Her brain admonished her to turn around and run—for her life, for her sanity, for Rube's job. But her feet were riveted to the rocky ground, and she couldn't tear her eyes from his, because her heart spoke, too, begging her to run straight back into his arms, to feel his body close to hers, to experience again the dizzying combination of strength and surrender she felt there.

Fortunately, her feet refused to do her heart's bidding. After what seemed like an eternity, a bit of reason broke through her reeling senses, her legs steadied, and she turned and walked away.

He watched her go, numbed by the experience they had shared, aware only of his erratically thumping heart, which followed her retreating figure with every beat, step by step, further and further away. She started slowly, then gradually gained speed, reminding him of one of her father's diamond-stacker engines pulling gracefully away from a station, methodically gaining speed as it gathered a full head of steam, until, finally reaching her horse, she mounted with such vengeance that he laughed.

"Maggie Britton, you're a woman to be dealt with," he whispered under his breath. The thought was sobering, and he clenched his fists into balls. "Indeed, I fear you are."

Chapter Two

By the time Meg rode into Hell on Wheels the sun was setting behind her, and she had finally managed to work herself into a righteous rage.

It had been difficult. For the entire ten miles she vacillated between utter contempt for Kalib whatever-his-name-was and an unfamiliar, inexplicable sense of longing for something, she didn't know what. No sooner would she succeed in convincing herself that he was indeed the vilest creature on the face of the earth, than she would find herself riding, reins aslack, reliving the dizzying sensations created by his lips on hers, the tumultuous, all-consuming yearnings his body had spawned within her own.

Furiously, she would toss her head this way and that in order to shake loose such dim-witted notions—notions which had taken hold so quickly. Soon, however, the stakes she followed faded in a haze of recollections, and she once more drifted in a state of moronic bliss . . . and consternation. One nonsensical question kept popping into her mind over and over again.

She couldn't recall where she had put her hands when he kissed her. Merely thinking on it, the memory of the feel of his muscles against her upper arms still weakened her through and through. The breadth of his shoulders enveloped her senses to the point of leaving her breathless, even now.

But what had she done with her arms? Had she put them around his neck? Her head sagged backwards against the remembered weight of his hand. Had she run her fingers through his hair, as he had hers? Why couldn't she recall such simple things? *Pray God, she had pushed him away with both palms planted firmly on his. . . .* She swallowed convulsively, recalling the hard, warm feel of his chest when he pressed her to him.

Why, oh why, couldn't she force this poppycock from her mind? Why, she demanded of herself furiously, had one kiss—one single kiss by a . . . a vile and vulgar, completely unscrupulous prospector attached itself so intrusively, yet so securely, to the inside of her very thick skull?

One kiss by a despicable, corrupt man who intended to ruin Rube's chances of proving himself to the railroad! That's what the prospector was, yet . . .

One blissful kiss. . . .

Flailing thus against an ever increasing fear of losing mastery over her own mind, Meg arrived at the Diamond-Stacker Palace Saloon with the majority of her hairpins strewn somewhere along her backtrail, together with a great deal of her senses.

A mile outside town, she had stopped at the construction train, hoping against hope to find Rube sober and on the job. She shrugged off her disappointment that he wasn't there and spoke briefly with Uncle Grady, telling him of her meeting with the prospector—well, she conceded, with guilt stirring in the pit of her stomach, parts of the meeting, anyhow.

"There's nothing wrong with the right-of-way contracts," Uncle Grady answered, after an exasperated sigh at the news that Meg had put her life in jeopardy by going alone to talk to the prospector, in spite of his own earlier warnings.

Meg sighed inwardly, hoping her discomfiture wouldn't alert Uncle Grady's suspicions about the things he *didn't* know concerning her visit with the prospector.

"Run along to the Diamond-Stacker," he advised.

"Tomorrow I'll give those contracts another going over, just to make sure."

Dust swirled around the sorrel's hooves when she drew to a stop in front of the Diamond-Stacker Palace. Finally, her real problems pushed aside those created earlier by the prospector's kiss . . . that damnable, contemptible man. He had no right handling her in such an untoward manner. She blanched inside, recalling her own demeaning reaction to him.

With a flip of her head she pushed open the tall, narrow outside doors and entered the saloon, chestnut hair aflying. Her state of indignant wrath, however, staved off any thoughts of personal appearance. She would deal with her own behavior later, she told herself scathingly. Right now Rube needed her—again.

The Diamond-Stacker Palace Saloon had been a part of Meg Britton's life since her earliest memories. Of course, it hadn't always been so grandiose. In the beginning the Diamond-Stacker Palace—regardless of its outward appearance, the establishment had always carried the same ostentatious name—had quenched its customers' thirst inside a tent, like other establishments in the Hell on Wheels terminus towns that followed the railroads. Tents were portable; they could be picked up easily and moved overnight.

The building housing the saloon now was new, one of Di's "improvements" during Meg's four years away at school. Designed originally for the long, narrow lots of new towns along the railroad's route, the mail-order frame building served the enterprising businessman's needs well, since he could never depend on such a town not going bust. Easily dismantled in one day's time, the building could be packed onto a flatcar and hauled to a new site, where re-erecting it took no more than two additional days. Using her inimitable business sense, Di made up for those three lost days by serving drinks in a temporary outdoor beer garden, regardless of the weather. "A good Irish whiskey or rye served neat is all a rust-eater needs," Di was fond of saying, "to chase away the chill of winter or the heat of a summer's day."

Meg stood in the saloon's anteroom, which Di referred to as the "cigar apartment," in reference to its large glass-encased counter where cigars and packaged liquors were for sale. She sighed. One thing about Di, she invested money in her business. She could hear Di's often-expressed sentiments even now: "The railroaders spend more of their hard-earned money with me than anywhere else, so I owe them something special in return."

Stepping to her left, Meg peered through the open door of Di's office. The only occupant was a young man sitting at the cluttered ledger desk, chewing the end of a lead pencil, while he studied a sheet of writing paper. He glanced up, gave her a startled look, and jumped to his feet.

She grinned in spite of herself, while the young man unabashedly took in both her disheveled state and the fact that she was very much a lady in a place where ladies were never seen.

Four years ago she wouldn't have recognized that look, she thought dismally. Until she went back East to school, entering a saloon was something she did regularly, unaware that ladies never, not under any circumstances, set foot inside such places. She sighed. What an eye-opener her education had been! She'd probably have been better off had she never left Hell on Wheels. Then she wouldn't know the difference between life here and what went on in so-called normal households. And that difference wouldn't have made such a shambles of her life.

"Where's Di?" she asked the young man, who shifted his gaze from her tailored outfit to her face.

He nodded toward the double-action rattan doors. Sounds from beyond—of scuffling boots and a piece of furniture hitting the oilcloth-covered floor—held their attention a moment.

"I'll fetch her for you, ma'am," the young man offered.

"Never mind." Meg turned toward the saloon proper with a smile befitting the lady he probably was thinking she wasn't.

The young man shrugged, then called tentatively after her. "Ah . . . ma'am? Could I trouble you with a question?"

Turning, she raised a skeptical eyebrow.

He blushed and looked quickly down at the sheet of writing paper that had held his attention before she startled him with her presence. "Miz Di lets those of us who're of a mind come in here and write letters to our . . . ah, back home, but I'm not much hand at spelling. Would you say 'pining' has one 'n' in the middle or two?"

In spite of her own spirits, which ranged somewhere between absolute gloom and total fury, Meg had to tighten her jaws to restrain a grin. "One, I believe," she answered, at which the young man thanked her and bent seriously over his letter once more, her own unconventional presence in this all-male domain forgotten.

Inhaling a deep breath of courage and cigar-perfumed air, Meg pushed through the swinging doors. The sounds of a fistfight increased, and suddenly the screen blocking one's view from the cigar apartment into the saloon proper toppled over onto her. She sprawled to the floor, deluged by recollections of the circus into which her life with Rube and Di usually degenerated.

"Sugar! What're you doing here? You're supposed . . ."

Rube's words ended in an abrupt grunt, as his opponent took advantage of his distraction. Grabbing him by the shirt, the much younger man pulled Rube to his feet, and the fight began in earnest once more.

Raising herself on one elbow, Meg inhaled a deep draft of the sweet smell of washing soda, kerosene, and furniture oil. No hint yet of the unwashed odor of the railroaders who would soon fill this room to the rafters.

A trickle of blood ran down Rube's tawny cheek from a cut below his eye. His nose also was bloody, and his knuckles split, but his face bore the smile of a man who loves a fight.

Meg struggled to stand. Sliding her fingers through her hair, she held it away from her face and steadied herself against the carved birch screen. How Rube did enjoy a rollicking good barroom brawl! Standing a bit under six feet tall, he was sturdily built, and his work had kept him agile. Assertive when sober, drunk he became the aggressor.

With a sigh of something akin to resignation, she stared around the establishment, forcing herself to regain a portion of the anger she knew she needed at this moment, wondering at the same time whether she was as dim-witted as she felt at still being taken aback by anything she found inside the Diamond-Stacker Palace Saloon.

Standing behind the extra-long curly birch bar, which ran a good three-quarters the length of the room, Di herself appeared oblivious of the conflict. Holding one glass tumbler firmly in each hand, she swung her arms in a wide arch, as though juggling, tossing, instead of balls, a constant stream of water blithely back and forth between glasses. Amazingly, most of the water traveled its intended course and ended up in the tumbler opposite the one from which it had been so ceremoniously thrown.

Working beside Di, apparently oblivious not only to the ruckus, but to his employer's odd form of entertainment, as well, one of the saloon's serving boys intently poured an amber liquid from a beaked pitcher into pint-sized liquor bottles.

The other serving boy worked behind them, pasting labels on the bottles his companion filled, his actions reflected in the twelve-foot beveled mirrors framed in cornices of matching curly birch. Since all three stood on the raised slatted-wood bar mat that ringed the bar both back and front, they appeared to be staging a theatrical.

Meg looked back at Rube. It seemed for a while he would take the fight, or at least extend it until both combatants were winded and unable to continue, but his age, or smaller size, or perhaps his advanced state of inebriation finally took their toll, and his adversary felled him suddenly with a sharp right to the throat.

Pitching backwards, he fell spread-eagled across the top of one of the dozen or so gaming tables. Shifting precariously for a moment, two legs of the table suddenly gave way, and Rube slid to the floor with it.

Before Meg could take more than one step toward him, however, Di rushed forward and dropped his opponent by a swift blow to the head with a sham glass. He crumpled, knees first, at Rube's feet.

"I've told you a dozen times you can't fight in here if you're going to break up the place," she shouted. Straightening quickly, she thrust fists to hips and addressed Meg. "Like he said," she continued in the husky voice Meg had once tried so hard to imitate, "you're supposed to be in Silver Creek."

Meg stared incredulously from the sham glass to Di's intimidating stance above the two men. "You could have killed him with that glass."

"What do you think I keep them around for?" Di asked, looking at the beer mug, which was made of such thick glass that it actually held only half the amount of liquid it appeared to. "I certainly don't use these mugs to cheat my customers out of the measurement they pay for." She considered the situation again. "Of course, now and then, when a gent has imbibed too heavily, I'll switch to a sham so he won't get so drunk."

Meg shook her head. "If you're concerned with your customers' welfare," she said angrily, "why don't you start by helping me keep Rube sober enough to build this railroad?"

Di studied her a moment, then turned her attention to the boys behind the bar, and her eyes widened. "No, no, no, Bart, Georgie," she instructed. "Those bottles contain St. Croix rum. You must put the proper labels on them. How else will the customer know what he is buying?"

The serving boys stopped momentarily, then continued their work as if they hadn't been interrupted.

Before Meg could speak again, Rube struggled to his feet. "Sugar, what're you doing here? You're supposed to . . ."

Meg inhaled furiously. "We're *both* supposed to be other places, Rube." She took his arm to steady him, but he pulled away. Looking at him, she struggled to turn her

38

anger into sympathy. The whites of his eyes were cobwebbed with red veins, and his nose was as red as a cherry pulled out of a Christmas pie, but his green eyes twinkled from his fifty-year-old face as mischievously as though he were a boy of five.

"I just came into town to pick up some gandy-dancers," he assured her. "I'm on my way back to the end of track."

Meg pursed her lips. "When was that, Rube?" she asked caustically. "When did you come into town?"

He squinted at her. When he spoke his tone was a trifle defensive. "This morn . . ." he began. "Well, maybe yesterday. But I'm heading on back right now."

"It was not yesterday," she told him. "It was every bit of two days ago."

"No." He shook his head definitely. "I haven't been here two days. It's only been . . ."

"Yes, you have. And you've been drunk from the moment you arrived. Would you like to hear what's gone wrong with the railroad since you started this binge?"

Rube fidgeted. "Now, sugar, don't go getting riled." A sheepish grin tugged at the corners of his mouth, and his green eyes sparkled briefly. When Meg refused to respond, however, he wiped his mouth with his sleeve, shrugged in a disgruntled fashion, and shuffled toward the bar. Taking up an empty glass, he poured himself a drink from one of the bottles the boys were filling. At the first sip, he wrinkled up his face, swallowed, then took a bigger swig.

Apparently oblivious of it all, Di watched her two employees a moment longer. "When you finish," she instructed the one called Georgie, nodding toward the multitude of wicks in the three kerosene chandeliers, "light the lamps. Customers will begin arriving within the hour."

That bit of business tended to, she looked at Meg. "Don't be too hard on him, dear. He's doing the best he can. He'll get the job done."

Meg turned furious, disillusioned eyes on Di. "You don't understand," she stormed. "How could you not, after all these years?"

The drink seemed to have revived Rube a bit, for this time his voice was stronger, his tone less defensive. "Now, sugar, don't go laying into Di. She had nothing to do with . . . with . . ." His words trailed off, dissolved into thoughts.

Suddenly, Meg could stand the charade no longer. Crossing the room in three strides, she jerked the glass from his hand and flung it, liquor and all, into one of the tubs set into the workboard behind the gleaming curly birch bar. Georgie and Bart jumped aside to keep from being hit. She glared at Rube, Di, then back at Rube, whose defensiveness returned in full measure. "You're . . . you're both disgraceful!"

"You've no right to talk like this, sugar. Di's been good to you, better'n you'll ever know. You should've stayed in Silver Creek. I'm taking care of everything."

"Like always," Meg agreed sarcastically. "You spend your time drinking and gambling and . . . and who knows what, while I'm the one who has to run around being accosted by strange men to get this damned railroad built."

Anxiety shone momentarily from Rube's sluggish green eyes. "What sonofabitch accosted my girl?" he demanded, a good octave below fighting range. Meg inhaled, immediately sorry she had spoken of the one thing she'd never intended to mention.

Di's small oval mouth fell open in the shape of a perfect heart. "What on earth do you mean? What's happened?" Her eyes traveled up and down Meg's frame slowly. "You do look a fright! Your hair . . ."

Meg's head swirled with unleashed anger, at herself as much as at Di and Rube and the whole miserable situation—mostly at Kalib what's-his-name. "I'm sorry. I didn't mean . . ."

"Sit down," Di insisted, trying to take Meg's arm.

"I . . . I didn't intend to say it that way," Meg continued. "Nothing happened to me personally." Why in heaven's name had she blurted out such a thing? she chastised herself. Stick to Rube's problems, they're enough—enough for a lifetime. She pulled away from Di's soothing hand. "I'm all right. Really. No one accosted me. But . . ."

"Then what the hell happened?" Rube asked cautiously, as though he didn't really want to know the answer. Di continued to scrutinize Meg from top to toe.

With a sigh Meg studied Rube. At length, she replied through clenched teeth. "Some befuddled old prospector is holding up the grading, Rube. You have to sober up and get rid of him." She told them, then, the story of Grady's appearance at the Hotel O'Keefe, and of her own subsequent visit to the prospector, leaving out obvious parts of their meeting.

"Did he . . . was he forward . . . ?" Di asked.

Meg shook her head, not trusting her voice.

Now it was Di's turn to be angry. "Grady should have known to look for Rube here," she fumed, taking Rube by the arm.

While Meg watched silently, Di removed her apron and handed it to Georgie. Using a damp cloth, she bathed Rube's face, then dried it with a clean linen moustache wiper from one of the dozen or so towel holders attached at two-foot intervals along the length of the bar just below the lacquered birch arm rail. Rube stood stockstill beneath Di's ministrations.

Meg inhaled a deep breath. It was almost impossible for her to stay angry with Di. She studied the woman's outlandish sable-brown hair, which was not over three inches long anywhere on her head. It's natural curls ringed her remarkably unlined face, resembling a furry brown cap much more than a lady's hair style. She'd worn it that way as long as Meg could remember.

Di had been like a mother to her. Perhaps not like a real mother, Meg thought now. Until she'd gone back East, she hadn't known exactly what a mother was, so Di had fit the bill while she grew up.

Her own mother had died when she was born, in a remote railroad camp somewhere in the Colorado Rockies while Rube was working on the transcontinental. Di had been there from the beginning, caring for her, nurturing, disciplining. Di was the only lady . . . woman . . . she had ever spent time around until going away to school—practically the only female she'd ever even seen, except for the soiled doves who worked on the fringes of Hell on Wheels, and whom Di and Rube forbade her to so much as look at, much less speak to.

Finished, Di handed the towel to Georgie and proceeded to lead Rube through the double-action doors at the rear of the saloon. Identical to the ones separating the cigar apartment from the saloon in the front, these rattan doors separated the saloon proper from Di's living quarters and storerooms.

Meg straightened her tired shoulders and followed, despair churning in the pit of her stomach. "He has a railroad to build, Di," she called after them. "Why can't you help me keep him sober enough to do it?"

Stopping in the doorway to Di's parlor, Meg leaned against the jamb. An unfamiliar wave of melancholy swept over her suddenly. She stared across the room and through the open door leading into Di's bedchamber. How she'd come to hate these encounters with Rube and Di, especially since spending time in the normal world.

Rube and Di's relationship had never entered Meg's innocent mind as worthy of consideration until she went back East to school, where she quickly discovered that no one else had a father who lived in railroad camps and enjoyed the companionship of a lovely friend who owned a saloon. Even now, she wasn't sure what went on between Rube and Di outside her presence. When she was around, they were as discreet as brother and sister. Still, she wondered. Yet, like Rube, she wasn't sure she wanted to know the answers.

Visions of Di's fluffy, feather mattress covered with a delicate lace-and-flowered counterpane swam in her head, and she began to feel awkward, standing there like an intruder. She'd spent many a pleasant afternoon curled up in Di's big bed, listening to the same three fairy tales over and over, until they both had them memorized word for word.

Why did she have to grow up? she wondered bleakly, still staring into the bedchamber into which Di and Rube had disappeared. Whatever problems she'd had at five she had at least been unaware of. Actually, even though she'd spent most of her time taking care of Rube and tending to railroad business with and for him until she went away to school, it wasn't until she left that she saw their life as abnormal.

It only *became* abnormal after she left, she reasoned, her hand stroking on the cool wooden door frame, still hesitant to enter this uncomfortably private domicile. The thoughts of it flooded her with obscure, yet at the same time vaguely familiar, feelings of incompleteness and longings . . . and dread.

Di stepped to the door of the parlor. "He'll sleep it off by morning."

Silently, Meg pushed past her and stared at Rube stretched across the familiar feather bed, fully clothed.

Well, what in heaven's name had she expected? she admonished herself, while expelling a sigh of relief. What nonsense had taken up residence inside her brain?

She shook Rube by the shoulders. "Can you hear me?" she demanded. "One more episode like this, and I'm through. Do you hear? The next time you get drunk, I'm leaving." Her breath caught in her throat, and she paused, recalling the innumerable times she had threatened to leave him, recalling, too, how miserable she had been when separated from him. "Tomorrow you must return to the railroad, Rube," she continued. "That prospector is holding up the grading. He even removed some of the stakes. And he . . . he fired at the crew . . . and . . ."

She shook his shoulders again, and his green eyes blinked open. "Tomorrow you have to ride out there and get rid of that vile old prospector. You ought to save your fighting for men like him."

As soon as she finished breakfast the next morning, Meg

43

and a contrite, quite hung-over Rube rode the one mile from Hell on Wheels to the construction train at the end of track.

After she'd left Rube virtually passed out on Di's bed the night before, the rest of the evening had passed with relative quiet, considering the bustle of the evening crowd, which resounded with clamor and din through the thin wall separating the saloon from the room Di provided for her to sleep in. Directly across the hallway from Di's parlor, the room served generally as a storeroom, but Meg suspected it had been used as a bedchamber before, since the single bed and small dresser were already in place. She wondered briefly whether this was the room Rube used while here in Hell on Wheels, then she quickly tore her mind away from such thoughts. She wasn't ready to tackle the question of Rube and Di's sleeping arrangements— not tonight. Nor anytime in the foreseeable future, she added to herself, certainly not before this railroad was built.

They had taken supper, she and Di, in Di's parlor, served by Georgie who brought in a platter of prairie chicken and rice from the HOW Cafe next door, a pot of steaming coffee for Meg, and a bottle of champagne with one hollow-stemmed goblet, which Di sipped while she dressed for the evening.

"Steady's the hand," she explained, pouring herself a second glassful of the bubbly liquid before stepping into a black watered-silk skirt and white basque jacket. The only thing that kept the costume from being the height of prim and proper attire was the neckline, which dipped low in front, exposing a goodly portion of Di's well-endowed bosom.

"I promised the boys a real Blue Blazer tonight." She looked wistfully at Meg through the looking glass while she tied a black bow tie around the creamy skin of her slender neck. "That's what I was practicing when you came in," she said, then added, "with cold water instead of boiling water and flaming scotch whiskey, of course. A real crowd pleaser, the Blue Blazer, when it's done right."

Adding a small, ruffle-encircled apron, and a black garter to each forearm, she curtsied to Meg. "What do you think? Do I make a reasonably passable mixologist?"

Meg grinned. "What happened to the red velvet dress? The one you wore when you sat in the red velvet swing and sang about 'Handsome Mary, the Lily of the West'?"

"Every good mixologist wears black and white," Di responded unequivocally. "Besides, the swing's gone, dear. Didn't you notice? It got in the way of the billiard table." She tripped lightly across the colorful rug and patted Meg's cheek, humming the tune Meg remembered from *Beadle's Dime Song Book*. "To tell the truth, that swing got a little wobbly. But, then, I don't warble like I used to, either. Years." She smiled. "They do take their toll, even when we refuse to give in to them entirely."

"Di, we have to talk about Rube."

Di studied her a moment with heart-shaped lips pursed into a thin puckered line. Then a bright smile brought dimples to her cheeks. "We will, dear."

"I'm serious, Di. If the railroad isn't finished in time for the new governor to make his address, Rube's career will be finished. You have to . . ."

Di held up a quietening hand. "Not now, Meg. I must go to work now. Not tonight. But soon. Soon, I promise."

Exasperated, Meg went to bed and tried to put the entire day out of her mind. Eventually Di and Rube and all their troubles faded, and she drifted off to sleep.

But an equally unwanted vision took their place, and she slept restlessly. Her dreams left no doubt. She definitely encircled his neck with her arms . . . in her dreams.

What circuses were to some children, construction trains were to Meg Britton. For as long as she could recall, they had fascinated and excited her. That is, until she spent four years in the civilized East.

Riding up to it now in the clear light of a pleasant fall day, she assessed the multicar train with new, much more judgmental eyes. Stretching out ahead of the pusher engine, nearest the point of construction, a number of flat cars carried tools, supplies, and a blacksmith shop. Next came several, in this case, two, three-tiered sleeping cars, referred to by the men as rolling bunkhouses. Slung beneath both bunkhouses were hammocks where men slept when no beds were left inside, or when hot summer weather or stale air drove them out into the night. Looking up she saw a couple of the ever-present tents— some men were reluctant to sleep beneath the steel monsters—pitched on the roof of one of the cars. After the bunkhouse cars came the dining car, and finally the only car she had ever been allowed to enter with any frequency while growing up, an enormous car housing a kitchen at one end and a storeroom and the engineer's office at the other. On the outside of the kitchen end of this car freshly slaughtered quarters of beef hung on enormous hooks, ready to be cooked for the evening meal, along with a number of casks Meg knew contained water for drinking and cooking. In this dry country potable water was sometimes unavailable, in which case, the casks provided the only drinking water for the hundreds of men who made up the various crews.

Even at midmorning, as now, when the crews were in the field, enough men remained behind engaged in the various activities required to keep this rolling combination of office, hotel, and storage cars working, that the train usually had a festive air.

Today, however, it looked only untidy . . . unkempt . . . seedy. Was that what drove Rube to the Diamond-Stacker Palace and Di's company? Did he need a spot of glamour in his life, even the sleazy glamour of Hell on Wheels?

They found Grady Thornton in the engineer's office perched on one of the high stools in front of the drafting table studying the right-of-way contracts.

Looking up as they entered, Grady ignored Rube's surly mood. Both he and Meg realized it took Rube a good twenty-four hours to recover from one of his benders. "These contracts look to me to be in fine order," he said.

Silently Rube perched on the other high stool and immersed himself in the contracts. He hadn't spoken a word on the ride from Hell on Wheels, and Meg certainly hadn't initiated any conversation.

Talking would come later. She knew from experience that a hung-over Rube, while not as defensive as his drunk counterpart, was nevertheless too irritable to reason with. If pressed, he would become contrite, sometimes desperate, in his attempt to reassure her he would never, never fall off the wagon again.

That was one thing she did not want to hear at present. The only thing in this whole topsy-turvy world she knew for certain was that Rube Britton would fall off the wagon again. And again. And again.

He needed her to keep him straightened out and on track. That was why she was here—her mission in life.

In addition to the drafting table and two stools, the office held two triple-deck cots, enough beds for six engineers at one time. Looking over their shoulders, she listened to Rube and Grady's conversation, trying to hear something they might not have recognized as a problem.

"We can always take him into condemnation proceedings," Grady said. "Provided he proves he owns the property."

"He plays hell owning that property," Rube swore. "We own it. I wouldn't have broke ground until we had passage across the river. That crossing is the only place for a mile up or downstream where the bridges won't give our monkey's more trouble than they've seen since the Stampede Tunnel up in the Cascades." As he spoke he jabbed the plat with his meerschaum. Then he turned to Grady. "Besides, you know well enough how I feel about condemnation proceedings."

Grady nodded sagely. "Make enemies for us ever' time," he drawled, quoting company policy. "Landowners along the railroad rights of way are to be considered neighbors. Antagonizing a neighbor leads to hard feelings and work delays. And taking a neighbor to court is an unsure thing, at best, since most cases are heard by local commissioners who generally favor the landowner. The only thing we can count on is winning more enemies, and we sure don't need any more of them animals."

Rube nodded. "Soon as this new governor takes office, I figure the heyday of the railroad barons will be a thing of the past. This hundred eighty miles may be our last hurrah."

He glared at the plat, then rifled through the contracts on the table. "And no lousy prospector is going to stop our last ribbon of iron. What's more, I intend to use the gorge on the far side of the Silver Creek crossing for a borrow pit."

Grady's eyes widened. "Sure enough?" he asked. "Have you checked it out?"

"Settled on it right off," Rube assured him. "That's why I'm certain the contracts are in order. There's enough high-grade gravel in that draw to provide ballast for the track from the river on into Silver Creek."

As morning gave way to afternoon, Meg settled herself on one of the cots and smiled contentedly. Rube Britton was back at work. How long he would stay on the job, no one knew, least of all she herself.

She sighed. She would insist on his returning to Silver Creek with her tomorrow. He could run the railroad from there, since he needed to spend most of his time in the field, anyway.

Finally, Grady left and returned from the kitchen with enough lunch for the three of them, the same lunch the crews took into the field: canned tomatoes, boiled eggs, and ham sandwiches, which they washed down with tin cupsful of thick black coffee. Rube's health revived before their very eyes.

Now that she knew he had already taken care of the right-of-way question, and, with it, the prospector, Meg tried to relax. If she kept vigilant, the railroad would be completed on time. They would leave the area, probably the whole state of Texas, since Texas wasn't building railroads much anymore, and she would never have to see that vile prospector again. In time, she would even stop thinking about him. Of course, she would.

After lunch the men, joined now by Meg, pored over the paperwork once more, determined to have everything in order before Rube confronted the prospector.

Toward evening Meg lighted the lamps. Suddenly Arny Perham, the grading crew foreman, burst into the engineer's office, breathless.

"Every damned stake," he blurted out, then drew breath at the sight of Meg. "'Cuse me, Miss Meg, I didn't aim to let go a string of cursin' with you around, but every one of our stakes clear on in to Silver Creek is missing—gone without so much as a trace. The whole derned survey will have to be reshot."

Chapter Three

By the time they rode away from the construction train the following morning, Rube Britton had returned to his gruff and crusty old self, and Meg relished the idea of his tying into that vile, contemptuous prospector. Rube Britton didn't scare worth a cent. He'd soon make jackrabbit stew of Kalib what's-his-name.

The nine miles from the work train to the river crossing took a good four hours, however, for Rube insisted on inspecting every inch of roadbed, the three-foot shoulders, and each and every man's work progress along the way.

Once recovered from a hangover, Rube always appeared to forget the spree entirely, taking charge of business in the maniacal fashion that had earned him the reputation—when he was sober—of being a task-driving perfectionist.

Studying him now, Meg wondered whether he had truly forgotten, or whether his contriteness of yesterday had instead burrowed inside, lodging itself deep within his conscience from where it needled him to make amends in the only way he knew: he could build a perfect railroad.

His disposition remained sunny while he studied each successive operation they passed, meerschaum clamped firmly between his teeth. Along the first few miles the rust-eaters were setting rail. Since he considered gauging track one of the most important operations in railroad building, Rube personally measured the gauge in a few places himself, with an anxious assistant foreman peering over his shoulder.

After checking to be sure the master gauge was not bent, he turned his attention to the assistant. "Watch the spikers," he told the man. "Don't let them spike too tight or too loose. Four feet, eight and one half inches—no more, no less."

The assistant nodded.

"Measure every rail yourself. Twice a day. Do you understand?"

The assistant nodded again, and Meg had trouble keeping a straight face. Of course the assistant understood, she thought. Three successive foremen before him had been fired from this very job, in the same number of days. If he didn't understand, he wouldn't last long in Rube's camp.

Traveling on, Rube dismounted periodically to study the work of the tracklayers. At each place he took up a shovel and measured for himself—two shovel widths between ties, no more, no less. When necessary, he instructed the ties be torn out and the distance adjusted.

Arriving at the grading operations, he surveyed the work with the same care, this time tamping into the prepared roadbed with a rod, then sifting the fill through his fingers. He listened amicably to the grading foreman who allowed as how he could do a faster job with four-up fresno to move dirt, or at least another two-horse slip. Rube replied that yes, a fresno, which could move about three times as much dirt as a slip in the same amount of time, would be faster, but that the foreman knew as well as he how difficult requisitions were to get through. It was hard enough to get a simple supply of buggy whips or a wheelbarrow.

By the time they came to the end of the work force, Meg's pride in Rube had returned in full measure. The prospector shoved to the back of her thoughts, she felt herself consumed with energy. Building a railroad must surely be the most exciting occupation in the world.

Rube's mood, however, altered as soon as the work played out. Morose, now, he instructed Meg to help him look for sign of the missing stakes.

"They were here when I traveled the route two days ago," she told him. Her mind returned reluctantly to the prospector. "I can't imagine him removing *all* the stakes. He said . . ." Thinking hard, she tried to recall the man's actual words. "He said something about the hill across the river being his, but that's all. He certainly didn't indicate he would try to halt work along the entire route."

"Well, someone has," Rube replied. "Twenty miles of stakes don't disappear without a little help."

Irritation at such a prank stirred inside her, then deviltry lighted her smile. She pushed a length of chestnut hair away from her face. No matter what his motives, the prospector's days were definitely numbered now. Rube Britton would see to that.

Although at times during the morning she thought they would tarry so long they wouldn't make it to the Silver Creek River before nightfall, when they finally did arrive, the noontime sun bore intensely down upon her head. She pursed her lips. Butterflies fluttered unexpectedly in her stomach.

While they sat their horses at the riverbank where Rube, following the advice of the bridge architects, had chosen to span the river, he studied the embankments on either side with care.

Meg concentrated on the steep sides of the bank, too, but for an entirely different reason than Rube. Terrified of what—or whom—she might see, she couldn't make herself look up and across the river.

At last Rube turned his attention to her. "Which way do we go to find your prospector?"

She bristled. "He is not *my* prospector."

"You're the one who found him, aren't you?" he laughed. "At least, you're the only one brave enough to confront him."

"I . . ." she began, then paled at her quaking voice. Yes, she had definitely confronted the prospector, she thought dismally. And how!

Inhaling a deep breath, she tried to order her thoughts.

"You're here now, Rube," she answered firmly. "You'll not only confront him, you'll give him what for, and he'll never bother us . . . or your railroad . . . again."

Rube leaned across and patted her shoulder. "I have a long ways to go to live up to my reputation with you, sugar." Then he asked again, "Which way?"

Steeled by a childlike image of Rube as protector, she indicated a dim trail to the south, which they followed across the river at the shallow crossing she had taken two days earlier. Without stopping, she led the way up the riverbank and onto the prairie where the line of hills the prospector and his friend had emerged from now loomed before them.

Rube whistled through his teeth. "Looks like we're expected."

Startled, but not sure why, Meg stared at the two horsemen who loped to meet them.

Two!

She squinted into the hazy distance. One of the riders was definitely the man called Tobin. But the other . . .

Her heart pounded erratically. The second rider wasn't large enough to be Kalib. Or had she forgotten?

No chance, she thought, warming from a sudden rush of heat within. Even though she had only seen him once, his image remained etched in her brain as though she had known him always.

"Is that your prospector, sugar?"

"I told you. He isn't *my* prospector," she snapped. "He isn't my anything."

The riders pulled up sharply in front of them, forcing Rube and Meg to draw rein.

"That's far enough." The speaker was a blond man she had never seen before. The man called Tobin stared hard at her.

She squirmed under his gaze. "This is my father," she said firmly. "Rube Britton, chief engineer for this railroad spur. He's come to see Kalib."

For a moment she thought both men might fall out of their saddles. They stared at her, then at each other. Alarm

53

buzzed almost audibly between them.

"I told you he'd gone plumb rabid," Tobin told his partner angrily, before turning his attention back to her. "Come with me."

Meg and Rube touched the flanks of their mounts simultaneously. Instantly, however, Tobin's companion spurred his horse between them, cutting Rube off.

"You," Tobin barked. "Come with me. Your father stays."

Meg's mouth fell open. She turned to Rube to protest. "You go," she managed to whisper. "I'll stay."

"Are you sure you'll be all right . . . ?" Rube began.

"Lady, I said *you*. Your father stays here with . . ." Instead of supplying his companion's name, Tobin merely jerked his head toward the smaller blond man.

Neither of them looked particularly menacing, despite their rifles held at ready and Tobin's obvious dislike for her. Yet, she wasn't about to see Ka . . . that prospector by herself. Rube was the one to set him straight. Not her. She'd already tried and failed.

Rube would handle him. Fury mounted within her. *What damned foolish game was that man playing, anyway?*

She swallowed against a sudden dryness in her throat. "I won't go." Looking at Rube, she expected an affirmation of her decision, but instead he studied her quizzically.

"One of us has to talk to him, sugar. You said you aren't afraid of him."

She shook her head. "It isn't that. . . ."

"Then what?"

Drawing a deep breath, she pursed her lips as if to hold the air inside. Slowly, she shook her head. She couldn't see him again. She didn't even want to see him again.

No. More important, she *wanted not* to see him again. Not ever. Never.

While she watched, scarcely seeing, Rube untied the flap on his saddlebag and withdrew the packet of contracts. "Here, sugar. Take these and show him. He'll understand. If he's intelligent, like you said, he'll understand."

"I said he *spoke* intelligently," she exploded, suddenly unable to hold her raging turmoil inside. "I never said he was an intelligent man. Surely, he must be the stupidest man alive!"

"Meg." Rube's voice was soft. "Go ahead. Perhaps you can convince him to talk to me. As things stand, you're our only chance to settle the matter peaceably."

She bit her lip, thinking . . . thinking . . . thinking. . . .

Then she followed the man called Tobin. Her heart thundered in her ears louder than the horse's hooves beneath her, but she knew, right or wrong, this was the only decision she could have made.

For Rube. For the railroad.

But not for herself.

Later, she realized that no matter what she might have expected to find beyond the crest of the hill, she could never have prepared herself for the scene that actually appeared, as she followed Tobin, like a lamb following a Judas goat, into Kalib's camp.

He stood in the doorway, and for a moment, he was all she saw. Although she hadn't thought it possible, the sight of him increased her heart rate by tenfold, and she became intolerably warm and faint. But she determined to keep her emotions to herself today, shamed even now by the dastardly way she had practically thrown her body at his feet two days earlier.

He was every bit as huge as she remembered, taking up most of the doorway to the tent . . . or house . . . or whatever the strange building was called. He stood on the ground with one foot propped on a stump beside the door, stockstill, leaning forward with a forearm resting on his thigh, staring straight at her with those same penetrating brown eyes, which today seemed to pin her to her saddle.

In fact, once she managed to tear her eyes away from him, she knew she would remain in her saddle. Likely, it was the safest place around . . . by a long shot.

55

"Light and set," he suggested easily, a grin tipping the corners of his mouth upward, bringing with them his lustrous black beard.

Lustrous! He had shaved. No, she recanted, he hadn't shaved. His face was still covered with thick black hair. But it was neatly trimmed and sparkled with cleanliness. He'd trimmed his beard, and . . .

Quite involuntarily her eyes drifted over him then from head to boot top. Trimmed and sparkling, she thought, amazed. From neat denim trousers tucked into glistening black boots, to his spanking white shirt, which draped open provocatively, curly black hair peeking lavishly, invitingly . . .

"Go on back and help Wash out," Kalib instructed Tobin without taking his eyes from her. "Miss Britton and I have some unfinished business to take care of."

"Have you gone completely loco?" Tobin's voice sounded bewildered. "Don't you even care that you're about to bring this whole operation flat down upon our heads?"

Kalib spoke curtly. "It's my operation, and I'm not about to bring it down on anybody's head. I know exactly what I'm doing." Although his words were spoken in his well-practiced, self-assured tone, Kalib felt anything but assured inside. What in hell *was* he doing? He didn't even know this . . . this incredibly beautiful, enchanting . . . his thoughts dissolved in an all-enveloping pool of desire as he stared entranced at her chestnut hair flying about her sun-warmed face. Her green, green eyes. . . .

Tobin interrupted his thoughts. "We agreed. . . ."

Kalib turned to Tobin with a broad grin. "Our agreement doesn't extend to . . . to certain areas, friend. Now, get on back out there and help Wash. Don't let Britton come another step closer to this camp. When we've concluded our business, Miss Britton will return to her father. . . ."

Without warning Kalib shifted impish eyes to Meg. ". . . unharmed."

Meg swallowed. Vaguely she heard Tobin ride away,

but his horse's hooves sounded muffled. Kalib moved toward her, as through a haze. Glancing up, she saw the large golden sun, shining brightly from a clear, blue sky, and she suddenly felt feeble-minded for coming into the enemy's camp.

"Light and set," Kalib suggested again, extending his hand toward her.

She stared at it. Somehow, then, from somewhere deep inside, she managed to summon a bit of sanity, and with it, a growing sense of outrage. Ignoring his intentions of helping her from the saddle, she thrust the packet of papers into his waiting hand.

"These papers will verify who owns this hill," she said firmly.

His grin faded a bit, but his eyes still gleamed—the sun glinting from the golden highlights in their deep, dark, depths, she thought, then chastised herself properly. Looking quickly back to the envelope of papers, she held them until she felt his grasp close around them.

Kalib stared at the papers a moment, then back to her, and suddenly, without another word, he turned toward the building and disappeared inside, carrying the papers with him.

Meg sat her horse, her hands gripped in a deathlike vise around the saddlehorn. Gradually, she forced herself to relax a bit. This wasn't so bad, after all. He would read over the contracts and realize she was right. He couldn't come to any other conclusion. The contracts were plain as the nose . . .

Funny, she thought, his nose and his eyes were about the only parts of his face visible beneath his heavy beard. Yet, she knew he was a handsome man.

Margaret Marie Britton! she screamed inside. *Enough. Enough.*

Forcibly she concentrated on the camp before her. She'd give him time to study the contracts, then they would be on their way—she and Rube—to Silver Creek. That was all there'd be to it. She'd never have to see him . . . to be humiliated by him . . . again.

On this side, the ridge of hills only gave way to more hills, with a small valley in the midst. Shin oak and mesquite and three or four large oak trees dotted the area. The building was set smack-dab in the middle of the little valley, with trails, some dim, some worn, running hither and yon into the hills.

She studied the building itself. Sitting at one end of the half-tent, half-frame structure, she couldn't determine its size, but it looked nearly as wide as the Diamond-Stacker. She squinted around the side, not daring to budge an inch from where she sat. Probably not as long as the Diamond-Stacker, she decided, looking now to the roof, where a chimney popped through the canvas and smoke circled lazily toward the sky.

She gasped. Smoke? How long had she been sitting here like a dimwit, waiting for him to read those contracts? He'd had plenty of time. . . .

Furiously she dismounted, tied her sorrel to the hitching rail, and stormed toward the open door of the building.

. . . more than enough time to burn the contracts. Then they'd be up a creek, for sure.

Her boots thudded against the plank floorboards, and she jerked to a stop. The room was enormous. Though, as she had suspected, not as deep as the Diamond-Stacker, it nevertheless gave a feeling of spaciousness even with the three cots at the rear and the various chests, the large dining table and ladder-back chairs, and the pot-bellied iron stove, before which . . .

Kalib turned from the stove and watched her admire the room, from the Indian rugs on the wooden floor to the simple cast iron chandeliers hanging at intervals down its length. When at last she looked at him, he bowed slightly, lifting a teapot in salute.

"Hot tea?" he inquired with a bow. "Strange how a cup of tea cools one off in the heat of . . . the day."

Her mouth fell open. Absently, she stroked her hair away from her face and held it in place with one hand. Glancing away from him, her eyes riveted on the packet of

58

contracts, lying bound as before on the table.

"You haven't even read them." Disappointment mingled with ire in both her tone and the shaking of her head.

"No need." His own tone was light. Carrying the teapot to the table, he proceeded to fill two china cups with the boiling liquid. "Sugar?" he asked, sweeping a chair back from the table for her to sit in. "Or honey?"

Quite without intending to, she sat. She looked from the iron stove to the teapot, then up the flue to the tented ceiling. Taking a deep breath, she supposed she should be grateful he hadn't burned the contracts. Wasn't that why she had barged in here in the first place?

But neither had he read them.

Ignoring the cup of tea Kalib placed in front of her, she reached for the contracts and untied the packet.

"If you'll read these, you'll understand. . . ."

"Maggie, Maggie, Maggie," he mused. Taking the packet from her hands, he retied it. "The outside is enough to convince me these contracts aren't valid."

She glared at him.

"The date." He tapped his finger on the date scrawled in bold black letters across the top of the packet. "July, 1889. It tells me exactly what happened."

Incensed, she tried to jump to her feet, but he pushed her back to her chair with gentle hands to her shoulders.

She jerked to free herself.

He held her firmly in place. "The railroad's right of way through here was granted this past July, wasn't it?"

She nodded.

Releasing her shoulders, he moved in front of her and perched on the corner of the table, from where he proceeded to explain in quiet tones. "My deed hadn't been recorded by then."

When she opened her mouth to object, he silenced her with one slender, sun-bronzed index finger to her lips.

For an instant, their eyes met, and she knew he felt her lips tremble beneath his touch. She looked away, and a second later, he removed his finger.

"I bought this piece of land back in June. It takes

59

months for a deed to be recorded. Do you understand?"

She pursed her lips, trying to find fault with his explanation. "You sound like some smooth-talking lawyer," she hissed. "Or one of those damned double-talking politicians!"

"Double-talking?" he queried with a grin. "No, can't say I've ever been accused of double-talking—before now. I'm just a man who's had experience buying land. I know what I'm talking about, Maggie."

She gripped the edges of the white porcelain saucer and stared into the depths of the still steaming tea. It made sense, she thought angrily. It really made sense.

"Drink your tea." Kalib slid his hip off the table and took a chair opposite hers. He sipped his cup of tea.

"You might be right," she conceded at length, still staring into the steam rising from her cup. He didn't respond, and she lifted her eyes to his. "But I'm not about to take your word. As soon as we get to Silver Creek, I'll wire the land office in Austin. They've surely had time to record your deed—saying you have one—by now."

He grinned and saluted her with his cup. "Fair enough. Now, drink up."

She sipped the tea, and, as he said, it cooled her. Her thoughts settled a bit, turning from obstinate denial to a grim curiosity.

"What harm would the railroad do you?" she asked. "It wouldn't even touch your camp here. Why are you so against progress?"

"I'm not against progress," he answered. "Far from it." He looked at her then for a long time, not in the sensual, teasing way she'd come to expect from him, but in a different manner entirely. She had the strange sensation of being sized up, as if he were trying to decide something within himself.

Finally, he rose from his chair, pulled her up, and led her to a chest on the far side of the room. Seating her on a hide-bottomed stool, he squatted before her and withdrew an old piece of leather from the chest. Closing the lid once more, he spread the leather flat on its surface.

"Look at it, Maggie. This is why I can't let the railroad through here. Leastways, not for a while yet."

She looked at the drawings on the leather—a map of sorts. "What is it?"

"A plat," he answered. "To the Lost Bowie Mine. Actually, the mine is called by various names—the San Saba Mine, La Mina de las Iguanas." He laughed up at her. "How's that for a name for a silver mine—Mine of the Lizards? Now, watch my finger."

As he spoke he traced his finger from one edge of the leather to the other—the same bronzed index finger that had so recently touched her lips, she thought, feeling a flush of heat creep up her neck. "This line represents the railroad."

Her eyes widened when his finger stopped on the very spot where the plat indicated the mine was located. For a moment he held his finger still, and she stared at it.

Then she jumped to her feet, anger flaming in her eyes. "Do you think I'm dim-witted?" she stormed. "If you intend to hold up this railroad for . . . for nothing more than the fantasy of buried treasure, don't ask me to understand it. And don't think you will get away with such a stunt, either."

She stomped to the table and reached for the packet of contracts. "Only a lunatic would try to hold up progress to look for a . . . a nonexistent treasure mine."

Then she thought of Rube, and her fury blazed like a flaming tumbleweed. Turning abruptly, she glared at him. "Why is it always some bastard like you who causes good men like Rube Britton to lose their jobs?"

Crossing the room swiftly, Kalib grabbed her arms with such force her head popped back. She stared into his enraged brown eyes. All the golden flecks had fled, leaving only seething fury.

"And how could a *good* man like Rube Britton allow his daughter to sleep in a place like Hell on Wheels?"

Flailing this way and that, she struggled to free herself from his grasp. "Unless, of course," he continued, "she belongs in one of the hurdy-gurdy houses there!"

His words hit her like a pail of cold water thrown in her face. With a mighty tug, she freed one arm and slapped him hard across the cheek. His beard was thick, though, and cushioned her blow. The silky hair trapped her open hand, reminding her of ants caught in the dishes of peppermint water Di set her fancy bottles of liquor in to repel insects. Inwardly she braced herself for his rebuttal. Her eyes flared open.

Their gazes locked.

The golden flecks had returned, she thought crazily, just before he crushed her in his arms.

This time she was sure. Her arms circled his neck. The bulky muscles of his shoulders rippled beneath her trembling fingers, which then lost themselves in the silky curls on his head.

This time it wasn't in her dreams.

His lips covered hers with an ardor made all the keener by the effects of their first kiss. He hadn't been able to put her sweet passion out of his mind. Tobin thought he'd lost his wits.

Well, maybe he had, he mused, tracing her parted lips with the tip of his tongue. If so, he only hoped he never regained them. Dipping within, he savored the last traces of tea from the contours of her mouth.

And she reciprocated. How she reciprocated, he thought wildly, feeling her small tongue enter and explore and twine with his own, leaving him heaving breathlessly, craving more, ever more, of her sweetness.

With no looking glass to guide her toilette this morning, she had foregone the rat and tied her hair with a single ribbon at her neck. Now he fumbled, then removed the ribbon. Tangling her long strands of chestnut hair through his fingers, he massaged the nape of her neck with the heel of his hand in a sensuous rhythm, sending waves of heat radiating down her spine.

Reeling with the headiness of it all, she clasped his head firmly in her hands and pressed his lips closer to hers. Suddenly, she felt more at peace than she had in her entire life. Suddenly, she was right where she wanted to be.

Kalib slipped his hands to the small of her back, then easily spanned her waist with his fingers. His thumbs rubbed gentle circles in her midriff, feeling the bones of her corset. Gliding slowly up her sides, he tenderly stroked the gentle curves beneath her breasts. Her fiercely beating heart throbbed against his thumb; her heightened passion ignited his own to even more intense levels.

Returning his hands to her waist, with the gentlest of pressure he drew her back, and, lifting his head, he stared longingly into her questing eyes. Opening his mouth to speak, his need for her choked in his throat, and he found himself utterly speechless, for the first time in memory.

"Are you a devil?" she whispered into the gloriously loving expression on his face.

"Are you?" he countered.

"Nothing like this ever happened to me before," she breathed, her lips brushing his as she spoke.

"Nor to me." Without taking his eyes from hers, he tenderly moved his hands back up her sides, until, reaching her breasts, he covered them with his palms. The heat from her body emanated through her layers of clothing, and he felt her heart throb into his hand and travel up his arm, reaching his own heart . . . his own soul.

"Who are you?" she whispered.

A wry grin tipped the corners of his mouth. "A bastard?"

Her lips curled inward, pursing in thought, then, when she spoke again, they brushed his, firing his body with trails of fire.

"Why are you hunting treasure?"

"Why are you building railroads?"

All this time she had been standing on tiptoe. Now, she dropped her heels to the floor, dislodging his hands from her breasts.

He grasped her shoulders, and held them firmly beneath his palms. The last two questions had broken the spell, yet he couldn't let her go. He spoke earnestly, wondering whether his words were intended to convince her . . .

or himself.

"The reasons we're here have nothing to do with this." Lowering his head, he kissed her again. Intensely, ardently, as though to leave an imprint she couldn't forget. And she returned his kisses in kind.

When he loosened his hold on her, she picked up the packet of contracts and walked to the door. Turning, she studied him at length, then spoke.

"We're going to build the railroad, Kalib. Right across that plat of yours. If we have to, we'll begin condemnation proceedings."

She left before he could answer, and he stood rooted to the spot. All the time she spoke, she had looked at him with fervid passion.

Now, he wondered whether her passion was for him . . . or for the damned railroad.

They arrived in Silver Creek in time to clean up for dinner in the hotel dining room. Meg pleaded fatigue, intending to order a tray brought to her room, but Rube insisted on dining downstairs, and she acquiesced, conscious of her role in keeping him sober.

If she didn't go downstairs with him, he might very well finish the night at the Woodcock Saloon across the street.

A bath in the newly installed bathing room at the end of the hallway did much to revive her, however. Reclining in the claw-footed porcelain tub, she smoothed the lavender-scented bubbles—which Mavis O'Keefe, the proprietress of this outlandish hotel, provided for all female guests— over her drying, dusty skin, striving all the while to keep her experiences of earlier today at bay. If she didn't think about him, maybe his image would disappear like the evaporating bubbles in her bath.

After drying herself vigorously, she wrapped her wet hair in another towel, turban-style, and lathered a lotion of fresh lemon juice, rubbing alcohol, and glycerine over her entire body. Tomorrow she would lie abed with a beauty pack on her sunburned face, she vowed, returning to her own room. What would the girls at school say if they could see the way she punished her skin with such abandon!

Dressing in a simple batiste shirtwaist with lace yoke and tuckings and a lightweight black wool skirt looped up at the hemline with velvet binding, she again tied her hair with a single matching ribbon.

Rube awaited her in their tiny parlor, and they descended the grand staircase to the dining room together. He had made a few improvements, too, she noticed, complimenting him on his fresh shave and haircut.

He studied her thoughtfully. They ordered—he a steak with potatoes and gravy, she, one of the specialties of the house, beef stew, both orders served with all the coffee and cornbread sticks with fresh butter one could eat.

Finally, Rube broke the lengthy silence. "Tell me about our enemy."

Meg looked into his faded green eyes. Some of the redness had already vanished. Funny, how quickly he recovered from his bouts with Demon Rum, both in body and in spirit. She hoped he wouldn't bring up the subject of the missing stakes again. Once had been enough to unnerve her. On the ride into town, when he asked, she'd suddenly recalled she hadn't thought to ask Kalib about the stakes. Her admission had elicited a strange silence from Rube then. *Let him keep that silence now*, she prayed.

Attempting an air of composure she didn't feel, she shrugged. "I've already told you. He claims his deed is valid."

"Tell me about the man, himself," Rube persisted.

Looking down, she studiously picked through her stew for a large piece of potato, which she speared on her fork.

"You're a good judge of men, Meg," he went on. "Since you were a tyke, you've been able to see right through to the heart of a man." He grinned. "Perhaps I should say to his conscience."

Inhaling a steadying breath, she chanced a look at him. "Not this one. He's an enigma. If you met him on the

65

street, he wouldn't strike you as a treasure hunter. I mean, he doesn't come across as some idle . . . ."

She shrugged again. "All men aren't predictable, Rube. You know that better than I."

"Is he trustworthy, sugar?"

A piece of beef caught in her throat, and she struggled to swallow against it. When at last she felt calm enough to speak, her voice came out reedy, and her words faltered.

"How could he . . . ?" She paused, gained a measure of anger, then continued. "How could he be trustworthy, when he is obviously lying about ownership of the property?"

Rube held her gaze with his own, and she trembled when he spoke. "I mean, can a man trust him with his only daughter?"

The next morning Meg accompanied Rube on an inspection of the construction work around the depot site. Thankfully, he refrained from broaching the now most uncomfortable subject of the prospector.

Actually, Kalib had long since—almost twenty-four hours now, she thought with a glance at the near noontime sun—ceased to be *the prospector* in her thoughts. Now he was Kalib, a sensual, demanding, passionate mystery.

The most mysterious part being her inexplicable physical capitulation to him, a stranger, when she had never been kissed . . . or touched . . . by a man before. What demon had taken hold of her senses?

The only two times she had seen him, they had been totally alone—except for Tobin's brief presence. It was as if he were a vision—a figment of some wild, unfulfilled dream. She had asked if he were a devil. Perhaps he was.

If so, she sighed, she'd be tempted to reside in the netherworld, forever, in his arms.

The heel of her walking shoe clacked against the boardwalk in front of the uncompleted depot, and she snapped to her senses. Wiping her brow with the back of her hand, she was thankful for the late-October sunshine. Perhaps anyone who noticed her flushed skin would think she had taken too much sun.

A number of townspeople accompanied them on their inspection tour, anxious to see if their efforts were pleasing to the railroad. The passenger depot and the freight house were well along.

"Another month, six weeks at the most," Dr. Jefferies told her. Standing at her elbow, he topped her by a good six inches, and she suddenly realized Dr. Hank Jefferies was likely the most eligible bachelor in town. His sandy hair and still freckled nose were wholesome . . . refreshing. . . .

And not in the least arousing in the romantic sense, she thought, suddenly realizing *that* part of her, the romantic part, was already spoken for, albeit only in her reveries.

She smiled at Dr. Jefferies enthusiastically. "It's a fine depot," she lauded. "You folks in Silver Creek really do things up right."

The group of six followed Jefferies through the open structure of the building into the area destined to become the freight house. He motioned widely about the room. "In a few short months this place will be bulging with goods."

Murmured assent traveled around the room. Libbie Lancaster, the Silver Creek banker, spoke above the din. "Mr. Fred Harvey has approached Mavis about purchasing her hotel. He wants to turn it into one of his popular Harvey Houses, you know, with those pretty young Harvey Girl waitresses and all that good food."

The room fairly buzzed with this news, which Meg suspected a good half of those gathered had heard before, with the speed with which word traveled in this community.

"Way things are going," Woody Woodson, the saloon-keeper, ventured, "a man's gonna have to spruce up his place to keep pace with progress."

The group laughed, agreeing, and Miracle Westfield, the wife of the hotel manager, added her piece of information in a dreamy, faraway voice. "Just think, the depot will be finished in time for the Christmas Ball on December tenth. We'll have enough room this year to invite everybody in the state of Texas."

Hank Jefferies squeezed Meg's elbow, while explaining. "We've decided to hold the ball in the depot. The proceeds will go toward our bond."

She laughed. "Rube'll be glad to hear that. He's always worried about a community's bond dept." Suddenly she had the uncomfortable feeling she was about to be invited to the ball—as Dr. Jefferies's date. Casting her eyes about for Rube, her mind flailed in search of a suitable change of topic.

As if on cue, Ellsworth Fredericks, the nosy editor of the *Silver Creek Sun*, came to her aid. "See you made it back to town without mishap, Miss Britton."

She squinted at him, wondering at his meaning, but before she could think of a reply, he spoke again.

"What's this about the missing stakes?"

Her eyes flashed.

"Word going around says all the location stakes along the right of way have disappeared."

Meg felt Hank Jefferies's eyes on her. She fumbled for an answer. "Wherever did you hear such nonsense, Mr. Fredericks?" she managed to mumble.

"Not nonsense, ma'am," he replied hurriedly. "Gospel fact."

She wondered at the sense of uneasiness that never failed to overwhelm her in Ellsworth Fredericks's presence. Staring straight across at him now, she decided her disquietude must stem from his height. They were so near the same size that every time she so much as glanced his way, she invariably stared directly into his always probing eyes.

That thought calmed her enough that she regained her composure. "I'm sure it would take a whale of a wind—likely a hurricane—to do away with *all* the survey stakes, Mr. Fredericks. And you don't have hurricanes in this

68

country, do you? Perhaps your varmints are large enough to abscond with our stakes. Though heaven only knows what their motives would be."

She looked inquiringly at Hank Jefferies. "What do you think, Dr. Jefferies? Could it be to shore up their dens?"

Ellsworth Fredericks bristled under the mockery. His eyes pierced her as he spoke again. "Word has it there's a man . . . claimin' to be a prospector of sorts . . . holed up in the area of the old mine shaft. Think I'll take a ride out an' see what he has to say. Might make interesting copy for the *Sun*."

Meg smiled, a feeble smile to be sure, while inside her heart beat a fierce staccato. She nodded slightly to the newspaper editor. "Do that, Mr. Fredericks. Be sure you do that. . . ."

Rube's clear voice interrupted her confused mumblings. "Yes, sir, you folks have come through real nice, real nice." He drew deeply on his meerschaum. "Looks like you'll have the pens and all ready by the time we roll our ribbon of rails into town."

He took Meg's arm and ushered her through a space between the wall supports of the depot. "Real fine," he repeated, then looked down at Meg. "Time for me to hit the trail."

She frowned.

"Can't tarry in town too long," he announced to the crowd in general.

"I thought you were staying a while," she inquired in a near whisper.

He shook his head. "No can do. Duty calls."

"Rube. We had an agreement." Instantly, those words brought Tobin's similar plea to mind. What had he meant? she wondered. Was his agreement with Kalib as pressing as hers with Rube? She sighed audibly. One thing for sure, neither she nor Tobin were having much luck winning compliance.

"We won't hear from the land office for a week or so," Rube told her later, as he led his mount from the livery stable. "I can't stay away from the tracks that long. You can bring me the word when it arrives."

She stared at him hard. He did need to see to the tracklaying and numerous other tasks involved in bringing this railroad to town. But could she trust him?

"Rube," she began tentatively, "stay off the bottle."

He patted her on the shoulder. "You can trust ol' Rube, sugar. I'm off it now."

She inhaled a deep breath. "Now," she agreed. "What about tonight, and tomorrow, and . . ."

"Don't worry about me," he said. "I know I have trouble. I don't understand it any better than you. Sometimes it's like . . . well, like a demon of some sort grabs hold and won't let go for a spell." He grinned at her, trying to look reassuring, she knew. "Suppose that's why they call it Demon Rum."

A demon. She recalled her own explanation for submitting herself so wantonly to Kalib's embraces. "You must be on guard, then," she told him firmly. "Constantly. This railroad has to be finished on time. You know what it will mean to your future otherwise."

"I know, sugar." He gave her a peck on the cheek. "You take care of things at this end, I'll see to the other."

She watched him mount and draw the reins into his hands. "Rube," she called after him, "stay away from Demon Rum."

He saluted her with his hat.

"And Di . . ." she ventured cautiously. "Stay away from . . . from the Diamond-Stacker."

His expression turned solemn, and his eyes glinted with a stony edge. "Di has nothing to do with my drinking, Meg. Nothing whatsoever. Di's a trustworthy woman." He held her gaze with his own until she recalled their conversation in the dining room the night before. Then he relaxed his features and smiled. "You can trust your ol' pa with her, sugar."

Sinking spurs into the flanks of his mount, he galloped away leaving her standing in front of the livery stable, her hands clasped to her very warm cheeks.

His parting message sank like a boulder into her senses. What was he telling her? To live her life and let him live his? How did he know what had happened to her at Kalib's camp? He didn't know! He couldn't!

Furiously, she stormed toward the hotel. But if he did know, how could he . . . how could any father condone such dastardly, wanton behavior?

Chapter Four

The next couple of days passed with relative calm, except inside Meg's head. Work on the depot, the freight house, and the pens progressed at a steady pace. The community's anticipation of the coming railroad ran at flood stage. Hank Jefferies never quite managed to invite her to the Christmas Ball, and Ellsworth Fredericks disappeared.

This last fact troubled her every time she recalled the nosy editor's threat to approach Kalib's camp, but she scoffed at such concern. Kalib, Tobin, and Wash, as Kalib had called their blond cohort, were certainly capable of protecting themselves from the likes of Ellsworth Fredericks. Hadn't they already proven their adeptness at such aggressive activities? And what difference did it make to her, anyhow?

She tried to worry about Rube. If he returned to the Diamond-Stacker, she knew well enough that Di would entice him with some of her fancy concoctions.

That she wasn't being fair to Di, Meg knew, also. But neither was Di's flaunting of Demon Rum fair to Rube. What, these days, was fair?

As her mind wandered for the umpteenth time to Kalib, a heavy drape of despondency fell over her shoulders, and she was incapable either of shrugging it off, or completely understanding it. She seemed to have run smack-dab into a dream, a dream the likes of which couldn't exist in the world she had in store for her with Rube and the railroad.

Not that she didn't plan to fall in love and even to marry, someday . . . she swallowed against a bitter taste of disappointment. When she did fall in love, it would have to be with someone associated with the railroad. How else could she look after Rube? After all he'd done for her—raising her under the direst of circumstances, taking her along on all his jobs, without the aid of a wife, providing her with an expensive eastern education—she couldn't abandon him when he needed her most.

Especially not for some lunatic treasure hunter! That thought jolted her from a restless sleep late one night. Springing from her bed, she stormed about the room in her bare feet trying to recall the details of her very realistic nightmare.

He'd called her a whore! That bastard! He'd called her a harlot! A scarlet woman! A soiled dove!

Well, practically, anyhow, she thought furiously, hearing again his dastardly words. He might as well have—it was what he intended, suggesting she belonged in a hurdy-gurdy house!

Returning to the bed, she gave the plump feather pillows several fierce jabs with her fist and tried to settle down to a more peaceful sleep.

Such sleep, however, eluded her. She did doze some, but over and over she found herself awake, staring into the darkness overhead, recalling the mounting inconsistencies about Kalib, the treasure hunter.

That bastard treasure hunter! she swore vehemently into the soft canopy above her bed. Who the hell was he? Serving *tea* in *china cups* at a *fancy oak dining table*, which sat on *refined woolen rugs* in . . . in a *miner's camp!*

The first thing Mavis O'Keefe noticed when Meg stumbled to the breakfast table the following morning was her distraught appearance.

"My sight isn't as good as it used to be, darling, but I'd

swear you have three dark circles under each eye. Don't these men know anything? Railroad building is their work. After breakfast we'll fix you a beauty pack of warm honey, lemon juice, and oatmeal, and you climb right back into bed and get the rest you should have gotten last night."

The idea sounded good to Meg. In fact, the mere thought soothed her as she finished breakfast and listened to the animated conversation around the long community table. The dining room proper of the Hotel O'Keefe was equipped with individual tables, but for breakfast Mavis used a long table in the rear of the room, claiming family-style dining gave her guests a feeling of belonging to the community, since they were joined by several of the town's tradesmen: saloonkeeper Woody Woodson, the ancient hostler, Slim Samples, the young Dr. Jefferies, and, when he was in town, newspaperman Ellsworth Fredericks.

Gripped by a sinking feeling at the thought of Fredericks's threat, Meg tried to sustain the idea that whatever harm Fredericks might bring to Kalib could not possibly make up for the turmoil that bastard treasure hunter had put her through. She tried to concentrate on the table talk concerning the growth the railroad was expected to bring to Silver Creek.

"I'm going to have to build me a new saloon," Woody insisted. "My old place won't do for the city slickers we'll have coming to town. They'll expect something finer."

"Yessirre, folks! Enjoy the peace and quiet while you can," Hank Jefferies enthused. "Life is sure fixing to light up around here."

Woody Woodson sat facing the doorway leading into the hotel lobby. Suddenly, he raised his hand and called over Meg's head. "Hey, Ellsworth, bring us a paper in here."

Meg turned to see Ellsworth Fredericks, rumpled and unshaven, drop a stack of newspapers on the registration desk and come forward, a couple of papers in his hand.

Woody took one, and the men around him gathered to read over his shoulder. Fredericks handed Meg the other copy, studied her a moment, then left the room.

The malicious grin on his face should have forewarned her, she thought later, as she snapped at the paper like a catfish at a worm-covered hook, her worries on Kalib.

Woody read aloud from the lead story, which dealt with plans for the inauguration of the new governor, including a ball several Silver Creek couples planned to attend, and the fact that Governor-elect Chaney was expected to return from his elk hunt in the Big Bend region revitalized and ready to tackle all the state's problems.

"Like straightening out them railroad higher-ups," Slim Samples offered. "Maybeso he can get some laws passed so common folk can afford to use the contraption. . . ."

"No offense, Miss Britton," Hank Jefferies broke in hastily. "We know real railroaders like your father aren't responsible for the excessive rates. It's the bosses at the top who're bleeding the little man and the businessman alike with impossible tariffs."

Meg smiled. "I'm well aware of the unfavorable sentiment toward railroad rates and practices, Dr. Jefferies. I'm not sure the answer lies in a politician's lap, though."

The men at the table mumbled agreement with her mistrust of politicians, and she looked back to the paper, half listening, half searching for the source of Fredericks's sly grin when he'd handed it to her. Then she found it.

At the bottom of the front page. The caption alone was enough to give her a case of the vapors:

Chief Engineer Britton Foiled
in Attempts to Complete Railroad.

The article itself represented slander at its worst:

According to officials in the Santa Fe's home office, the railroad has long been plagued by Chief Engineer Rube Britton's inferior performance. Sources in the field have now learned there is little

75

Britton can do to complete the Summer Valley-Silver Creek spur in time for Governor Chaney's scheduled dedication speech.

She read the first paragraph twice, then finished the article, which stated in strong terms that Rube was both unqualified and incompetent to perform the duties of chief engineer. The writer—Fredericks, no doubt—left the clear impression that someone from the Austin office—presumably under the direction of General Manager Leslie Hayden—had been sent to spy on Rube.

Her heart lurched, then thumped wildly. *Kalib!*

Eggs and sausage scrambled with buttermilk biscuits and peach preserves in the pit of her stomach. *No! No! No! No!*

Racing from the table, she fought to prevent both her breakfast and her fear from bursting forth. On the front porch she clung to one of the newels, the newspaper crumpled in her hand, her eyes steadying on the dried-mud ruts of Main Street.

Finally, her racing thoughts stilled and the quaking in her flesh subsided. She breathed deeply in and out.

Her initial impulse was to lay into Ellsworth Fredericks, but more important matters cried out to be tended to. Rube must be warned. What if that rattlesnake, Leslie Hayden, *were* behind this? Rube must be told immediately.

But what would such news do to him? She shook her head dismally, holding her hair back from her face. This news would provide the very excuse he needed to return to Demon Rum.

Donning her mahogany wool riding habit, which only last night she had dusted with warmed powder and brushed clean, she wished absently for the luxury of a local scourer such as she sent her clothes to back East. They always looked and smelled so fresh—with no bother on her part.

After tying her hair back with a matching ribbon, she hastily repacked her tapestry satchel. This time she would

76

stay with Rube, she decided, until the railroad was completed. If Leslie Hayden intended to destroy Rube's chance to make a comeback, he would have to step over her to do it!

Hiring the sorrel she'd ridden before, she left town in haste, her mind in a whirl. She would stay with Rube and not let anything happen to him. He deserved as much chance as the next man to straighten his life out once more.

The miles sped beneath her horse's hooves, while her mind raced with her fears, Rube's problems, and plans . . . plans . . . plans. . . .

Plans to silence Ellsworth Fredericks. Plans to defeat Leslie Hayden. Plans to bring the railroad in on time.

Quite without warning she came upon the Silver Creek River, and new thoughts assailed her . . . unwanted thoughts of Kalib.

Sickening thoughts. The realization that she had been taken in by such a man both embarrassed and infuriated her. It was as though she had consorted with the devil while he skewered Rube on his poisonous prongs.

As disgusted as she was with her own weakness, her personal disappointments paled beside her fears for Rube. The question of how she managed to find herself emotionally and physically entangled with such a man as Kalib—a stranger, at that—made her feel even more dim-witted. But being the practical person she was, she understood that some things, such as emotional entanglements, were beyond the scope of her own more earthly abilities to comprehend.

Her fears for Rube were not. How could she have been so blinded that she hadn't seen through Kalib? Looking back on things now, she realized he had given her all the clues she needed.

Along with covering them over with an ample layer of charm and passion! She'd known all along he didn't belong in a prospector's camp. Not that his camp in any way resembled the normal shoestring operation one associated with miners.

Hot tea! China cups! Chandeliers!

How could she have been so stupid? How could she have let him drug her with his . . .

Berating herself wouldn't do, she admonished. Action was what was needed. Action. Quickly.

Rube was the one to handle matters from here on out. Rube, with her beside him to keep him strong in spirit. But they must act with haste.

How far the *Silver Creek Sun* circulated, she had no idea. Likely, only in the immediate area. So, if they acted quickly, the word would probably not travel too far. To Austin, specifically, she thought. If they acted quickly, they could still finish the railroad, even if Leslie Hayden *had* sent Kalib to spy on Rube. She sighed, as a mingling of disgust and disappointment throbbed inside her. In light of the missing stakes and other overt acts against the railroad, sabotage was likely a more accurate term than spying.

Sabotage! Her heart beat a painful dirge. If Rube and a group of his brawny Irish tracklayers could attack Kalib's camp before . . .

Shaking her head at her own simple-mindedness once more, she stared at the sparkling waters of the Silver Creek River and thought of the sheriff.

Why hadn't she thought of the sheriff before she left town? He could have gone to Kalib's camp while she rushed to Rube's side.

Once aware of her nearness to the river, she had skirted the valley where Kalib's men had encountered her both times she had ridden this way before. Coming now to the shallow crossing, she relaxed a bit, protected by the low hills along the riverbank, and dismounted to allow her horse to drink. After he finished, she held the reins firmly in her hands and lowered herself, stomach resting on a sun-warmed rock, and scooped some cooling water into her mouth.

She grinned in spite of her plight, thinking that with practice, she might get the hang of this yet. She'd certainly managed to do more than wet her lips this time.

Rising, however, her pleasure vanished, replaced by wholehearted self-denunciation.

Kalib offered her a hand as she rose. "Wish for an angel, and you get a mermaid!"

His voice rumbled along her spine, and her first thoughts were traitorous—to Rube. Feeling herself grow weak at his nearness, she gritted her teeth forcibly and tried to submerge her emotions—her dreadfully *misguided* longings. *Would she had been forewarned of his presence!* She would at least have come armed against disloyalty to Rube.

But she hadn't been aware of his presence, and his eyes reflected the sparkling river, and she lifted a limp hand to his, all the while reviling herself for her racing pulse.

Just before flesh touched flesh, however, she regained her anger and withdrew her arm, scrambling quickly to her feet and out of his reach.

He stared silently, mildly amused.

"Traitor!" she hissed. "Saboteur! Spy!"

Kalib cocked his head, wet his lips tantalizingly with the tip of his tongue, and Meg turned swiftly away.

When he didn't respond, she chanced a look and was startled by the way he studied her. She could fairly see his brain whir.

Tightening her fist around the reins, she glared at him one last time. "Don't pretend to think too hard," she chastised. "You know perfectly well what I'm talking about."

He shrugged, and the muscles on his broad chest flexed visibly beneath his work shirt. "I was just trying to decide whether I've been promoted or demoted," he replied lazily. "Is a traitor, saboteur, and spy higher or lower than a bastard devil?"

His mocking banter fired her anger to the boiling point, and she glared at him through the filtered autumn light.

He shrugged again, this time with a curious grin. "I thought so . . . a demotion. Mind telling me what this is all about?"

"You know well enough!" Turning toward her horse,

she started to mount, then thought of the newspaper in her saddlebag. Without really intending to, she jerked it loose and handed it to him. Deep inside her a need stirred . . . a desperate need to show him she knew of his scheme against the railroad and Rube. Emotions closer to the surface berated her for it.

Kalib studied the paper, scanning the lead article. Finishing, he looked at her strangely, then asked in a quiet voice. "What does this inauguration stuff-and-nonsense have to do with me?"

She jerked the paper from his hand. "Not that," she snapped, turning the paper over so the bottom half of the front page was exposed. "Here. And don't even attempt to tell me you don't know what it means."

He read the article as she spoke, mouthing the words. Finished, he scrunched the paper into a ball in one fist. "So you think I . . ." he began slowly, wondering how the hell a little thing like looking for a lost silver mine could have suddenly embroiled him in the middle of a matter he had no desire to be caught up in.

"I *know* you're the spy," she spat at him. "Nothing else about you even remotely makes sense."

Kalib sighed with a sheepish grin. Tobin had warned him against bringing her into camp. He shouldn't even have gone out to meet her that first day. Staring at her now, with the sun glinting off the rosy highlights of her enticing chestnut hair and so fiercely from the depths of her green eyes, he grinned more broadly. Oh, yes, he should have, he rejoined silently. He'd just have to work things out so she believed in him again.

Jerking her reins from her hand, he stepped into the saddle of her horse and stretched his hand out to her, his smile forced, his eyebrows arched.

"Take it," he barked. "Step on my foot and pull yourself up behind me."

Her head spun in maddening circles. "You're crazy. . . ."

"Get on up here," he ordered. "I'm going to show you once and for all what I'm doing in this country. Then maybe you'll leave me alone."

His last sentence did the trick. If he would leave her and Rube alone, she told herself fiercely, she'd gladly leave him alone.

Seated behind him, she tried valiantly to hold on to this conviction, as well as to keep herself on the horse without touching him. Finally, she gripped her fingers over the cantle.

He let her ride that way while they loped along the riverbank. Then when they started up the steep embankment, he reached back and dislodged first one of her hands, then the other, until he had them around his waist.

"Maggie, Maggie." His voice rumbled to her, reverberating through his body into hers behind him. "How will I be able to convince you I'm not a spy or any of those other damnable things if you fall off and hit your head on a rock and die on me?"

"You'll never convince me." She spoke vehemently to his back, but her efforts to keep from bouncing about painfully on the back of the horse and the weakness that gripped her at being so close to him took much of her breath away, and she had no idea he could hear her. "You even admitted to taking all those stakes."

She felt him chuckle beneath her arms. "A few stakes?" he asked, turning his head so she could hear him. "Is that your evidence against me, ma'am?"

His insolence in the face of such behavior further infuriated her. Would it *were* all she had against him! "I'd call twenty miles' worth of locating stakes more than a few," she retorted.

He didn't answer, and afterwards they spoke no more. Leaving the embankment, they entered the valley, where he spurred his mount to a gallop, forcing her to grip him ever more tightly about the waist.

They raced thus over the crest east of his cabin, where they slowed and then took off in a demented fashion up one of the lesser-used trails.

Vaguely, she wondered where he was taking her. At first, she supposed to the cabin, but when they passed it, she became tense.

Not frightened. For some strange reason she felt no fear of this man—not in the physical sense, leastways.

Emotionally, she was already in shambles, she admitted to herself. What more could he do to her emotionally than to woo her—for that was exactly what he had done on their two previous meetings—and then betray her. Anything in between would be easy to take.

Or so she thought.

By the time he drew to a sharp stop, they were well back in the hills. Without warning, Kalib swung one leg over the saddlehorn, dropped to the ground, and reached both hands to help her down.

She stared at him momentarily before accepting his arms, and her brief glance assured her she need not fear his holding her in his arms—only that he would *not*.

Turning loose her waist after the briefest of contact, he dragged her by the hand up an even dimmer trail than the one they had traveled on horseback.

Twenty or so rods from where they left her horse, his boots ground to a stop in the loose earth. He jerked her forward.

"See for yourself," he demanded.

She stared into the gaping hole in the side of the hill. "See what?" she asked, furious that she had allowed him to sidetrack her from her rush to Rube's side.

"It's a cave. . . ."

"I can tell that!"

"Go on in."

When she hesitated, he nudged her with a hand to her rear. Instead of being suggestive, however, or even intimate, his touch more nearly resembled a push one would give a balking child, and something inside her felt suddenly empty.

The cave wasn't deep, not over ten or twelve feet, and only high enough to allow her to stand comfortably. Kalib hunched over, then squatted on the floor.

Nodding his head toward her, he spoke his instructions in clipped tones. "Kneel on down here," he commanded.

"You can't very well see from up there."

Kneeling reluctantly, she took the rocks he offered and turned them over in her palm. "What are they?"

"Silver," he answered, staring at her intently.

She looked around the cave. "Is this the mine?"

He shook his head. "Just some silver carried up here, probably by ancient miners."

Inhaling a lungful of dusty air, she squinted at the dull gray stones. A tiredness of sorts settled over her, and she recognized it at once—disappointment. She had been expecting proof—irrefutable proof that Kalib was who he said he was, a treasure hunter. What a fool she was!

"How do you know who carried these rocks up here? Or from where they came?" she demanded. "They could have been left by anyone . . . carried in by who knows who . . . yesterday or a hundred years ago. You can't tell such things."

His heart stood still at her words. He sensed her disappointment and was glad for it. Yet, he was sorry at the same time. She would be hard to convince. She was too damned smart.

"I realize that," he said at last. "But they fit the pattern . . . the old stories. Tobin and Wash are out looking for the mine shaft at this very moment. Fact, that's what I was doing when I saw you ride past."

Meg rose and stepped outside the cave, sucking in large drafts of fresh air. Funny, she thought, how little it helped to revive her smothered spirit.

When he took her arm, heat raced all the way to her brain and she flinched. He gripped harder, jerking her around to face him. Her feet slipped on loose rocks along the hillside, but she quickly caught her balance.

"Maggie, listen to me. . . ."

Pulling away, she turned from him and stood facing the afternoon sun, but the heat was at the back of her neck, where the fine hairs stood on end, begging for his touch. Lifting both hands, she swept imaginary strands of hair from her face and held them with her fingers on top of her head. Inside her a battle raged, urging her to mount her horse and ride away now, urging her to turn back to him. Instead, she simply stood still.

Kalib stood beside her, hands on hips, making no attempt to touch her. "I don't suppose you've ever run into a treasure hunter before?"

She pursed her lips between her teeth. Still, she was unable to move toward her horse. She wasn't at all sure her legs would carry her the four or five paces required.

He studied her, wondering how much he could get away with telling her . . . how little. Watching her stand there, so still, like a statue, her raised arms accentuating her tiny waist, her uplifted breasts, he was hard put to keep from taking her in his arms.

"We're not a bad lot, treasure hunters." He spoke quietly. "All we ask is a little time to find what we're looking for, then we'll be gone. We don't aim to hurt anyone."

Her spinning brain took in only parts of what he said, listening as it was for the things he didn't say . . . something, however small, to extricate him from involvement in the sabotage. But his last statement hit its mark, spreading fury through her ragged emotions. Incensed, she whirled to face him.

Her eyes swept him from head to foot. "Don't insult my intelligence. You're no treasure hunter. I can see that now. I would have seen it before, if only I hadn't been . . ."

Quickly she pursed her lips over the truth that had threatened to blurt from her mouth. "You're no treasure hunter," she repeated. "And you certainly *do* intend to stop this railroad, no matter who you have to harm to do it."

"That's a damned lie," Kalib stormed, slamming one fisted hand into the other. "You wouldn't know a treasure hunter if he slapped you in the face. Or . . ."

He glared hard at her . . . *or kissed you on the lips . . . wildly, madly. . . .*

She stared back at him, finishing his sentence silently . . . *or kissed me on the lips . . . passionately, desperately.*

Neither of them moved a muscle, until at last he spoke again. "I have no intention of stopping the railroad, Maggie," he argued, quieter now. "I need a railroad through here as much or more than any man in the country. How else will I get my ore to market?"

Staring at him still, Meg felt her rigid muscles begin to relax, and in relaxing, to tremble. "You're infuriating," she retorted, though her voice was not loud enough for her threat to carry much weight.

She stepped toward her horse. With a gentle hand to her arm, he again stopped her in her tracks. The touch sent tremors through both their bodies, and each felt the other's turmoil.

"I know," he agreed, in answer to her description of him, reluctantly dropping his hold on her arm. "But we can work around it."

Inhaling deeply, she at first refused to meet his eye. "No, we can't." Her voice was firm, then it abruptly changed to bitterness. She stared into his pleading brown eyes.

"If you're helping Leslie Hayden put Rube out of business, you'll live to regret it. I promise you. I'll do everything I can to ruin you, treasure hunter or not!"

Like a cool breeze sifting through the shin oak leaves above them, a premonition swept briefly through his body, giving him a start. *What in hell was he doing?* Fortunately, neither Wash nor Tobin were around to hear her threat.

"Damnit, Maggie, listen to me. I'm not trying to stop the railroad."

She glared at him, her mouth ajar.

Staggering backwards a step, he grinned and held up his hands, as if to ward off her blows. "I know . . . I know. It sure enough looks like it. I even owned up to removing some of those stakes, but I told you why. I also told you this little interruption is only temporary. As soon as I find what I'm looking for, the railroad can pass, either along its intended course, or on another path, away from the mine."

Her chin tilted upwards and slightly to the right, giving her the effect of snubbing him, when in fact she was straining fiercely to keep from looking into his mesmerizing eyes. Once she did, she had the dreadful feeling she would lose Rube's case for sure.

"I'm not trying to ruin Rube's business," he told her emphatically. "You could, at least, *try* to believe me."

Lowering her gaze, she studied the rocky ground at their feet, thinking how drab everything was this time of year. Although they had yet to see the first freeze, all the grass had browned long since, from the heat and dryness of summer.

"And while you're at it," he added, his voice rising in ire, "try *not* believing everything you read in the damned newspaper. In the brief look I got at this issue of the *Silver Creek Sun*, I saw more than one item I know for a fact to be wrong."

At his words, the picture of Ellsworth Fredericks and his ever-negative probing crossed her mind. Quickly, she reached her horse and mounted. This time Kalib stood stockstill, making no move to touch her even by way of helping her into the saddle.

Without speaking, she touched her heels to the flanks of the sorrel, but suddenly he caught her reins and jerked hard, causing the animal to rear and pitch, sending rocks flying down the hillside.

"Where are you going?" he demanded.

She answered through clenched teeth. "To Rube."

"To Hell on Wheels?"

She squinted at him through narrowed eyes, hardly believing her ears. "Isn't that where hurdy-gurdy girls work?" Jerking the reins furiously from his limp hands, she turned and headed down the hillside.

With the first day of November fast approaching, the days had already begun to grow shorter. Even though she had left Silver Creek before midmorning, by the time she stayed a while with Kalib, then stopped at the construction train, she didn't arrive in Hell on Wheels until dusk. Lamps outside and inside the Diamond-Stacker glowed in the twilight, lending a feeling of gaiety to the otherwise drab and dreary tented terminus town.

Although during her growing up years she had never been allowed inside the saloon proper once the evening crowds began to appear, she'd never given much thought as to why. Kalib's accusation, however, stung her with the truth that girls who grow up in terminus are not likely to be considered ladies, in the proper sense of the word.

The denunciation stirred a vengeance inside her she hadn't known existed. Usually even-tempered, she was becoming more and more volatile with each passing day.

Checking herself in full stride, she paused just outside the main entrance to the Diamond-Stacker and instead turned and entered the building from the rear, by the door leading into the hallway to Di's living quarters and storerooms.

Admonishing herself fiercely for this further proof of her inclination to desert Rube's camp, she forced herself to think on the future. . . .

The immediate future . . . such as: the easiest way to tell Rube about the news article.

Voices greeted her when she opened the door and stepped inside the dimly lit hallway.

"No, no, no," Di's gravely authoritative voice instructed. "That cask is to contain St. Croix rum."

Meg stopped in the door. The small storage room was filled with casks and other paraphernalia used by liquorists—or mixologists, as Di preferred to call herself—to produce practically any drink a customer might call for.

Of course, she justified her bogus concoctions by insisting she used *real* whiskey in her liquors, not grain alcohol like bartenders of dubious moral character were known to serve. The fact that she cut cheap rye whiskey with water until it had no taste, then added ample measure of essences of whatever flavorings she desired, seemed not to enter into the question of authenticity.

Di looked up and blinked. "Meg, dear. What are you doing back so soon?"

Meg's concern began to build, and she covered it with a

veneer of irritation. "Where is he?"

Di rummaged about the countertop nervously. "He's asleep," she answered, nodding across the hallway. Then turning her attention back to Georgie, she handed him a vial of amber liquid. "Use this sparingly. And let me taste the results before you bottle them."

Despair welled like a geyser inside Meg, and she could hold it off no longer. Ever since she'd stopped at the construction train, she'd known she would find Rube drunk. But until now, with their confrontation imminent, she'd been able to hold back her emotions.

Along with her unfamiliarly conflicting thoughts. Why did she insist on throwing her entire life to the wind for a man who cared so little about her that he stayed drunk all the time?

Stopping before Di's closed parlor door, she realized suddenly that she wasn't even quaking, as before, at the idea of finding Rube in Di's bed. What did she care who or even how many women he slept with?

He could sleep with Di morning, noon, and night, for all she cared! Never mind that she herself had just rejected the man she loved. . . .

Loved? Confusion fluttered like white heat through her entire being. Suddenly, another line of Burns's poem sprang to mind, and she stood still, transported as in a dream back to Kalib's arms:

> Had we never lov'd sae kindly,
> Had we never lov'd sae blindly,
> Never met—or never parted—
> We had ne'er been broken-hearted.

Burns, she thought with a sigh. The way that man wrote of love turned all the girls at school into quivering masses of femininity, dreaming romantically of unrequited love.

Love? Meg shook her head furiously, as though to relieve it of such an objectionable idea. She'd never loved anyone, not in the romantic sense, anyway. Never.

Especially not that bastard treasure-hunter!

Never met—or never parted—

And she wasn't broken-hearted, either. Certainly not over Kalib whatever-his-name-was.

Inhaling a deep, tremulous breath, she pushed open the parlor door and stepped inside. She was tired, that was all. Simply bone-tired.

Brokenhearted over Rube? Well, of course. Sighing, she pushed straggling lengths of hair away from her face and considered him, lounging on Di's horsehair sofa with a bottle of whiskey on the table beside him.

Looking up, he stared at her a moment before finding his wits. "Sugar, what're you . . . ?"

"Is that all anyone around here can ask?" she stormed. "What do you *think* I'm doing here, Rube? I don't come to this place for my health. The only time I come is to drag you out of this damned saloon when you're in trouble."

Rube tried to rise, but he only managed an inch or so before falling back onto the sofa. "What's trouble. . . ."

Closing her eyes against a wave of despondency, she steadied herself against the door frame. Her hand tightened on the newspaper, which first she, then Kalib had crumbled in frustration, and she wondered why she had bothered.

"He'll be all right in the morning, dear," Di said, moving Meg with a gentle nudge so she could close the door. "I've ordered supper brought in here. Georgie will deliver it directly." She crossed the room to Rube. "Why don't I help you to bed now, rounder. Tomorrow you'll feel like tackling the world again."

Rube shrugged Di's hand away and patted the sofa beside him. "Come over here, sugar, and tell ol' Rube what's matter."

"We can talk about it tomorrow," she told him.

Rube gave her a lopsided grin. "You can tell me now. My legs might be wobbly, but my brain's all right."

"Your brain is pickled, Rube," she retorted. "Like all the rest of you. I don't know why I . . . why I even thought you wanted to build railroads again."

"I do," he insisted, becoming increasingly agitated.

"What makes you say I don't want to build railroads, sugar?"

His words were so slurred she could hardly understand them, an indication he'd been drinking even more than usual.

"You're only upsetting him, Meg," Di said. "Whatever the problem is, it'll have to wait until tomorrow. In all my years on the railroad, I haven't found many things that don't improve with setting overnight. Drunk men and whiskey top the list."

Infuriated by Di's lack of sensitivity to Rube's problem, Meg turned raging eyes to her. But before she could think of anything even remotely appropriate to reprimand the woman with, a loud commotion erupted from the saloon proper.

Di rushed from the room, and as the noise increased, Meg followed. Rube stumbled behind them.

"What's going on in here?" Di demanded above the din.

Meg had just recalled, incongruously, that for a small woman Di had an uncommonly powerful set of lungs, when she heard the excited reply.

"The fanciest goddamned train you ever seen just pulled into town," one of the saloon patrons enthused.

Georgie, who had evidently gone to fetch their meal from the HOW Cafe next door, rushed in, his face glowing with the news. Meg smiled at what a stir a little thing like a fancy train pulling into the station caused in out-of-the-way places like this. In Northampton, where she had attended school back East, such things were too common-place to be noticed.

Nevertheless, she followed along as the saloon emptied, finding herself standing outside in the middle of the wide space that served as the main street, with her inebriated father clutching at her sleeve.

The train was indeed fancy. The engine, a sleek diamond-stacker polished to a fine gloss, pulled only one car.

As she watched, her heart rate slowed to a deathlike pace, but each beat pounded violently against the constraints of her corset.

The *Texas Star!*

"My God, Rube, get back inside. Quick. It's Leslie Hayden. We can't let him catch you drunk!"

After Maggie rode away, Kalib squatted on his haunches and absently chewed a sprig of dried grass. The sound of her horse's hooves faded and a serenity settled over the hillside, but his own calm exterior belied the turmoil inside him.

He should be worrying about himself, he chastised himself, recalling vividly Tobin's fury upon discovering that he had given her his name, to say nothing of taking her inside the cabin and showing her the plat.

"She'll blab everything you said and she saw all over town, mark my word. I've never known a female yet who could keep her mouth shut about anything!"

Maggie's different, Kalib thought, but he kept his own counsel, because he knew only too well that she could indeed tell everything she heard and saw.

"I was careful, Tob," he explained. "She didn't hear or see anything out of the ordinary . . . leastways, nothing she could link to any of us."

He hadn't been able to soothe their ruffled feathers, though, neither Tobin's nor Wash's. And what he had in mind now wasn't going to set well with them, either.

But he'd made up his mind, and that was all there was to it. Walking down the hill, he crossed the valley to where his two companions searched for the old mine shaft. His thoughts rode with Maggie Britton.

The idea of her riding into Hell on Wheels gave him the all-overs. Terminus towns weren't safe for anybody, male or female, peopled as they were by the scum of creation— professional gamblers, dive-keepers, prostitutes, gunmen, and thieves.

That Maggie had likely spent time in terminus towns before occurred to him, since her father was a railroader, but he brushed the thought aside as irrelevant, since that

91

was before he knew her . . . before she had gotten under his skin, in a way that promised to create one hell of a problem, as Tobin assured him more than thrice daily.

A beautiful, young, independent woman like Maggie Britton riding into a terminus town would be viewed as fair game—like a bull elk sporting a perfect rack of horns to the hunter. Chuckling at the comparison, he stumbled over a rock, caught himself, and hurried on.

"You want what?" Tobin stared at Kalib incredulously.

Wash thrust fists to hips and eyed Kalib with a knowing grin. "I knew that woman was bad news the instant I set eyes on her. The pretty ones always are. And the prettier, the . . ."

"Think what you want," Kalib told them. "I've made up my mind. And don't look so gloomy. Have I ever let you down? Trust me."

Tobin snorted. "I've always trusted you, friend. You know that. But this is the first time you've acted like a lovesick calf, since . . . since that little black-eyed filly named Carmen when you were eight years old."

"You ain't eight years old any longer," Wash put in, grinning from ear to ear. "And with your advanced years, and your . . . ah, station in life, you can't afford . . ."

Kalib cut his friends' good-natured mockery short. "My mother is sure to be pleased. She's been most unhappy with my single status."

"Pleased you've fallen for some railroader's daughter, who's likely never seen the inside of a schoolroom?" Tobin snorted.

"Is that your impression of her?" Looking from one to the other, he addressed his question to both his friends.

"Listen, Kalib," Tobin argued. "Neither one of us has spent time with her. We're just saying what's probably true. No matter what you think you feel for this . . . this admittedly very pretty young lady . . . she isn't worth derailing the whole operation."

Kalib inhaled deeply, then slapped each of the men in

turn on the back. "Lighten up, boys. I'm not about to derail us. I merely want you to help me keep this *very pretty young lady* safe while she's in Hell on Wheels. You know as well as I, those terminus towns didn't come by their name accidentally, they earned it. Now, set to it."

He watched them leave, Wash to Hell on Wheels, with instructions to keep Maggie in his sights but stay out of hers, and Tobin to Austin, with instructions to tend to business, while keeping out of sight of anyone who knew them. Then Kalib went on searching for the mine shaft. The sooner he found proof of the mine, the sooner he could get on with the important matters of running his life.

Chapter Five

One look at that sleek crimson and gold railcar sent white-hot terror chasing cold anguish through Meg's veins. Only her many disciplined years of placing Rube's welfare before anything else allowed her to function.

First, she had to get Rube out of sight. Leslie Hayden must not, *could* not, find him here . . . drunk.

The anguish that mixed with her terror at watching the general manager's magnificent traveling car, the *Texas Star*, pull onto the side railing to take on water and fuel was secondary . . . it *had* to be. Rube's job was at stake now.

Rube's job took precedence over Kalib's betrayal. Kalib, who had spied and sabotaged. Now his master had come to collect his dues—Rube's job.

Her earlier anger at Rube evaporated under pressure of her fear; her accusations that he didn't want to build a railroad lay forgotten, as mindless barbs thrown in warfare, intended only to wound, never to destroy.

Rube Britton was the best damned railroader in the business. Drunk or sober he could outbuild any other man, living or dead.

But drunk or sober didn't count with Leslie Hayden. Only sober. The general manager had made that quite clear to Rube with Meg standing by his side before they left Austin.

One time. If he caught Rube drunk on the job one time,

he was gone.

The two women hastily shoved Rube back into the Diamond-Stacker, where they secreted him within the safety of Di's living quarters. Leaning her back against the closed parlor door as if to bodily stop anyone from entering, Meg strove to catch her breath, all the while issuing a stern warning to Rube to confine himself inside these two rooms for as long as that rattlesnake Hayden remained in town.

Then she turned stormy eyes to Di. "No one . . ." she demanded, ". . . no one is to know Rube is here. Everything must go on like always, business as usual, but . . ."

"Meg, dear, there's no need to be hostile. What do you take me for?"

Filled with the urge to tell Di exactly what she took her for, Meg expelled a great sigh. "Leslie Hayden didn't just happen to come to town," she told them both. "That's why I'm here. He's had a spy among us all along—the pros . . ."

Swallowing quickly, she hesitated, suddenly unable to accuse Kalib out loud. Instead, she retrieved the newspaper from the floor where it had fallen in their haste, and thrust it into Di's hands. "The missing stakes . . . Hayden's behind it. He's trying to get rid of Rube. As you'll read, his spy has all but finished the job for him. He's taken care of everything, except firing Rube."

Di smiled down at Rube, who had sunk to the sofa where he sat slumped forward with forearms resting on his knees, his head cradled in his own hands. "Hayden will have to find him to fire him, dear." She spoke with such force that Meg had trouble deciding whether the woman wasn't enjoying the hullabaloo. Recalling the number of scrapes the three of them had been through before, however, she knew Di was merely rising to the occasion, as in their previous ordeals with Rube.

"I'm going to borrow Georgie from you for an hour or so," Meg added, her mind now racing to the next hurdle Leslie Hayden's arrival had erected in their path. "He can ride out to the construction train and warn Uncle Grady, while I try to stall Hayden."

Di raised her perpetually arched eyebrow. "You'd best stay in here with Rube. I'll see to things . . ."

"No," Meg insisted. "I must get to Hayden before someone in town has a chance to tell him about Rube's . . . condition."

Di was already at the door. Opening it now, she called to Georgie, then turned her attention to Meg. "You brought a change of clothing in this satchel?"

Meg nodded. "But I certainly don't have time . . ."

"Indeed you do," Di countered. "You can't meet the general manager in such a tumbled-up state. Give Georgie instructions, while I press something for you to put on, and your hair . . . I do hope you brought your rat, dear. You look a fright . . . like you've skirmished with the devil himself."

Meg inhaled sharply at the reminder of her encounter with Kalib. "I did," she answered mournfully, "on the way out here."

In the precious few minutes it took Meg to issue Georgie both instructions and warnings, Di tidied her clothing with one of the several irons she kept continually on the fire to freshen moustache cloths and other linens for the saloon. First, a white linen waist with gathered-on sleeves and a high lace-trimmed collar, then a bengaline gored skirt of the deepest myrtle green. While Meg fashioned her hair awkwardly around the rat, Di struggled to fasten a tightly fitting magenta belt just below her tiny waist with a filigreed belt pin.

"There you go, every inch the lady." Di patted the pin in place and stood up. "Come on."

Even though the entire operation had taken less than five minutes, Meg followed Di into the saloon proper with trepidation. She must get to Leslie Hayden and keep him from disembarking here in Hell on Wheels. Her work was certainly cut out for her, she realized now, for she couldn't allow him to travel to the construction site tonight, either—not before she and Uncle Grady had an opportunity to synchronize their stories.

As the double-action doors at the rear of the saloon swished behind them, the commotion inside engulfed the two women. Strains of a bawdy tune, the melody of which Meg had often heard but never the words, drifted above the din of men's unrestrained voices:

> The miners came in '49,
> The whores in '51.
> They rolled upon the barroom floor,
> And begot the Native Son . . . ooo . . . on. . . .

"Bart!" Di snapped immediately upon hearing the song. "Cut the frontier genealogy."

"Ah, Miz Di. . . ." the guitar player began.

"You heard me, Bart. Can't you see there's a lady present?" Then, as an afterthought, she added with emphasis, "This *isn't* a bawdy house."

Meg's head reeled. Her only thought was to get to the *Texas Star* before Leslie Hayden decided to disembark.

Suddenly Di stopped short in front of her. Thinking she had stopped to speak to someone in the throng of customers, Meg pushed around her. At that instant, she heard the Diamond-Stacker's proprietress's throaty voice, and her stomach flip-flopped.

"Why, if it isn't Mr. Leslie Hayden himself! Come in, come in. Let me find you a table."

Meg's hastily made plans tumbled before the general manager's appearance in the saloon—the saloon, where any number of well-meaning patrons could and would tell him of Rube's presence . . . and of Rube's condition.

Interjecting herself between Di and the general manager, Meg faced him, praying her knees didn't give way. She quickly stifled her first impulse, which was to favor him with a smile. A smile from her would only further arouse his suspicions. Offering him her hand instead, she strove for a businesslike demeanor.

"Mr. Hayden." She paused, then adjusted her voice so she could be heard above the clamor of the crowd. His ramrod-straight posture and stern features reminded her of an army general encountering, not his own troops, but the enemy. "I was just coming to welcome you. Things are going so well, Rube will be pleased. . . ."

"Miss Britton?" Hayden squinted through the haze of smoke. Leaving her, his gaze traveled around the saloon, searching, then settled again on her with obvious distaste. His voice was flat, emotionless. But his words rang as a death knell in Meg's brain. "Will we find Rube here in town or at the construction train?"

Her mouth felt cottony, and she had trouble shouting above the crowd this time. "At the construction site."

Suddenly she became aware of the other men in Hayden's party, older men, graying, bespectacled, attired as Hayden himself, carrying Homburg hats and wearing suits to match, their eyes bright with anticipation. One of them reached for a loose strand of her hair.

She slapped his hand away.

Hayden bestowed a knowing, tight-lipped smile on her, then spoke to the man beside her. "May I present Miss Britton? Our *esteemed* chief engineer's daughter."

The man closed his gaping mouth, but he continued to ogle her over the wire rims of his eyeglasses.

Di rescued her from the unseemly situation. "Miss Britton came in search of some wayward tracklayers." Taking Hayden and Meg by one arm each, she babbled on. "I'm sure she will be delighted to fill you in on the magnificent progress of the rails. I'm sorry I can't provide a wine room where it would be more appropriate for her to visit with you. Perhaps my office will do." With that she maneuvered them around the screen, through the swinging doors and the cigar apartment, and into her always cluttered office.

The din settled to a low rumble. "Seat yourselves," she told them cheerfully. "I'll see to a round of drinks."

"And women," one of the men in Hayden's party added. "Bring on the ladies."

Di's look could have melted a mile of steel rail in the dead of winter, and Meg stifled a grin.

"This is a drinking establishment, sir. Our entertainment includes billiards, faro, keno, poker, and singalongs. We can offer you beer or ale, fancy drinks, cocktails, cobblers, flips, fizzes, smashes, a fine milk punch, or a *pousse-café*. As to ladies, there are only two on the premises, and believe me, sir, we are both that—ladies. Cross the line with either of us, and you will go home with a splitting headache, totally unrelated to our outstanding stock of liquors."

The five men in the room stared at Di in absolute silence as this diatribe rushed from her inviting lips. "Now," she finished sweetly, "if you'll be seated here where the crowd noise isn't so pressing, I'll return with your drinks." Without waiting for them to place individual orders, she sashayed from the room, and they heard the swinging doors swish behind her as she re-entered the saloon.

Meg turned level eyes on Leslie Hayden. "As I was saying, Mr. Hayden, Rube will be delighted you've come to inspect the railroad. In fact, you couldn't have arrived at a better time. Everything is going so well. . . ."

"This isn't an inspection tour," Hayden began, and Meg froze. She tried to steel herself for what she knew would follow.

His tone was more cordial now, and, as on other occasions when she had met with the man, she wondered briefly whether his stern demeanor wasn't just the natural expression of his severe facial features. Two vertical wrinkles of bare skin formed a natural frown just above the bridge of his nose, interrupting unnaturally straight brown eyebrows. Clean-shaven, his upper lip receded beneath a razor-straight nose into a tight, thin-lipped mouth, giving him the appearance of continually pursing his lips. His chin was covered by several inches of fuzzy hair, which fell somewhere between a goatee and a full beard.

Looking at him now, Meg suddenly thought of Kalib and his faceful of hair. Her head reeled. *Kalib.*

Was he spying for Leslie Hayden? Was that what she sat here waiting so painfully to hear?

"These gentlemen are investors," Hayden told her, turning to introduce his retinue of bankers and businessmen. "They've come to see firsthand the fine railroader we have in Rube Britton." His smile, no more than a thin curved line three-quarters of the way down his face, reflected for a moment in his glassy eyes. What an actor, Meg thought, again finding herself hard-pressed to keep a straight face. But there was nothing comical about a snake skimming smoothly through the grass, concealing his vengeance until he was ready to strike.

She couldn't allow her guard to slip. Yet, if Hayden's trip really had been prompted by a need for investors—for capital—perhaps he hadn't seen the *Sun*, nor spoken with Kalib, yet. If she could keep him occupied the entire time he was here. . . .

". . . what a dependable man we have in Britton . . . how fortunate we are to have him on our side. . . ." Hayden continued smoothly, like a slithering snake, and she waited, listening for the deadly sound of his rattles. "He's at the site, you say?"

Pushing a loose strand of hair away from her face, Meg nodded and tried for a convincing tone of voice. "If he has returned from his foray into the countryside," she lied. "He went in search of timber contractors. You know how dreadfully difficult it is to find reliable contractors."

Hayden nodded shortly, then spoke to the men around him. "We'll stay overnight here on the siding. In the morning we'll fire up the *Star* and take a looksee. I know you're going to like what you see." He turned back to Meg.

"How far away is the end of track?"

She hesitated, hoping its close proximity wouldn't change his mind about going on tonight. "A mile . . . maybe a bit more." If she lied this time, she'd only be caught out in the morning when Hayden arrived at the site. Then, he's be less likely to trust anything else she told him. And one thing she knew beyond a doubt, Rube Britton would not return from his fictitious sashay into the countryside until Leslie Hayden was well on his way back to Austin.

Di returned, followed by Bart carrying a silver tray laden

with stemmed goblets of champagne, into which had been stuffed an array of fruit—grapes, orange slices, and cherries. "Champagne juleps," she announced.

"A veritable dessert," one man complained.

Ignoring him, Di dispersed the drinks, then left the room, only to return a moment later bearing two ornate decanters of amber liquid, along with what appeared to be a calling card.

"St. Croix rum," she told Hayden. "For your guests, when you retire to your car. Of course, you're welcome to gamble with us this evening. However, I'm sure you'll be more comfortable in the quiet surroundings of the *Texas Star*."

Hayden took the bottles, studied the card, then thanked her with a curt nod. "Indeed," he responded, draining his glass of all but the fruit. "Gentlemen, what say we down these cocktails and get to our supper. Our mess of quail is languishing in the wine sauce even now."

Meg rose along with the investors, wishing desperately she could think of some way to hold him here until morning. Di, it appeared, had effectively sold them out, sending them away so soon. Now, Hayden had ample time to meet with Kalib before he inspected the railroad tomorrow.

Held back by the agony of indecision, Meg stood, awkwardly watching them leave. Would the man dare fire Rube *in absentia*?

Turning at the door, Hayden bowed slightly. "We expect your company on our little excursion in the morning, Miss Britton. Six o'clock sharp." Without waiting for a reply he pushed through the outer doors of the Diamond-Stacker and disappeared into the night.

"Don't worry about a thing, dear," Di whispered, placing a sympathetic arm around Meg's waist. "My little message informed our Mr. Hayden of the bevy of ladies from under hill awaiting him and his investors in the *Texas Star*."

At Meg's horrified stare, she quickly added, "And the ladies have instructions not to leave the gentlemen alone

101

until daybreak, especially not the esteemed general manager.''

Sighing, Meg headed for her sleeping quarters in the storeroom. Try as she might, she couldn't find fault with Di's unorthodox manner of keeping Leslie Hayden under guard. The shady ladies would relieve her of worrying about Hayden's whereabouts all night.

Georgie had returned by the time she checked on Rube, so she sent him back to Uncle Grady, this time with a message bearing her exact fabrication to Leslie Hayden and warning him to expect them early the following morning.

With that accomplished, she retired to her room, brushed her hair one hundred strokes—an act that never failed to relax her—and tumbled into bed, exhausted. But sleep eluded her once again, and she tossed and turned, anticipating the dastardly events she would most surely face come morning: the loss of Rube's job . . . the proof of Kalib's betrayal. Kalib's betrayal.

The thought never failed to startle her. Somehow this man Kalib had worked his way into her subconscious in an entirely unwelcome fashion. Somehow he had become important to her—far too important for the short time she had spent with him.

Likely that was it, she assured herself, dressing the next morning in her brushed grenadine suit. Smoothing her hair around her rat, she tucked the ends in with ample pins to hold it secure. No need giving Hayden's investors another excuse to manhandle her.

That was it, she assured herself, again. She hadn't spent enough time with Kalib to become thoroughly appalled by who and what he was.

His kisses had been heavenly, merely because they were the only kisses she had ever known. Likely if she were to be kissed by someone else, she would discover how distasteful his kisses actually were.

When she was kissed by someone else, she reproved herself, anchoring her bonnet by a ribbon beneath her chin. *When*. She definitely intended to remedy the fact of

102

her inexperience as promptly as possible. It was way past time for her to fall in love—with some suitable gentleman, not a pleasure-seeking treasure hunter. A suitable gentleman with a railroad career. Surely, such a man existed . . . one who could take Kalib's place in her heart.

In her heart! she swore, accepting a china coffee cup engraved with a golden emblem from Leslie Hayden. She had come to the coach trembling at the mere thought of what this day might hold for Rube. But as important as Rube's job was—important enough that she found herself caught up in all sorts of lies and playacting—all she seemed able to think about, nevertheless, was the prospector!

For a moment the lavish brocade and gilt-trimmed interior of the *Texas Star* took her mind off other matters. No wonder railroad barons had such despicable reputations among the general populace! Their board members traveled in luxurious and free accommodations on the same rails the public was required to pay through the nose to use for business.

Hayden attended his group of investors like a mother hen. He even smiled at Meg. "Sit yourself, Miss Britton. Sit yourself. You must look out the window and describe your father's progress to us as we go along."

Her legs trembling from the fear in her heart, Meg sank to a horsehair-stuffed red brocade banquette, grateful the man nearest her was the one she judged most ancient in the group, and the only man present who had not paid her the least bit of attention. She blushed at her thoughts, momentarily wondering whether he had enjoyed the favors of one of the under-the-hill gang last evening.

The engine fired. She braced her arms against the windowsill in an effort to keep from spilling the contents of her coffee cup onto her lap. The velvet window draperies had been pulled to the side where they were held with gold-tasseled cords, and she watched the dismal little settlement of Hell on Wheels begin to move outside the window. Several people stood around the dusty streets watching the ornate train. Di held open the back door of the Diamond-Stacker, shading her eyes with one hand against the morning sun.

With pursed lips Meg looked for Rube, but true to her word, Di had kept him out of sight. As she turned her head slightly, a blond-bearded man came into view suddenly, and she gasped, sloshing coffee into the porcelain saucer.

As quickly as she saw him he disappeared, but she needed only a brief glance. Even though she had seen him but once before, she recognized him instantly—Kalib's friend Wash.

Distracted by disturbing questions that wouldn't be quieted, she had trouble concentrating on Leslie Hayden and his carload of investors. Had Wash met with Hayden? Why else would he have come to town?

And most important of all, had he discovered Rube's temporary confinement in the Diamond-Stacker? If so, she could rest assured Leslie Hayden knew, as well.

They arrived at the construction site well before midmorning, and Uncle Grady greeted them with an appropriate mixture of surprise and pleasure.

Hayden took Rube's absence in good humor, and encouraged Grady to show the investors the railroad's progress. The investors, in turn, questioned Grady about rails and ties, ballast and fill. Simple questions the average man in the street could answer. Hayden kept his own counsel, leaving all the questions to his investors. By noontime they had checked into everything of interest at the construction site and declined to take horses farther into the field. Grady invited them to wait until evening when Rube and the crew foremen would return, and Meg held her breath for fear Hayden might accept. He could easily ride from here to Kalib's camp during the night.

He declined, however, after consultation with his investors, who obviously were more at home in boardrooms than at construction sites, and they partook of the noonday meal on a leisurely trip back to Hell on Wheels in the salon car, where a rotund uniformed chef had set the two gaming tables with white cloths, napkins, silver, and crystal services.

Sickened almost to the point of swooning, a thing she never did, Meg expected each word Hayden spoke on the way back to be followed by Kalib's name. With great effort, she concentrated on the lavish meal of oxtail soup, roast venison, boiled sweet potatoes, green corn, and for dessert, coconut pudding in wine sauce, *edam* and roquefort cheeses, Bent's crackers and fruit. The dry red wine served with the meal was bitter, but Meg drank her full glass. Champagne accompanied the dessert, and she quickly consumed two whole glasses before she realized it.

The investors showed more interest in the champagne than they had in anything all day. It was too warm for their palates. It seemed the *Texas Star* was running low on ice.

"We'll replenish in Hell on Wheels," Hayden told them. "I'm sure the saloon can spare us enough for our journey back to Summer Valley."

Hayden's suggestion suddenly gave hope. She pushed a length of hair back with unsteady fingers, planning. . . . These grumbling men were unlikely to tarry long in a place where they couldn't find enough ice for their drinks.

Later, she grinned, watching them pull away from Hell on Wheels. She hadn't won the war, not by a long shot, but one skirmish had definitely gone her way. And all it had taken was a quickly whispered sentence to Di with Leslie Hayden hot on her heels, after which Di informed him with regret in her voice that her own ice shipment was two days overdue and her regular customers would have to do with room-temperature drinks until it arrived.

Before he left, Leslie Hayden actually patted her shoulder and thanked her for showing his investors the railroad. "From their comments, I'm certain of the funds to complete this spur, counting the Silver Creek bond money, of course."

She smiled, feeling a bit light-headed from the wine. "Rube will be sorry to have missed you," she said.

He eyed her sternly. "Be sure to have him in Austin for the board meeting on January twenty-first. The railroad will be completed by then, and I have assured the directors

Rube will be present with his final report. We purposely set the meeting for Inauguration Day, so you will want to come along for the ceremonies. A good time to celebrate Rube's completion of this spur—two weeks before the new governor dedicates it."

Meg nodded weakly. The reminder of the short time remaining to finish the railroad flooded her with the multitude of problems they faced.

Rube wasn't in Di's quarters, and Meg's depression sank to a familiar feeling of pure dread. Pushing through the double-action doors into the saloon proper, she stared dismally at the billiard table where he was engaged in a game with a young rust-eater.

Georgie had already lighted the chandeliers, and the room was filling rapidly with men and noise. The lateness of the hour surprised her. She hadn't realized they had tarried so long over luncheon.

Rube was well on his way to being drunk. He sprawled across the far bumper of the billard table, maneuvering his cue in a precise mannerism Meg knew so well she could practically see his thoughts in words.

There came a point in Rube's inebriation when his mental, physical, and verbal coordination operated as from three separate bodies, and the struggle he went through to coordinate the three into one movement rivaled General Grant's ability to stage the Battle of Vicksburg.

Rube's opponent, however, was obviously under no such handicap. He ran four balls easily before missing a pocket and standing aside for Rube to shoot again.

Rube was the picture of concentration, never mind his movements resembled those of a wind-up tin toy. Finally, he pursed his lips, blew air into his cheeks, and popped the ivory ball with the small leather tip of the cue. His expression went through three stages also, while he expelled his breath, deflating his puffy red cheeks. His eyes, round as dollars, followed the slow progress of the ball. It rolled along the green felt covering toward the general vicinity of a pocket at the opposite end of the table.

But general vicinity was all it was. Rube straightened, sucked in his breath, and smiled broadly at his opponent's triumphant stance.

Holding back a wayward strand of hair, Meg inhaled an angry breath of stale, smoky air. Rube Britton had never been a sore loser, at least. Why couldn't she be satisfied with that small fact?

But she wasn't. His whole future was at stake, and here he was playing pool and drinking rye whiskey.

Rube's opponent smoothly refitted the long slender cue in its stand, then did the same with Rube's. Rube handed him a handful of coins, which the young man pocketed, and the two shook hands.

Meg strode across the floor, her heels clicking off beat with the strumming guitar, of which she was only now aware. Listening, she heard no singing, though. No bawdy ballad tonight. Nothing but soulful, mournful, out-of-tune regrets.

"Rube . . ." she stopped suddenly, eyeing the man who sidled up to Rube from the other side, writing paper and pencil in hand. Her eyes widened. "Mr. Fredericks!"

Fredericks flashed Meg a winning smile, then turned his full attention to Rube. "I saw the general manager of this spur just leave town," he observed. "What happened between the two of you?"

Rube's legs wobbled ever so slightly. He reached for his glass of whiskey, which rested on one of the drink pockets attached beneath the corners of the table.

"I understand you've run into a bit of a problem finishing the railroad." Fredericks's high-pitched voice shot barbs through Meg's nerve endings. His obvious intention was to badger Rube into saying something he shouldn't, but before she could stop him, Rube spoke up.

"If Hayden told you that, he's a bloody liar."

Meg grabbed Rube's sleeve. "Come on, let's go."

He jerked loose. Squinting through slitted eyelids at the

newspaperman, he continued. "What're you driving at, Fredericks?"

Ellsworth Fredericks shrugged. He favored Meg with a guileful smile. "There's rumors going 'round, Britton—rumors of fraud and . . ."

Rube's face went red, and his unsteady eyes found their mark. "Say it in plain English. Are you accusing me of trying to hornswoggle the railroad?"

Fredericks stumbled backwards half a step, but otherwise he stood his ground. His eyes fairly popped when he opened his mouth to speak. "What about the missing stakes, Britton?"

Rube stepped in, eager for a fray. He swung a punch, obviously intended to land on the newspaperman's left jaw, but Fredericks ducked, throwing Rube off balance. Rube regained his footing. "Ain't no buffalo chip printer with a shirttail full of type going to call me a swindler." He swung again, this time landing a punch to Fredericks's right shoulder.

Fredericks sidestepped the worst of the blow. "Hey, don't fly off the handle like this. I'm just looking out for the community's money. They can't be forking over bond money for a railroad that's never going to get finished."

Rube's next punch hit its intended spot and Fredericks sprawled to the floor. Di and Meg both stepped in this time, each taking Rube by a sleeve.

He shrugged them off and reached for Fredericks's collar. Dragging the man to his feet, he grinned at Di. "If it won't inconvenience you, darling, I'll just kill the bastard here and now."

"Rube, for God's sake, he's a newspaperman. . . ." Meg's words suddenly caught in her throat as someone grabbed her around the waist and dragged her bodily from the scene. Her feet flew out from under her, and her furious eyes met Kalib's serious ones when he swung her over his shoulder like a sack of grain.

"Put me down," she shrieked.

Without stopping, he moved swiftly toward the back of the room. His chest heaved against her stomach, and she could feel the fierce beating of his heart.

"That man is a newspaper editor," she demanded. "Let me go to Rube." He didn't stop, so she pummeled his back with her fists and kicked her legs against his.

He tightened his hold on her legs. "Hold still, Maggie. I'll set you down directly."

The doors swished behind them again, and Di rushed into the hallway. She grabbed Kalib's sleeve, and he swung to face her. Meg stared into Di's troubled face.

"I won't hurt her, ma'am," Kalib told Di. "I'm just taking her back to Silver Creek where she belongs."

Gasping, Meg struggled to free herself. Wash came into the hallway, then, and she saw a look on his face somewhere between dismay and fright. Kalib saw him, too. "Go back in there and make sure Rube doesn't get himself into any more trouble. Tell him Maggie's safely on her way to Silver Creek."

"Like hell I am!" Her flailing had stopped momentarily, but now she began her struggle again in earnest. "Put me down, you . . . you . . ."

She felt him chuckle beneath her, increasing her anger tenfold. "Which am I tonight, Maggie? A bastard or a devil?"

Suddenly Meg gasped again. She felt color hot and red heat her face. Her discomfited gaze was held by Di's startled brown eyes. "Maggie?" Di mouthed.

Infuriated, Meg resumed pounding his shoulders and demanding to be put down, but to no avail. As they exited the hallway into the darkness outside, her last glimpse was of Wash speaking earnestly to Di and Di shaking her head solemnly, her eyes still wide with disbelief.

One horse stood hitched to a low-growing mesquite bush behind the saloon, head dragging. Kalib untied it with one hand, then set Meg on the ground, stepped into the saddle, and pulled her up behind him as before.

Although for a moment he held her by only one wrist, her head spun so rapidly she didn't even think to try to escape until she was sitting securely behind the cantle and he pulled her arms around his waist. Fury seethed within her, then, at her own ignorance. She gripped her hands into tight fists across his belly.

"Don't you dare ride out of this town with me," she demanded, squirming behind the saddle.

"Quiet down now, Maggie. You'll spook ol' Abe."

"Abe?" she questioned, without thinking. "What kind of name is that for a horse?"

He chuckled and she could have strangled herself. "Put me down. I can't leave with that dastardly Fredericks still here."

"Rube's doing a fair job at handling Fredericks," he told her. Gathering the reins with his left hand, he clasped both her fists in his right, pulling tightly enough that, although she squirmed behind him, she couldn't get enough leverage to dismount.

"He needs me," she insisted against his broad back.

"The only thing Rube needs tonight is a bed," he answered.

Squeezed between the cantle and Kalib's full saddlebags, her legs were forced forward, so that the only thing separating her body from his was the curved ridge of the cantle. Her knees brushed the backs of his thighs. When she moved, she kicked him.

"Hold still, wiggle-worm," he cautioned, sinking spurs deep into the flanks of his mount.

Panic rose inside her as the horse bunched, then sprinted forward. "You don't understand," she pleaded. "I must stay here. I have to. Until the railroad is finished."

"No, you don't," he called harshly over his shoulder.

Infuriated at his obstinacy, she fought to loosen his grip on her hands. "I belong here," she said fiercely.

"No, you don't," he repeated.

"It's my home."

Kalib swallowed against his bobbing Adam's apple, and Meg felt his body tense. "Not anymore, it isn't."

"Have you gone mad?" she questioned, but he didn't answer.

They raced through the chilly autumn night, and for a while all she could do was hold on. His body warmed hers,

110

and she suddenly found herself relaxing against him.

As quickly as she realized this, however, she drew back and stiffened her backbone, a position that caused her to bounce unbearably on the back of the saddle. "I can't ride all the way to Silver Creek like this."

Turning loose her hands, he patted her leg where it touched his thigh, sending tremors like thousands of tiny fireflies racing along her spine. "Relax, Maggie," he soothed just above the clattering of the horse's hooves. "Relax and move with the horse. It won't be so hard on you."

Instead of answering, she held her breath, waiting for him to remove his hand, but he didn't for a long time. Then, when he finally did, her leg grew suddenly colder than before.

They rode on in silence, and, at last, she gave in and rested her head against his back.

The sky overhead was inky black. Millions of stars twinkled gaily. The moon appeared as a mocking, cocky grin on a giant black face. Despair filled her at the sight of so much beauty. Her plight was merely that—her own problem. One tiny drop of misery in a world chock-full of larger concerns.

Kalib's appearance tonight clinched his guilt in her eyes. What reason would he have had for coming to Hell on Wheels, other than to see Leslie Hayden? She doubted not that he had succeeded.

Fury swirled in her muddled brain. Didn't he succeed at everything he set out to do? Including abducting her from beneath the nose of her very own father . . . her very drunk father.

At last they approached the river. He guided the horse across, splashing water on her boots and clothing. When he turned toward the north, she protested in a reedy voice.

"Where are you going?"

Shifting his weight in the saddle, he looked over his shoulder. "You said you couldn't ride all the way to Silver Creek."

Her heart leaped to her throat, and she clamped her

teeth over her bottom lip to contain her rage. "Bastard!" she hissed.

His chuckle reverberated against her, filling her with even more indignation.

"I certainly am not going to your camp in the middle of the night."

Reaching back, he patted her leg again. "Now, Maggie, calm down. I don't figure you have much choice."

He hadn't bargained for the fight that ensued, however, and it took all his strength to hold her on the horse without losing his own balance or dropping the reins.

By the time they rode up to the camphouse, they were both struggling more for breath than freedom.

"How 'bout we call a truce?" He slid her to the ground, then followed her. "Over a cup of hot tea?"

Glancing from him to the camphouse, then quickly away, she held her hair back from her face and tried valiantly to steady her racing pulse.

Kalib studied her, knowing her thoughts, her fears. He grinned. "I'll behave myself. That's a promise."

She looked toward him sharply. Moonlight played across his face, clinging like dewdrops in the fine hairs of his black beard. He looked so harmless. Nothing like a man who would sabotage a railroad and bring the engineer down to ruin, not to mention abducting the engineer's daughter in plain sight of everyone in the saloon. All this, and still the nearness of him caused her blood to run hot in her veins. *I'll behave myself, too*, she prayed.

In spite of herself, she grinned and preceded him into the dark camphouse.

"Stand still, while I get a lamp lit in here." Again, his casual, friendly voice belied the night's previous events. She listened while he shuffled about the room, followed by golden halos as one by one he lighted every wick in the three chandeliers, then stoked up the fire.

"The water'll boil while I tend the horse." Moving to the door, he turned and grinned in a totally disarming fashion. "When I get back, I'll scare up some grub."

112

Forewarned, she repeated to herself. *Forewarned is forearmed.* By the time he returned, she determined to have her rebelling emotions under control.

He found her standing over the stove, cooking supper in a skillet. From the doorway he watched, damning himself for causing her such a scare tonight. He'd intended to wait until he found her alone, but how in hell did you catch someone alone in a place like that?

He'd intended to convince her to come away willingly . . . he'd intended to . . .

Shaking his head to rid it of the nonsense she filled his brain with, he stepped into the room. Tobin was right. A girl like this—a girl from a terminus town—had no place in his life.

She'd never fit in. It wouldn't be fair to her. In fact, it would be downright cruel, no matter how lovely and genteel she appeared. Her past would always interfere . . . it would never be forgotten. Life with such a woman was, for him, impossible.

Except, as Tobin suggested, for a one-night stand. A roll or two in the hay, was the way Wash put it.

She turned to face him, and guilt washed over him like a raging flood in springtime. Quickly, he pushed it aside.

Why should he feel guilty? He certainly couldn't be the first, not with a girl from Hell on Wheels . . . especially not with one so beautiful from a place like that.

"See you found the grub."

She nodded, consciously gripping her newfound resolve. "Sausage and eggs. Your water is boiling for the tea."

He crossed the room in lengthy strides, peered into her skillet, and grinned. "Smells good."

"Your cupboard is dreadfully bare, for a man with your tastes. Perhaps you should have petitioned your employer to replenish it with some of his delicacies."

Kalib frowned. "Who?"

Fury at his treachery flamed as hot as the fire within the pot-bellied stove over which she cooked. "Leslie Hayden!" she snapped. "Your employer."

"I've never even met the man," he declared. "You're the

113

one who enjoyed the comforts of his special car today. Perhaps he's *your* employer."

Her eyes popped, but she tried to conceal her outrage by studiously finishing their supper.

He began to steep the tea leaves. "You're a good cook," he offered quietly.

She watched him while he set the table, wondering how she could still ache to touch and hold this man . . . traitor that he was. *"We* eat, too."

Frowning, he carried the skillet to its place between their two plates. After holding her chair, he took his seat opposite. "What?"

She stared at him. "Women from Hell on Wheels. We eat like everyone else; therefore, we cook."

"Maggie, I didn't mean . . ."

"Yes, you did." Her voice was flat. Picking up her fork, she took a bite of sausage. "Eat," she commanded, "or my work will have been in vain."

Anger mixed with guilt inside him, making it difficult to swallow. After a few bites, he threw his fork in his plate. "You said the Diamond-Stacker was your home. Well, I didn't see any kitchen there, so I . . ."

She stared at him so intensely his words died off. Then she sighed. "I'm sorry. I know I'm too defensive, but . . . I've spent time in the outside world. I know well enough what people think about those of us who follow the railroads."

Her words stung to the very core of his guilt, and he busied himself eating the meal she had cooked for him. The idea of . . . of this beautiful young lady, as Wash called her, being shunned by the rest of the world sickened him. But wasn't he as guilty as the next man? Hadn't he thought along these very lines earlier tonight? And didn't he himself plan to take advantage of her terminus-town upbringing later?

Sickened by his own insensitivity, he sought ways to extricate himself from the web of deceit he'd woven around them. "Following the rails must be exciting. Tell me about it . . . about your life."

His eyes probed hers with an unsettling sort of inquisitiveness, and his voice had softened dangerously.

Somehow she managed to smile. "No, indeed. I'm much smarter than you give me credit for. I wouldn't dare jeopardize my position here in the midst of the devil's own camp by giving away all my secrets."

Her lighthearted jesting assuaged his nagging conscience a bit, and he smiled broadly, revealing his magnificent white teeth, gleaming from their luxurious nest of black beard. "How you've relieved my mind. I definitely prefer the role of devil to that of either saboteur or traitor."

His words affected her powerfully. He could see it immediately. "I'm not off the hook yet?"

Rising, she carried the plates to a cabinet at the far side of the room with trembling hands. "I should say not."

"Put the dishes in that tub." He came to stand behind her. "In the morning I'll wash them in the river."

Without speaking, she did as he instructed. Then, suddenly, he grabbed her by both arms and swung her around to face him.

Panic raced through her veins, up her neck in fiery spirals, stirring nervously in the pit of her stomach. "Please," she whispered. "Please, don't touch me."

His hands burned rings around her forearms, but he made no move to release her.

"I don't work for Leslie Hayden." He spoke fiercely. "I'm not out to destroy the railroad, nor Rube Britton. In fact, I hardly know him."

Releasing one of her arms, then, he tipped her chin so she had to look into his eyes. "But what I know, I like."

It took her a moment to gain her senses back. Why was he so good at stealing them away? she wondered desperately. Clutching her teeth over her bottom lip a moment, she found her voice. "You fired on the grading crew," she accused, "and you stole the stakes. You've admitted as much."

"That's right," he said softly. "I also explained my reasons, and I thought you understood."

"I'll never understand. . . ."

115

"You can understand without condoning," he suggested.

"All the stakes? All the way into Silver Creek?"

He nodded.

"Why?"

"Time, Maggie. I need a little more time, that's all. I'm not out to destroy Rube or anybody else. Do you think, knowing you, I could hurt you? Or anyone you care for?"

Heat spread across her skin like a grass fire, leaving her nerve endings scorched and begging for more. Quickly, she pulled away and fled from his touch.

Instead of moving to recapture her, he refilled their cups with steaming tea, and when she chanced a look, he smiled as platonic a smile as she'd ever seen and motioned to her cup.

"You're infuriating," she told him, slipping into the chair again.

"So you've told me before . . . among other things," he mused. "Of course, the same can be said about you."

She frowned. "I'm only doing my job."

They sipped tea, and she relaxed her guard a bit. Finally, she pursed her lips and sighed. "I suppose it's too much to ask you to listen to all the facts . . . I mean, truly listen."

"Not at all," he agreed readily. "On one condition."

She looked at him, silently questioning, her breath caught, as in a vise, somewhere between her lungs and her throat.

"That we first dispense with this matter of my involvement with Leslie Hayden."

"How do you propose we do that?"

Wetting his lips with his tongue, he held his breath a moment before answering. "Simple. You agree to take my word."

Her mouth fell open, then she laughed out loud. But her laugh was bitter, and he did not join in.

"Maggie, I have nothing to do with the man. I promise you. Nothing."

"And I'm to . . . to simply take your word."

He nodded.

116

"Because you're so trustworthy, I suppose?"

"Because I have never lied to you. And I won't start now."

She stared at him blankly.

"I have never lied to you," he reiterated. "I told you the truth about the stakes; I admitted firing on the crew."

Shaking her head in disbelief, she scanned the elaborately furnished camphouse. "You're not a treasure hunter," she whispered accusingly.

"Yes, I am," he responded sharply, then he shrugged and his tone intensified. "That might not be all I am. I never said it was. And I never claimed to be a lifelong treasure hunter. But right now I'm looking for the Lost Bowie Mine."

"In Hell on Wheels, I suppose," she retorted, infuriated by his obstinate refusal to admit to the obvious. Staring at him relentlessly, she continued. "Or were you representing your *other* interests when you and your cohort met with Leslie Hayden . . . and then abducted me?"

Now it was his turn to stare her down. Running the tip of his tongue around his lips, he held her furious gaze until she began to squirm. "Definitely my *other* interests."

Although his deep voice sent tremors of anticipation resonating through her body, she suppressed them. "So, you admit it? You're Hayden's spy."

"Maggie, you're the one not listening. I've never even spoken to Leslie Hayden." His voice rose in anger now. "In fact, the only time I ever saw him was when you returned from your little excursion with him today, a mite too tipsy for one returning from a simple business trip, I might add."

As his allegations became clear, she bolted from her chair and stormed to the far side of the pot-bellied stove. "Bastard!" she hissed, turning her back to him, clutching her arms across her heaving breasts.

"Maggie . . ." Coming up behind her, he placed a hand gently on her back.

She flinched from his touch and resisted with all the strength in her.

117

"I'm sorry. . . ."

Speaking through clenched teeth, she abhorred her quivering voice. "Leave me alone. This is all so stupid. The only thing I care about is Rube . . . and his job."

His superior strength won out, and he swung her around to face him. "Let Rube take care of himself," he demanded into her furious face. "He's your father, for God's sake, not your child. He can very well handle his own life."

Struggling fiercely to free herself, she finally succumbed to his hold on her, bowing her head so only the top of her hair touched his chest. Her scalp fairly burned at his nearness. But her anger was so great, she knew she had never been so out of sorts with any person in her whole life.

Kalib stared at the top of her head. Most of her hair had come loose and now hung in a chestnut curtain about her face. In his mind's eye, he saw her sweep it back in her simple gesture so full of sensuality that even recalling it made him want her all the more.

At length, he let go his hold on her arms, but before she could escape, he ran spread fingers under her hair and held it back her face in the same manner she always did. Gripping the sides of her head firmly, he raised her stricken face to his.

"My *other* business in Hell on Wheels was you, Maggie."

His soft, rumbling voice sent tremors through every part of her body, and she knew he felt them, too.

"You," he repeated, lowering his lips to hers ever so slowly. "Only you."

She struggled to retain her anger, but in the end it was to no avail. His lips, firm and moist and demanding, were what she'd ached for these last miserable hours, and she submitted shamelessly to them.

Her arms encircled his neck, her fingers twisted in his curly black hair, and her face nuzzled into his soft black beard. Suddenly, all her cares stood apart, and she felt separated into two different persons. One, a responsible,

118

sensible young woman called Meg Britton who built railroads and cared for a wayward father; the other, known only to one person in the entire world: Maggie—wild and free and sensual.

His lips left her mouth, laved her face with kisses, and found her ear, where he nibbled mercilessly, running his tongue around inside. "Maggie, Maggie. What you do to me."

Sliding her quivering hands along either side of his head, behind his ears, she felt tremors shake him. Cupping his firm jaw in her hands, she pulled his face back and looked playfully into his pleading eyes—eyes that sent tormenting messages to the very core of her being.

"You must be a devil," she whispered. "You've made me forget everything but you."

A light touched his eyes, and he grinned. "You'd laugh if I told you my reason for hunting treasure. It's very similar to your reason for building railroads."

"Tell me," she breathed into his face. "I need a laugh."

Overcome by the emotions she evoked in him, Kalib shook his head solemnly. His fingers nimbly unbuttoned her jacket and discarded it. "No, Maggie, my love. I know what you need, and right now, it isn't laughter."

Then, kissing her all the while, he expertly discarded her overskirt, breeches, and waist. Suddenly she stood before him attired only in stays and pantaloons.

With a twist of her head, she broke the kiss and stared anxiously into his face. "No . . ." Her eyes darted to the door of the camphouse and back to him.

"We're alone," he whispered, fumbling now with the ties of her corset. "No one would dare bother us tonight."

She blushed, confused, as irritation stirred within her. So that's what he thought she was? She should have known. "I see. Your agreement with Wash and Tobin concerns the use of the cabin."

"Maggie," he soothed. Bringing his hands to her face, he ran his thumbs sensually around her tightened lips. "You're the first woman who ever set foot inside this cabin. Much less . . ." His eyes caressed hers, and in spite of herself, she found her need for him grow to alarming heights.

At her first sign of surrender, he claimed her lips again, arousing her fully with kisses so sensual he knew this night would end sooner than he had planned. His palms massaged her breasts through their confining garments, and when he felt her nipples peak rigidly through her clothing, he held her back, and gently finished the job he'd begun.

She didn't know quite what to expect. She had no idea why she stood so still and unprotesting under his wanton ministrations. But she did know one thing for certain: she could no more have stopped Kalib from removing her clothing than she could have stopped the moon from rising tonight.

And she had no desire to stop either one. Her body radiated heat more powerfully than the little pot-bellied stove, and watching him tenderly touch her, she knew he was warmed by it, too.

The wonderment this knowledge brought was entirely new and fascinating to her. She'd never suspected a person could have so much control over another human being. But tonight it was as though she and Kalib had changed bodies—he controlled hers, and she, his.

As her pantaloons dropped to the floor around her ankles, Kalib swept her in his arms and carried her to the bed. Without a word, he removed her boots and stockings and cushioned her head on a pillow with her long hair framing her face in a sunburst, her legs straight on the bed, naked as the day she was born.

Kneeling beside the bed, he gazed in obvious approval at her unclad form. Then ever so gently he swept one hand over her skin from her toes to her head and back again, sending unbearable tingles along her nerve endings.

"Maggie, Maggie, Maggie," he muttered, moving at last into her outstretched, beseeching arms. "You're so fine . . . so fine."

Instead of claiming her lips, however, as she expected,

his mouth covered one breast and he suckled there lustily, while he kneaded her other breast with his fingers until she writhed from the torturous flames of pleasure.

Moving his mouth back to hers, he delved between her parted lips and plunged inside her offered sweetness. Her fingers bit painfuly into his back as she pulled him toward her, wrestling herself closer and closer to him.

But he held her back and with one hand explored her questing body. When his fingers reached the soft curls below her abdomen, her hand swept out and stopped his.

A groan of apprehension escaped her lips, and he shushed her by intensifying his kisses. Finally, her legs relaxed and his fingers entered her warm, moist body, and he reveled in her inviting response.

Lifting his lips so they whispered against hers, he looked into her eyes and watched tumultuous passion dance within them.

"I've never felt . . ." she murmured.

"I know, love. I know."

The realization of what he was about hit him then. Competition. Pure and simple. He might not be the first, but if he could make her feel as she'd never felt before . . . if he could cause her body to reel and tumble with passion as no other man ever had, at least he would have given her something to remember.

If he could have her but this one night, he would make it a night she would remember the rest of her life and hold above all others, forever.

And he, as well. The thought absorbed him. Selfish? Selfless? Quickly he removed his clothing and stretched along the single bed beside her. Unbridled passion, more likely, he thought, wondering at his sudden sentimentality.

When at last he lay beside her, her body still cried for more. Snuggling ever closer, she nuzzled her throbbing breasts into the soft mat of hair on his chest. Her arms clung to him. Her hands traced his hard muscles and smooth, smooth skin.

His arms tightened around her then, drawing her so

121

close their heartbeats throbbed as one. He wrapped one leg sensuously across her hip and drew her close. Then suddenly she stiffened as his rigid arousal brushed near the center of her own erotic yearnings.

Sweeping his hands up and down her back, he felt her body stiffen, then relax and nuzzle his in such a frenzied manner that without further ado, he shifted her to her back and plunged desperately inside her deliciously fiery sheath.

As suddenly as he entered, he stopped. But not in time. Not before he felt the barrier.

The horrendous tearing of fragile skin.

The frightful tensing of virgin muscles.

The anguished cry of surprise and pain.

Supported on trembling arms above her, his eyes flared open.

She studied him, the undulating light from the multitude of flickering wicks writhed in his stricken eyes.

The pain she felt when her flesh tore shot white-hot fire through her brain, then subsided as quickly as it began, leaving her body as it had been before, still aching with desperate, unfulfilled passion.

"Don't stop," she whispered.

His expression didn't change, and neither did he move, either to withdraw or to continue, so she swept her hands down his back, and, pressing him to her, undulated her hips beneath him.

Finally, closing his eyes to cover the anguish he felt inside, Kalib continued, and in continuing felt his body, at least, recover from the trauma enough to seek and find the summit they both sought.

Afterwards, he rolled to his side, cradled her head in the crook of his shoulder, and rocked her back and forth. He'd never deliberately hurt anyone before in his life, and the knowledge that he had done so now brewed inside him insidiously.

What he'd done to Maggie tonight, though, was different even than setting out to hurt another person.

What he'd done to her just now was cruel—unforgivably cruel and insensitive. Hadn't she told him what people on the outside thought about terminus-town women? And hadn't he thought he knew all the answers?

Damn him! he raged inside. Damn his eternal soul! He'd been so sure he knew all the answers. Now . . .

Now, he'd hurt her beyond all repair. Why, he might as well have called her a whore to her face.

He sighed heavily, shamed beyond his ability to comprehend. He'd wanted to give her a night she would remember. Well, he'd certainly done that. She'd not soon forget such treatment—not soon—not ever.

She stirred in his arms, and he felt her looking up at him. But he couldn't open his eyes to face her. Not now.

"Kalib," she whispered, scooching herself upward so her face was level with his. She kissed the tip of his nose lightly, sending even more shame flashing through his body.

"It only hurt the briefest of moments," she said. "Then . . . then it was . . . fine."

Opening his eyes, he stared painfully into her sweet, innocent face. "I wanted it to be wonderful," he whispered.

The agony in his voice pierced her own hurt. Reaching up her hand, she ran her fingers lightly through the fine hairs of his beard. She knew well enough what he had been thinking . . . why he had done what he did.

But it didn't change a thing for her. If her feelings were strong enough that she could love him in spite of the multitude of difficulties in their lives, one more barb couldn't hurt . . . much. Their chances of having a life together were nonexistent; but they had been so before tonight.

Pecking his lips playfully with hers, she stared lovingly into his eyes. "Then we'll just have to try again."

A tenderness completely foreign to his nature took hold of him at her words, and moisture sprang to his eyes, but he was unaware of it. Awkwardly, he stroked her hair back from her face. Bloodlines and education be damned, he thought. The woman in his arms stood so far above the crowd of bluebloods and eastern-educated women of his acquaintance, that not a one of them could touch her if they were standing on top of the Capitol Building down in Austin.

He ran the tip of his tongue absently around his lips. "What else have I been wrong about?"

She smiled at him as honestly and frankly as she knew how. "Everything."

Chapter Six

Not everything, Maggie, my love, Kalib thought, staring into her begging eyes, which once more stirred desperate longings inside him.

They loved again. This time much more slowly, but every bit as desperately. He eager to teach, she, to learn. Both impassioned with a need to give to the other—pleasure, fulfillment, gratitude—forgiving and forgiven.

And when at last they lay satiated, they still clung to each other, not in desperation now, but for the simple, incomprehensible joy of touching.

He extinguished the lights, and the night passed in glorious passion, as they alternated sleeping and loving. Once she awakened to find the fire had died down and Kalib was gone. When she sat up, he called, reassuring her.

"I'm coming, Maggie. Just getting us some blankets." And when he returned, they loved again.

Toward morning, he stoked up the fire and returned to nuzzle her awake. "Good morning, Maggie Britton."

She smiled, stretching lazily, reveling in the brush of skin on skin. "Good morning, Kalib. . . ."

He kissed her firmly on the mouth, but she wriggled loose. "You *do* realize that I still don't know your name."

"Yes, you do," he mumbled, pulling her closer and kissing her again.

Again, she broke away, studying him with half a smile. "Not all of it. Besides, Kalib is such a common name, you could have merely borrowed it."

"Could have, but I didn't." He reached for her lips.

She twisted away. "How do I know you're telling the truth?"

A grin broadened on his face. "Tobin and Wash would like it a hell of a lot better if I hadn't."

This time he succeeded in distracting her totally, and afterwards, when she lay damp and thoroughly sated with his love, she pulled his face close. "Mr. Wonderful," she whispered. "Mr. Kalib Wonderful."

Staring into her loving face, he choked back rising emotions—sentimentality was an unfamiliar item for him to digest. "You mean after trying all night," he teased, "I finally succeeded."

Her soft laughter sang through his senses. "For the time being."

Rising, he found his saddlebags on the far bed and pitched them to her. "A surprise."

Inside she discovered her satchel, much to her relief, for she'd had dreadful visions of returning to Hell on Wheels in her rumpled riding suit.

Kalib busied himself preparing breakfast while she dressed hastily in an equally wrinkled riding skirt and blouse. Bending from the waist to brush her hair, she suddenly looked up at him.

"How did you know where to find my satchel?" Although she recalled his claim to have gone to Hell on Wheels for her, she didn't begin to understand what he meant.

He grinned. "Wash told me where your room was, and while the ruckus was going on in the saloon, I had him pack your belongings in my saddlebags."

She studied him curiously. "What was Wash doing in Hell on Wheels?"

Ignoring her question, he broke a half-dozen eggs into the sizzling skillet.

"What did you mean last night . . . about why you went to Hell on Wheels?"

He shrugged. "I . . . ah . . ." Without finishing, he

126

studiously returned to cooking.

Coming close, she faced him from the opposite side of the stove. Was he actually blushing? she wondered curiously, or was it the heat rising from the stove? "You what?"

Scrambling the eggs with vigor, he suddenly looked at her helplessly. "Hand me a plate. These eggs are going to ruin."

"I'm waiting," she prodded softly, after they had seated themselves at the table and had begun to eat.

He inhaled deeply and studied her. "Damnit all, Maggie. Someone had to watch out for you. I can't stand to think about all the things that could happen to you in that town."

"I'm flattered, Kalib, but . . ."

"Don't be," he fumed. "It's true. You don't see the ogles those men give you. You don't know what's running through their minds." As she watched, he tore a piece of wheat bread in two and stuffed half of it into his mouth. "I do!" he finished, talking around the bread.

Her eyes danced at his discomfiture. "I grew up there, Kalib. . . ."

"Don't remind me," he swore dismally. His gaze found hers, seeking solace, she could tell.

"Quit blaming yourself," she told him. "You made a very natural assumption. . . ."

Reaching across the narrow table, he laid one slender index finger on her lips, silencing her. "Don't," he whispered. "I'm not ready to discuss that . . . I hurt you too badly."

Pushing her tongue through her closed lips, she tipped his finger playfully. "You didn't hurt me . . . you made me feel . . . wonderful." And loved, she sang silently. I've never felt so loved in all my life.

About the time they finished eating, they heard horses ride up. "That'll be Wash," Kalib said. "He's bringing your horse from the livery stable."

Her eyes widened. "You think of everything when you abduct a woman, don't you?"

Coming around the table, he drew her into his arms. "Not *a* woman, Maggie. *My* woman."

Laying her head against his chest, she listened to his heart beat in her ear—a rhythmical sound, pacifying, secure. The kind of feelings found only in fantasies.

"I'm going to insist on something." He drew her back to watch her reaction. "You're to take your horse and ride straight to Silver Creek. And you're to stay there until . . ." His words drifted off and she cocked her head.

"Rube can take care of himself," he told her. "It's time you let him grow up . . . cut the apron strings."

"You don't understand," she implored. "This railroad spur has to be finished by the end of January. It's a political job, pure and simple. That damned new governor conceived it as a vehicle to buy votes, that's all. Railroad reform was the most passionate issue in the campaign, and he knew to get elected he had to appease the voters. You don't understand the power these damned politicians hold over everybody's heads, Kalib. If Rube stays drunk and this spur isn't finished in time for Governor Chaney to dedicate it, Rube will never work again."

He studied her a long time with one of those preoccupied looks of his, neither sensual nor suggestive, instead appraising. Then he smiled. "You've certainly formed some mighty strong feelings against politicians."

"I've lived with their quirks and instant changes of whim and fancy all my life. Regardless of what you think, living in a terminus town can be an education in itself."

Kalib nodded thoughtfully. "So I see," he mused, then turned more serious. "I understand that you want to help Rube keep his job, but only he can do that. Besides . . ." Stopping abruptly, he pulled her to his chest. "One of these days you're going to have to leave him . . . you're going to *want* to leave him. This is as good a time as you'll find to let him test his wings."

She sighed against his chest, waiting for anger that didn't come. She wanted to tell him she could never leave Rube, not again. But she didn't. He certainly wouldn't understand that.

"You're taking a big interest in someone you won't even trust with your last name," she teased.

Holding her back, he gazed deeply into her eyes, sending her senses reeling. "You'll learn it before long, my love. One day soon it'll be yours, too."

For an eternity they stood locked together by this intense, insane pronouncement. She watched the vein in his neck throb and knew she was seeing a reflection of her own longing. For this one glorious moment she denied herself the right even to *think* of truth, of reality. That would come later. For now, she wanted to feel the need this man had for her in its keenest sense.

"Promise me you'll go to Silver Creek."

"If that's what you want," she mumbled.

He grinned then, an enticing, delicious grin, full of all the sensuousness they had shared this past night. "It's not at all what I want. But it'll have to do for now."

He rode with her a piece, not because he didn't trust her to keep her word—as he said, she could well double back as soon as he went his own way—but because he couldn't bear to spend one more second away from her than he actually had to.

"All for the love of a woman," she sighed. "A woman you still won't trust with your name."

"I have to save something to bargain with later," he teased. "Besides, you haven't told me all your secrets, either."

She grinned, dimming the sun in his estimation. "I'll save my secrets for bargaining power, as well. For when I have the sheriff serve you with condemnation papers."

Back at camp Wash inquired about his raucous evening, and Kalib silenced him with a harsh stare.

"Be careful, Wash, old friend. You're talking about the woman I intend to marry."

"Marry? Kalib Chaney, you've gone plumb loco. You'll never get away with marrying a girl like that."

"A girl like what?" Kalib challenged.

"You know perfectly well what I mean."

Kalib shook his head. "Wait until you get to know her, Wash. She's . . ." He felt his face flush recalling his words, and hers. "She's feisty and beautiful and intelligent and understanding . . . and wonderful."

"She's a girl from a terminus town, Kalib, and you're the governor-elect of Texas. You have an obligation to the people who elected you. You can't flaunt their support—to say nothing of their morals—in their face. You aren't your own man any longer. You belong to the state of Texas."

"Maggie Britton is the best thing that's happened to me in my entire life, Wash," he answered simply. "And she'll be just as good for the good people of Texas."

"They won't stand for it."

Kalib grinned again. "Then I won't take the oath. If I have to make a choice between Maggie and Texas . . . consider yourself the first to know, old friend, now that I've found her, I sure as hell don't intend to let her get away from me."

Wash studied him, a frown creasing his usually unfurrowed brow. "Good God, Kalib. I believe you're serious. Does she know? I mean, about you being governor and all?"

Kalib shook his head. "And I don't intend for her to find out anytime soon." He laughed, hearing her voice again. "The only people on this earth she considers lower than Leslie Hayden, whom she refers to as a rattlesnake, are politicians. No, indeed. Maggie will have to become a lot more attached to me than she is right now, before she learns the facts about my life."

Later, in Silver Creek, Meg Britton came to her senses. The town was astir with word of the general manger's visit to the terminus town, and every man, woman, and child, or so it seemed to her as she fielded questions right and left, wanted to know the latest on the progress of the rails.

130

Excusing herself briefly to change into fresh clothing, she found Uncle Grady waiting patiently in her parlor.

"Rube sent . . . truth is, missy, we're all worried over your whereabouts. Are you—?"

"I'm fine," she mumbled, her mind scurrying to grasp some noncommittal phrase that would set his mind to rest. "Tell Rube I'm fine. In fact, my . . . visit with the prospector will likely help resolve the railroad's problem."

Then, giving up all thought of changing, she took Uncle Grady's arm. "Come with me. We must see what the townsfolk are so anxious to show us."

Ellsworth Fredericks dogged their every step. Rumors flew concerning her abduction from the Diamond-Stacker, rumors aided and abetted by the sensation-seeking newsman. She had trouble quelling them, until she discovered that Rube had kept Fredericks so busy he hadn't actually seen Kalib carry her out of the saloon itself, only into the rear hallway.

"Really, Mr. Fredericks, you're making a mountain out of an ant hill," she chastised him as he put still another biting question to her in the midst of a crowd of Silver Creek business leaders who insisted on showing her the progress of the two enormous yards for loading cattle to be shipped to market. "After all my years with the railroad, do you think I have no friends? The bearded gentleman to whom you refer is one of our loyal employees, who graciously removed me from the unsavory atmosphere you men tend to create in a saloon."

She led the way to the depot, and he followed.

"I should say he removed you, Miss Britton! In a most ungentlemanlylike manner. Why . . ."

Carrying a notebook with her, Meg studiously noted the progress of the two-story depot. Now she straightened from examining a partially full keg of square-cut wrought iron nails and marked down the exact number of kegs left to finish the job. "Mr. Fredericks, I surmise from your questions that my *abduction*, as you insist on calling it, will make front page news in this week's edition of the *Sun*. If so, let me warn you, if you print one slanderous

131

statement—even one—I'll sue."

Fredericks's mouth gaped, but as usual, he had a ready response. "Like it or not, Miss Britton, my job—my vocation, if you will—is to act as the community's conscience."

"Conscience?" Meg turned on the shrill-voiced newsman in fury. "I fail to see how the chief engineer's drunkenness or sobriety or his daughter's chastity—or lack of it—concerns the community's conscience. What is of decidedly more concern is whether this railroad gets built."

"But . . ."

"Let me assure you, Mr. Fredericks," she rushed on, "if you succeed in turning the community against us, they will withhold the bond money, and this railroad won't be completed. That, for your information, is what the general manager's visit was all about. Capital to complete the spur."

After that, Fredericks let her finish her examination of the depot and stockyards without further questions. Seething inside, she struggled through the remainder of the morning with no more reminders of Rube's, Kalib's, or her own outrageous behavior.

The outer walls of the depot had taken shape in the short time since Rube led the last inspection. "Your progress is impressive," she praised some of the workers, running her hands along the rough masonry. With precise detail, she made careful notes of each phase of construction. Not only would Rube be pleased with the progress, Uncle Grady assured her as he tucked her notes into his saddlebags and prepared to return to Hell on Wheels, but such a record would furnish irrefutable proof of the work should Leslie Hayden call Rube to account for any portion of this spur.

Thoughts of Leslie Hayden never failed to recall Kalib to her mind also, as did any number of other things, she admitted dismally to herself while soaking in tepid water

132

and almond oil one evening a few days later.

Convinced of his lack of involvement with Leslie Hayden, she now wished, preposterously, that he were. It would give him *some* link with the railroad, however dastardly. Even that sort of connection would leave her with something positive to hope for.

As it was, any future with him was out of the question. She could never leave Rube.

Although she had no intention of following Kalib's instructions to the point of remaining in Silver Creek until the railroad was completed, every time she started to leave for Hell on Wheels, something arose to demand her attention.

One morning she arrived at breakfast to find a message from Rube. The shipment of bedsticks, a term he used for railroad ties, that they needed to finish the track all the way to the Silver Creek River hadn't been delivered, and work would have to be halted unless he received some soon. His message asked Meg to contact the contractor who was to furnish "burnettized" ties for the ten miles of track from the river into Silver Creek, and see if he could come up with three miles' worth of extra ties for them to use now. According to his message, if the contractor, a man by the name of Trace Garrett, could furnish the extra ties, Rube would send carts to collect them in the next couple of days.

She read the message aloud over breakfast, and as chance—or luck—would have it, Dr. Jefferies was on his way to the Ranche Santa Clara immediately after breakfast to examine the rancher's wife, Mrs. Garrett, whose third baby in the same number of years was due any day now.

"I'll hitch the buggy while you fetch a wrap," Hank Jefferies told her. "We'll kill two birds with one stone, and enjoy ourselves in the process."

Although Meg worried over the consequences of such a trip, she knew well enough that she couldn't find her way to the Garrett ranch alone. Neither could she refuse to travel with Dr. Jefferies, then turn around and hire someone else to guide her.

Much to her surprise, the day proved relaxing and

enjoyable. Hank Jefferies was splendid company. He had been born and raised in this country, and all the way to the Garretts' he regaled her with stories of long ago, "before the country grew up and became overpopulated," as he put it.

She laughed more than in recent memory and was reminded of the times back at school when she'd met schoolmates' siblings. Often, she'd thought how nice it would have been to have had an older brother with whom to share experiences.

Hank Jefferies, she decided, would have made the perfect big brother. He told her about leaving home to attend medical school in Louisiana, at a place called Tulane University, and of the trials and tribulations associated with being a boy from a one-horse town out in the sophisticated world.

She, in turn, reflected on her own similar difficulties at Smith College up in Massachusetts. Hank took her proper eastern education in stride without so much as a raised eyebrow, and she enjoyed sharing her experiences with him.

The experience left her dispirited, however. Once during her wild, wonderful night in Kalib's camp, she had started to tell him about her four years of eastern schooling, but for some reason, she couldn't bring herself to discuss it. Now she knew why.

Unlike Hank Jefferies, Kalib would have been shocked that a girl from a terminus town had received such an education. And she knew she couldn't have endured seeing that shock register on his loving face.

Hank Jefferies, who had had like experiences, understood, possibly because he didn't go about with preconceived notions of terminus people.

Kalib judged harshly. Still, her feelings for the two men were worlds apart. Dismally, she wondered why. How could one's affections be so entirely separated from one's faculties to reason? Unless, as was entirely possible, she admitted grimly to herself, her faculties for reasoning were marred by too much fantasizing.

The ranchhouse on the Ranche Santa Clara, named, she discovered, for Mrs. Garrett, whose given name was Clara, impressed her with its unpretentious elegance. Built of native stone, it sat on a hill with one entire side overlooking a peaceful valley.

"You must return in the springtime," Clara Garrett told her. "The wildflowers are magnificent."

Clara appeared to be only a few years older than Meg herself, and as Hank had indicated, she was in the very last stages of confinement. Unused to being around children, Meg fell instantly in love with the Garretts' two toddlers: a dark, curly-headed little boy of about two years addressed by the improbable nickname "Four," and a tiny girl no more than a year old, whom her father called Clarita.

The day was marred only by its many reminders of Kalib. Every time Trace Garrett affectionately draped an arm across his wife's shoulder, Meg thought of Kalib. And Clara was just as bad—catching up her husband's hand in an instant, encircling his waist with her arm.

The Garretts insisted Hank and Meg join them for dinner. Afterwards, because of her advanced state, Clara stayed behind at the big house while Trace showed Meg and Hank the cottonwood railroad ties his hands had already begun "burnettizing."

"This old dipping vat provided a natural pit for the process," Trace explained, showing how, after being cut to the proper length and width, each tie was submerged into the solution of zinc chloride, which preserved it against rapid deterioration, an operation devised by a Scott named William Burnett.

"Rube will be relieved to learn you have enough ties finished to complete the track all the way to the river," Meg told him. "He has enough good and durable ties to intersperse with these treated cottonwoods at a ratio of about four to one."

"Four junk to one good and durable?" Trace asked.

Meg nodded. "He sent word that he'll bring some carts and men in the next couple of days to pick up what they need."

On the way home, Hank heaped vociferous praise on Meg for her knowledge of railroad building. Suddenly she found herself so comfortable with him that she even confided a bit of Rube's problem. But when he broached the topic of the Christmas Ball, she immediately made the excuse that she would likely be in Austin tending to railroad business during the holidays.

Dismally she recalled the first time the ball had been mentioned, and how then she had thought of herself as being spoken for. She felt even more so now, since her night with Kalib. But, even though his words of commitment still rang in her ears, she knew the situation was impossible.

From her own standpoint, as well as from his. Likely, after the heat of passion wore off, he had either regretted those words or forgotten them. Whichever, she would never know, for she had vowed to stay clear of him as long as work continued on the railroad. Hopefully, Rube could find work next on a railroad a million miles away from Texas. She sighed. Africa would be wonderful, or Australia, or China. Perhaps Rube could build a railroad along the Great Wall. That would take her far enough away from Kalib.

Compounding her worries since meeting the lovely and pregnant Clara Garrett, was the possibility that she carried Kalib's child, a thought that depressed her beyond measure. If that eventuality came to pass, their glorious, yet all too brief, encounter would have indeed turned into a skirmish with the devil, as Di had suggested.

Fortunately, a few days later, her own body relieved her of this worry—but only this one.

Rube was already two days late coming for the ties, and her concern grew by giant leaps. What if he had never even left the Diamond-Stacker? She knew better, because his messages concerning the ties confirmed that he was tending to business, but still she worried.

Vacillating between knowing she should wait in Silver Creek for a reply to their wire to the land office and the great desire to leave before it arrived, she dithered about until her dilemma solved itself at midmorning a couple of days later.

Ellsworth Fredericks, who had kept a low profile since her dressing down of him at the depot the first day she'd arrived back in town, raced panting into the hotel, grinning like a possum.

"I knew the bearded feller who carried you out of the saloon wasn't a gandy-dancer like you said," he announced triumphantly.

Her eyes flashed. "What do you mean?"

"He's the prospector, that's who he is?"

"No," she answered quickly. "I mean . . . how would I . . . ? I thought I recognized him," she shrugged. "But I don't know his name."

Fredericks grinned at her confusion. "You *truly* don't know?"

She shook her head, wondering how she had managed to put herself in the untenable position of lying more often than she told the truth these days.

"Your abductor is the prospector all right. Remember, I told you a couple of weeks back about the prospector who's been digging around out at the old mine shaft?"

Nodding slowly while her mind raced hither and thither, Meg finally channeled her multitude of emotions into a single one—raging anger directed at the nosy, shrill-voiced newspaperman. "What difference does all this make to anyone, Mr. Fredericks? You're forever chasing up the wrong tree. You're like a coon dog with a defective nose or something." Slinging her hair back from her face, she started to turn, but his next words brought her to an abrupt halt.

"Sticks and stones, Miss Britton. Sticks and stones. And they're being thrown by both sides now. The bridge monkeys and the prospector and his two cohorts are locked in mortal combat out by the river."

If someone had physically knocked the breath from her lungs, she couldn't have felt any more woozy. "How do you know?" she demanded. "Did you see him?"

Fredericks shook his head. "Not up close," he admitted.

"But I got a good enough look to be sure he's one and the same—your abductor and the prospector, I mean. He keeps himself hidden beyond those hills, him and his two cohorts. But your pa's bridge monkeys are fixing to show him who's boss of this railroad."

Not until she was halfway there did she question why Ellsworth Fredericks had come all the way into town to inform her of the fight, instead of staying where he could get firsthand copy for his sleazy newspaper. The thought didn't linger long, however, once she considered the odds Kalib faced against the bridge monkeys.

Jerry Sullivan's bridge gang numbered a good three dozen, all large, husky, bearded Irishmen, built along the general lines of blocks of granite, used to manhandling steel and masonry—happy lads, ripe for such lawless adventures as fighting for rights of way.

With a deep sigh, she realized the situation could well be out of her hands. Jerry Sullivan's monkeys could protect Rube's interests without her jumping into the middle of the fracas. Coming before all else in her mind was her strong loyalty to Rube and her responsibility to see this spur to its successful completion.

But her heart was a different matter. As though they were two organs in separate bodies, heart and mind pulled one against the other. Three treasure hunters were no match for three dozen of the toughest bridge monkeys in the business. The resulting clash would undoubtedly escalate into a full-fledged war. Knowing as she did the resoluteness with which Kalib approached his search for that dratted mine, she had no doubt at all he would fight to the finish.

Riding pell-mell for the river, her mind raced with indecision. Should she talk first to Jerry Sullivan? What would she tell him? Not to kill the man she'd fallen hopelessly in love with?

This was business. Regardless of the unfortunate turn it had taken, this railroad job must be looked at from as professional a standpoint as possible.

Should she approach Kalib? Pursing her lips over a deeply inhaled breath, she tried in vain to push aside her own hurt and disappointment. No matter his profession of love after a stormy night of passion, she doubted not that he would stand his ground now. She would have no chance persuading him to leave the bridge monkeys alone to do their job.

Through her hopelessness his words rang clear, words he'd spoken that first day in the cabin. *The reasons we're here have nothing to do with this.* Then he kissed her. Suddenly she felt all quivery and weak and wished more than anything in the world to have a normal life in a normal family, well removed from the discord of life with Rube—from the conflicts of life without Kalib.

Nearing the river, she heard sporadic gunfire, and her heart lurched with painful reminders of the conflict and discord in her present life. Just when she decided she'd find Kalib, she heard a horse approaching behind her and turned to see Ellsworth Fredericks approaching fast. Her desperation grew.

Drawing rein sharply, she looked hard at him. "What are you doing?"

He grinned, and she wondered for a moment whether he were a scoundrel by design, or simply a grown man whose scruples hadn't fully developed. Right now, he resembled a kid going to a parade more, much more, than a reporter riding into battle.

"I hear you talked to him once before, Miss Britton. Are you going to face him again? As a negotiator?"

A rejoinder sprang to her lips and she bit it back. This was no time to tackle the paltry Ellsworth Fredericks. His presence here solved one dilemma, however. She had no intention of leading him to Kalib's camp, which was obviously what he intended.

"Talk to the prospector?" she quizzed. "He's the enemy, Mr. Fredericks. Or had you forgotten?"

From the look Jerry Sullivan gave her when she and Fredericks rode into the bridge monkeys' encampment along the east side of the Silver Creek River, she thought for a moment she had made a grave error coming to him first.

"What in tarnation are you doing here, Miss Meg?" the red-faced Irishman stormed. "This ain't no place for a female."

"I quite agree, Jerry," she placated, "but Mr. Fredericks indicated you have a little trouble on your hands, and I thought I might help."

The foreman raised skeptical eyebrows. "Help?"

She nodded seriously. "How did it all begin?"

"We got out here about sunup and started in determining what bed material we'll need to erect the trestles. Then before you could ask who shot Cock Robin, these sonsa . . . these good-for-nothing treasure hunters commenced to firing on us. My boys don't stand for such nonsense."

Meg sighed, surveying the heavily armed bridge camp. A few rifles were in sight, but most carried shovels, tamping picks, lining bars, track chisels. In fact, she'd have wagered every type of tool used in railroad building was represented in this assemblage of fighting men. Her stomach churned at the thought that they would get close to Kalib, Tobin, and Wash. For these men would fight to the finish. They wouldn't faint at the sight of blood, whether their own or that of their enemy.

"I thought Rube decided not to start the bridge until we receive an answer to our wire about the ownership of this land."

Jerry Sullivan shrugged. "If we're going to finish this line of rails on time, we have to have the bridge up and ready to cross when the tracklayers get here."

With one hand, Meg pushed a length of hair away from her face, thinking. . . .

Ellsworth Fredericks hounded her heels like a puppy dog afraid of being left, which was exactly what she intended to do to him. But how?

Finally, strolling idly from one group of men to the next, she paused long enough that Fredericks got sidetracked by one of the more talkative members of the crew, allowing Meg time to whisper a plan to Jerry.

"I'm going over to talk with them, and I don't want Fredericks tagging along."

Jerry Sullivan's round eyes popped. "Not on your life, you're not."

"I've met with the man three times already," she confided. "Nothing came of it, but . . . well, whatever the outcome today, it'll look better for Rube if we try to negotiate."

"I can't let you. . . ."

Meg smiled, remounting. "I'll be in no danger, Jerry, as long as you keep Fredericks out of the way. I can't promise how they would treat *him*."

Actually, she knew exactly how Kalib would react to Ellsworth Fredericks's entering his camp, she thought, riding across the river and waving a white handkerchief high in the air to appease Jerry Sullivan.

In spite of the fact that she knew Kalib would not shoot her, nor allow his men to, the hairs along her spine still stood on end. Slowly she nudged the sorrel forward, holding her back straight, her shoulders high, in spite of an overwhelming desire to stay right where she was and wait for Kalib to come to her.

As she neared the crest, Tobin and Wash stood up, straight and tall, still as death, their rifles trained not on her, but on the opposite bank of the river beyond her. Guiding her mount between them, she searched each face in turn and found nothing remotely resembling a welcome in their eyes.

Topping the ridge, she rode into the campsite and sat her horse. After a moment, Kalib stepped from behind the building.

"Are you alone?" he barked. His deep voice resonated with accusation through her entire being.

"Of course." She dismounted and walked to meet him.

He stopped within five feet of her, and she stopped, too. "You'd best stay out of this, Maggie."

"So had you," she spat at him.

He was furious, she could tell that at a glance. She'd never seen him in such a rage.

"I will not allow them to build that bridge until I'm finished here. I thought you understood."

Indignant with him, enraged with Rube, and infuriated with herself, she stared hard at him. Why did his presence weaken her so? She wouldn't have a chance fighting him if she couldn't control the enormous sensual cravings welling inside her at the very sight of him. And the fact that he appeared to be adjusting to her nearness with ease further filled her with anguish.

"If you hadn't insisted I go to Silver Creek, I might have prevented it . . . for the time being, if only until we receive a reply to the wire we sent to the land office. I have more to do with running this railroad than you choose to believe."

Quickly he strode forward and grabbed hold of her arm. She broke away furiously. Clutching the rough branch of the mesquite with both hands, she hung on for dear life. If he touched her she would dissolve. Of that, she had no doubt.

His voice softened dangerously, and she resented the way he played with her emotions. "Send the bridge gang away, Maggie. Please."

"If I do," she ventured, "what will we get in return? Will you allow the tracklayers to build up to the opposite bank, unmolested?"

"I can't do that. Not just yet."

Fury swirled inside her. How could she even think she cared for such a stubborn man? He wanted exactly what he wanted, and he didn't intend to give an inch to get it. "And if I don't?" she stormed. "How do you intend to stop thirty-six armed bridge monkeys?"

He studied her turbulent features, aching inside at the misery he caused her. "I'll do it, love. Trust me."

She caught her breath at his appellation. How dare he interject tenderness into the heat of battle! "Then you'll live to regret it," she vowed, turning to her horse.

This time when he took her arms, he made sure she

didn't get away. Turning her to face him, he stared deeply into her stormy eyes. "Remember what I told you, Maggie. . . ."

For a moment her heart pounded so hard she couldn't respond. Biting her lips between her teeth, she struggled for presence of mind. "You were wrong, Kalib. The reasons we're here make a great deal of difference. I've come to build a railroad, and you're trying to stop me, for whatever devious reasons you might have. Those reasons have everything to do with us . . . with all that we are . . . with every tiny part of us. . . ."

Her words choked, and she ducked her head, but not in time. His lips found hers, and suddenly they were players in a very different, yet just as tumultuous, game. Lovers now, instead of enemies.

After an eternity, he broke his lips from hers and laved her face with ardent kisses. "Maggie, Maggie, how I love everything about you, even your fiery spirit."

Unsteadily, she lifted her face so she could see his eyes. "Kalib, let them work on the bridge until the telegram comes, then if . . ."

"No," he mumbled, kissing her hair, her cheeks, returning to her lips.

Finally, she jerked away. "This is insane. Insane," she insisted. "Do you know how I found out about this ruckus? Ellsworth Fredericks, the newspaperman, came to town to get me. He knows about you, Kalib. . . ."

His sudden frown stopped her. "Knows what?"

"Not your secrets," she assured him, "whatever they may be. But he knows you're the prospector, that you're looking for the mine, and that you're the man who abducted me from the Diamond-Stacker. He would have come with me now, except I persuaded Jerry Sullivan to keep him back."

His adoring expression sent shivers down her neck. Drawing her to him, he held her close and propped his chin atop her head. "Be patient, Maggie, be patient, just a little longer. I'm almost finished here, and then we'll settle down to a nice, peaceful life. Someday we'll sit in our rocking chairs and laugh at how our life began."

Joy surged through her veins like fireworks on the Fourth of July. He hadn't forgotten. Not at all. But what good would it do? she wondered, feeling her joy fizzle like the rockets, spent. She had Rube.

Kissing him quickly, she turned in his arms. "I have to get back. I can't see what harm the trestles could possibly do you, so I'm going to tell them they have your word they won't be fired upon while they're constructing them. If the wire says you own this property, then we'll simply begin condemnation proceedings, and . . ."

He squeezed her to him again. "Maggie, love, you're a hell of an opponent. I can't wait to have you on *my* side."

She grinned weakly, letting happiness wash over her. "Do I have your word?"

"On what, specifically?" he teased, smiling at her now with those wickedly handsome brown eyes.

"That neither you, nor Tobin, nor Wash will fire on the bridge monkeys."

A grin tilted the corners of his mouth, tipping his beard so it caught glints of the sun. "We won't fire on the bridge monkeys," he told her. "You have my word."

Kalib climbed the hill behind her and stood with Tobin and Wash, watching until she was out of sight.

"I can see a hellcat like her in the Governor's Mansion," Tobin mused.

Kalib studied him with a curious grin. "You will, my friend."

Then he told them of the promise he had given her, and they stared him down.

Holding up his hands as though to ward off their blows, Kalib smiled. "I have a trick or two up my sleeve, too. I figure we'll have enough proof of the mine before long. In the meantime, one of you will have to stand guard, so those bridge monkeys don't wander over and get too close a look at us."

General grousing erupted from Tobin and Wash, but

Kalib cut in again.

"I haven't finished. My agreement with Maggie was that we wouldn't fire on the men. Nothing was said about the trestles. Way I figure it, they won't make too much headway building trestles by day, if we burn them by night."

His friends groaned in unison.

"You've made a pact with the devil," Tobin accused.

"We'll wind up having to fight those goddamned bridge monkeys yet," Wash swore. "And all for the love of a . . . lady."

Chapter Seven

Heady with the excitement of having seen Kalib, with the thrill of winning this latest round in their continuing struggle, Meg approached Hell on Wheels with new determination. Perhaps Kalib didn't work for the railroad, she reasoned, pushing a strand of hair back from her face, but why couldn't she entice him to apply for employment?

He obviously didn't have much of a job anywhere else; not one that required his presence, leastways. The short time she'd been with him showed her he was a man with strong convictions, a man who would be steadfast and loyal, a man whose intelligence would lend itself well to leadership and great accomplishments. The railroad could use such a man.

Her mind twisted and turned this way and that, fretting over positive things now, however, instead of problems such as had plagued her previous rides to Hell on Wheels. Rube wasn't at the construction train. He'd gone to the Diamond-Stacker on a mission, Uncle Grady assured her, a mission for the railroad. Their shipment of beef cattle was overdue, and the construction crew had only one more day's worth of meat. So Rube had ridden into Hell on Wheels to discover what happened to the shipment.

She smiled. Uncle Grady reported that sending Jerry Sullivan to the river to begin work on the trestles had been Rube's decison. Obviously, Rube's fighting spirit had resurfaced.

It always did, at some point in a project. Rube played by the rules as long as he could, then some event would transpire—large or small, worthy or unworthy of drastic action—to set him off like a mustang stallion suddenly reverting to the wild. Cautiously, he had advised waiting for an answer from the land office before tackling Kalib again; he never liked to antagonize the railroad's neighbors if other means could be found to solve the problems they faced. Now he himself had reversed this decree. Meg sighed, unsettled, yet relieved at the same time.

Once stimulated by this fighting spirit, Rube rarely touched the bottle again until a project was completed. The intoxication of battle apparently curbed his appetite for Demon Rum.

She and Rube were very much alike. They both needed a mission, and they both seemed to have found one. Actually, she had a couple, depending on whether Rube did indeed stay away from the bottle. Her first obligation would always be to him. But this new idea—Kalib joining the railroad—gave her hope deep down inside her heart.

Pursing her lips together, she refused to let herself look on the dark side of such a proposition. If she handled things right, how could he refuse?

Railroading was certainly no more nomadic than living in a tent hunting buried treasure. Yes, she decided, she had come upon the perfect solution to their problem. And she would certainly leave no stone unturned in her efforts to convince him to join the railroad.

She smiled dreamily to herself. With her success today, she had every hope that her plan contained more reason than fantasy.

Of course, if he should find the Lost Bowie Mine, all hope of his working for the railroad would be gone. But considering fantasies—finding a lost treasure mine was definitely more fiction than fact. Why, even Kalib admitted the Bowie Mine had been sought in vain since the days of the Spanish Conquistadors. What chance did one man alone, or even with his two helpers, have of finding something that had eluded men for centuries?

147

The late-afternoon sun sat on the horizon like a giant fireball, spraying golden streaks in an arc across the ruby-red sky. Shivering against a chill in the air, she vowed not to go out again without a heavier wrap. This being late November, winter would be soon upon them.

A dog nipped at the sorrel's legs as she entered the main street of Hell on Wheels, dust stirred in the twilight, and she felt at peace with the world for the first time since she could remember. Then a queasy feeling unsettled her stomach at the thought of facing Rube for the first time since Kalib carried her out of the Diamond-Stacker Palace. Uncle Grady had reassured him, of course, but would Rube guess what had happened, just looking at her? Had Kalib's loving left telltale signs on her face, in her eyes?

Suddenly all such thoughts vanished. She jerked the reins tight in her hands and sat in stunned silence, staring at the passenger car standing in ominous stillness on the siderail.

The *Texas Star!*

Blood, hot and fierce, stirred in the pit of her stomach. *That damned Leslie Hayden,* she cursed beneath her breath, while she glared without comprehension at the fancy car belonging to the general manager. *What mischief had he cooked up for Rube this time?* Had the spy come forth? If it weren't Kalib, who then? And if it were . . . ?

Forewarned, she reminded herself for what seemed like the hundredth time lately. Fortunately she wouldn't walk straight into his path unprepared.

Where moments before her entire being had been suffused with a feeling of sheer enchantment, desperation now overwhelmed her. Riding straight to the livery stable, she left the sorrel, then, swinging her satchel in angry slashes by her side, she strode to the Diamond-Stacker, preoccupied with the capricious nature of life. Was there to be no end to the trouble on this spur? Nothing lasted very long, she soothed herself. Neither pleasure nor pain. Nor even peace.

Try as she might, her efforts to retain a semblance of

optimism faltered beneath the disappointment of losing her earlier sanguinity. Entering the saloon, she pursed her lips between her teeth to still their quivering.

Inside, Georgie had lighted the lamps and Bart strummed to the small early-evening crowd. A few rust-eaters stood around the bar regaling one another with tales of the latest skirmish between the bridge monkeys and the three reprobate prospectors. Rumors surely traveled fast inside the terminus community. Although the various crews were forever feuding and competing against one another, they wouldn't hesitate to unite against a brother under attack.

With a grim sigh, she knew Kalib, Tobin, and Wash would be in real trouble should a delegation from the Diamond-Stacker decide on revenge.

Finding neither Di nor Rube in the saloon proper, Meg's despair raced toward panic, and she pushed through the rattan doors and burst into Di's parlor without giving a thought to what she might find within.

Standing near the center of the room, Di and Rube hastily broke away from an obviously ardent embrace. Meg's hands flew to her face, and she closed her eyes in an effort to shut out her own embarrassment.

"Sugar?" Rube questioned, his voice anxious. "Has the sky fallen in?"

Meg opened her eyes, but avoided theirs. Visions of her night with Kalib swam in her head and flushed her cheeks. She'd probably have been embarrassed catching them together before, she thought, but now . . . now that she knew in intimate detail what went on between a man and woman. . . . How could she have been so thoughtless? Dreading Rube's rebuke of her own indiscretion, here she had completely ignored his and Di's right to privacy.

Di stood unnaturally silent with Rube's arm firmly about her shoulders. Her face, too, was flushed, and Meg suddenly felt an empathy for the woman she hadn't known before.

Thrusting aside her own embarrassment, she tried to concentrate on the present. Her voice faltered, then tumbled from her lips. "I'm sorry . . . truly sorry. I wasn't thinking." Taking a deep breath, she plunged ahead. "What's Leslie Hayden doing back so soon?"

Di and Rube exchanged glances, then grinned in a curious manner. "Come, dear," Di began, obviously relieved to have something to take their minds off the discomfiture of the moment. "Let us show you."

Following with trepidation, Meg tried unsuccessfully to quell the fears raging inside her head like a tornado in springtime.

Crossing to the railroad siding, Di swung onto the rear of the ornate passenger car. Without so much as a knock, she pushed through the door into the elegant, now empty, salon.

"Where is he?" Meg asked, inclined to whisper as though they might at any moment be caught trespassing. "What . . . ?"

"Come over here," Di motioned from beside a round walnut table Meg remembered from her earlier visit. In fact, the entire salon looked the same to her, although as she recalled, her emotions had run so high the day she rode in this car, she was unlikely to recall every detail.

When Di moved to hand her a card from the table, Meg saw the enormous bouquet of red roses. Their sweet aroma filled the car, conquering the stale cigar smoke that had permeated the air the last time she visited this salon.

She stared at the card, confused. Raising an eyebrow to Rube, she finally admitted, "I don't understand. What does it mean?"

Rube shrugged. "I don't know any more than what you see on that card, sugar. The general manager has sent his personal car for our use until the spur is finished."

Meg squinted, trying to decipher the meaning. Leslie Hayden never did anything without a reason. What could he possibly expect in return?

"And the car isn't all, dear." Di drew her by one arm through the rest of the extra-long customized railcar. Two doors, gilded with brass fittings, opened across from each other off the narrow hallway.

"Sleeping compartments," Di said. "Each with its own water closet. One for you, the other for Rube."

Before Meg had a chance to do more than peer into the sleeping room on her left, Di drew her further along the hallway and into a small, shining kitchen. "Chou Ling calls it his galley," Di told her.

"Chou Ling?" The name was one she had never heard Di mention before, and for some reason she dreaded learning who its owner might be.

"Your chef," Di proclaimed, stepping aside to reveal not the rotund chef from Leslie Hayden's last visit, but a middle-aged Chinese man clad in starched white apron and hat.

Chou Ling bowed formally from the waist, and Meg awkwardly mimicked him, feeling for all the world as though she were participating in some sort of charade, wishing desperately that she would awaken without further ado.

"Tea?" Chou Ling inquired with a smile.

"Tea?" Meg's eyes widened.

Di laughed. "The Chinese always drink tea, dear. You certainly don't have to take up their habits, though. A chef is supposed to serve *your* preferences."

Weakened by this unexpected turn of events, Meg suddenly recalled how revitalizing Kalib's hot tea had been. "Yes, Mr. Ling," she mumbled. "Tea would be fine," she waved a hand to include Di and Rube, "for all of us . . . in the . . . ah, in the salon."

For some reason the tea had none of the relaxing effects Kalib's had had. In fact, it was quite bitter, and she didn't even think to ask for sugar or honey until much later.

Neither Di nor Rube had the slightest explanation for Leslie Hayden's sudden generosity. "Except," Rube told her, "he expects us to use this car to travel to Austin for the stockholders' meeting in January."

Meg shook her head. "He's determined you won't miss the meeting, but he wouldn't go to these lengths." Her gaze traveled slowly around the room, taking in the velvet and brocade and gilt . . . gilded everything, she thought

151

with exasperation. "This car is his most prized possession. He wouldn't send it for us, unless he expected something in return . . . something of enormous proportions. Something he couldn't wheedle out of us by conventional means."

Slowing her racing brain as best she could, Meg turned the heavy vellum card over in her hand, examining it as if for clues. The message was printed in gilt script . . . what else, she thought sarcastically . . . and unsigned.

It is our wish that Miss Margaret Britton, accompanied by her father, have the use of the *Texas Star* for the length of her stay in Hell on Wheels. Also that Miss Britton and her father use the *Texas Star* for their journey to Austin in January.

Meg stared at the card until the gilt script blurred before her eyes and she could no longer decipher the words, much less their hidden meaning.

Suddenly she sat bolt upright on the red brocade banquette. *Unsigned.* "That low-down, conniving rattlesnake!" she cried, startling both Rube and Di with her outburst. "Do you realize what this will look like?"

Her thoughts raced with Kalib's accusations . . . to his denunciation of her lifestyle here in Hell on Wheels. What would he think when he learned of Leslie Hayden's . . . she didn't even know what to call it . . . a gift . . . a gesture? And he would learn of it, no doubt about that. He had Tobin and Wash spying on her all over the place.

After his charges that she had stumbled out of this very car, inebriated on Hayden's wine. . . .

Her eyes flared in horror. Her heart beat so rapidly she felt light-headed. "I won't stay here!" Jumping to her feet she threw the card on the table. "I won't." She stared from Rube to Di, silently imploring them to understand. "Don't you see what it would do to my reputation? I don't know what message Mr. Hayden is trying to put out about me, but I won't let him succeed. I will not stay in this car one more minute!"

With that she raced from the elaborate railcar, into her own little room at the saloon, and flung herself onto her bed. Later, she stirred at Di's urging, but she steadfastly refused to take dinner in the *Texas Star*.

"Very well, dear, we'll let Chou Ling bring dinner to us." At Meg's furious response, she added, "We can't very well let the little man's efforts go unrewarded. I'm sure he has nothing to do with Mr. Hayden's decision. He merely works for the man."

"Well, I don't . . . not in any capacity," Meg retorted. "And I don't want anyone to think I do." She did agree, however, to Di's proposal. After washing her face and brushing her hair, she joined Di and Rube in Di's parlor, where Chou Ling served them a delicious roast leg of venison with prairie onions and scalloped potatoes with lemon and parsley.

The roses, however, were too much to tolerate. When Chou Ling presented them to her, she was hard-pressed not to fling them back in his face.

Realizing his innocence in the whole affair, she waited until he retired to the *Texas Star*, then stood in the back door of the Diamond-Stacker and hurled them to the hard ground, crystal vase to boot, with all the fury the situation had created inside her.

During dinner Di and Rube finally agreed they saw her point.

"We wouldn't let anyone compromise your reputation, dear," Di said. "We just hadn't looked at it in that light."

Meg smiled, keeping her own counsel. They hadn't had her reputation thrown brutally in their faces, as she had so recently. Still, she seethed inside, wishing she could get her hands on that rattlesnake Leslie Hayden, while at the same time praying she never had to set foot in the same room with the man again in her hopefully long life. Finally, both Rube and Di stopped trying to cheer her up.

"Tell you what, sugar," Rube told her after Di left to attend her customers in the saloon. "Why don't you ride out to the Varner ranch with me tomorrow. I need to see why our beef shipment is overdue before those rust-eaters

153

get hungry and walk out on me."

Meg didn't feel much better in the morning. All night she had flailed about in the small bed, worrying over Leslie Hayden's motives behind sending the *Texas Star* off for two whole months without him.

Once during the night she realized she hadn't even told Rube about Kalib's agreeing to let the bridge monkeys work unmolested until they received word from the land office.

She dressed quickly in one of her more updated riding habits, a Hussar blue split skirt of a fine twill-weave brilliantine and matching jacket. With nothing more than loose pleats in front and back the garment was obviously not a regular lady's skirt. But since she'd become accustomed to riding astraddle now, it would be more comfortable than her habits with button flaps front and back or the more bulky outfit with trousers and overskirt.

She'd just tugged on her mahogany boots and taken up her bonnet when Di knocked at the door, and announced with a grin. "Breakfast is served, ma'am."

Inhaling a deep sigh of chagrin, Meg opened the door to find Chou Ling bearing a tray full of steaming platters—eggs Benedict, flapjacks with maple syrup and honey, and a side dish of strawberries, no less, in the middle of November.

"I'll say this for him," Di enthused. "Leslie Hayden has connections."

"Not to me, he doesn't!" Meg hissed furiously.

Meg and Rube left immediately after breakfast. The sun shone through the hazy fall morning, sparkling as though at half-intensity on dew-dampened mesquite grass and cactus. They spoke little until Meg remembered to tell him about her visit with Kalib.

"Kalib agreed not to fire on the bridge crew," she told him.

"Kalib?" he inquired.

She felt her face flush. "The prospector, that's his name."

Rube continued to stare at her, and suddenly her ire

154

began to rise. "That's the only name I know, Rube," she stormed. "If it's really his. He protects his identity like . . . like he was escaped from Huntsville prison or something."

After a smile she couldn't decipher, Rube turned to survey the country before them. "You seem to be getting on pretty well with him," he mused. "For a man whose name you don't even know."

"We're not getting on at all," she retorted. "He just agreed to let the bridge monkeys work undisturbed, that's all."

Rube didn't broach the subject again, and before long they arrived at the Varner ranch. The family was about to sit down to the noonday meal, so two places were hastily added, and Meg found herself in the midst of another sample of ranch-country hospitality.

The Varner house was of native stone, like the Garrett ranchhouse, only of a much different design. When she commented on it, Anne Varner laughed and nodded to her husband.

"Jed's the stonemason for much of the county . . . in his spare time. He's built six or seven ranchhouses, the Silver Creek Bank building, and so many dipping vats these last two years, I've lost count."

Meg was also startled to learn that the Varners were parents to the lovely young wife of the hotel manager, Miracle Westfield.

Finally, Rube got a chance to state his case, much to Jed Varner's surprise.

"One of your men rode out here special to cancel the contract," he told Rube shaking his head in disbelief.

"Not one of *my* men," Rube corrected.

"Well, he sure claimed to be," Jed told him. "Said you'd found beef for a better price. When I suggested I'd consider going lower, he told me he had nothing to do with it, he was just delivering the message, but the other deal was already struck."

"I don't do business that way," Rube told Jed Varner when Meg accompanied the two men to the pens where a couple dozen head of cattle were penned, waiting to be driven to Summer Valley for shipment. "You still have a copy of the contract we signed?"

"Somewhere, I reckon," Jed replied.

"Well, I'll take all these cattle here, if you can deliver them to the construction site by sometime tomorrow. At our agreed-on price."

Jed nodded.

"If anyone else comes around claiming to speak for me, make sure he has it it writing with my signature affixed."

Not until they were in the saddle, ready to ride away from the Varner ranch did Meg find the courage to ask the question that had been on her lips since Jed first told them of the deception. "Can you describe the man who canceled the contract?" The moment the question left her mouth, she regretted asking it, for before she even heard the answer, she knew she wouldn't like it.

"Sure can, Miss Britton. He wasn't a large man, but what there was of him was covered with long blond hair and a bushy beard."

Kalib's friend, Wash. Numbly she thanked Mrs. Varner for her hospitality, and they rode away from the ranch. Her despair was so great, she couldn't talk. Of course, the contract had been canceled before she won Kalib's agreement. On the other hand, he might have agreed so rapidly because he knew he had already struck at Rube from another angle.

Rube broke the silence. "I reckon this blond feller is the same silver-tongued scoundrel who tried convincing Di and me that the prospector wasn't really abducting you when he carried you out of the Diamond-Stacker like a possum in a sack."

She mumbled agreement, but offered nothing more, and he didn't prompt her until they had ridden several miles further. He cleared his throat, but his words were still gruff. "What are you not telling me, Meg? Who is this man, Kalib? What does he want . . . besides my daughter?"

Meg swallowed convulsively. Running her tongue around her dry lips, she took her time answering him. The words *besides my daughter* rang in her ears like a church bell . . . tolling a death, she thought furiously. "I don't know what he wants, Rube. He says he's looking for the Lost Bowie Mine. He showed me the plat; it indicated the entrance to the mine is located precisely where the railroad crosses the river. He says as soon as he finds the mine, then the railroad can pass, either along the intended route, or by another, depending on where the mine is. But he intends to hold up the railroad until he's certain where the mine is."

"You believe him?"

"Yes. I mean, no. I mean . . . I don't know, Rube. I don't know what to believe." Her stomach churned and she hoped desperately he would drop this insane topic . . . not insane, she countered to herself . . . necessary . . . regrettable. . . .

"Di says he has a . . . a special name or something for you. He calls you . . . Maggie?"

Her breath choked in her throat, and she thought for a minute she might actually strangle. While she stared straight ahead, she felt her face draw up in a manner she knew he could read as acute embarrassment. Her cheeks burned.

"What happened that night he carried you out of the Diamond-Stacker, sugar?"

When finally she was able to answer, her voice surprised her by its strength. "Nothing you should be concerned about, Rube. He . . . ah,"—she shrugged helplessly— "he's afraid of what might happen to me in Hell on Wheels."

She gave him a brief, sickly grin. "I know it sounds silly, but that's what he says. Anyway, he was taking me to Silver Creek. He didn't think it was *proper* for me to stay in the saloon, but . . . well, Silver Creek was so far away that we . . . we ended up staying overnight at his camphouse."

"What . . . !" Rube began, but Meg quickly stopped him.

"Don't worry, Rube. He's a gentleman. Really. About everything except the railroad, anyway. He even served me tea." Thoughts of the evening suffused her, easing some of

157

her embarrassment. Suddenly, her mind switched from her and Kalib to Rube and Di, and she relived the instant she'd barged into Di's parlor. She knew exactly what Rube was asking her.

"You have nothing to worry about," she assured him again. "I did nothing I'm ashamed of." She had no doubt about what he was thinking had gone on, but neither did she intend to admit to it. The evening was too special . . . it would always be special, no matter how things turned out between them.

They didn't speak again until they reached the outskirts of Hell on Wheels. "He's the kind of person you'd like . . . under different circumstances," she said.

Rube grunted.

"I know what I said the day we rode out there, but I was angry. He *is* intelligent . . . and decisive . . . and . . . well, after this is over, I hoped maybe you could find him a position with the railroad."

When he didn't reply, she turned and found him staring at her with a curious smile. "Why don't we finish this railroad spur first, sugar. Then we'll discuss finding work for an unemployed treasure hunter."

Although she hadn't actually told Rube anything about her relationship with Kalib, she felt more comfortable that night than she had in a long time. She still refused to sleep in the *Texas Star*, but Chou Ling's dinner was as delicious as the previous meals he had served, and he seemed quite agreeable to bringing them to the Diamond-Stacker. Of course, by the time he carried them fifty yards through the nippy fall air, some of the heat had been lost.

Nevertheless, the following morning she awoke feeling rested and optimistic again. Then, as if under orders to restore her black mood, Ellsworth Fredericks showed up bearing the wire from the land office in Austin.

"What does it mean, the land is *tied up?*" she stormed. "I've never heard of such a thing. They don't even give the names of the people who have *tied it up.*"

Rube shook his head. "It doesn't make sense to me, either. This is one ruse I've never run up against in all my years dealing with rights of way."

"I know who's behind it, though," Meg hissed through clenched teeth. "And he's going to hear about it."

Rube raised an eyebrow. "Want me to come along?"

"I'll handle it. For once and for all!" she vowed, storming across the hallway into her room, where she flung on her blue riding skirt from yesterday and a clean waist. Donning the matching jacket, she stuffed her hair into a Hussar blue fur-rimmed bonnet to ward off the November chill.

She reached the river in record time, neither stopping to confer with Uncle Grady at the construction site, nor at the river to let her winded horse drink. The bridge crew was busy with shovels along the embankments where they would soon begin erecting trestles, but she didn't even take notice.

Galloping up the crest of the hill she saw Tobin and Wash position themselves to stop her, but neither of them did. Kalib wasn't in view, so without pausing longer than necessary to make certain he wasn't at the campsite, she rounded the house and raced up the dim trail where he had taken her once before.

Suddenly there he was, standing before her in magnificent . . . She gulped back the desire to leap from the saddle straight into his arms. She'd been duped before, she reminded herself angrily, but never again. Never again would she be hoodwinked by this man.

Sliding to the ground she waved the telegraph message toward him. "Bastard," she hissed, but as soon as he opened his mouth, she bit her lip over her outburst. "Don't say a word," she demanded. "This is not a joking matter. The games are over . . . finished."

He stepped forward to take the paper from her hands, and she panicked. "Stay where you are. Don't come one step closer."

Cautiously, he held up his hands. "What's the problem, Maggie?" His eyes held hers, caressing, teasing.

"And don't call me by that name . . . not ever again. Not . . ." Inhaling a deep breath, she finally allowed herself to close her eyes for one instant in an effort to calm her shattered senses.

"What is it, love?" His voice rumbled along her spine and tumbled precariously inside her brain. *The problem is I love you,* she thought desperately. *I love you, and I mustn't. I can't.*

"This." She shook the paper in his face. "The answer to our wire. What exactly did you do to have your name obliterated so completely from the records?"

He shrugged. "If you'll let me take a look, I'll try to explain it."

Gingerly then, she handed him the paper, holding it by one corner, while thrusting the opposite edge toward him. As soon as he touched it, she jerked her hand away.

"I won't bite you, Maggie. I never have."

Her cheeks flamed, and she gritted her teeth so hard the pressure traveled all the way down her neck. *That's all you haven't done,* she thought viciously, watching him study the telegram.

"This says the property is tied up," he told her. "Like I said."

She smiled wickedly. "Exactly like you said," she agreed. "Except the names of the parties responsible are . . . what does it say? . . . *Confidential?* What the hell does that mean?"

He shrugged. "Confidential. It means they're not at liberty to divulge . . ."

"Not at liberty to divulge," she mimicked. "That's mishmash. You're the party responsible. I know you are, even if I can't prove it. But you won't stop us. This time we're coming through here, whether you like it or not. Our army of bridge monkeys and rust-eaters, and . . ."

"Gandy-dancers," he supplied.

She glared at him, quivering all the way to her toes. "Joke if you want to, Kalib. We have over two hundred Irishmen who are itching for a fight. You and your two cohorts won't stand a chance against such odds."

He cocked his head and scrutinized her so intensely her knees began to wobble. "Is that what you want, Maggie?

160

What you truly want?"

Surging with heat, her body responded to the full timber of his voice with desperate longings, desires, and passions that would never be fulfilled. "You bastard!" she whispered through her teeth.

Their gazes held, while she tried to make herself remount and ride away. He came a step toward her, two steps. . . .

"Don't, Kalib. Don't come any closer. This time I mean it. You're despicable . . . perfidious . . . contemptible, and I don't want any part of you. Not any part," she stammered, backing to her horse.

He stopped when she spoke and watched her mount the sorrel without taking his eyes away from hers. Try as she might, she couldn't tear hers away from him, either.

Once more he moved a step, and she drew the reins around. Just before she sank her heels into the horse's flanks, he spoke again.

"So you don't like roses?"

Her eyes found his in a flash. Then her heart hardened, at last. "Spy on me all you want. You'll never find anything untoward about my behavior or my life. Unlike you, I have nothing to hide."

He watched her ride away with more sadness in his heart than he could ever recall feeling. At the same time, his entire spirit droned with the magic of being alive . . . of loving Maggie Britton.

If he'd needed proof before, he now had it: this was definitely the woman for him. The excitement generated by political opponents couldn't compare with the thrill of challenging Maggie. Her magnificent spirit was dauntless.

Tobin and Wash rode up with grins on their faces.

"Wipe those cock-eyed grins off your faces, boys, we've got a silver mine to find."

Tobin and Wash exchanged glances. "Glad to see you've finished moping about," Tobin said.

Wash winked. "Guess that's the end of our little

terminus-town filly."

Kalib frowned at his two friends. "Not on your life, boys. Maggie's in for the long haul. She just doesn't know it, yet."

After that he intensified his search for the Lost Bowie Mine, wishing he'd never made the promise to find the thing in the first place. Every day the search lasted was another day Maggie would spend in turmoil. And he hated being the source of her anguish.

Looking on the bright side, though, he realized it was going to take a major effort to separate her from her dependent father. Perhaps this battle was the very thing she needed to show her Rube could make it on his own— and that she could live without him. She already knew she would have a difficult time living without her prospector—he could see it in every expression on her lovely face.

Chapter Eight

Meg rode away from Kalib as though she were trying to
outrun the devil himself. Racing past the bridge crew, she
didn't stop until she came to a little creek where she had
previously watered the sorrel. When the animal persisted
in tossing his head now, she finally realized she'd
practically run him into the ground, without allowing
him so much as a drop of water all day.

Dismounting, she let him drink and became conscious
for the first time of tears streaming down her face.
Gloomily, she tried to recall the last time she had actually
cried tears, but couldn't. Not since she was a child, for sure.

Plagued by her miserable state of affairs, she tied the
reins to a low-growing oak limb, where the horse could
graze while she rested. She had no desire to return to the
Diamond-Stacker anytime soon. All she wanted was to be
alone.

Propping her back against the trunk of the ancient tree,
she gazed through tear-streaked vision at the big, clear sky
and into the endless space stretching beyond her in every
direction. The world was so huge—so grand—her own
situation should pale in consideration.

It should, she thought wretchedly, but it didn't. Her
own situation closed in on all sides, smothering her very
spirit with an all-encompassing desperation such as she
couldn't remember ever having experienced before.

How could she have been so misfortunate? The two men

she loved most pitted against each other. One who needed her desperately; one whom she needed with equal fervency.

Long she sat, unaware of passing time, until the rays of the afternoon sun dazzled her into action, and she dried her eyes with the backs of her hands. Heavy-hearted, she remounted with grim determination and rode toward Hell on Wheels. She would see this wretched endeavor to its conclusion. Until then, she would think of nothing else.

Afterwards, she could brood over what might have been; afterwards, she could pine for a love found and lost in the space of a few short weeks.

Afterwards, she would plan for her future. But right now she had a job to do. Sitting beneath the tree her thoughts had jelled into a couple of firm plans: first, she would convince Rube to begin building the railroad out from Silver Creek to the river. They would have to resurvey, since Kalib had removed all the stakes, and they would need to set up a command center of some sort in Silver Creek. But it could all be accomplished in less time than it would take to wait around for condemnation proceedings, which looked to be futile, since they couldn't even confirm ownership of the land.

By the time the right of way was determined, the rails would be far enough along that they could meet at the river. In fact, they could even plan a ceremony, a joining of the rails for the new governor to preside over, like at Promontory. The Silver Creek townspeople would be pleased.

The second thing Meg decided while sorting things out beneath the ancient oak tree concerned herself. As soon as she returned to Hell on Wheels, she would move into Leslie Hayden's *Texas Star*. That would show Kalib she didn't care a whit for his opinion of her! Tears stung the back of her eyelids, then slid down her parched cheeks. *Would she didn't!*

Di came into the room while Meg rushed this way and

that, throwing clothing into her satchel.

"Whatever are you doing, dear?"

Without looking up, Meg answered briefly. "Moving into the *Texas Star*." Her arms loaded, she rushed to the door, where Di stood with a quizzical expression on her face.

"Is your tail on fire?"

Meg shook her head quickly and changed the subject. "Where's Rube?"

When Di shrugged, Meg squinted at her. "Send him over to the railcar. I have a plan. You can join us for supper."

Inside the *Texas Star* she tossed her belongings onto the blue brocade-covered bed and looked in on Chou Ling.

"I'd like tea in the salon, Chou Ling," she told him. "And there'll be three of us for supper. Here in the salon."

Chou Ling grinned and bowed as though he had been serving her in the salon every day. "Anything special you would like for supper, miss?"

The question surprised her. "Whatever you want to prepare will be fine, thank you."

Pacing the salon once, twice, three times, she looked impatiently out the window for Rube, but didn't see him. *Pray God, he isn't drunk,* she thought, returning to her bedchamber where she began unpacking her satchel.

Much to her surprise, the wardrobe was already full of clothes— a couple of lovely dressing gowns, three different riding habits with matching accessories, and several silk day costumes, also with matching accessories. Checking the small walnut bureau, she found it full of undergarments, stockings, and toiletries.

Everything a lady would need. . . .

Her curiosity rose quickly as she rifled through the garments in the wardrobe. Everything was new, pressed, and ready to wear. Holding one costume against her, her curiosity turned to uneasiness. A perfect fit.

"Chou Ling," she called, still clutching the garment in her hands, while she rushed to the galley. At his astonished

165

expression, she hesitated, then continued, slowing her words with purpose.

"The clothing in . . . in my bedroom," with her head she nodded backwards to the blue sleeping compartment, "to whom . . . ah, to whom does it belong?"

He looked at her quizzically a moment, as if trying to interpret her meaning. Then he edged past her, apologizing, and scurried to the salon, where he took an engraved card from the drawer of a walnut table. Grinning his perpetual grin, he stood patiently while she read.

"For me?" she asked, sinking to a brocade banquette. "Why for me?"

He shrugged. "The card says . . ."

She bit back a sharp reply, recalling Di's admonition that Chou Ling had nothing to do with any of this nonsense. "I know what the card says," she answered politely. "Did Mr. Hayden put these clothes here for me?"

Chou Ling shook his head. "Not Mr. Hayden. A lady bring . . ." He pointed to the card.

Meg studied it. "Mrs. R. Smith, seamstress," she read aloud. "But why for me?"

Chou Ling shrugged again and returned to the galley. In a few moments he came back, bearing a tray with tea pot and complements. "When you finish tea," he asked her, "you take bath? The water tank is full of hot water. All you do is . . ." lifting his hand, he pulled an imaginary chain, ". . . pull chain, and water will come."

Mumbling her thanks, she barely heard him, so engrossed was she in determining why Leslie Hayden would have outfitted her with an entire wardrobe. Fury began to mount inside her, a fury the hot tea did nothing to quell. How had he known her exact sizes *for everything?* She heard again Chou Ling's suggestion to take a bath, so she did.

The bathing room was tiny, only large enough for the bare essentials—small porcelain tub, sink with mirror, and water closet. But here again everything she could wish for was laid out ready for her use, from fluffy bath towels to rose-scented soaps and shampoos.

True to her chef's pronouncement, when she pulled the copper chain hot water diluted with cold shot forth from a pipe into the porcelain tub. Soaking in the tepid water loosened not only the grime from her body, but a number of unwanted thoughts from her mind.

The rose scent reminded her of Kalib's last sharp remark, and she had to press the hot wash cloth firmly to her eyes to keep tears from flowing down her face.

What would he think of her now? After this . . . ? She stared around the compartment outfitted just for her. What would he think of her? Desperation flooded her senses for a moment, but she fiercely gained control once more.

She wasn't a kept woman. She knew as much. Rube and Di knew as much. Even Leslie Hayden knew it, regardless of what this looked like. And that was all that mattered.

Back in her tiny but exquisite bedchamber her resolve wavered, and for a moment she decided to forego this dim-witted notion she'd taken to show Kalib she could do as she pleased. She'd be more comfortable in her own wrinkled garments, in her own room.

Chastising herself properly, she searched the wardrobe for a costume suitable for dining in the salon of the *Texas Star*. After all, she admitted reluctantly, her only armor against Kalib was anger, and every instant she stayed in this railcar, every moment she attired herself in Leslie Hayden's clothing added that much more fuel to her anger.

And she definitely would need tinderboxes full of anger to make it through these next few weeks.

The costume she chose was a simple green and beige plaid wool with pleated skirt and wide Empire waist encircled low with a great green sash. The sleeves were full to the elbow, then tapered to a tight-fitting beige point de Genes lace cuff at her wrists. A matching lace bertha added the finishing touch.

167

By the time she completed her toilette Rube and Di had arrived in the salon, Di dressed for the evening's work in her black skirt and starched front—what there was of it, Meg thought distastefully—basque.

Chou Ling had draped one of the walnut tables with a crisp white cloth and adorned it with gilt candelabra and . . .

She caught her breath and held it behind pursed lips. Roses. More of those blasted red roses.

Ignoring Di's oohs and aahs, she turned furious eyes on the mild-mannered chef. "Where did these roses come from?"

He shrugged, his eyes wide with astonishment. It occurred to her he'd probably never seen a woman who reacted so violently to roses before in his life.

"The supply train brings flowers, miss. I keep them in the ice box."

"Roses?" she demanded, thinking for the umpteenth time of Kalib's biting remark.

Chou Ling nodded and bowed vigorously. "This trip, miss, roses."

She sighed, knowing if she were to throw them out the door, Kalib or one of his spies would only see them again. "They're lovely," she forced herself to reply, thankful for one more item with which to reinforce her anger.

Over a supper of succulent roast beef, cabbage, and hot rolls, topped off by ice cream with fresh strawberries, Meg explained about the clothing.

"I suppose Mr. Hayden outfitted Rube, too?" Di inquired with a wry smile, indicating the room set aside for Rube's use.

Meg shook her head. "Not very well. A smoking jacket or two, for your *leisure* hours, I suppose." She grinned sardonically. "You'll have to make do with your old wardrobe, Rube."

Di waved a fork about the elegant surroundings, then nodded toward Meg's dress. "What made you change your mind about all this, dear?"

Resentment flashed through Meg at Di's offhand acceptance of the outrageous arrangement. It would have been far more appropriate had she ranted and raved, had she insisted that Meg should not put herself in a position to be ridiculed. But that was Di, Meg thought. Di's mores were certainly not to be confused with those of polite society.

For a moment, she held Rube's inquiring gaze. He looked so sympathetic, her despair formed as teardrops in her eyes, and she quickly busied herself with the remaining strawberry in her dish of ice cream. Finally, she shrugged lightly. "I figured it was a shame for this car to sit here unused. Why, I'll probably never have an opportunity to live in such grandeur again." She looked quickly to Rube, seeking reassurance.

"I know what it looks like," she admitted. "But since you and I . . . and you, Di . . . know the truth, what difference does it make?"

She paused. They said nothing. Then she continued. "We all know Leslie Hayden doesn't do anything without expecting repayment, but he's never given me the slightest feeling that he . . . well, you know what I mean. So, I decided the investors must have come through grandly, and . . . well, this is his way of repaying us for impressing them."

Di and Rube exchanged looks, then nodded in agreement.

"Besides," Meg added, "we've built his only miles of railroad all year. He owes us something for our dedication and hard work."

Rube laughed, and she joined in. "I know, it'll be a cold day in hell before Leslie Hayden feels any obligation to any of us," she continued. "But if he expects more than a railroad in return for the use of his prized *Texas Star*, he has a surprise. Both of you know how I feel about that man."

Chou Ling cleared the table and brought them coffee. "Di tells me you have a plan, sugar."

Di excused herself to tend to business at the Diamond-Stacker, and Meg told Rube the plan she had dreamed up that afternoon. He was delighted.

"Outstanding!" he exclaimed. "Outstanding. We'll get the surveyors in the field first thing in the morning. Joining the rails at the river will make headlines all over the country!"

She sighed. "Hopefully this will give that abominable Ellsworth Fredericks another slant on our activities. I warned him if he turned the community against us this spur wouldn't be completed at all."

"Good for you, Meg. Good for you." Rube studied her silently. When he spoke again, his voice took on such earnestness, her heart lurched.

"I know you've been through some rough times lately, sugar," he told her. "But they're over now, far as I'm concerned, anyhow. You don't have to worry about me. I'm going to finish this railroad without so much as a drop of Kickapoo Indian Worm Killer, much less Demon Rum."

She smiled ruefully, knowing he meant this pronouncement with all the fervor he delivered it; knowing, too, that he could well fall off the wagon before the night was out.

"Why don't you camp out with the surveyors?" she suggested. "They're likely to be a bit uneasy, what with all the stakes disappearing once and . . ."

His jubilant expression changed instantly to a defensiveness she knew well. "I just thought . . ." she began.

"You thought to keep me away from Di," he said flatly.

Here we go again, she thought. Inhaling a deep breath, she expelled it in exasperation. "Rube, she's not good for you. I know she probably has the right intentions, but . . . Can't you see what being around her and the Diamond-Stacker does to you? The temptation is too great . . ."

"You've certainly become wise these last few weeks," he accused.

"I've always known . . ."

"You've always known Di," he finished for her. "She's a

170

good person, and she's been like a mother to you, Meg. To me . . ." He stared hard at her, as though seeing clear to the core of her heart. When he spoke again, she squirmed on the red brocade banquette. "After these last few weeks, I should have thought you would understand what Di means to me . . . and what I mean to her."

He left immediately—for the construction train, he told her. She lay awake long into the night, however, in the luxury of her blue and gilt bedchamber, worrying over whether he had indeed gone to the construction train, or whether even now he was sharing Di's big feather bed. Somehow, after his accusation tonight, the thought of his relationship with Di left her more devastated than she had been before . . . and lonelier, too.

And these thoughts, in turn, were even more unsettling, since they called to mind in distressing detail the night she had spent on the small cot in Kalib's camphouse . . . the happiness and security she had felt in his arms.

When, at last, morning arrived, she found herself in a more distraught state than when she had retired. The small spaces here in the *Texas Star* stifled her. She brushed her hair, threw on an elegant beige cashmere breakfast coat from Leslie Hayden's gifts, and took breakfast alone in the salon, where the rich, sweet perfume of the roses filled her with unbelievable sadness.

And even more, loneliness.

Chou Ling cleared the table, and Meg decided to ride out to the construction site and see the surveying crew off. It would take them a few hours to collect all their materials, instruments, and get their tents in order, so she had time to make it before they left for Silver Creek.

Arising, she had started for her bedchamber when Di appeared. Although Di was the last person she wanted to see this morning, for Rube's sake she knew she could not be rude. Summoning Chou Ling, she requested more coffee.

Di came right to the point. "We must talk about Rube, Meg."

Meg smiled indulgently, recalling how Di had refused her this exact same request a few weeks earlier. She nodded toward a banquette.

"You . . ." Di began in a shaky voice. Meg was startled by the woman's hesitancy. "I know how much you worry over him," Di said, slowly. "But . . . well, dear, you . . . you're overprotecting him. You must . . ."

Fury rose quickly along Meg's hitherto defensive senses. Kalib had used almost the same words, and at the time she had wondered why her ire hadn't been aroused. Now it definitely was. "How dare you say such a thing, Di," she fumed. "You're the one to blame."

Di's lips formed an open heart. "Me? Why, I . . ."

"You," insisted Meg. "You're the one who feeds him liquor by the keg. You're the only one who . . . who . . ." Her words trailed off, and she pushed a wayward strand of hair out of her eyes. Rube would be furious with her for laying into Di in such a shameful manner. Yet . . .

"The only one who does what?" Di demanded. "What sort of wicked things are you accusing me of?"

"Let's not argue, Di. Rube wouldn't like it; you know that." She took a quick breath. "You also know what a terrible time he has staying away from the bottle. And you insist on providing him with an endless supply."

Di's face drooped. She was obviously distressed. "You're right, Meg. He wouldn't like us carrying on in this fashion, but we have a few things we must settle. I know Rube has a problem with the bottle. The Lord only knows how much I wish he didn't. But your badgering and belittling him won't keep him away from it."

"Neither will your blind acceptance."

Di caught her breath. "Your father would do anything for you, dear. And he can't bring himself to tell you how much your attitude hurts him. You've been treating him like a child. And it's . . . well, frankly, it's getting the best of him. You must learn to accept him as he is."

"As a drunk, you mean?"

"As a fine man," Di retorted. "A grown man, and a very

172

intelligent one, at that. A man capable of finishing this railroad on time. He's operated like this all your life. You should know . . ."

"While I was growing up, I didn't realize what went on around here," Meg admitted sorrowfully. "Now that I know . . ."

"Your education may turn out to be the biggest mistake we ever made," Di told her. Taking a couple of deep breaths, she continued in a more formal manner. "I know what you came to think about me . . . and my lifestyle . . . while you were back East, dear. . . ."

Meg's eyes flew open. Had her feelings been so obvious? "Di . . ." she began, feeling things suddenly rush out of control. Rube wouldn't like this at all. He would be furious. He might . . . Gulping, she wondered crazily whether he would choose Di over her, given an ultimatum.

"Maybe your judgment of me is right," Di continued. "I've certainly never claimed to live an exemplary life . . . one fit for a proper lady. But I've always tried . . . Rube and I have tried . . . to see that *you* grew up to be a lady. We haven't forced our lifestyle on you. In fact, we've bent over the other way. . . ."

"Di, please. . . ." Suddenly, Meg had the overwhelming sense that she must stop this conversation before it got out of hand . . . before she said something that would forever damage her relationship with Rube. She could never let that happen.

"Listen to me, Meg," Di insisted. "I know you resented being sent away to school. Rube showed me your letters. Well, he wasn't totally to blame, dear. I thought . . . I knew you couldn't learn all the things you would need to know when you go out in the world alone here in a raucous terminus town. I realized what would happen, even then," she sighed. "Once you saw proper young ladies from proper homes . . . I knew you would begin to question your life here with us. It was a chance we had to take. You had to have such a background to be able to live a life of your own outside a terminus town. I knew the

173

consequences, but even now I wouldn't change the decision."

Meg stared at her, her mind in a whirl. For so long she had blamed Di for sending her away . . . for separating her from Rube. Now the woman actually admitted her guilt.

"We missed you dreadfully while you were gone," Di continued. "Until you have children you'll never know how much. But you've returned now, and you can't change things here to fit that other world. You can't change me. I'm who I am. . . ." Shrugging, she ran a hand through her outrageously short curls. ". . . a saloonkeeper. Just what I've always been. And Rube is what he's always been, too. He's a fine railroader; he's a loving father; and he's a man who on occasion drinks too much. You're going to have to accept him like he is, or . . ."

Di's words struck terror in her heart. She jumped to her feet. "Or what?" she demanded, fists on hips. "Or you'll send me away again? That's what you've always wanted, isn't it? Rube, all to yourself. Well, I won't let you send me away again. When I returned this time, his life was in shambles. I won't let that happen again. I intend to stay . . . forever . . . to be sure he has a chance to live a good, productive, sober life. After all he's done for me, I owe him that much."

Gasping for breath after her outburst, Meg stared angrily into Di's startled face for a moment, then whirled and ran from the salon to her bedchamber, where she hurled herself onto the blue brocade bed Chou Ling had already made up and sobbed.

Bitter, wretched, desperate tears. Tears of despair. Tears of loneliness. Tears of fear.

Fear of finding herself alone and abandoned . . . rejected by her own father.

How could he have taken up with someone as heartless as Di? Someone whose intent was now obvious—to get rid of her?

She didn't ride out to the construction train that morning; her ears still burned with Di's accusation that she treated Rube like a child. In fact, for several days following their argument, she stayed close to the *Texas Star*, reading books from a well-supplied bookcase in the salon and wrestling with her problems. She did recall the letter Di had mentioned, one she'd sent Rube shortly after arriving at school, in which she'd accused him of letting Di send her away. But during the four years back East, she had pushed the thought aside, replacing it with a determination to return as a lady of whom Rube would be proud.

But she had returned to chaos . . . to the muddle Di had made of their lives. Thinking on it these days alone, Meg admitted she should give Rube credit for his own drinking sprees, if nothing more.

But the fact remained clear in her mind—if he didn't insist on keeping company with a saloonkeeper, he wouldn't be as exposed to Demon Rum.

Unaccustomed as she was to the idle life, Meg grew more restive as the days passed. She didn't dare go to the construction site, for fear she'd be accused of mothering Rube. And she had no desire to face Di, so she read, and thought, and read some more.

One morning she arrived in the salon for breakfast wondering how much more of this isolation she could stand before Rube returned. Chou Ling had been quietly attentive during this time, paying special notice to every detail, as if he served ten people instead of only one. The night before had been a particularly restless one for her. Until now, she had managed to worry so much over Rube and Di that she had been able to push thoughts of Kalib aside. But that night she had dreamed of him. Sweet dreams. Only to awaken time after time to find them merely that—dreams.

The first thing she saw when arriving at the breakfast table this morning were the ever-present fresh red roses.

For the umpteenth time she resisted the impulse to throw them from the salon door. "Where do they come from?" she demanded of Chou Ling. "Does the supply train have nothing but red roses?"

He bowed convulsively, his grin fading beneath the starch in her voice. "They are set aside with our order, miss. With our ice and the other fresh foods."

"Why do they always bring red roses?" Deep inside a sickening feeling told her the answer, and she despaired of trying to find a solution to the dilemma of Leslie Hayden.

Shrugging, Chou Ling returned to his galley. She was well aware of the supply trains that arrived every couple of days with supplies from Summer Valley. That was how Di got her ice and fresh fruits, too. But roses? How could even Leslie Hayden afford the luxuries he provided for her? And why? *Why?*

Disgruntled with the world in general and red roses in particular, she settled on the banquette and looked out the window into the dusty street of Hell on Wheels, while Chou Ling filled the table with breakfast foods.

Suddenly she sat bolt upright and stared at Rube, who emerged from the rear entrance of the Diamond-Stacker and sauntered toward the *Texas Star.*

By the time he reached the salon, she'd regained a measure of composure. Nevertheless, when she spoke, her voice sounded reedy to her own ears. "When did you get in?"

"Last night," he answered, taking a seat at the table. Chou Ling hastily brought an extra plate and coffee cup.

"Where . . ." she began, then bit her tongue.

Rube grinned at her a moment, then picked up his fork. "Di says not to wait breakfast on her. She had a long night at the saloon and wants to stay abed this morning."

Meg flushed and busied herself eating Chou Ling's scrambled eggs with *champignons.* How are things going with the survey?" she finally asked.

"We've had trouble," he admitted. "That's why I'm here. If that prospector of yours isn't inclined to let up on us soon, we'll have a full-fledged war on our hands."

This time she denied nothing, but stared at him, her heart frozen with the fear his words instilled within her.

"Every damned stake we set by day is stolen by night. A man can't make progress at that rate."

"What about the bridge monkeys?" she asked.

"He's kept his word on that part," Rube answered. "So far, anyhow. They're still busy adding fill and making the embankment secure. Haven't gotten started on the trestles yet."

Meg took a sip of coffee, thought instead of tea and Kalib, and swallowed her bitter mouthful. "What are you going to do?"

"I've already talked to Grady," Rube told her. "We'll split the crew in two, set half the graders directly behind the surveyors, so we won't have to depend on locating stakes to do the grading." He shrugged. "Work'll go faster that way, anyhow."

Meg was reminded of Di's accusations and she blanched at the truth of them. Rube was carrying on as the skilled engineer and leader he was propounded to be. He could indeed get along without her.

"What can I do?" she asked slowly.

"That's why I came to town, sugar." Looking around at the fancy salon, he winked. "That is, if I can persuade you to come back to Silver Creek and feed the grading crew for a few days."

Her heart leaped unexpectedly, then she recalled how she liked to be in the middle of things, involved in the action. "I'm ready to leave this minute," she sighed. "It's been dreadfully boring around here."

He studied her carefully. "Di said she hadn't seen you about town in several days. You sure you're feeling up to it?"

She nodded enthusiastically.

"The depot is finished enough that you can stay upstairs and do the cooking. The crew won't number over twenty, so it shouldn't be too hard on you for a while. Grady'll see that plenty of supplies are brought down from the construction train, so you won't have to worry about anything except the actual cooking. Fact . . ." He paused,

177

reflecting, then continued "Ling Chou might . . ."

"It's Chou Ling," she corrected him with a laugh. "And, no, I don't think Leslie Hayden's generosity would extend to having his chef cook for the grading crew."

"Not likely," he agreed with a grin, watching as she dashed her napkin to her plate and rose to her feet.

"When do we leave?"

"Straightaway," he said. "I'll get our horses from the livery while you dress."

Chapter Nine

Meg rummaged through the wardrobe of fine clothing Leslie Hayden had so conveniently provided for her use. Of the three riding habits, she had trouble deciding which one to wear, they were all so fetching.

Finally, however, she chose a brash costume of brown velveteen with wide Turkish trousers that drooped deeply on gaiters of brown cloth to be stuffed into her boots. The short double-breasted velveteen jacket buttoned over a brown plaid sateen vest, collar, and tie. Quite the thing to wear while traipsing around the country, she mused sardonically. What would the quiet, unsophisticated citizens of Silver Creek think should they discover these outrageous garments had been given to her by a gentleman? And not even a gentleman *friend*, at that.

As she stuffed her hair beneath a brown fur cap, she heard horses outside the railcar, so with a word of adieu to Chou Ling, she hurried outside, swinging her satchel, only to come face to face with Di.

"Have a nice trip, Meg," Di offered without looking at her directly.

Mumbling a hurried thanks, she mounted and waited for Rube, who spoke to Di in hushed tones, then, showing an aplomb she had never witnessed in him before, he bent from his saddle and planted a firm kiss on Di's lips. "Miss me," he instructed her.

Flushing, Meg turned quickly away, but not in time to

179

escape the enraptured look on Di's face. "You bet, I will, rounder," she whispered.

The intimate scene stunned Meg into a subdued silence, which lasted until they arrived at the construction train. Except for the recent occasion when she'd burst into Di's parlor and caught them in an embrace, she'd never witnessed so much as a handclasp between Rube and Di in all these years. Now a kiss—and, much more, a mutual exchange of intimacies, right there in front of her and the entire population of Hell on Wheels!

Uncle Grady had the wagon packed and the graders ready to roll when she and Rube arrived. "I'm taking along everything you'll need, missy," he told her. "Including a couple of younguns to help you with the heavy stuff. All you need do is see to the meal preparations, they'll carry your water and wood and do all your chopping and cleaning up, too."

She thanked him, then retreated into her self-imposed silence once more. All she could think about was that kiss. The closer they came to the Silver Creek River crossing, the more graphic it became in her mind, until at last, she admitted to herself that instead of Rube and Di, her reflections centered on herself and Kalib. Every time she saw Rube's lips touch Di's, it was Kalib's lips on her own that she felt.

Every time she heard Rube's intimate remark to Di, it was Kalib's voice speaking to her, Kalib's eyes searching hers, Kalib's hands tantalizing her senses.

Crossing the Silver Creek River, they rode west, and it took every ounce of concentration she could muster to keep from turning to stare in the direction of the range of hills, to keep from searching the horizon for him . . . or for Tobin . . . or for Wash. Recalling as from a dream the times he had stopped her when she crossed the river, she longed for him to appear now. But, of course, he didn't.

Although he didn't materialize, that fact didn't keep her from wishing, nor from reliving those other times—the times he had taken her in his arms, crushing his mouth to hers, held her as though he would never let her go. But, of course, he had let her go.

By the time they rode into Silver Creek the afternoon sun was well down on the horizon, and her entire mental process was in shambles.

Disembarking at the depot, she hardly noticed the finished look of the building, with its deep verandas along the street side, and deeper loading docks skirting the side where the railroad track would eventually run.

The men carried the supplies inside, and she stood listening, responding with difficulty when absolutely necessary, agreeing perfunctorily to everything Rube and Uncle Grady suggested.

"The living quarters are not as finished as I thought," Rube told her after inspecting the site. "We'll let the men sleep upstairs on cots. You'll be more comfortable in our suite over at the hotel."

Uncle Grady made a chore of inspecting the cook stove and getting the equipment stashed in the proper places. When one of the boys brought a load of wood, he put him to work building a fire and sent the other boy for water from the town cistern.

"I'll handle supper for the crew myself," he told Meg. "You can help me out with breakfast, then we'll leave you on your own. I think. . . ."

"Uncle Grady," she pleaded. "I'll be fine. You act as though I've never cooked or. . . ."

"I don't figure you did much of this type of work while you were off at school, missy. This here cooking will tire you out faster'n laying rail, if we don't get things set up right."

"You're pampering me, you and Rube. And you both know I don't need pampering." Lifting the heavy lid on one of the two enormous black pots Uncle Grady had been so careful with, she inhaled the delicious aroma with a smile. "I've always loved construction train stew."

"Let me scare up a batch of sourdough biscuits, and we'll have meal enough for supper," Grady told her.

Against both his and Rube's protestations, Meg helped make the biscuits. When the Dutch oven was filled, she

181

popped it in the heated oven and began another batch.

By the time the meal was hot, the graders had put together a plank table and drawn up enough nail and spike kegs to serve as chairs. But they'd no more than sat down to eat, when Ellsworth Fredericks burst into the room.

Meg sighed. She'd been so engrossed in her own misery she'd forgotten the nosy newspaperman. With him around, her stay in Silver Creek took on much less appeal.

He sniffed the pot of stew and peeked at the biscuits, and Rube—in a pleasant voice, which belied the last meeting she had witnessed between these two men—invited Fredericks to grab a plate and eat with them, an invitation Fredericks immediately took up.

"You ever find out what's happening to those survey stakes?" he asked Rube.

Meg kept her face to her plate, afraid she would snap at him and end any truce Rube might have achieved with the man. She sighed angrily. Ellsworth Fredricks would likely keep her on the proverbial pins and needles these next few weeks, for she had no doubt he intended to hound her every footstep.

"We aren't even trying to find out about the stakes," Rube answered, after a brief glance Meg's way. We've got us another trick up our sleeve. Fact is, regardless of our opponent's strength, we're confident we'll always be able to come up with something to outwit him—or her—or whoever the perpetrator might be."

Meg finished her meal, and while Rube and Fredericks sat over coffee, Uncle Grady showed her how he had arranged the kitchen she would preside over. True to his word, the two boys busied themselves cleaning up after the meal.

"Don't you worry about fancy cooking, now, missy. These men aren't used to it. Why, I reckon, even if you went to the trouble, they'd prefer the plain and simple. I'll send beef, and the boys here will do a little hunting and fishing for variety. They'll dress out and clean anything they bag, have it ready for the skillet. If you run out of

182

anything, like coffee or flour, before we get it to you, stop in at Herman Crump's Mercantile. He's agreed to fix you up and bill the railroad. And eggs, now, you can purchase them and milk, too, from the Widow Evans over behind the hotel there. She makes her living selling eggs and milk and will be grateful for the business." He paused to hand her a sack of what he termed "egg money." "We're always on the lookout for grateful citizens."

She followed him from one box to the next, one cabinet to another, while he carried on as though she had never seen a kitchen or anything in it before. "Your biggest trouble will be baking enough bread, since these men take sandwiches in their lunches every day. Promise me you'll get the younguns to help with everything. They know to fetch and carry and to clean up after meals, but they're also here to do anything else you ask." He gave her shoulder a squeeze. "Be sure you ask," he admonished. "We don't want you laid up from too much kitchen work."

Uncle Grady and Rube left the following morning after breakfast shortly behind the grading crew. Both men intended to return to the construction train—and Rube to Di, Meg thought dismally—but she knew they would find excuses to drop by regularly to check on her. Their concern unsettled her a bit. At the same time, though, it was flattering. She worried that Rube had told Uncle Grady his suspicions about her relationship with Kalib. Why else would they be hovering over her to such an extent?

Popping the last batch of the day's baking in the oven, she sighed. No need worrying over that now. Or anything else. She was certain Di had confided their discussion to Rube, although in what detail, of course, she didn't know. Neither did she want to know. For the entire length of their journey from Hell on Wheels to Silver Creek, she had ridden in fear that he would bring up the subject. And what would she have said? Angrily, she admonished herself. She must not think of such things. She *must* not. These worries were beyond her control . . . out of her hands . . . and she must put them out of her mind, as well.

As soon as they finished washing the dishes and mopping the floor, the younguns, as Uncle Grady called them—she finally asked and learned their names were Rob and Jim—left to fish in the Silver Creek River, promising a mess of catfish for supper.

The week passed in a flurry of activity. Looking back on it later, Meg figured she spent most of her time wiping her brow.

And baking bread. True to Uncle Grady's predictions, a good portion of her day was spent mixing, kneading, and baking. Breakfast consisted of sausage or bacon Uncle Grady purchased from local ranch wives, eggs from the Widow Evans, and pancakes with fresh butter and milk. The fresh milk, as opposed to the canned they normally were served, pleased the graders, and their praises made her more conscious of trying to lighten their drudgery-filled days by sending along special things for their lunches, in addition to the usual sandwiches, boiled eggs, and canned tomatoes.

So, in addition to baking bread, she took to making pies, using canned peaches and apples. For every man to have a slice of pie large enough to enjoy, she needed six pies for every meal.

By the end of the first week, her routine had become regular: she arose before dawn, prepared breakfast, and packed lunches. Then as soon as the men left, she visited the Widow Evans to purchase the next day's supply of fresh milk and eggs. Her job kept her so busy she rarely saw any of the Silver Creek citizens, except for Ellsworth Fredericks, who became less of a nuisance after she learned to be inanely boring company, as well as infuriatingly uninformed about railroad business.

And the young doctor, Hank Jefferies. Always gracious, Hank appeared every morning in his buckboard, to take her to the Widow Evans and back with her supply of milk and eggs. The times she spent with Hank Jefferies became even more pleasant after she learned he had no more designs on her romantically than she had on him.

It happened one day when they returned with the

supply of fresh eggs and milk. The new wrought iron benches with green-lacquered slats were in place on the veranda in front of the depot. Hank noticed them first.

"We can be the first to use them," he suggested, helping her alight from the buckboard. After depositing their purchases in the kitchen, he led her back to the porch, where they sat laughing on one of the green benches. Meg, however, was not laughing inside.

Inside she trembled at the possible effects such closeness could have on their friendship. Lazily reclining with his long legs outstretched in front of him, feet crossed at the ankles, Hank laid his arms along the back of the bench in both directions, his left arm behind her in a most distressing gesture.

After a lengthy silence, during which she could think of nothing to say, he cleared his throat, and she gritted her teeth, fearing the worst.

"The Excelsior Reading Club ladies have decided to sponsor a box social before the Christmas Ball," he told her. "The proceeds will go to their scholarship fund."

Meg nodded, chewing her bottom lip.

"I . . . ah . . ." Hank began. Later, she knew if she hadn't been so nervous herself, she would have sensed his anxiety. But at the time, all she could think of was that rejecting his romantic overtures would put an end to a friendship she had come to cherish.

"You know how I've talked about my little sister, Katie, who's a student at the University of Texas down in Austin?" he asked.

"Uh-huh," she finally managed.

"Well . . . I . . . ah, I never told you about her room-mate."

Meg's eyes flew open. Her mouth broke into a wide grin. "Her roommate?"

He nodded. "Mary Sue," he added. "She's come home with Katie a few times. She's coming again for the Christmas Ball, and . . ."

"Why, Hank Jefferies, you mean you've had a sweet-heart all this time, and you've kept if from me?"

Ducking his head, he gave her a sheepish grin.

"That's wonderful. However did you manage not to talk about her?"

"I wanted to," he confided. "Katie and I have always been close. I've really missed having her to talk to . . . then you came to town. You've . . . well," he shrugged, "you've sort of taken her place."

Tears sprung to Meg's eyes. "That's the nicest thing I've ever heard, Hank. Remember the day you drove me out to the Garretts'? I thought the same thing about you then. I never had any brothers or sisters . . . and I always knew I'd missed a great deal."

He dropped his arm from the bench and pulled her to him playfully. They sat in silence a moment, then she drew back and grinned broadly into his face.

"Tell me about Mary Sue," she demanded. "And don't you dare leave out a thing."

His face brightened with a light Meg knew well, too well, she thought, as her stomach turned flips at the nostalgia his happiness created within her.

"You'll get to meet her at the Christmas Ball. I know you'll like her. She's . . . well, she's terrific. Most important, I suppose," he confided with a blush, "she feels the same way about me. In fact . . . ah, I haven't told anyone this, not even Katie, since she's away, but I plan to . . . ah, to ask for Mary Sue's hand during the holiday. Since the Christmas Ball is a couple of weeks before Christmas, I'm going to take off the rest of the holidays and spend it with her family."

Meg shrieked with delight and threw her arms around Hank Jefferies's neck. He hugged her in return, and she felt truly happy—for him, at least.

The incident filled Meg with two disparate emotions: her happiness for Hank Jefferies was strong and sincere, but it was definitely overshadowed by her longing for the same kind of relationship in her own life. That, she knew, was impossible, for the only man to whom she would ever want to be betrothed was . . . lost to her.

Lost to her.

Toward week's end Rube returned and stayed in the hotel a couple of days. He worried about her slaving over a hot stove, but she convinced him she could stand anything for a limited amount of time, wishing the end to her desolate loneliness was as firmly in sight as the end to her cooking for the grading crew.

One morning after Rube left with the graders, and Rob and Jim had finished their chores and gone deer hunting, Hank Jefferies popped his head in the door.

"Won't be able to drive you to the Widow Evan's this morning, Meg. Trace Garrett sent word for me to come pronto. Clara is showing signs of delivering the youngun." He shook his head. "That Trace, after two healthy, normal deliveries, he still worries over Clara as though this were her first."

Meg laughed. "The same way you'll worry over Mary Sue before long."

Raising his eyebrows at the inevitable, he agreed and left for the Ranche Santa Clara. Suddenly she was alone, and her mind whirred with a new thought.

She loved having Hank around. Not only was he great company, but his presence kept her from dwelling on her own misery. He also kept her from contriving ways to end that misery.

Or ways to prolong it, she thought furiously, as she baked several peach cobblers in record time.

For some time now, she'd considered taking lunch to the men in the field . . . they worked so hard. . . . Her heart pounded feverishly. Her true goal, of course—the slight chance she might get a glimpse of Kalib, in the process.

Since the men had taken their lunch with them, she settled for extra dessert, making sure she had enough cobbler to serve not only the grading crew, but the surveyors, as well. Although the surveyors had their own cook shack and food, she couldn't travel all the way out there, she reasoned, without including them in her plans. Besides, they were out ahead of the graders, closer to the river . . . closer to Kalib.

Knowing how ridiculous she would look, while the last

of the cobblers were baking she rushed back to the hotel and dressed in a flared ankle-length split skirt of black English wool, widely belted in ivory, and an ivory linen waist with an elaborate lace jabot and cuffs. Covering it all with a sweeping black wool cloak, which, she insisted to herself, would allow her freedom of movement, she stomped into polished black boots and stuffed her hair beneath a black Persian lamb turban. Giving herself one last look in the glass, she plucked wisps of hair here and there, softening her face. Catching her own eye in the looking glass, she swallowed convulsively. What if he didn't . . . ?

Stifling all negative thoughts with a stern reprimand, she loaded the wagon and proceeded to her destination, quivering like the Widow Evans's mustang grape jelly.

Rube glanced up at her arrival, then squinted, alarm showing on his face.

Forcing a smile, she hurriedly shushed him, "Don't worry. Nothing's happened. You've all been working so hard, I decided you deserve a treat."

Crossing to the wagon, he peered inside the bed and a proud smile beamed on his face. "My, my, what have we here. Smells like peach cobbler, boys. Come help us unload it, and we'll break for lunch."

"Not this part," Meg cautioned, then at Rube's startled expression, she hurried on. "This is for the surveyors." She gulped, knowing her intentions were as clear as Silver Creek River water. "I couldn't very well come all the way out here with dessert and not include them, now could I, Rube?"

He raised a quizzical eyebrow, and his mouth twitched in a smile.

Abashed, she looked around. "Where are they? I hope not too far ahead, I must get back in time to fix supper."

"Not far, sugar," he told her, shaking his head in a hopeless attempt to conceal his amusement.

Flushing with embarrassment at being found out, Meg nevertheless refused to admit the goal of her trip aloud. *Not far enough* was what he meant, she thought dismally.

Regardless of what Rube thought and she knew her destination to be, she knew the men were pleased at her attempt to indulge them with dessert in the field. Their praise lightened her spirits considerably.

She found the surveying crew more strung out than the graders. The foreman, Scotty McCaa, working the transit when she arrived, turned it over to his number two man at sight of her.

Realizing for the first time the extent of the tension Kalib's sabotage had created for the various crews, she grimaced. Her presence in the field automatically alarmed them all.

Jumping from the wagon seat, she smiled reassuringly and extended her hand. "Nothing's wrong, Scotty. Rube thought the same thing when I arrived at the grading site. I bring no bad news, only a bit of dessert, although I won't vouch for the quality of the home cooking."

Scotty helped her unload the remaining containers of cobbler and sat with her beneath an oak tree on top of a slight rise while the surveyors chained the line they were reading.

"It won't be long," he told her. "We were fixing to break for dinner directly, anyway." She assured him she didn't mind waiting in the least.

Wasn't that why she had come? she thought, feeling conspiratorial. But at the same time, she idly scanned the distant hills for movement, for a familiar form. . . .

As she watched far ahead, Scotty described the actions of the surveyors. "That's Kendall at the tripod," he told her, then immediately pointed in a straight line with his arms outstretched. "Can you see Joe Lee there in the distance? With the flagpole?"

She nodded, inattentive, but hoping Scotty wouldn't notice.

"When he raises it horizontally over his head, he'll be signaling he's ready to set a hub. Afterwards, they'll come on in."

As she watched, Kendall gave the line, surveyor talk for signaling where the stake should be set, she recalled, and the men in the distance bent over, pounded something into the ground that she couldn't see from this distance, but what she knew to be a wooden stake with blue keel numbers marked on it. "What distance is it?"

Scotty shrugged. "We're calling it twenty-six thousand four hundred feet—'station two sixty-four—measured from Silver Creek running east."

Below her, Kendall motioned for the back flagman to come forward, then he pulled up his instrument and made his way across the rocky, unlevel ground to the new hub. Afterwards the men drifted over to the tree to see what had occasioned a visit from the chief engineer's daughter. Usually, such a visit meant trouble somewhere along the line.

As from the grading crew, her cobbler brought praise and appreciation from the surveyors, warming her heart, but failing to lift her spirits, which by this time were becoming more dejected by the minute.

She tarried as long as she could without arousing undue suspicion. In a show of enjoying the enormous open spaces, she strode to the summit of the hill, where she inhaled drafts of fresh fall air and stared into the distance far beyond the surveyors' position, wishing . . . wishing for a mere glimpse of him. Wishing . . .

At last, *willing* him to appear, and finally, her body weak with denial—

With the loneliness that daily closed about her in ever tightening circles—

With the absolute knowledge, now, that what might have been would never be—

She returned to the grading crew, then to Silver Creek, where she prepared supper for the graders and listened to Hank Jefferies describe in joyous detail the fine baby boy Clara Garrett had this day delivered, trying all the while to respond as the occasion warranted, with a measure of cheerfulness.

Life went on, she told herself during her nightly soak in water scented with Mavis's favorite lavender oil. Life went on, as well it should, and soon—someday, she corrected herself, holding tears inside with a tepid cloth—someday she would again relish every moment of it, as she had, not so very long ago.

For now, about all she could find to be thankful for was that Mavis's favorite scent wasn't roses.

Using field glasses, Kalib watched her from the hill, and the strength it took him to keep from charging after her would, he knew without doubt, fuel every skyrocket that would soon be fired at his inaugural celebration.

She was searching for him, too. He could tell. And that fact cheered him considerably, since Tobin returned from Silver Creek almost daily now with reports of the young doctor squiring *his* Maggie about town.

He studied her exquisite form as she stood on the hillside, cape tossed back from her shoulders, looking, from the distance, at least, the part of a swashbuckler from one of Alexandre Dumas's romantic novels. He watched wisps of hair flutter about her face, and when she reached to hold them back, his heart skipped a beat. In his mind's eye, he could see her expression every time she held her hand that way, a sensual expression that never failed to set his blood to boiling through his veins. Even now, so many yards away.

She turned to go, and he jammed his field glasses back in their case. If he should be thankful for small favors, he thought furiously, he supposed he would have to be satisfied with the knowledge that she hadn't forgotten him.

But such knowledge, however necessary for his future plans, did nothing to alleviate his present suffering.

Nor hers, he thought regretfully. Nor hers.

Tobin had also kept him informed about the Christmas Ball, a mere week away now. His stomach tightened at the thought that Hank Jefferies, doctor or not, would most likely escort Maggie. *His* Maggie. Tobin had even reported, somewhat with glee, that Maggie and Hank Jefferies had been seen in an embrace on the veranda of the

191

new depot.

Returning to camp, he wished desperately that he'd never even heard of the Lost Bowie Mine, especially that he'd never given such a foolhardy promise as to try to find it.

Drawing rein in a cloud of dust before the camphouse, he dropped to the ground and hitched his mount. Then another thought struck him.

If he'd never given such a promise, he would never have met Maggie Britton. And no matter how dark things looked for them at the moment, he knew his world would be a much bleaker place indeed without her in it.

──── FREE ────
B O O K   C E R T I F I C A T E

ZEBRA HOME SUBSCRIPTION SERVICE, INC.

YES! Please start my subscription to Zebra Historical Romances and send me my free Zebra Novel along with my first month's Romances. I understand that I may preview these four new Zebra Historical Romances Free for 10 days. If I'm not satisfied with them I may return the four books within 10 days and owe nothing. Otherwise I will pay just $3.50 each; a total of $14.00 (a $15.80 value—I save $1.80). Then each month I will receive the 4 newest titles as soon as they come off the press for the same 10 day Free preview and low price. I may return any shipment and I may cancel this arrangement at any time. There is no minimum number of books to buy and there are no shipping, handling or postage charges. Regardless of what I do, the **FREE** book is mine to keep.

Name _____

(Please Print)

Address _____ Apt. # _____

City _____ State _____ Zip _____

Telephone ( ) _____

Signature _____

(if under 18, parent or guardian must sign)

Terms and offer subject to change without notice.

3-89

MAIL IN THE COUPON
BELOW TODAY

To get your Free **ZEBRA HISTORICAL ROMANCE** fill out the coupon below and send it in today. As soon as we receive the coupon, we'll send your first month's books to preview Free for 10 days along with your **FREE NOVEL.**

GET
FREE
FREE
GIFT

ACCEPT YOUR FREE GIFT
AND EXPERIENCE MORE OF
THE PASSION AND ADVENTURE
YOU LIKE IN A
HISTORICAL ROMANCE

Zebra Romances are the finest novels of their kind and are written with the adult woman in mind. All of our books are written by authors who really know how to weave tales of romantic adventure in the historical settings you love.

Because our readers tell us these books sell out very fast in the stores, Zebra has made arrangements for you to receive at home the four newest titles published each month. You'll never miss a title and home delivery is so convenient. With your first shipment we'll even send you a FREE Zebra Historical Romance as our gift just for trying our home subscription service. No obligation.

BIG SAVINGS
AND FREE HOME DELIVERY

Each month, the Zebra Home Subscription Service will send you the four newest titles as soon as they are published. (We ship these books to our subscribers even before we send them to the stores.) You may preview them *Free* for 10 days. If you like them as much as we think you will, you'll pay just $3.50 each and *save $1.80 each month* off the cover price. *AND you'll also get FREE HOME DELIVERY.* There is never a charge for shipping, handling or postage and there is no minimum you must buy. If you decide not to keep any shipment, simply return it within 10 days, no questions asked, and owe nothing.

Chapter Ten

The week of the Christmas Ball dawned clear and sunny, and the citizens of Silver Creek held their collective breath, hoping the fine weather would continue until after the celebration. In deference to the season, however, two mammoth iron stoves, one for either end of the depot's large reception room, were put in place, their flues connected, and a supply of wood laid in.

The day following Meg's trip to the field with her peach cobbler, Rube left for the construction train in search of another wayward shipment—his supply of good and durable ties was running dangerously low.

In addition to her regular duties, Meg now found herself busy with details for the upcoming celebration. Several Silver Creek ladies spent hours in the depot, creating wonderful decorations for the party—an enormous cedar tree reaching to the ceiling was erected in one corner and trimmed with strings of popcorn and yellow chinaberries, and hundreds of tiny candles.

They draped cedar boughs over the doors and windows, and one lady even parted with enough red velvet ribbon to tie festive bows on each bough. The grading crew had a good laugh upon returning from the field one night to find sprigs of mistletoe hanging from every doorway.

Two days before the ball Hank Jefferies's sister and sweetheart arrived. The girls stayed in the hotel until after the ball, giving Hank and Mary Sue a chance to spend some time together, and Meg an opportunity to get to know both girls.

It turned out to be the closest thing to dorm life she had experienced since leaving school—giggling and woman talk, about men, naturally, and midnight snacks in the parlor of Meg's suite.

One night as they sat cross-legged around the room stuffing themselves with roasted pecans and hot chocolate and quoting a bit here and there of Robert Burns's romantic poetry, Meg suddenly recalled a classmate living in Austin.

"You may know her," she told the girls, "Sara Ann Chrystal?"

"Know her!" the girls shrieked in unison. "Everyone in South Texas knows Sara Ann. She's from one of the old ranching families. Why, Sara Ann Chrystal is Miss Texas personified."

Meg laughed, recalling the manner in which the beautiful Sara Ann portrayed the ultimate Texas character. "She did shock a few people back at Smith College."

"Well, they won't be exposed to her outrageous behavior anymore," Katie said. "She's working on the ultimate marriage—ultimate for a Texas woman, that is."

Mary Sue agreed. "She came home and immediately set her cap for the most eligible bachelor in the state."

"And the handsomest," Katie sighed.

"I'll give you an argument about the new governor being the handsomest man in Texas," Mary Sue challenged.

Meg laughed. "I don't suppose your vote would be for a local physician, by any chance?"

Mary Sue blushed, and Katie and Meg teased her mercilessly.

The next two days passed in a whirlwind of pleasant activities, marred for Meg only by her tumbled-up state of affairs. Every moment she spent with Hank and Mary Sue, her thoughts were on Kalib, and her spirits remained low.

In turn, she chastised herself soundly for not feeling the proper amount of happiness for these two people who had become dear friends in such a short space of time. But how could she be totally happy, she countered to herself, when inside the gnawing ache to see Kalib . . . to hear his voice . . . to touch his face . . . plagued her at every turn?

At night her dreams of him were even worse, for in them they often shared the sweet love they had once known, and from them she always awakened, alone and crying.

Once again Ellsworth Fredericks became an annoying factor in her life. Since her trip to visit the grading crew, he had dogged her every step, asking exasperating questions about the prospector and the missing stakes, quizzing her endlessly about what Rube would do if the prospector refused to allow them to join the rails.

Finally one day, she could take it no longer. Turning on him in front of the Hotel O'Keefe, she laid into him with all the fury that had amassed inside her heart and soul since she last saw Kalib.

"Why don't you do what you said you would, Mr. Fredericks? Why don't you ride out to the mine shaft, or to the river, or wherever you think you can find that old prospector and ask *him* your silly questions. You should realize by now I don't know the answers."

While she talked, Fredericks watched her with an ominous intensity, further setting her ire on edge. Then, when she finished her tirade, he clamped his hat back on his head, adjusted its angle, and eyed her triumphantly.

"Oh, you know, all right, Miss Meg. You know a lot of things you aren't saying."

Pursing her lips, she gave an exasperated huff, and gathering her skirts in her hands she swept down the steps and into the street.

"You make a pretty sight, Miss Meg," he called after her. She stopped in her tracks and turned to observe him curiously. In all these months, the man had never made one personal comment to her, so why would he start now? Was this a new tactic to try to learn whatever it was he thought she knew? Or . . . heaven forbid . . . was he beginning to notice her as a woman? "What did you say, Mr. Fredericks?"

He tipped his hat. "I remarked how stunning you look, your hair sparkling red in the sun and all. If you don't mind me saying so, Miss Meg, anger brings a becoming flush to her cheeks."

Recounting these remarks to Katie and Mary Sue later, she expressed her indignation. "I can't decide whether he was issuing a compliment or fielding a new offensive attack."

Katie shook her head vigorously. "We can do better for you than Ellsworth Fredericks, Meg. You don't have to settle for the likes of him."

Meg smiled ruefully. "I'm not going to *settle* for the likes of anybody. At least, not . . ." With a deep sigh, she suddenly wished she could confide her secret to these new friends. Yet, she couldn't. For many reasons.

The most obvious being they would hardly understand. Two girls from upstanding families could never grasp, not in their most romantic fantasies, why she had given herself—heart, body, and soul—to a reprobate of a man like Kalib . . . and a stranger, to boot. A stranger whose name she didn't even know.

A stranger who would always occupy the most special place in her heart. At this last thought, she cringed. *Pray God, not always. She couldn't stand this torment forever.*

On the day of the ball the sun shone in all its glory, warming the nippy December day by its mere presence. The town fairly crackled with excitement and anticipation.

Meg's own expectations for the celebration were anything but festive, however. She had actually planned to return to Hell on Wheels and spend the evening in the *Texas Star*, but her friends' insistence, coupled with the fact that she wasn't at all sure she possessed the will power she would need to ride *past* Kalib's camphouse, changed her mind. She certainly didn't intend give herself an opportunity to ride out to see him, inadvertently or otherwise.

So, under direct orders from Hank, Mary Sue, and Katie,

she prepared to attend the ball, with less than desired enthusiasm. She and Katie would go together.

"There'll be oodles of dancing partners," Katie assured her. "Every cowboy in all West Texas is coming tonight."

"At least let me skip the box social," Meg pleaded. "I've prepared enough lunches the last couple of weeks to last a lifetime."

The three girls had followed an insistent Mavis O'Keefe to her storeroom, where the sprightly sixty-year-old hotel proprietress climbed on top of box after box, tossing things down into their expectant arms—hat boxes and tissue paper and embroidered linens.

"You certainly can't miss the box social," Katie insisted to Meg. "That's the perfect way to meet gentlemen and impress them with your culinary skills. Why, who knows, your box might be bought by some handsome, dark-eyed stranger who . . ."

"Some what?" Meg gasped. "What do you mean . . . some handsome, dark-eyed stranger?"

Katie shrugged lightly. "It's just an old expression." Then her eyes searched Meg's. "You've been keeping something from us," she accused with a laugh. "You have a handsome, dark-eyed stranger in your past, and you haven't told us about him! You must, Meg, you absolutely . . ."

At that moment Mavis dropped a clump of vibrant-colored ribbons to the floor at their feet. "I need the blue ribbons for my box!" Mary Sue exclaimed. "Hank insists I wear a blue gown, and . . ." She paused and stared helplessly into the others' startled faces. A blush crept up her cheeks. "He won't say why," she added shyly. "Is blue his favorite color, Katie?"

Katie scoffed. "He doesn't have a . . ." Then she shrieked and hugged Mary Sue. "Goodness gracious! I know why! I know! That scoundrel! He hasn't even told me!" She looked at Meg. "Has he told you?"

Meg shook her head weakly, still recovering from her recent fright that she had been found out.

197

The rest of the morning was filled with deciding what to put in the lovely hat boxes Mavis provided for their box suppers, and then the actual cooking.

"Lace cookies," Katie said. "We must have lace cookies, and . . ."

"And pecan tortes," Mary Sue added. "Small, individual pecan tortes, and perhaps some molasses. . . ."

Meg laughed. "I fear your gentlemen friends will fret if they pay hard-earned money for nothing but boxes of fluff."

The others agreed, so at last they settled on fried chicken, cole slaw, pecan tarts, and lace cookies. Meg thought of Chou Ling and his endless supply of strawberries and other delicacies, but this secret she kept to herself, also.

Suddenly the secrets she felt obliged to keep from these new friends increased by the minute, and so did her despondency. By the time the boxes were packed and the three girls returned to the hotel to see to their dancing dresses, Meg knew all she really wanted to do was take to her bed.

But no respite was in sight. With an eagerness born, Meg soon discovered, of an innate curiosity, Katie persuaded Mary Sue to use the bathing room first. "Since you're being called for by a beau, you mustn't be more than fashionably late."

No sooner had Mary Sue closeted herself in the bathing room, however, than Katie spirited Meg away from the hotel. Clasping hands, they raced to Hank's small cottage behind his doctor's office, where they found him preparing to dress for the evening.

"Show us," Katie demanded of her startled brother. "We know why you insisted Mary Sue wear a blue dress. So show us."

"Girls," Hank pleaded. "You're not supposed to. . . ."

"Oh, yes, we are, Hank Jefferies," Katie insisted excitedly. "Now, show us, or we'll hold you down and search your pockets."

Meg paled a bit, doubting only that she would be able to indulge in such an activity, never for a moment that Katie meant every word she said.

"All right," Hank finally agreed. "But you can't tell a soul. Neither one of you. It wouldn't be the least bit proper, since I haven't had an opportunity to ask for her hand yet."

While he spoke, Hank took a small box from his bureau drawer and flipped the lid open.

Both girls gasped.

"I've never seen anything so beautiful," Meg whispered, staring at the lovely robin's-egg blue stone set in a delicate gold band. "What is it?"

"Blue topaz," Katie pronounced triumphantly. "I knew it all along. It had to be."

Hank studied Meg's enraptured look. "Did you notice Clara Garrett's pendant the day we visited the Ranche Santa Clara?"

She nodded.

"This blue topaz comes from their ranch. There's not much of it, but it's . . . well, it's a special gift for a . . ."

"For a very special lady," Meg told him, smiling. "She'll be so pleased."

He inhaled a bit shakily. "Do you think so? Really?"

"Hank Jefferies," Meg admonished. "That girl adores you. And well you know it. Don't you go getting jelly-kneed on us."

All the while they dressed—Katie in a stunning gown of dahlia brocade with a deep purple velvet bodice and yards of dahlia ruching, and Mary Sue in blue velvet and moire with intricate embroidery and a deep ruffle of Belgian lace sweeping across the tips of her shoulders and dipping to a low vee in front—Meg could tell by the way Katie squirmed about that it was only with the greatest difficulty that she was able to keep this magnificent secret from her roommate and best friend.

Meg herself chose a plain gown of white satin with a pleated tulle ruffle edging the skirt, but her new friends contested such a bland choice.

"It looks every bit the proper graduation gown it probably was," Katie told her, rifling through the wardrobe of new clothes Meg had bought before leaving school. "Not at all the kind of gown you need to attract attention." Triumphantly, she withdrew an elegant gown of emerald satin bordered with black fur, and sighed. The pointed waist draped low across the bust and ended with short puffed sleeves of dotted mousseline de soie, which were covered with double ruffles of beaded satin. The graceful skirt fell in godet pleats and extended to a short train in back. Both skirt and bodice were trimmed up the sides with crystal beads embroidered in an intricate iris design. "This one is perfect!"

"Oh, no," Meg insisted. "Not for tonight. I'm saving this one. . . ."

"For what occasion?" Katie demanded, withdrawing the matching cloak of emerald satin and crystal beading with fur-trimmed hood. "A romantic interlude with your handsome, black-eyed . . . ?"

"Stop," Meg pleaded, laughing, though inside she felt far from mirthful. "I'll wear it. Anything to shush this crazy notion you have of some . . . some black-eyed . . . *monster* in my life."

The depot was filled to the rafters by the time the girls arrived. An auction, the likes of which Meg had never envisioned, began the evening's activities.

Hotel manager Davy Westfield served as auctioneer. The first item up was a lovely painting of local wildflowers by Clara Garrett. The bidding was spirited. The winner, banker Libbie Lancaster, was greeted by remarks of how many of Clara's paintings she already owned.

Next, a dipping vat donated by Jed Varner, to be built anywhere on the winner's ranch; then a tooth extraction by Hank Jefferies, a bolt of calico from Herman Crump's Mercantile, and an overnight stay for two at the Hotel O'Keefe, including dinner and champagne, donated by

Mavis O'Keefe.

"You'd better hurry and use this one," Mavis whispered as the out-of-town winner passed her in his haste to collect his prize. "If I decide to sell to Fred Harvey, he may not serve champagne."

Pausing, the young man grinned over his shoulder. "How 'bout tonight, ma'am?"

Meg smiled delightedly, as Mavis challenged his choice of companions. "As long as you bring your wife, cowboy."

The thought had just crossed her mind that the evening was turning out to be more enjoyable than she'd dared hope, when Davy Westfield shouted to listen up: bidding would begin immediately for the box suppers. As the bidding progressed, and one by one each winner claimed not only the fancy box of supper, but also the company of the lady who had prepared it, Meg wished she were somewhere else. Worry about whom she would be required to share the meal with buzzed senselessly through her head, filling her with dread. Turning this way and that to find an avenue of escape, she suddenly saw Rube standing in the doorway behind her.

He'd come. Like he'd said he would, in order to show his support for the community's efforts! Quickly, she made her way to him. "Buy mine," she implored.

He squeezed her arm. "Why, sugar, you don't want to spend the evening eating with old pa when there's so many handsome cowpokes around."

"I do, Rube. . . ." she began, then her breath caught as Davy held up her box. The bidding began, she heard shouts here and there about the room. "Please, Rube. . . ."

He looked down at her with a sympathetic grin. "Too late, sugar." Meg turned her back, mentally preparing herself for the inevitable, but the instant she heard the high-pitched voice, she knew she could never adequately prepare herself for a meal with Ellsworth Fredericks.

"Hope you put in some peach cobbler like you carried out to the surveyors the other day," he said amicably.

Her eyes raked him incredulously, then swept the room,

searching now for an empty place at the long plank tables, near friends. Finding one, she stepped toward it, but Fredericks grasped her arm, pushing through the throng of milling revelers, and guided her onto the long back veranda of the depot. He didn't stop until they came to the bench farthest from the crowd.

"We might as well sit out here away from the noise, where we can enjoy the moon along with your fine cooking."

Meg seethed. She wasn't afraid of untoward advances from Ellsworth Fredericks. Although she doubted he would try anything, she figured she could hold her own with him, but she had no stomach for his endless, mindless questions.

"Why don't we join one of the other groups?" she suggested, nodding toward the reception room. "It isn't neighborly to sit way over here alone."

"You'll have your fill of all those other fellers before the evening's done," he observed, nodding for her to take a seat.

While she eyed him silently, he balanced her box on the railing and untied the bows, then took out a chicken drumstick and seated himself beside her.

"Why are you always so angry with me, Miss Meg?" he asked, handing her the box. "I know my questions needle you, but I'm only doing my job."

She stared at the box, wishing she had put only half the amount of food inside. Then he would finish sooner, and she could be rid of his company. "Now?" she retorted at length. "This is a party. What information do you want from me tonight?"

Turning, he stared at her, the chicken still held to his lips. "I bought your company. Supper with the loveliest lady at the ball."

She laughed. "You can't bribe me with flattery, nor with much of anything else, as you should have discovered by this time. Besides, after you've dragged me away from the crowd without a chaperon and damaged my reputation . . ."

"You didn't give your reputation much consideration the day you went traipsing off without me to see the prospector."

His statement surprised her so much she gasped before she thought, then tried to cover it up with lighthearted repartee. "Would you have come along to protect my honor?"

Wiping his greasy fingers on the embroidered linen napkin, he took the box from her lap and examined its contents in the dim light. "You know darned well I would have. Why did you run off and leave me?"

"I didn't run off from you," she protested.

"Yes, you did," he observed casually. "But I'll think about forgiving you if you tell me about the prospector."

She frowned, stalling for time to think. "Why are you interested in him?"

He shrugged. "I'm always interested in people who aren't what they appear to be."

"Why, Mr. Fredericks!" Meg enthused. "What about you? You bring me way out here under the guise of a romantic supper for two, and all you want to talk about is some . . ."

At that moment two strangers approached them from around the darkened corner of the depot. Dressed in city top coats, one black, one fawn, the men wore dark Homburg hats and carried elegant walking canes. They stopped in front of Meg and Fredericks, their backs to the depot.

Clean shaven, except for waxed moustaches and long sideburns, she recognized neither man—until the shorter of the two spoke. Then her heart almost stopped.

Wash and Tobin. Spit and polished. A new disguise? Or was this their true identity? Were they actually sophisticated city-slickers instead of reprobate treasure hunters? And if so—her heart lurched—what did that make Kalib? Where was . . . ?

"You Ellsworth Fredericks?" Wash demanded. Neither he nor Tobin paid the least bit of attention to Meg.

Fredericks nodded, frowing. "Say, don't I know . . . ?"

"Not likely, Mr. Fredericks," Tobin told him. "We've just ridden into town. We were told you're the local newspaper editor, and we have a story for you."

Fredericks's eyes popped.

Wash reached for his arm. "If you'll accompany me over to the telegraph office, we'll confirm it. A scoop, Mr. Fredericks. A real scoop."

"Can't it wait until morning, Mr. . . . ?" Fredericks looked questioningly at Meg, who sat deathly still. Her mouth was so dry, she ran her tongue around her gums to loosen her lips from them. She dared not let her mind stray from this moment.

Yet, she couldn't help herself.

Tobin spoke reassuringly. "Run along, Mr. Fredericks. I'll keep the young lady safe during your absence."

"What's this all about?" Fredericks asked.

Meg found her voice. "I suppose you'd best go find out. If these gentlemen have gone to so much trouble to locate you, they must have something newsworthy."

Fredericks frowned, but acquiesced. Meg could see his eyes spark with unanswered questions. "You sure . . . ?"

Meg nodded, holding her breath for fear her runaway imagination would prove wrong. Joy and despair vied within her these days, like the hills and valleys surrounding Silver Creek, but never had she felt herself on so high a precipice, nor so feared being dropped, disappointed, from its height.

Tobin stood beside her watching until Wash led Fredericks around the corner and out of view. Then he bowed from the waist and extended a crooked elbow.

"Would you care to stroll along the riverfront, Miss Britton?"

Her heart pounded so furiously she thought for sure she would burst out of her corset. Glancing up, she saw a conspiratorial grin tip Tobin's lips. He looked down at her with a softness in his eyes she'd never seen there before, and she thought crazily that she had finally won him over.

Rising on wobbly legs, she clutched his offered elbow and let him lead her from the loading dock and away from the depot. The shaped heels on her green mesh slippers teetered on the rocks, and he clutched her arm more tightly.

She tried to think of something to say to him, but her mind was too occupied with where he was taking her—with who waited at the end of this . . .

If her spirits hadn't been soaring with the stars, she would have been in danger of swooning, she decided, as her breath came shallow and her eyesight blurred and she peered deeply into the enveloping darkness.

First, he appeared as a dark familiar shape in the distance. At the sight of him her heart lurched against her rib cage with such force her body actually jerked, and Tobin patted her hand, reassuringly.

She wanted to run to him, even now, as his face began to take form, but she felt stiff—frozen to Tobin's arm. Her legs would barely support her, much less move with any speed.

When at last they stood within ten feet of each other, the moonlight streamed in a fragile shaft of white light through the bare branches of the pecan trees, and she could but stare at him and he at her.

Gently, Tobin pried her fingers loose from his arm and moved apart.

"Be sure her doctor friend doesn't come after her," Kalib told his partner.

"It wasn't the doctor," Tobin responded with ill-suppressed laughter in his voice. "She was eating with that blasted newspaperman. But don't worry about a thing. Wash and I have it all under control."

Although he hadn't even spoken to her, his voice nevertheless rumbled along her spine, loosening her frozen muscles with the heat of anticipation. She heard Tobin leave, the dry leaves crunching beneath his boots, and Kalib turned his full attention to her.

"Maggie."

The instant he called her name, she raced to his arms. Burying her face in his chest, she tried to still her raging heart, but his own heart beat frantically against her cheek.

His voice, weak and beseeching, spun in her brain, and she pressed herself to him shamelessly, longingly, transmitting to him all the fear and desperation she had felt these long days and nights, receiving from his strong arms and erratic breathing the same message.

Kalib crushed her to him. His arms folded about her; his face nestled into the cold satin of her fur-trimmed hood, her very presence redemption enough for this elaborate hoax his cohorts called foolhardy. For a moment they stood without talking, their bodies communicating their mutual fears, finally settling more peacefully into the reality of the moment.

They were together again—for how long didn't, at this instant, matter. Lost in the stillness of time; they were together again.

Lifting his hands to her head, he drew her back and stared into the pools of swirling green fire that were her eyes. Gently, he swept her hood from her head, twined his fingers into the curls she had pinned on top, and lost himself in the wonder of her beauty.

Silently her hands crept up his chest, and she stroked his silky beard . . . at last . . . thinking how desperately she had longed to see him . . . to touch his face . . . to . . .

Her touch ignited sparks where he thought there was no more room for desire, and suddenly their lips met in a desperate kiss of passion denied, passion reclaimed.

They communicated now through their lips, their tongues. She twined her fingers in his hair, stroked the muscles on his shoulders, and pressed her face closer to the satiny mat of hair surrounding his tender, loving lips.

His hands delved beneath her satin cape and roamed her trussed-up body, teased by the smooth satin of her gown, the softness of the fur trimming at her shoulders, her snug, form-fitting bodice. Dropping his fingers, he spanned her tiny waist; his hands traveled enticingly over the beading, the boning, finding at last her sheltered breasts. Their heaving brought a groan of desire to his lips.

"Maggie, Maggie," he mumbled against her lips. "How I've missed you. How I've missed you."

At his words tears sparkled in her eyes, and she squenched her lids tight against them. *How I've missed you, too, my love,* she thought.

"Here," he said suddenly, holding her at arm's length. "Let me look at you." His fingers fumbled at her neck, then expertly unfastened the frog closing on her cape and held it aside. His breath caught in his throat at her loveliness. He'd never seen her hair swept up in curls, exposing a graceful neckline that looked even lovelier for being unadorned with gaudy jewels. "Majestic!" Lifting one of her hands by the fingertips over her head, he twirled her around in front of him, giving him a complete view of her exquisitely shaped and attired body.

When she stood facing him once more, she smiled at the chagrined look on his face. "What's the matter? Don't you approve?"

His eyes roamed her body unabashed, taking in the shimmering satin gown, which gleamed even brighter with the moonlight playing off the crystal beading. "You shine like a jewel," he said quietly, "like the emerald my grandmother never removes from her finger."

The words caught suddenly in his throat, and he pulled her into a tight embrace and buried his face in her curls. "But you're more dear to me than any jewel," he whispered, bringing more tears to her eyes. Releasing her once more, he cupped her chin in his palm and brought her face to within a hair's breadth of his own. "I'm sinfully selfish, my love. I can't bear the thought of you dressing up like this for another man."

At that she laughed delightedly, recalling the events that had led to her wearing this particular gown tonight. "Actually, I didn't wear it for *another* man," she told him, then recounted the story of Katie's insistence that she had a "handsome, dark-eyed stranger" in her past.

The story pleased him, she could tell by the way he ran his tongue idly around his lips while listening. But he quickly went on to another concern. "Katie Jefferies, you say? Is she related to . . . the doctor who's been squiring you about town?"

She laughed. "You mean Hank Jefferies?"

Kalib's face hardened, not in anger, she thought, recognizing his expression as one she so often grappled with these days herself—anguish. Very carefully he draped her cloak back over her shoulders and secured the frog beneath her chin. "Why didn't he buy your box tonight?"

Her eyes brightened. "Kalib, are you jealous of Dr. Jefferies?"

He gripped her shoulders and studied her with deadly seriousness. "I'll always be jealous when handsome men pay attention to my wife."

Her heart actually leapt for joy inside her breast. He hadn't forgotten. He was serious about marriage, about her; and he was jealous. "Kalib, Hank Jefferies is eating with his soon-to-be fiancée. At this very moment, perhaps, he's gifting her with an exquisite promise ring of blue topaz."

Kalib's brow knit about curious eyes, causing her to laugh again.

"No, he didn't jilt me, if that's what you're thinking. We're friends, great friends, but nothing more." She considered a moment, then corrected herself. "Really, we're more like brother and sister. He's wonderful. You're going to like him, I know."

While he listened to her, his face softened, and by the time she finished, he was smiling with her. "Perhaps I will," he agreed, moving his hands inside her cape now, where he encircled her waist with his strong hands and lifted her toward him. "But I'll never approve of my wife embracing another man on a bench on Main Street."

She clasped her arms about his neck, letting the edges of her cloak fell back from her shoulders. Playfully, she reached her lips to kiss his briefly. "I'm not your wife, or do you always forget such aggravating legal complications?"

Their eyes held while he answered her, his urgent tones trilling insistent yearnings along her spine. "You will be, love. Before a month has passed, you will be Mrs. Kalib—"

Abruptly he stopped, then, with a sigh of regret, he set

208

her back on her feet.

"Mrs. Kalib Who?"

Almost imperceptibly he shook his head, then he dropped his lips and kissed her fiercely. When she tried to break away, to question, he silenced her with still more ardent kisses.

"Talk to me, Kalib," she pleaded. "Talk to me . . . please."

He nuzzled his face against her, kissing her eyes, her nose, her hairline. "No, love, talking only gets us in trouble. Just let me love you."

Her lips trembled, then opened beneath his demanding, passion-filled kisses, and she felt her senses sway. But for his strong arms about her, she would crumble to the ground, she knew. But for his arms, she would be left empty and alone.

Her breath whispered from her lungs as weak and fluttery as butterfly wings. But for his arms . . . she would surely die . . . but for his love.

Leaving her lips, he traveled down her neck, where he lifted her cape away and kissed her throbbing pulse points, her skin cooling in his wake. He nibbled along the top of her exposed breasts, while his tongue dipped below the fabric, tantalizing, torturing her with long denied yearnings.

When she pulled his head toward her breasts, he trembled with desire, desire he knew would be hard to fulfill here outside the depot in a pecan grove on a chilly December evening.

"Smuggle me into your hotel room," he suggested. While his hands pressed her tender breasts together from the sides, his face delved beneath the gaping fabric to better taste her sweetness, to further torment them both with a torturous desire.

Visions of their being discovered sneaking into the Hotel O'Keefe, to say nothing of his being found in her room by Rube . . . or Mary Sue . . . or Katie . . . swarmed in her head. She snuggled her face in his dark hair, reveling in the feel of his lips on her breasts, nipping now at a sensitive nipple. She inhaled deep drafts of unbridled passion. "Only if when we're caught, you promise to own up to being my handsome, dark-eyed stranger," she whispered.

"I'll never deny loving you," he mumbled, returning his lips to her mouth. His hands swept down her back, pressing her gussied-up frame to his, increasing, as he did, the torment wracking his own body. "But I'd have to deny knowing myself, and that would pose a problem of a far different nature." Moving back, he searched her begging eyes, seeing his own desperate yearnings reflected in their emerald-green depths. "Come home with me."

"Rube's here," she said quietly. "And there's Katie and Mary Sue . . . Mary Sue will rush in tonight to show me her ring. My absence would be impossible to explain."

"Then Tobin can take a room in the hotel," he said. "I'll sneak in when no one is watching, and later, after everyone is in bed, you can pretend to go down the hall to the bathing room, and instead," his eyebrows waggled suggestively, ". . . instead, you'll come to my bed . . . to me. . . ." With a fierceness that shot quivering flames through her body, he clasped her to him and snuggled her body into a perfect fit against his own. ". . . and we'll finish this wonderful . . ."

"No," she sighed. Looking up at his handsome face, into his eyes, which glowed with the same desire she felt inside, she knew she would go to any lengths to protect him from whomever he feared, for whatever reason. Even if it meant denying her unbearable yearnings to be with him once more. "It's too dangerous for you. I don't know what you're hiding—I don't even care anymore—but I'm not going to let you get caught for my sake. Ellsworth Fredericks is suspicious enough already. Seeing you in town, at the hotel, would only arouse his suspicions more."

Catching her face between his two hands, he studied her lovely, tortured features. His heart practically burst with joy at her unconditional acceptance of what she could only think of as his folly. "I love you, Maggie Britton.

210

How I love you, you can't begin to imagine. When this is over, I'll spend the rest of my life making up to you for all the torment I've caused you. I promise, my love. I promise."

After a while, they walked arm in arm beside the river, silently. She thought of his remark that they usually got in trouble when they talked. Perhaps. But his last words would comfort her for a long time to come. She didn't think for a single moment that his appearance here tonight, his pronouncements of love and commitment to her, represented a change in his attitude toward the railroad. They still had trouble ahead, somehow she knew that without a doubt—as surely as she knew he meant every word and gesture of love he had given her tonight. And the last would help her through the rough times. That, and her idea, which had been greatly strengthened tonight—her plan to persuade him to accept a position with the railroad.

Dance music drifted toward them from the depot, and she tensed, knowing she should go soon. Too many people would be looking for her. Tobin and Wash were only concerned with Ellsworth Fredericks. But there were Rube, and Katie, and possible even Hank and Mary Sue. Tobin and Wash knew only to worry over Fredericks. But when she suggested leaving, neither of them was ready to part.

He cocked his ear toward the depot, then suddenly bowed from the waist. "A waltz, ma'am. We can't let a waltz go to waste." At her laugh, he swept her into his arms, and they twirled about under the pecan trees, a bit awkwardly, considering all the fallen nuts on the ground, but she could tell he was a superb dancer.

He gazed into her eyes so longingly that for a time all she could do was search her mind for someplace she could spend the night with him—alone and loving.

"Always remember this night, Maggie," he whispered. "No matter what grand ballroom we find ourselves dancing in, no matter how elevated the company or our station in life, always remember where we first danced."

For a long time she couldn't answer. Wondering what elevated company and station he had in mind for them, she nevertheless rejoiced in his words, in his perception of the importance of this glorious moment in their lives, in his readiness to tell her of his feelings.

For that, she knew, would keep her sane until they could be together. The music ended, and she raised on tiptoe and kissed him deeply, passionately.

"What a strange fantasy this is," she whispered, thinking of the real world, which raced pell-mell all around, while the two of them moved as in a separate universe, outside the realm of reality.

"It's no fantasy, love. This is you and me. Two real people who are in love and," he grinned and pecked her lips, ". . . and in terrible pain because of it at the moment."

A noise at the edge of the pecan grove startled her.

"It's only Tobin," Kalib assured her, responding to the sound of a man clearing his throat as though it were a butler announding a caller in the parlor of a mansion somewhere.

"The troops're getting restless," Tobin told them. "There's lots of out-of-town folks, too."

Kalib turned to face his friend, holding her tightly beside him. "Anyone recognize you or Wash?"

Tobin shook his head. "But they'd be likely to recognize you. We'd . . . ah . . . we'd best hit the road."

Kalib sighed. "I'll meet you in one minute, by the horses. I want you to escort Maggie back to the dance before we leave."

They kissed again, long but not long enough, their desperate parting made bearable, as she had thought, only by their professed commitment, which carried the promise that they would one day be together.

"I'm going to the hotel," she told him as they approached the horses. "Our dance is enough for me. I'm going to bed," she caught her bottom lip between her teeth a moment, wondering whether she dared be so brash as the finish the sentence, ". . . and dream of you."

His step faltered at her words. Although he kept walking, he bent forward and kissed her lips soundly. "You're a wicked temptress," he whispered. "Leaving me in an state of unbearable pain wasn't enough. Now, you fill my mind with visions of you snuggled in bed ... gowned in sheer lace and ruffles ... while I ride alone through the cold night with only my trusty steed for company ... in physical agony!"

Chapter Eleven

Rube was pacing the floor of the tiny parlor of their suite when Meg arrived back at the hotel, and for a second she was glad she hadn't given in to her overwhelming desire to roll among the leaves and pecans in Kalib's arms. Not that he'd suggested such a thing, but since it had been on her mind, she didn't doubt the same thing figured into his own desperate longings, as well.

When Rube heard her enter, he turned to stare with unfeigned relief. "Thank the Lord you've turned up safe and sound, sugar. Whatever happened to you? We've been out scouring the streets."

At the thought of being caught in Kalib's passionate embrace by the local citizens, she flushed so deeply that Rube squinted, then clamped his meerschaum more tightly between his teeth.

"You're . . . all right?" he asked, hesitating now.

She nodded. Raising her hands to unfasten the frog closing on her cloak, her fingers lingered there, recalling Kalib's hands so recently at her neck.

"Ellsworth Fredericks's tale left us . . . wondering," Rube began. Meg interrupted him.

"What did Mr. Fredericks say?"

"Said while you were on the loading dock eating, a couple of strangers approached the two of you with tales of a story for this week's *Sun*." He grinned at her. "I gave him a regular rust-eater's cursing for leaving you alone with a stranger."

"You blistered his ears?" She sank to the sofa, where, kicking off her shoes, she tucked her green-stockinged feet beneath her skirts and hugged an embroidered pillow to her chest.

"I suppose," Rube began again, "this is another episode you don't want to discuss."

She looked down at the pillow and thought how she should get up and hug him for being so understanding. "Not yet," she admitted. "There isn't anything to say . . . at the moment."

He sat opposite her, smoking idly, and she wondered whether he intended to wait her out. Then her anxiety began to rise. "Did . . . ah, did Fredericks say he recognized the men?"

Rube studied her silently—long enough to let her know he understood her unspoken question. Finally, he shook his head. "Said they were city fellers, come to town with some cock-and-bull story about the governor's hunting trip."

Meg considered the situation, thinking Kalib could surely have come up with a more sensational story than that. However, she recalled, Fredericks had made the governor's hunting trip headline news, so perhaps a story about the governor was something to pique his interest.

"I talked to the one who ate your box supper while Fredericks was off at the newspaper," Rube told her.

She smiled, thinking of the softness Tobin had shown her tonight. She hoped he liked her cooking. "Did you . . . ah, did *you* recognize him?"

Rube pursed his lips between his teeth, then reinserted his ever-present meerschaum. "Not right off, I didn't," he admitted. "But since you mention it, I reckon he's one of the two fellers who stopped us at the river that day."

"What'd he tell you?" she asked. "I mean, about where I was?"

"Said after Fredericks went off with his friend, you ran back into the depot and he hadn't seen hide nor hair of you since."

She sighed. "Oh, what a tangled web we weave. . . ." Then suddenly her mind flitted from Sir Walter Scott to Milton—*Hearts . . . tangled in amorous nets. . . .*

Letting her head fall dreamily back against the cushions, she recalled the day Rube had seen Tobin and Wash—that was the first time Kalib had ever kissed her. That glorious day! This glorious night! Would they entangle themselves hopelessly in their own amorous webs of secrecy and deceit?

"How was your prospector tonight?" Rube asked quietly.

Her head snapped up, and she studied his beloved face. How she wished she could tell him about Kalib . . . as much as she herself knew, anyway. "You're going to love him, Rube. You'll be the best of friends in no time."

He laughed sardonically, shaking his head in disbelief. "If you say so, sugar. But we've sure had a hell of a shaky beginning."

When a knock came at the door, Rube rose to retire. "That'll be your friend, Miss Jefferies," he told Meg, kissing her cheek before he vanished into his own bedroom. "She's been here looking for you three times already."

Katie stood, fists on hips, looking Meg curiously up and down. "How dare you disappear without a trace!" She pushed past Meg and closed the door behind them. "Now, tell me everything. How did you manage to slip away from Ellsworth Fredericks? Were you abducted? Did you run off with your . . ."

"Shush!" Meg laughed. "Katie, dear friend, your imagination runs wild. Mr. Fredericks was called away from our little tête-à-tête on business, and I, having developed a splitting headache from his nagging questions, came home. It's as simple as that."

"Not quite," Katie declared. "You've been gone for hours."

Temporarily shocked, Meg recovered quickly. "Not hours, Katie. I'll admit I didn't return immediately. The fresh air was so invigorating, I walked up the road a piece, letting it relieve my head."

"Well, you must come back to the dance now," Katie encouraged. "You haven't met any of my friends yet . . . I mean, my hometown friends. They're here from ranches all over the country. They'll love . . ."

Meg pushed a strand of hair away from her face. "I'm sure they'll be here tomorrow, too. You run along and have fun and introduce me to them tomorrow."

As soon as Katie left, Meg gathered up her things and hurried to the bathing room, where she soaked in Mavis's lavender oil and dreamed lazy dreams of Kalib—of their ardent passion, of their hazy future. She sighed, recalling his idea to let Tobin take a room for them to use tonight.

And her response still baffled her. Not that she'd refused to sleep with him in so public a place as the Hotel O'Keefe, especially on the night of the Christmas Ball. One of them had to keep his head about him. But her desperate attempts to protect this man and his charade confounded her every time she thought about it. She'd even won Rube's silence, and for what?

For love? For the love of a man who was as much a stranger to her tonight as he had been the first time she ever saw him. *Oh, what a tangled web we weave, When first we practice to deceive,* she thought again. Pray God, Kalib wasn't deceiving her about . . . about his love.

By the time she dressed, in flowing flannel instead of lace and ruffles, and turned down her bed, more visitors had arrived. She'd been expecting these, too.

Katie burst in without even knocking, towing Mary Sue by an arm—giving Meg heart failure just thinking on the scene had she smuggled Kalib to her room, as he'd suggested. Mary Sue, aflush with excitement, held her ring finger aloft as though she wore an episcopal ring. And the next hour was spent oohing and aahing in the sincere adoration one friend bestows upon another in times of great joy.

Early the next morning Rube left for the end of track, abandoning Meg to the belligerent Ellsworth Fredericks.

"Why didn't you wait for me?" he stormed. "You knew I

217

would be back straightaway."

"I knew nothing of the kind, Mr. Fredericks." she responded, returning to her baking, which he had interrupted. "Why did *you* leave me alone so readily . . . and with a stranger, at that?"

"I returned as soon as my business was completed," Fredericks explained. "That gentleman who was to stay with you said you'd gone back inside the depot, but I couldn't find you."

"I had a headache, so I returned to the hotel," she said simply, sliding the last batch of bread dough into the oven and slamming the door. *And I'm getting one now*, she thought, *from your incessant whining*.

"He even had the gall to eat all my supper," Ellsworth Fredericks complained. "Can you believe that? Supper I bought and paid for?"

At this last Meg was unable to keep a smile from her face. He was obviously more distressed over being deprived of her cooking than of her company. "Was your visit with the stranger worthwhile?"

He sighed. "Somewhat. Mr. Sanders, that's what the man called himself, claimed to have an inside scoop on the governor-elect. I hope to have the story in print before anyone else in the state."

"Good for you, Mr. Fredericks. Good for you." *You take the governor, I'll take the prospector, every day of the week, and Sunday, too.*

By the time her baking was done, Katie Jefferies had descended upon the depot with those of her hometown friends who had stayed overnight in town. Their introductions were interrupted by the arrival of Mary Sue and Hank, who were on their way to South Texas.

"Keep your fingers crossed," Hank told Meg. "Her folks have never even seen me."

"Stop worrying, Hank. You're worse than a woodpecker on a tree full of ants. They're going to love you." Then, on the spur of the moment, she stood tall, and whispered in his ear, "When you return I may have a surprise for you, too."

His eyes widened in response. "I thought we shared secrets. What have you been keeping from me?"

"Shush! Don't let Katie hear, or I won't have another moment's peace!"

He laughed, she hugged Mary Sue and wished them both God speed, and they were off.

By afternoon Katie and her friends had all returned to their respective ranch homes, and Silver Creek became once again the sleepy little town it had been before the Christmas Ball.

"What a nice place to live," she confided to Mavis at noon. "When things get too quiet, you liven them up with a humdinger of a party. Everyone in the country comes; they all wear themselves out; then they return home, and we go back to normal . . . for a while."

"That's about the way it is, darling. Now you know why I've stayed around these last twenty-five years."

Returning to the routine of cooking for the grading crew was easier, Meg discovered, than returning to the way she felt about Kalib before he'd appeared the night before and taken her senses away with him. Although before she had thought she was desperate to see him, to feel his nearness, her decision not to see him again had helped her keep her mind off the future. But now that he had come— and gone—she was left with more unbearable longings than before. His avowed love for her, his commitment to marry her, filled her with not only intense joy, but also with an overwhelming sense of needing to be with him constantly . . . always . . . forever. Whatever was she to do?

Her question was answered quite unexpectedly one morning as she took the last of the loaves of bread from the oven and set them on the plank table to cool. Rob and Jim had already left for a couple of hours of hunting, and she was alone. But suddenly, as she stood with her back to the rail side of the depot, the feeling of his presence caused the fine hairs along her neck to stand out like they'd been starched.

Her heart lurched to her throat, and she caught her breath. She knew it was he even before she turned and saw him lounging in the doorway.

Her hand flew to her head. "Ka . . . !" As quickly as his name blurted from her lips, she closed them over it. "What if someone sees you? People are forever dropping by. . . ."

"Hurry, then." He pushed away from the door and extended a hand to her. "I have something to show you."

"You shouldn't have come here. You might get . . ."

His lazy, sensual grin shot pure passion through her trembling body. "Sometimes a man has to take a chance, love. Hurry, now."

Grabbing her cloak from the hook beside the door, she followed him silently. In fact, she didn't speak again until they escaped the depot, exited the far side of the pecan grove, and started to mount the horses he had waiting for them. Grasping the saddlehorn with one hand, the cantle in the other, she stepped into the stirrup, then stopped short.

Although the skirt of the old cotton wrapper she wore was wide, it wouldn't stretch *that* far! Her eyes met his across the saddle, where he swung onto his own horse. His wicked grin trilled up her spine and fired her scalp.

"Hopefully, nobody's around to see your ankles but me, Maggie. And I've already seen a great deal more of your loveliness than that."

Her face aflush with the knowledge that what he said was very true, indeed, she quickly mounted and followed him from the grove of trees, across the river, and over the rise on the opposite side.

When they were far enough away not to be seen, he slackened his pace and waited for her. She pulled up beside him, her heart pounding fiercely at his nearness. She stared, enamored, at his rugged features, his captivating smile, the loving light in his eyes, and he studied her in return.

Reaching toward her, he swept the white cotton cap

from her head and fingered her silky hair. Then he leaned way forward in the saddle and planted a firm kiss on her anxious lips.

"That'll have to do for now," he whispered in his husky voice, which never failed to turn her to a quivering mass of jelly. "I have something to show you."

They rode silently then, her curiosity tempered by the unbounded joy she felt at being with him. Nothing he could show her would be half as wonderful as his presence.

The Silver Creek River flowed in lazy S's from above Silver Creek itself to she knew not where. They traveled north, then east in the general direction of Kalib's camphouse, sometimes following the river, crossing it once. After cutting across a bald-open prairie littered with nothing more than a few clumps of mesquite grass and thousands upon thousands of limestone rocks, he pulled rein beside a large cedar brake.

She sat her horse, watching him hitch his own, then hers. When he lifted her by the waist from her saddle, her body trembled beneath his touch.

But his eyes were alight with more than her presence, she could tell. He moved like a child who had just found a new kind of lizard and couldn't wait to show it to his best friend.

Setting her to the ground, however, he noticed her slippers and frowned. "I should have given you time to change," he said. "Those thin-soled slippers weren't made for climbing over rocks and cactus."

She shrugged and clasped an arm about his waist. "You can carry me," she suggested playfully.

"You think of all the right things," he laughed. Then, without further ado, he swept her into his arms and carried her to a point near a circular clearing in the midst of the cedar trees, where he sat her on her feet and squatted to examine a tangled mat of vines. "Hog persimmon," he muttered, tearing them away to expose a broad slab of limestone.

When next he looked at her, his expression of guileless sincerity took her breath away. Tugging gently on her

221

hand, he pulled her down beside him.

"After the night of the Christmas Ball . . ." His deep voice played sensually with her wits and she had trouble concentrating on anything except the nearness of him.

". . . I came to a couple of important decisions," he went on. "I meant it when I told you I hope to be finished here within the month. Since then, I've redoubled my efforts to find that damned mine."

Pressing her lips lightly between her teeth, she stared at him through the bright winter day. *How had she ever managed to find someone like this man . . . someone she could fall so hopelessly, wonderfully in love with?*

"I also realized how selfish I've been," he admitted softly. "You've given me your love and your trust, unconditionally. All you've asked in return is an explanation for the trouble I'm causing you and Rube."

She watched his Adam's apple bob when he spoke, and she squeezed his hand reassuringly. "I . . . I know you'll tell me when you can, Kalib."

"I can right now," he whispered. "That's what I'm fixing to do." Now, his voice became more animated, and he rushed forward, bringing a smile to her face, an ache of pure happiness to her heart.

"Look carefully at this rock." As he spoke, he pulled her fingers forward and traced them across the slab. "See these three crosses?"

She nodded. Indeed, the faint form of three crosses appeared to have been etched into the gray limestone surface.

"They've been marred by weather and time," he went on. "But they're here, exactly like on the plat I showed you in the cabin."

Dropping her hand, he began to tug at the rock slab. "Tobin found this cedar brake two days ago."

She edged back, squinting through the dust kicked up by the rock, then stared in awe at the enormous hole he uncovered.

"Is this the mine?"

He shook his head. "It's connected with all the old

stories, though.

"How?"

He shrugged. "Either the Indians or the Spaniards stored silver here."

Scooching forward, she peered into the depths of the hole. It didn't look big enough—a couple or three yards in diameter, the same in depth. "What did you find down there?"

"Nothing," he answered, returning the rock to its resting place over the hole.

"Then why . . . ?" she began.

"Because it fits the pattern." Rising, he pulled her behind him, then as quickly as he had moved forward, he stopped and quirked an eyebrow at her. "Sorry," he mumbled, scooping her into his arms once more. "As you can tell, love, I'm not used to looking out for anyone but myself . . . but don't give up on me. I'll learn."

"You're doing fine," she encouraged, reaching to kiss the soft beard along his cheek, not intending to discourage his treasure hunt, to the contrary, she thought now, she was enjoying it almost as much as he—although, she quickly admitted, she would likely enjoy anything that brought her this close to him.

He carried her down a bluff, across a rocky draw, and deposited her before a circle of fire-blackened rocks.

Kneeling on her own, she asked, "Now, what are we looking at?"

"To the uninitiated eye it would appear to be nothing more than an old Indian kitchen midden—a circle of rocks in which they did their cooking."

"To your trained eye, what do we have?" she laughed.

"Laugh if you wish, ma'am, but I'm going to impress you, yet. Just wait and see." With a wink he fished a pocket knife from his trousers, and using the razor-sharp point, dug around until he turned up some spent bullets. "They're not silver, like I'd hoped, but I'm sure this is the smelter."

"The smelter?"

"Where the Indians melted down their ore and poured it

into bars."

She cocked her head and studied him. It occurred to her suddenly that he was making this all up, trying to impress her with the sincerity of his cause. "There seem to be a lot of things you *haven't* found," she mused.

"It's on the plat," he reiterated. Then silently he led her fifty yards or so up the draw to a gaping hole in the side of the hill. "This should be more convincing."

On closer inspection, she could see that the mouth of the hole was actually supported by aged timbers. "It's a . . . shaft?" she questioned.

Nodding, he led her inside the mouth, which dropped off quickly into a pitch-black hole.

"I don't think I . . ." She clutched his hand tightly, and he squeezed her fingers in response.

"Don't worry," he assured her. "It's perfectly safe. Stay right behind me, and we'll take it slow." They edged forward in a slow fashion. "Notice the steps are wood," he told her.

She stared back at the shaft of light streaming through the opening. Rough wooden steps were visible through the hazy beam of light. "Who . . . ?"

"According to Jim Bowie, who later became a Texas hero when he died in the Alamo, the Lipan Apaches mined the ore from the mine," Kalib called over his shoulder. "Bowie joined their tribe, became an adopted son of the old chief, Xolic, who, one day when the other Indians were away, showed him this very spot. Bowie claimed to have seen millions here."

She frowned in the darkness. "Millions of what?"

Kalib hesitated, then answered, "Silver." The feigned lightness in his tone, acknowledged to her, in spite of his words, that he didn't know much more about what Jim Bowie had found or where he had found it than she did herself.

"Silver what?" she prodded.

"That isn't exactly clear," he finally admitted. "It may have been ore, or he may have seen a room full of silver bars ready for shipment, or . . ."

"If you don't know what you're looking for," she asked, "how can you be so sure this is the place?"

"The steps cut into the live oak log," he answered readily.

"Oh," she whispered. "And what else did you find in here?"

His sigh echoed in the darkness around them, then she felt his hands on her shoulders, turning her back toward the opening of the shaft. "You're full of questions," he murmured.

"Unfortunately, you don't have many answers."

Outside she watched him stand, legs apart, hands on hips, searching this way and that.

"Kalib," she began quietly, trying to keep her bitter disappointment from showing, "I know treasure hunting gets into a man's blood. I've heard it can even distort his thinking."

He stared down at her with a distressed look on his face, and suddenly her disppointment turned to anguish.

"How are you ever going to find this damned mine," she demanded, "if you don't even know what you're looking for?"

He swallowed convulsively; she watched his Adam's apple bob; he dug the toe of his boot into the side of the draw and dislodged a stone, which he kicked down the hill.

"I'm not looking for the mine," he told her.

Her mouth went dry, her head spun, and she tried desperately to determine what he meant. "My God," she cried in despair, "don't you ever make any sense?"

At length, he drew her to him, and she felt his heart pound against her face. "It's a long story, Maggie. Why don't I tell it to you over a cup of tea."

Although she knew they had ridden far this morning, she was surprised when they came to the camphouse before traveling more than a mile west of the cedar brake.

Tobin and Wash were nowhere to be seen, and when she asked, he told her he sent them on errands.

"Obviously not to spy on me," she quipped. Hanging

her cloak on a hook, she helped him prepare tea. The delicious feeling she got being in the cabin again settled over her like a warm blanket.

He looked chagrined. "They don't *spy* on you, Maggie," he insisted. "I . . . well, let's just say I rest better knowing you're safe and sound."

She laughed. "The strange part is . . . I don't really mind."

Seating her at the table, he sat across from her and studied her with a knowing grin. "You'd better not mind," he told her with a softness in his voice that reminded her instantly that she would be his willing captive anytime, anyplace. "One day soon, you're never going to be out of my sight again." With a sip from his cup, he changed the subject. "Now, let's see if I can do a better job of explaining things. Back before the Texas war for independence from Mexico, Jim Bowie . . ."

At her groan, he paused. "I'm not rehashing old stuff, Maggie. Bowie plays an important part in this story. My grandfather was a member of an ill-fated expedition Jim and his brother Rezin put together to find this confounded mine in the first place. That's why I'm here."

She grinned. "You inherited your grandfather's treasure fever?"

"Be patient, woman," he commanded lightly, then continued. "Bowie left the Lipans, intending to get a company together and return for the silver. But by the time he got his expedition on the road, old Chief Xolic had died and a young warrior by the name of Tres Manos, that's Three Hands in Spanish, had assumed power. According to the story, Tres Manos distrusted Bowie from the beginning. Perhaps he was merely jealous of the old chief's love for Jim, no one knows for sure. Anyhow, Bowie and his company of nine men, including my grandfather, set out to find the silver mine, but they were attacked somewhere around this very spot by a combined force of several Indian tribes—Tehuacans, Wacos, Caddos, and some unfriendly Lipans, possibly made more unfriendly by Tres Manos's resentment of Bowie. Bowie's party never made it to the mine. After patching up their wounded, the expedition limped back to San Antonio in time to join in the fight at the Alamo, and I'm sure you know the rest. All the men except my grandfather died in the Alamo. My grandfather was one of the men wounded by the Indians, so he didn't make it to the battle of the Alamo. Instead, he died in my young grandmother's arms before the battle even got underway good.''

Meg sipped her tea, listening intently now as this most private man opened a part of his life to her.

After a moment, he continued. ''Of course, the men didn't bring anything back to prove their expedition hadn't been in vain. And since all of them died shortly after returning, no one ever knew what, if anything, their mission accomplished. My grandmother, left a widow at twenty-four, with six children to raise, was intensely bitter for a long time. She always believed if she could have proof the mine existed, she would be satisfied that her husband hadn't died for some empty dream. Of course, no amount of knowledge, or for that matter, no amount of silver itself, would have brought him back, but . . .''

Stopping, he gazed across the table into her eyes. ''She has this ring, my grandmother . . . it's an emerald as big and green as your eyes, Maggie. My grandfather gave it to her for their betrothal, and, would you believe, she never takes it off.'' He laughed softly. ''It's so big a glove won't fit over it, so she never wears a glove on her left hand.''

Meg listened, enthralled. He'd never shared so much of his life with her before. Then, suddenly, she understood what he was trying to tell her. ''Why you, Kalib?''

He ran his tongue idly around his lips. ''You mean, why am I the one appointed to provide proof of an elusive silver mine?''

She nodded. ''Surely someone before now . . .''

He smiled. ''I'm the first male born into the family in all these years. Neither my mother nor my aunts could persuade their husbands to forsake jobs or to expend the fortune it would have taken to look for the mine. From the earliest time I recall, I'm sure from the instant I was born, if truth were known, I was destined to fulfill this wish of my wonderfully eccentric grandmother."

Meg sipped the last of her tea and studiously examined the bottom of her empty cup. She looked up, and a grin tipped the corners of her mouth. "So, it's your eccentric grandmother against my besotted father."

He sat very still a moment, allowing the sensual passion of her smile, her voice, her very presence to stir invitingly inside him. "Something like that," he murmured. Without taking his eyes from hers, he rose and came around the table. His hands whispered against her shoulders, as he pulled her tenderly into his arms.

"Why can't we let them fight it out between themselves, leaving us to . . . ?"

"Wouldn't work," he breathed against her face. "We both have to do what we must do." His hands clasped her face and held her in a heated vise. "But we'd best give thanks everyday for the rest of our lives, Maggie. Without them we wouldn't have found each other."

Her lips met his hungrily, opening beneath the fiery insistence of his questing tongue, melting from the intensity of her need for him . . . for his love . . . for his loving touch.

His arms wound about her quivering body as though to prevent her from escaping—ever again. Finally, he loosened his grip and took the pins from her hair. It fell in waves like drifts of sand down her back, tangling in his hands and arms as he pressed her to him, as he kneaded her supple form, melding it to his own.

Ever since their interrupted lovemaking in the pecan grove, his need for her had grown steadily, until now, he felt as though they'd started in the middle of the game— half over, near, too near, the finish line.

Moving his hands to her waist, he untied the sash of her free-flowing wrapper, which, once loose, hung from her shoulders. Crumpling the cloth in his hands, he found his way beneath the yards of fabric and massaged her skin, separated from his own by the inner lining of her dress.

With trembling fingers he found the front buttons,

fumbled them out of their buttonholes, and felt her tender breasts drop loose and hot into the palms of his hands.

At the touch of her hot skin on his, he shuddered in her arms, and she tightened her arms about his shoulders. "I'm shamefully underdressed," she whispered, thinking of her lack of corset or chemise.

Kneading her breasts in his palms, he peered into her passion-filled eyes, hardly able to see her for the glaze in his own. "And I'm shamefully overwrought," he whispered, sending shivers down her spine. As quickly as he could make his awkward fingers work, he unfastened the neckline of her dress and stripped it over her head, then hastily disrobed her of petticoat, bloomers, stockings, and slippers.

Weakened by the grip of this fierce passion, he lifted her in trembling arms and carried her to the bed, where he sat beside her and tried to slow his racing pulse.

Her senses reeling, she lifted her fingers to undo his shirt, then, quickly, he discarded the rest of his clothing and lay beside her, Her fingers ran up and down his skin, igniting him with fiery sparks.

Laving her face with kisses, he whispered her name between each one, and she arched her naked body against his own, writhing with unfulfilled desire.

"I've needed you too long," he whispered, kissing now her neck, now her chest, cupping one breast to suckle at its ripened tip. "Wanted you too long. . . ." Shifting over her, his hand lifted her other breast to his mouth, and he moved from one to the other, sending unbearable fingers of desire shooting through her abdomen, causing her to move her hips against him in a desperate attempt to seek relief.

When he could stand it no longer, he lifted himself over her, and with a look of helplessness, entered her body in a desperate thrust, a demand . . . for release . . . for requital . . . for fulfillment. "I'm sorry, Maggie," he breathed against her lips, as he began to move inside her. "I've needed you too long . . . loved you too long."

Lifting her hips in response to his, she sought his lips with hers. "Never, Kalib. You can never love me too long."

Later they lay in each other's arms, damp, exhausted, filled with the wonder of their love, and for the moment, sated with the expression of it.

Turning in his arms, she twined her fingers lazily in the curly black hair on his chest, then moved to stroke his silky beard. "You said within the month," she told him.

In response, he nudged his chin against the top of her head, in a gesture she recognized as his way of thinking. "What must you find to satisfy your grandmother?"

He loosened his hold a bit, so he could look at her, but they lay still twined together, like the vines of the hog persimmon, she thought sillily. How good it felt to be happy enough to be silly.

He nipped her forehead with his lips. "Something silver," he answered, then corrected himself. "Something that originated in this area. A piece of ore, a bit of a silver bar. The Lipans were rumored to have used silver bullets. Something like that."

"I don't see how you'll ever find it. I mean, this is such a big country . . . and what if . . . ?" As she spoke, her lightheartedness turned quickly to despair. "Who ever heard of finding something as small as all that? The chances are so remote. . . ."

"Shhhh," he whispered, kissing her nose, then her lips, calming her with his strength, with his love. "It'll work out, Maggie. Trust me."

"But Kalib," she persisted. "The railroad *must* be completed . . . the governor is . . ."

"To hell with the governor," he breathed against her lips.

To hell with the silver mine, she thought, but she didn't say it. Instead she snuggled against him, wishing she were as confident of their future as he seemed to be. What he didn't know was that if Rube lost his job with the railroad, she wouldn't be able to get *him* one, either. Then none of them would have a job. Then . . .

He pulled her chin up so he could look into her troubled green eyes. "Hey, what's going on inside that noggin of yours? You're stirring like a hive of bees."

"Kalib . . . I . . ." Suddenly she reached and kissed him desperately. "I don't want to lose you. I couldn't bear to lose you."

"You won't, my love," he assured her, then in a more lighthearted vein, he added, "Maggie Britton, let me do the worrying. Now that we've found each other, nothing's going to separate us. You couldn't drive me off with a stick."

Chapter Twelve

As they lay in each other's arms, their passion quickly mounted once more, and this time they loved slowly and long. He sent tremors down her spine, brought chills to her skin, ignited her through and through with unbearable yearnings and incredible beauty.

His every touch increased her sense of desperate longing—his breath behind her ear, his lips against her skin, his teeth tormenting the aching tips of her breasts.

And his hands—she melted beneath his exquisite hands like clay beneath the fingers of a master potter, while he shaped and molded her ragged senses into the most magnificent offering—her gift . . . of herself . . . for him alone.

But she didn't lie passively beneath his touch, taking and not giving. Instead she reciprocated with her own hands, her own lips, until he became her willing slave, eager to please and be pleased.

When at last she cried to him, begging him to come to her, to fulfill the promises of his hands, his lips, he held her with his eyes, watching the green fire smolder with love and desire. Their bodies laved from the exertion of their frenzied passion, his hands slid slowly up her slick skin, lingering over her abdomen, at her breast, upon her heaving heart. Then as he purposefully lifted himself above her and entered her fiery, proffered sheath, watching still, he saw the smoldering fire enkindle in her eyes, and together they soared in a world of flames where everything exploded into a fire of brilliant green.

Exhausted now, they clung, each to the other's love-glazed body, again fulfilled for the moment, conscious of the fact that their passion would forever require fulfilling.

Kissing his damp chest, she raised her head from where she had snuggled against his shoulder. "I think you're a better lover than you are a treasure hunter."

He laughed and nipped the tip of her nose, then firmly kissed her lips. "I certainly hope so, my love. I'd hate to disappoint you in everything."

"You don't," she sighed with such sincerity that he felt sure, whether they were rejuvenated enough or not, they would soon love again. "I couldn't bear for you to find the silver mine. It would ruin everything."

He stared at her, curious now. What did she know? Was it possible . . . ? No, he decided, at last. If she knew who he was, she'd have told him by now. "Do you remember the plat I showed you?"

She nodded.

"According to it, the mine is under the river, and I plan to leave it there."

"You sound like you really take that plat seriously. How could you?"

"Easy," he assured her, running a palm lazily up and down her spine. "I've found almost every landmark on it—the old shaft, the smelter, the hole in the middle of the cedar brake. It all fits." She squirmed, and he shushed her with a smacking kiss, then continued. "When the Lipans left or were driven away from this country, they supposedly diverted the course of the river to cover the mine so their white enemies couldn't find it."

"Supposedly," she scoffed.

He grinned, snuggling his damp body wickedly against her. She shivered within his embrace, and they kissed, deep and long. Drawing back, he gazed lovingly into her upturned, rapturous face. "Do you take my word for nothing?" he teased. "One of these days I'll show you where I found the old riverbed."

Then with regret he rose and tossed her his shirt. "Share my clothing," he suggested, tugging on his pants.

His soft cotton shirt caressed her bare skin with a sensualness that made her shiver. Pulling her to him, he basked in the feel of her unbound breast against his chest, their skin separated only by his thin shirt. Unable to resist, he moved his hands beneath the shirt and swept them up her thighs, over her hips, tightening around her small waist, then, sighing into her waiting lips, he closed his palms over her breasts. "This is a hell of an enjoyable way to spend a day, Maggie Britton," he breathed before kissing her hungrily, yet again. "But it won't get us on the road to solving our problems, will it?"

Releasing her, he took out the skillet and began looking around for something to fix for dinner, but she stopped him.

"I can't take you home hungry, Maggie," he insisted.

With a grin that fired his blood, she threw her arms around his neck and kissed him fiercely. "Then you'll have to keep me here," she whispered. "The only thing I'm hungry for is you."

Holding her tightly, he returned her kiss, bathing her face in kisses, while his hands massaged her fine skin beneath his shirt. Finally, she drew back.

"I really must go," she told him. "I have to cook for the grading crew, and Tobin and Wash will return, and . . ."

He laughed. "I know, love, but go knowing I don't want you to."

Pushing a strand of hair away from her face, she smiled, happily. "Neither do I." When she picked up her clothing and faced the corner, he caught her shoulders and turned her to face him.

With a tempting wink, he said, "I'm hungry, too." And taking her clothes from her hands, he proceeded to dress her himself. First removing his shirt, button by slow button, then, holding her bloomers for her to step into, tying them at the waist. Her petticoat followed, which he buttoned before moving his hands to caress her bare breasts once more, dipping to kiss each in turn.

Then he lifted her dress over her head, and with the skirt draped on top of his own head he tantalized her shamelessly as he fumbled with the buttons of the lining that fit snugly across her bosom.

When at last she stood before him fully clothed, they stared at each other, transmitting such an intense longing that each knew above all else the only thing they both wanted at the moment was to disrobe and return to their loving bed.

With great joy over what they had shared this day, with regret that the day had to end, they left the camphouse and rode back the way they had come that morning. Not so much now to look for landmarks from the old plat, as to stay out of sight of the surveyors and the grading crew. Sitting their horses at the top of the draw, he pointed, and in the distance she saw the workers. The railroad, he told her, would dissect the circle on the plat.

The afternoon was warm, and they rode easily, if reluctantly, toward town. Only one cloud marred her clear, blue sky of happiness, and it she put down to the fact that everyone had to have something to worry about. At the moment, her life was *almost* perfect. Before they reached Silver Creek, however, Kalib gave her the opportunity to put this concern to rest.

"How long are you planning to stay in Silver Creek?" he asked.

"Why?" She glanced at him apprehensively. For a man who knew her every move, who appeared endlessly curious to the point of being downright critical at times of her activities, he had remained strangely silent on one issue.

The *Texas Star*. Not once had he mentioned it, and that made her uneasy. She certainly didn't want him to form the wrong idea about her relationship with Leslie Hayden.

He shrugged at her question. "You haven't been back to Hell on Wheels in a few weeks now."

She squinted to get a better look at him. His large hat drooped low over his eyes, and his full beard covered the rest of his face. The only way she had to guage his attitude was by his tone of voice, which in this case he kept bland. She tensed as a dull uneasiness began to undermine her feeling of well-being and joy. "I'm feeding the grading crew," she reminded him.

"And when they finish grading?" he asked.

She stared hard at him now, wondering what he knew, fearing what he thought. They rode a while in silence, then she turned to him with a different question. "What did you mean when you suggested that I don't . . . ah, like roses?"

Shifting in the saddle, he returned her stare, his reins limp in his hands. Their eyes held—questioning, challenging. At length, his lips curved in a grin. "Our minds run in the same direction, love."

"The *Texas Star*," she sighed.

"The *Texas Star*," he acknowledged.

Her words poured forth, as water from a primed pump. "It's very simple, Kalib. There's nothing to it at all, actually. I mean . . ." His eyes fastened on hers with such a wicked gaze that she blanched. "You're laughing at me!"

His smile softened, and he reached over and squeezed her shoulder. "Never at you," he told her. But when her frown reproached him still, he recanted. "Perhaps I was. I'm sorry. You're beautiful, even when you're in a dither."

"Kalib," she seethed. "I am not in a dither. I'm merely trying to explain a delicate . . ."

He raised his eyebrows. "Delicate? I thought you called it simple?"

She sighed. "It is simple. Leslie Hayden sent the *Texas Star* for our . . . for Rube's and my use while we're finishing the railroad and to travel to Austin in for the stockholders' meeting in January."

He nodded, running his tongue around his lips. "Simple?" he repeated. "My wife sleeping in a luxurious . . ."

"I'm . . ." she interrupted, only to have him stop her.

"Excuse me. My *future* wife, sleeping in a luxurious railcar furnished by another man . . . a man who also

236

provides her with fresh red roses and strawberries. . . ."

"Bastard!" she hissed, uneasy with his teasing words, the way he couched them in accusations. Then her eyes flew open. "How did you know about the strawberries?"

He waggled his eyebrows. "My spies? Every bastard needs a couple of spies . . . to protect his interests."

Turning her face from him, she held a strand of hair back and chewed her bottom lip. "I was afraid that's what you'd think."

Immediately he nudged his horse beside hers and pulled them both to a stop. "Look at me, Maggie," he commanded softly.

She complied, and his gentle expression brought tears to her eyes.

"I'm sorry to have teased you. I . . ."

She sighed. "I know how you felt about me . . . before," she began in a faltering voice. "I . . . I've been desperate for you to understand that I did nothing. . . ."

With a firm hand he turned her chin toward him, then lowered his face and kissed her long and hard. "I didn't mean to hurt you with my teasing," he whispered. "I know there's nothing between you and Hayden . . . except a lot of animosity. Frankly, if he's the one responsible for bringing the *Texas Star* to Hell on Wheels, I'm grateful to him. It gets you out of that confounded saloon."

"And the roses . . . ?" she asked. "You don't . . . ?"

He smiled, then, while the horses stamped restlessly beneath them, he kissed her eyes, her nose, and once more, her supple mouth. "If I could, I'd give you roses every day, too. Only . . . perhaps not red, the way you loathe red roses."

"I only threw them out because *he* sent them," she admitted shyly.

Kalib grinned, a broad, beaming grin, telling her all was well. "Yellow roses would be more my style," he mused. "Yellow roses for Texas."

By the time she returned to the depot, Rob and Jim had two venison hams prepared and a tubful of potatoes chopped and soaking in spring water. "We'll make stew," she told them quickly, and while they chopped the venison into bite-sized pieces, she filled the giant iron pot with the meat and vegetables and started the fire.

Somehow supper came and went, and she finished the day in her usual fashion, first soaking in a tub of lavender-scented water, then drifting off in the feather bed in her hotel suite . . . alone.

Alone with her dreams. Dreams in which Kalib worked for the railroad and came home to her every evening. Dreams in which Rube stayed sober, and he and Di became doting grandparents to her and Kalib's growing brood of beautiful black-haired children.

Dreams . . . comforting, reassuring, unfettered by the problems that would necessarily interfere with such peacefulness for a time yet, she thought the next morning while she dressed hurriedly and prepared the grading crew's breakfast.

Before she finished baking the day's supply of bread and pies, Trace Garrett pulled up to the depot with three wagons loaded with burnettized railroad ties.

"Tell Rube to send the wagons back when they're empty, and we'll reload them," Trace told Meg.

Shortly afterwards, Rube himself arrived with a crew of brawny tracklayers, and the rest of the day was spent in a frenzy of real progress.

Meg's spirits soared. The railroad would be completed on time, she was sure of it. Kalib, by his own admission, had narrowed the field where he must search for the evidence of silver for his grandmother, and she was sure now, very sure, that he loved her too much to jeopardize Rube's job. Not that she expected him to submit before he absolutely had to. She neither expected it, nor did she want him to. His commitment to his grandmother was as great as hers to Rube. She acknowledged the fact simply, confident now that he would allow them to complete the railroad before the deadline. No matter what he thought about the new governor.

She sighed. The completed railroad would definitely intersect the area bounded by the three landmarks he had shown her. But hadn't he told her not to worry? Hadn't he assured her everything would work out?

By the following evening when she heard the combined grading and tracklaying crews arrive for supper, she knew the only demon she fought now was her intense desire to be with him constantly—every waking moment, every minute spent in bed.

Flushing as her last thoughts became graphically real in her imagination, she wiped her hands on a cup towel and placed heaping platters of fried venison down the length of the table.

Item by item she set the meal out, and as she did, her own thoughts became more ordered, as well. She would manage her loneliness as she had managed all other insufferable events in her life. As long as she could see the end to the ordeal, as long as she knew she and Kalib would one day be together—he'd said within the month!—she could stand the loneliness until then. Its bitterness would only make the rest of their lives the sweeter.

She smiled to herself. In a day or so, she would ride out to see him. They hadn't even spoken of Christmas, yet it was a mere five days away. She doubted he'd be returning to his grandmother's for the holidays . . . that was what she would do, she assured herself. She would ride out and spend Christmas with him—their first Christmas together.

Then the men tromped into the depot, and her well-laid plans fell apart.

The instant they entered the room, she sensed the change in them. Usually they came dragging in, exhausted from a grueling day in the field. Tonight, the air fairly crackled with unspent energy, as they stomped their feet and shouted and cursed.

The last, their cursing, which they always curtailed in deference to her presence, tonight burned her ears. Silently she went from one man to the other, filling his coffee cup from her black pot, taking care to stay clear of waving arms and twisting, turning bodies.

Rube was the last to enter, and she caught him as she returned to the kitchen area of the large room. "What has happened?" He had trouble hearing her, but only partly because of the din of shouting men; her voice was weakened by a paralyzing fear—fear of his answer. Even before she asked, she knew Kalib was at the root of the problem.

"Nothing we can't handle, sugar," he told her, squeezing her arm.

"What?" she demanded.

He shrugged. "Those wagonloads of ties Garrett sent out . . . ah, someone turned them over, scattered ties all the way to kingdom come."

She sighed.

"Took the tracklayers all day to repair the wagon and reload the ties." He grinned sheepishly at the grousing crew. "Don't mind their manners tonight. They've had a troublesome day."

Without joining their harangue, Rube took his place at the table and ate quietly beside the men. From the kitchen, Meg listened to the escalating anger with a concern that quickly grew to fear.

"It's that damned fool prospector."

"I say shoot 'em!"

"Shootin's too easy, I vote to hang the sonofabitch!"

"Him an' his two henchmen."

"The three of 'em."

"I know just the place . . . an oak with three nice strong limbs."

"Rube!" Meg rushed into the room, her hands clamped over her ears. Suddenly the uproar ceased, and every man in the room turned a pair of inquiring eyes on her. She swallowed, then continued in a quieter voice. "Rube," she pleaded. "Come with me, please."

Scraping back the keg he sat on, Rube followed her outside where she stood on the loading dock, her arms crossed over her chest. Each hand gripped the opposite arm in an effort to stem her trembling.

"It's all right, sugar. Let 'em talk it out. They won't cause him any trouble. . . ." Pausing, he sighed deeply, then finished, ". . . leastways, no more'n the man deserves."

"Rube, please stop them. I'll talk to him, first thing in the morning. Tonight, even. I'll go tonight."

"No, Meg. I don't want you involved in this again." He took her by the shoulders and gently shook her. "Look at me. Your talkin' hasn't done any good. This is war now, plain and simple. Man's work."

She could do no more than stare at him, her eyes pleading, her mind abuzz. "He said practically the same thing the first time I ever saw him," she whispered, recalling how Kalib had accused Rube of sending a girl to do a man's job.

Tears brimmed in her eyes. Her shoulders shuddered against the chilly night air, and she thought of Christmas and cried. Rube pulled her into his arms and patted her back.

"It'll be all right, sugar," he reassured her. "We'll work it out."

Sniffling, she drew back and looked at him. "How? What are you going to do?"

"We're not going to lynch the man, if that's what's worrying you."

She didn't laugh. Lynching or shooting weren't really the problem; she knew Rube held a tighter rein on his crews than to let something like that happen.

Kalib was the problem. Why couldn't he let them get on with their work? Why, oh why, was he so pigheaded?

"What are you going to do?" she asked finally, taking a handkerchief from her apron pocket and drying her eyes.

"We left guards in the field," he told her. At her gasp, he hurried on to ease her mind. "They won't shoot him, Meg. They're there as a preventive measure. No man in his right mind. . . ." He paused and again forced her to look at him. "You did say Kalib is an intelligent man, didn't you?"

She nodded, and he continued. "Well, no intelligent man is going up against an armed guard. Come morning I want you to go back out to Garretts' ranch and arrange for another delivery of burnettized ties."

Studying him closely, her thoughts were on how she could convince Kalib to let them continue laying rails to the river, unharassed. Then Rube's suggestion that she arrange for the ties from Garrett registered. "Where are you going?"

"To the construction train," he answered. "I promised Scotty McCaa I'd have him a load of trestles shipped out tomorrow, and with this latest trouble, I plumb forgot it. He's ready to start building the bridge."

The next few days passed in a blur for Meg. She arranged for ties from the Garrett ranch; she cooked for the crews, both the graders and the tracklayers, who reported progress every night.

From appearances, all seemed to be going well, but she now had grave misgivings about the outcome. Several times she started to hire the sorrel and ride out to Kalib's camphouse.

Rube explicitly forbade it, however. His parting words, as he rode off for the construction train, were for her to stay in Silver Creek and not go near Kalib. She was reminded of her telling him practically the same thing about Di.

She sighed. He had ridden straight to Di with her plea still ringing in his ears. Di spelled trouble for Rube; now Rube felt the same way about her relationship with Kalib. But Kalib was trouble for the railroad, she argued, not for her. Yet, was there any difference? She'd been fooling herself believing they could separate their personal lives from the railroad. It couldn't be done; it shouldn't be done.

The sickening thing, though, she realized one night while she soaked in Mavis's tub, was how blinded she had been by him. She was so enamored with the man that she actually believed he would let the work progress, when, in fact, he had never said anything of the kind.

When she'd expressed her wish that they could leave the fighting to Rube and his grandmother, Kalib had replied that they—he and she—had to work it out. Why? She cried into the pillow that night.

Why couldn't he at least be reasonable? Again, she saw

the plat. Again she saw the line he drew through the center of the circle of landmarks with his fingers—a line representing the railroad. But surely, surely building a railroad wouldn't destroy every last bit of evidence—every single piece of remaining silver. If there were so few pieces of evidence left, he'd never find them, anyway.

This last thought troubled her even more than the previous ones. Now, she was certain she had been wrong about him—about his giving in when the time came to join the rails.

Now she knew he wouldn't. Not even for her. Not even for them. His stubbornness was preposterous; his dedication to some flimsy dream of his old befuddled grandmother, ridiculous.

That night in her dreams, he told her the same thing—about her stubbornness to let go of Rube; about thinking it took her to run Rube's business, to keep Rube sober.

He had asked her about it more than once, and she relived the scenes in her dreams. But where in real life he had held her unclothed, love-dampened body close to his own, in her dreams they sat across from each other at his table, drinking bitter tea.

"How long have you been taking care of him?" Kalib asked. In reality he had kissed her here, and his tone had been loving, gentle; in her dream his voice was mocking and the two emotions struggled within her.

"All my life," she'd answered, kissing him back.

"Why?" In real life he had pecked her nose with his lips; in her dream he glared across the table, and finished the question with, "Why don't you turn loose of him?"

"I owe him a lot, Kalib," she replied. "He struggled to raise me, to . . ."

"In a terminus town?" he barked in her dream, whereas in reality, he'd merely commented on her carefree life following the rails.

"Yes," she'd replied, catching the fine hairs on his chest between her lips and pulling playfully. "He raised me alone. . . ."

"With the help of the town whore!" he shouted across

the table in her dream.

"No," she cried in her sleep. "Not the town whore, the woman who served as my mother . . . a kind, wonderful, happy woman . . . or so I thought until they sent me away to that fancy girl's school."

"You what?" In her dream his dark eyes pierced her like the point of a Lipan lance.

Tears formed behind her lids at his scorn. "I . . . I went to school," she stammered, anger building within her at his self-important air. "I'm not stupid, uneducated. I spent four years at Smith College in Massachusetts. You probably don't even know where that is!" After the words escaped her lips, she shrank back in the chair, feeling . . . dirty . . . used . . . cheated.

"You never went to school," he scoffed. "Not a girl from a terminus town. *Not you.*" His eyes became black as coal, hard as uncut diamonds, and the contempt they rained upon her was as she had always feared. Tears formed in her eyes, burning, blurring. Suddenly she was angrier than she had ever been in her life.

Angry at being duped by so shallow a man; angry at the terrible feelings he created within her.

And she had called it love? Love didn't turn on those who were closest and dearest. Love didn't suddenly see one's family as beneath them simply because of where they lived, how they made a living, the fashion in which they cut their hair.

Love didn't reject out of fear. And that's what Kalib had caused her to do to her family. She saw them as dirty, because he thought she was.

But she had brought shame only to herself.

In the name of love. Looking around the table at the pretentious camp house, at the callous man who sat across from her staring her down with even more scorn than she had imagined he would feel when he learned of her proper upbringing, in spite of the circumstances . . .

Because of the circumstances, she cried inside. She was who she was because of Di and Rube. She owed her life to them . . . not to him. . . .

Suddenly she jumped to her feet. Her chair clattered to the wooden floor. Returning his stare with all the anger and humiliation he had wrought inside her, she screamed back at him. "Bastard!" And with that she flung her tea in his face and walked out.

She awakened, wet through her flannel nightgown, trembling, tears streaming down her face. For a long time she could do nothing more than hug her knees to her chest and cry, wondering what had called forth such a nightmare . . . a nightmare more real than life itself. Finally, she reached to light a lamp and discovered the table beside her bed overturned. Righting it, she found a light and walked around the chilly room, trying to calm her nerves enough to return to bed.

The dream was nonsense, she told herself. Yes, she had worried over his reaction to discovering she had a proper education, but not enough to bring on such a torrent of rage. Yes, she had been afraid of the scorn in his eyes, but she'd never seen it.

Yes, she had been ashamed of Di.

But she wasn't anymore. Sighing, she returned to bed and tried in vain to sleep. At least, the dream had taught her something.

The next morning, however, she awakened angry with Di once more . . . and with Rube. He was probably washing away his own troubles in the Diamond-Stacker at this very moment.

Through bleary eyes, she prepared breakfast for the combined crew, packed their lunches, and sent them on their way to work. All the time she kneaded and shaped the dough and baked the bread, she worried over her dream about Kalib. She'd been angry with him for turning over the wagonloads of ties. But not *that* angry.

After a while, her uneasiness vanished, only to be replaced by a nagging sense of guilt. He had treated her with such loving care, how could she have dreamed of him in such a manner. At last, she decided, Rube's admonition or not, she would ride out to see him this morning. Probably her nightmares stemmed from her desperate longing to see him, rather than from anything else. Longing for him, craving his nearness, yearning to hold him, to touch him. . . .

Later that morning she did ride out to see Kalib, but the circumstances differed greatly from her well-laid plans.

No sooner had she taken the last loaf of bread from the oven than a horse clattered up to the depot, and one of the tracklayers slid to the ground.

"Is Rube back yet?" he asked hastily.

Warily, she shook her head. When she answered, her voice sounded like tin ringing in her ears. "What's gone wrong?"

"Them damned ol' prospectors," the man began. "They've done tore up all the track we laid the past two days. Portis has gone to find 'em."

Her eyes fairly popped from her head. Portis Flannery, the tracklaying foreman, was the brawniest of the brawny tracklayers. Her mind raced. "Ride to the construction train to find Rube," she instructed. "If he isn't there, go to the Diamond-Stacker; tell Di you have to see him, no matter what condition he's in. Tell her I told you to say that."

"Yes'm," he answered. "You coming?"

She shook her head. "But would you stop by the livery and have Mr. Samples saddle the sorrel for me? I'm going to find that prospector. If there's anything left of him."

Chapter Thirteen

Meg dressed in record time, throwing on the first riding costume that came to hand, the brown velvet she'd worn from the *Texas Star*. Stuffing her hair beneath the matching cap, she raced toward Kalib's camp, her heart heavy with trepidation.

A norther had blown in overnight, and its biting wind soon chilled her nose and stung her eyes, while inside her brain echoes of the grumbling crew pealed with the doom of a tolling bell—*hang him, shoot him, hang him, shoot.* . . .

Through it all, her own guilt grew and plagued her with the unfairness of her dream. How could she have dreamed such things? How could she have felt such anger in her heart for one she held so dear?

When she approached the area where the ties had been set, an ominous stillness settled over her. Like a pall, she thought, seeing no sign of man or activity. For a good mile, she rode solemnly through a jumble of railroad ties scattered helter-skelter across the entire width of the right of way.

Rube's voice echoed through her numbed brain: *three thousand ties to the mile.* Three thousand ties? It must have taken them all night!

Panic rose hot inside her as she imagined three exhausted men facing fifty or more of the toughest tracklayers and graders in the country.

At the end of the clutter of ties, the ringing inside her head grew to such proportions that at last she recognized it for what it was, voices of angry men—guttural German shouts, lyrical Spanish curses, ancient Irish war cries. She thought suddenly of words she had heard used to describe America. Some called it a melting pot, and she now envisioned masses of men, all from different countries, melding together in the heat of battle.

By the time she came to the cedar brake where Kalib had shown her the empty hole in the ground, she began to understand his reasoning. The railroad would eventually cut through the circle of landmarks between the cedar brake and the smelter. Obviously, he didn't intend to let them come within that circle until he found his grandmother's silver.

Riding on toward the increasingly loud ruckus, she became more and more apprehensive herself, as the human voices were now accompanied by the clatter and clash of wood striking wood. Immediately, she shrank against visions of ax handles, pick handles, shovels, and spike mauls—all the tools missing from the work site.

Then they came into view—the milling mass of frenzied men—and she drew rein so abruptly her horse shied and reared in the air.

Bringing the sorrel under control, she scanned the crowd for Kalib. At first all she could see was the circle of men standing three and four bodies deep, chanting, calling, beating their tools against, not other men, but tool on tool—creating a clamor and clatter that drowned out even their own voices.

The first person she recognized was Ellsworth Fredericks. The sight of him with his tripod and black-hooded photographic equipment sent fury chasing anguish through her veins. *Would Rube were right*, she moaned inside, that Fredericks possessed only a buffalo chip printer with a shirttail full of type. His presence here today filled her with premonitions.

Quickly, however, her search continued for Kalib, and when she found him all thoughts of Fredericks and type and premonitions fled.

He stood, shoulders heaving, in the center of the ring of men, facing another heaving, belligerent man—Portis Flannery.

Dismounting, she fastened the reins of her horse to a limb of one of the cedar trees, then pushed defiantly through the throng of angry, swearing men. At the edge of the clearing, she stopped and stared helplessly into the circle occupied by the two men alone.

Both were gasping for breath, as if they'd been at this fight a while. Portis faced in her direction, and she could see blood trickling in a sweaty stream from a wound above his left eye. Kalib crouched in a ready position with his back to her. His shirt hung in wet rags from his shoulders. Lifting one arm, he wiped it across his face, and she wondered whether he was blotting away blood or sweat.

To either side of her men pressed in, trampling, elbowing, vying for better positions from which to cheer Right, as they saw it—Right embodied in their leader, Portis Flannery.

Portis Flannery—big and stout at fifty, given to choleric outbursts—was near impossible to restrain once his rage took hold. More likely than not, he'd flattened every cheering rust-eater in the crowd with his ham-like fists, at least once.

One fight in a lifetime with Portis Flannery was enough for most men. As far as Meg knew, Rube was the only man alive who'd ever taken Portis in a fight, and that at a time when Portis was the drunker of the two. Afterwards, Rube became the only man who could calm a riled Portis Flannery. And not even Rube succeeded every time.

Besides, she realized despondently, Rube wasn't here now. She thought for a moment to call to Kalib, but at the instant she opened her mouth, the fight began in earnest once more. Catching her lips between her teeth, she moved her own body with the fighters, as she concentrated on keeping Kalib away from Portis's deadly fists.

Kalib was ready for the fray. He dealt a sledge hammer blow to Portis's jaw, stepped in close, and delivered a solid left-hander to the burly man's midsection.

The case-hardened tracklayer was not to be denied, however. A left jab to the chin jerked Kalib backwards, and he followed it with a powerful wallop to Kalib's stomach, which caused Meg to double at the waist herself.

"Kalib, watch your eye," she called amidst the uproar. "Move to your right!" "Duck! Duck!" Doubling her fists like a puppet on a string, she sought a means to end his torture, or at least to keep him alive.

Kalib landed a solid shot to Portis's right chest, then, when the man tottered, instantly swung his boot behind Portis's knee and jerked him off balance.

Portis floundered a moment, grabbed what was left of Kalib's shirt, and pulled him to the rocky ground on top of him.

They rolled in a clench, kicked, struggled, and Kalib, who was shorter than the tracklayer by a head, finally managed to butt the man in the windpipe, momentarily forcing him to loosen his grip.

Kalib rolled out of Portis's clutches and sprang to his feet like a black cat. But instead of retreating, as Meg wanted him to—later she wondered where she had expected him to retreat to in this crowd of rust-eaters and gandy-dancers—he poised in a fighting position, and, when Portis gained his footing, struck him on the jaw with a wicked side cut.

For an instant it appeared that Portis would lose his balance, but such was not to be the case. He crouched, the two men circled, heaving, eyes only for each other.

Shouts intensified, reverberated from her eardrums, ricocheted like bullets from railroaders on the opposite side of the ring and back again. Shouts ever more threatening in nature; shouts beseeching their leader to *Kill! Kill! Kill!*

Across the way she saw Tobin, and down the row a bit, Wash, each being held by belligerent tracklayers. She could see their movements, their mouths issuing cries, cries that could not be heard above the melee.

The circling men stopped—Kalib first, then Portis,

ready, watching, each inhaling precious draughts of air, waiting for the other to strike again.

Kalib found an opening, feinted with his left fist, then landed a solid blow to Portis's jaw. Portis instantly returned the blow, staggering Kalib back a step. Then the two men struck at once, toe to toe, exchanging blow after blow.

Facing her direction now, Kalib's face streamed blood from a cut on his forehead. One eye was swollen almost closed, and his mouth was so bloody, all she could see was a gash of red in the midst of his stained black beard.

Her pain for him was physical—in her chest, in her stomach. Her legs shifted as her feet stamped in place, and with only the most ardent effort did she stop herself from running into the circle and flinging her own body between these two fierce men.

Her fear was even greater than her pain. Around her the men recharged each other with ever increasing violent threats and crude humor.

"He's a fightin' sonofabitch, I'll give him that!"

"Hell, he won't last Portis out."

"Lot of good it'll do him, if he does. There's fifty more of us waiting to take him on."

"Yee-haw! We'll fight till the sun goes down tonight!"

"An' bury 'em by lantern."

"Bury 'em? Hell, we'll just toss 'em under the ties, and spike the rails atop 'em!"

"Bed 'em with the ties! Sonofabitch! What a shindig!"

Desperately she cast about for some way to stop the fighting. If she had a gun, she could fire it into the air. If she had a bull whip, she could crack it loud enough to gain their attention.

But, of course, she had neither. She'd just begun to chastise herself for coming out so unprepared, when she saw Ellsworth Fredericks's photographic flare explode. Perhaps she could use it to gain attention. But a quick glance told her the flare neither disturbed the two combatants in the ring, nor their cohorts massed around. What would it take . . . ?

At that instant Portis caught Kalib on his right ear, staggering him sideways. Kalib regained his footing, sidestepped Portis's next blow, and landed a weak jab to Portis's shoulder.

Both men were tiring. Even though the temperature had dropped considerably, the massed ring of bodies blocked the north wind from the fighters, who were streaked with perspiration and blood, and covered with dirt from when they rolled on the ground.

Portis countered with a hard lick to Kalib's unprotected midsection, which, though less powerful than his earlier blows, nevertheless sent Kalib teetering backwards.

Again he caught his balance, eyed Portis from beneath swollen lids, and took a moment to rest his hands against his flexed knees, breathing raggedly.

Meg watched him. Whether he actually swayed on his feet, she wasn't sure later. But at this moment, she saw him sway, his eyes appeared to close, and Portis moved in.

"Kalib!" she screamed.

In the split second it took for her voice to register in his muddled brain and for him to look in her direction, Portis Flannery was able to land the final blow in this hard-won, fight-to-the-finish match.

Kalib's head snapped back. His body collapsed spent to the rocky ground, as though a plug had been pulled on a dirigible letting all the air swish out.

Within a hair's breadth of an instant, Meg was on her knees beside him.

"Better move on out of the way, Miss Meg, an' let us finish what we come for." Portis breathed heavily between each word, but his intention was clear.

Swiftly she shielded Kalib with her own body. "Leave him alone," she demanded of the panting, bloody warrior hovering above her. "All of you," she reiterated, "leave these men alone and go back to work."

The crowd closed in. Panic rose quickly in her breast, but she stifled it with reason. Time was short, as short as these men's fuses.

"Portis," she reasoned, "take your men back to the work

252

site. Thaddeus has gone for Rube. He and Uncle Grady will be here any moment.

Portis stood tall, bleeding fists on his hips. He surveyed the graders and tracklayers, then he moved toward her. "Get on up, Miss Meg. These fellers have caused too much trouble for us to stop now."

"Portis," she demanded again. "Take your men away before Rube gets here You know how he feels about fights with neighbors."

"Neighbors?" Portis scoffed.

Catcalls greeted her from all sides.

"Move away and let us at the sonofabitch!"

"Whose side you on, anyhow, Miss Meg?"

The crowd pressed in. Kalib stirred beneath her, and she realized with a start that she was actually sitting on top of him.

Portis reached for her shoulder, and she jerked away. Kalib spoke beneath her, but she couldn't decipher his words through the noise raging inside her head and out.

Reaching blindly to shush him, her fingers touched the sticky blood on his beard, and the heightened fear this reality instilled within her strengthened her resolve.

"Portis Flannery, if you want to continue working for this railroad, you take your men back to the work site this minute. And don't ever let Rube catch you starting a fight!"

"Starting . . . ?"

"Portis, you *know* I'm right. Rube expects you to keep your head. He wouldn't have put you in charge, if he didn't trust you to use good judgment."

Portis cleared his throat and shuffled his feet, rolling a loose rock back and forth beneath the sole of his work boot. Suddenly, she heard a distinct voice rise above the grumbling men. Arny Perham, grading foreman, stepped up beside Portis.

"Portis has learned these scoundrels enough lesson today, boys," he told the crowd. "Let's get back to work and wait for Rube to give us fightin' orders."

Some of the crowd—graders, she knew—began backing

253

off. Portis looked toward Arny, then back to Meg. If looks could kill, she knew she'd have fallen immediately under the fury in his hard eyes. Portis Flannery didn't like being stopped in the middle of a fight, she thought, recalling her earlier premonitions.

"When Rube gives the word, I won't stand in your way," she told him. "You know I'm only doing this for Rube."

Dust balled from the heels of retreating men. Meg sat stockstill, watching Portis change his mind. When his muscles relaxed, she nodded toward Tobin and Wash. "Leave them, too."

Portis jerked his head toward the men who held Kalib's cohorts, then stomped off. With a force signifying a shaky truce, at best—certainly not an end to the war—the angry tracklayers threw Tobin and Wash at her feet and tramped away behind Portis Flannery.

Still she sat, breathing in the stirred dust, stunned for a moment, half-expecting the angry mob to turn on them. Tobin and Wash picked themselves up and began dusting themselves off.

"Guess you were right, Kalib," Tobin observed. "She's a good one to have on your side."

Anger flashed through her suddenly, warming her spine against the blowing north wind, swelling her lungs with unspent fear . . . and fury. "I'm not on your side," she shouted. Moving from where she perched on top of Kalib, she swung around to tend his wounds. "I couldn't very well stand by and let them kill you. Don't you have any water?" she demanded of the startled men.

Then their own eyes flashed. "Fetch the canteen," Tobin told Wash. "I'm going to find that damned newspaperman."

Wash brought the canteen, unscrewed the cap, and watched while she stripped the scarf from around her neck and began bathing Kalib's battered and beaten face.

Kalib struggled to gain a sitting position but settled for resting his elbows on the rocky ground beneath him. At her angry swipes, he winced. "Hey, you don't have to take off the rest of my hide," he argued. "That damned giant did a good enough job on me without you adding to . . ."

"You didn't have to start this stupid fight," she fumed. His face was a mess. Every time she got the bleeding staunched in one place, it broke out in another. Furiously, she rubbed blood from his beard, blotted his split lips. His beautiful face, she cried inside. So mauled and mangled. "You're lucky to be able to see from this eye. He could have blinded you. Then how would you see to find something silver for your . . . grandmother?"

Kalib struggled beneath her ministrations. Through his limited vision he watched concern etch her face, worry that belied the anger in her voice. Scooching up, he reached for her arms, then doubled forward, his forehead dipping to her shoulder.

"You okay?" Wash asked.

Kalib caught a ragged, painful breath. "Maybe a broken rib or two, but otherwise I'll make it." Raising a hand, he waggled his jaw, satisfied that nothing was broken there.

It pained her to look at his rapidly swelling hands, his split knuckles. When he stroked the side of her face, she turned and buried her lips in his palm. Tears sprang hot in her eyes, and she squeezed her lids against them.

"Maggie," he said softly. "I'm all right. It's all over now."

"Don't lie to me!" she demanded through clenched teeth. "You're not finished, and you know it. You have no intention of letting . . . letting us through here peacefully."

He grinned, and she quaked at the pain it must cause him to move his lips. "This won't last forever, love."

"You're right about that!" she stormed, her eyes fierce with anger . . . and hurt. "They'll kill you next time."

"No . . ." he began.

"Then it *will* be over. All of it. We'll build the railroad, you'll be . . . I'll be . . ." Jumping to her feet, she turned away.

Kalib rose and stood behind her. "Maggie," he whispered into the wisps of chestnut hair that had escaped her cap. "Maggie . . ."

Tobin burst into the clearing. "I couldn't find the sonof . . ." His words stopped short, and he inhaled a deep sigh. "You know what that means, Kalib. He took photographs of you. Several. They'll be spread all over God knows where."

"We'll go into town and . . ." Wash began.

"No," Kalib told them. "Let's get on with this damned expedition. I'm ready to be done with it."

"Everyone in the whole cock-eyed state will likely see those photographs," Tobin complained. "Eventually someone is sure to recognize you."

"We'll be finished before then," Kalib replied.

"We'll *be* finished, you mean. Your whole life . . ."

"Enough!" Kalib hissed through his swollen lips.

Turning, Meg had taken in the scene with astonishment. "You're more concerned over one newspaperman than you are over fifty enraged railroaders. Don't you know they're coming back? This isn't the end. They'll be back in full force." She stared from one to the other. "You don't make sense, none of you . . . unless . . ." Her words ground to a halt like a mill wheel coming to a screeching stop. Her eyes searched Kalib's, but all she could see was pain. "What are you running from?" she whispered, breathless with anxiety. "The law . . . ?

At her words the three men burst out laughing. Kalib grabbed his side to hold in the pain. "No, Maggie, not the law."

Their laughter turned her anger to shame. Whirling away from them, she suppressed her tears, but they were tears of humiliation this time.

"Maggie." Kalib took her shoulders and held them against her struggles to be free. Knowing his pain, she stilled her body, but inside their mockery stirred as bitter dregs from the tea she and Kalib had shared in her nightmare. Her nightmare, she thought. *This* was her nightmare. Being with him, loving him, standing up for him against her own father, all the while knowing he hid some dreadful secret from her.

256

"It's best you don't know everything right now, love," he murmured, and she tensed beneath his tender, battered hands. Turning her by the shoulders, he raised his hands to her face, capturing it, turning it to his. "Very soon now, you'll know all my secrets. And I promise, I'll never keep anything from you—not ever again."

From the corner of her eye, she saw Wash and Tobin turn to go. "Don't," she cried against his face. With a gritty determination she dredged from somewhere deep inside herself, she called to them. "Don't leave him. You must stay together."

Twisting from his grasp, she staggered backwards, then caught her footing. "If you know what's good for you, you'll pack up and leave right now. They'll be back. You can count on their returning and . . ."

When Kalib spoke, his voice was stern. "I won't let them through here until I find what I'm looking for. I thought you understood that. If you'll just buy me a little more time with Rube. . . ."

Her heart felt as though he had actually grabbed it in his fist and twisted it. Her mouth fell open. "Then we're both fools!" she spat at him. "I thought you understood, too. Rube has to finish this railroad by the appointed time. And believe me, he will."

"You will, you mean," he snapped. "It was *your* harebrained idea to start the railroad out from Silver Creek."

"Harebrained! It was a brilliant idea, and you know it. Not only will the spur be finished in time, but we'll have a gala celebration to link the rails; the new governor will have a heyday of publicity to thank me for. Why, he'll be so grateful, Rube will probably get a wonderful new contract."

Kalib stared at her, wondering whether he should laugh or cry or shake her until her teeth rattled in her pretty head. "And me?"

"You can go to hell," she blurted. "You and your damned obsession with . . . with lost mines and possessive grandmothers."

"*My* obsession?" he challenged hotly. "You're the one

257

obsessed. Possessed is more like it . . . possessed by some misplaced love for that rogue of a father of yours.''

Through one lone, miserable gaze they exchanged bitter good-byes. *Bastard!* she thought. The word was on her lips, but she didn't say it. That word had become a strange sort of endearment . . . at least, he always took it as such. Today he wouldn't, and she couldn't bear losing the surge of joy the light in his eyes always brought her.

She didn't cry until she was well away from the cedar brake, and then she couldn't decide what exactly it was she was crying for. A love like this wasn't really love, she told herself. It was one-sided and selfish. She loving him; he using her. It wasn't true love.

But it felt like it. It *felt* like it—in the profound sense of joy thinking about him created inside her, in the abandonment and freedom she felt in his arms, in the intense physical pain she experienced at his. . . .

At his rejection. Over and over his words echoed in her brain, reverberated from her broken heart, sang a melancholy tune through her senses . . . *buy me a little more time with Rube . . . buy me more time . . . buy me . . .*

He had used her. Her body and her influence. From the very first day in the valley, he had mesmerized her with his sensual, charismatic powers, until she became clay in his hands.

She'd thought the same thing before, she reminded herself, and the remembrance brought an overwhelming sense of embarrassment and shame to her, warming her with such heat she didn't even feel the bitter cold.

Not a mile distant, she came upon Rube and Uncle Grady. Hastily drying her eyes, she tried to tell them what had happened in dispassionate terms. Recalling the disgruntled rust-eaters' contentions that she was on the wrong side, she wanted to let Rube know she stood with him and with the railroad. Later, she knew he had seen through her words, straight to the hurt inside her heart and soul.

"Go on back to Hell on Wheels," he advised her. "It's only three days till Christmas. Rob and Jim can cook for the men until then."

Knowing he had not only her own good in mind, but probably the morale of the men as well, she consented, and turning the sorrel about, she headed straight for the *Texas Star*, relieved to be able to spend some time alone.

If she ever needed to be alone, it was now. But the closer she got to Hell on Wheels, the more she thought about Di and the injustice she had done this woman who had been such an important part of her life for so long. . . .

Ever so much longer than . . . her heart was heavy and recoiled from calling his name, even in silence. A part of her came to his defense: he hadn't been the cause of her feelings against Di, those had started back at school, when she'd learned how real families lived.

But her wounded pride wouldn't let her defend him for long at a time. What claim could he have on superiority in any form, anyway? she fumed. At best, he was no more than an idle treasure hunter. More likely, she decided, thinking back on their revealing, if painful, conversation today, he was a fugitive.

A fugitive from what, she had no idea. But the realization that she hadn't given this possiblity serious thought until now baffled her. She had known from the first day she met him that he was hiding from something . . . or from someone. Yet every cockamamie excuse he came up with she lapped right up, like a puppy eager for attention from the hand that slapped it.

This train of thought led her to examine the things he had said, the things she had witnessed, in search of the truth about this man she'd once described to Rube as an enigma.

Every person had a little bit of mystery in his life, but Kalib was different: his entire life was a mystery. Thinking back, she began to doubt the story about his grandmother. And the search for the mine. The plat was probably a fake. Why, Ellsworth Frederick, whom they had laughed at, whom she had thwarted at every turn, had been suspicious of him since the beginning. Why? What did he know? What did he suspect?

By the time she rode into Hell on Wheels, she was determined to find out. If Ellsworth Fredericks knew anything about Kalib, she intended to discover what it was. Perhaps then she could rest, assured she was better without him in her life.

Until then. . . .

The north wind blew with a vengeance down the dusty main street of the tiny terminus town—her town, she thought fiercely. Fighting back bitter tears, she stabled her horse and crossed the street in the last dim light of day.

A man stepped from the door of the Diamond-Stacker Palace and she glimpsed the warm yellow glow within. Turning abruptly, she entered the cigar apartment, and tentatively pushed through the double-action doors into the bustle of the saloon proper.

Chinese lanterns flickered around the room in celebration of the Christmas season. Pushing back a wayward strand of hair, she surveyed the room. Attired in her revealing black and white mixologist's costume, Di stood behind the bar tending to business.

Meg leaned against the wall and let the festive spirit of the room and the season wash over her blue feeling of melancholy. Bart strummed a lively holiday tune on the guitar; several customers sang alone, off key. And Di—Meg watched her fondly now, seeing for the first time since she had returned from school the woman's beauty and vitality.

Di held her audience around the bar transfixed as she expertly concocted the drink Meg had only seen her practice before—the Blue Blazer. She tossed the flames back and forth from one glass to the other, and the mixture looked like a continual stream of blue fire. She placed the finished drink before the customer, smiled radiantly, and bowed in appreciation for the outbreak of applause.

Her eyes found Meg, who clapped along with all the men in the room. "Drink 'er up, Joe," Di told the customer. "This one's guaranteed to shake you down to your gizzard."

Then she quickly left the bar and crossed the room to

Meg. They stood for a moment looking at each other, then Meg fell into her arms.

"Di, I'm so . . ."

"Shuuu . . ." Di murmured, pulling Meg back to inspect her closely. "Have you been to the *Texas Star*? Does Chou Ling know you're here for supper?"

Meg inhaled a deep breath. Eating was the farthest thing from her mind. "I want to stay in here a while," she said, then added hastily, "It's so cold outside."

Drawing her to a quiet table at the far end of the bar, Di spoke to Georgie, who immediately left the saloon. "Georgie will let Chou Ling know you've returned," she told Meg, then she grinned. "This is a good night for an apple toddy, dear. I've been making them all evening."

With that she returned to the bar where Meg watched her take a baked apple from a covered container. After placing the apple in a glass, she added some powdered sugar, then "one gill of brandy, to one-half pint boiling cider." Setting the concoction triumphantly before Meg, she returned to the bar where customers began calling for first one drink, then another. "As soon as Chou Ling sends word your supper is ready, I'll come with you."

Although she didn't feel hungry in the least, Meg sipped the brandy, took a small bite of apple, and before she knew it she had consumed the whole thing. Watching Di, her own vindictiveness gone now, she became enthralled with Di's expertise in the field of liquors. One drink in particular held her spellbound. She crossed to the bar and watched up close. Di smiled brightly at her, as if, Meg thought, they'd never exchanged such hateful words.

"This particular *pousse-cafe* is called Stars and Stripes." Taking out a long, thin liqueur glass and a spoon, she set around her all the ingredients, then began the slow process of layering the drink. "Star and Stripes," she repeated, holding the spoon upside down just inside the lip of the glass. "You'll see stripes in the glass when I finish it, and stars in the sky after you drink it." The men clapped, Meg smiled appreciatively, and Di never seemed to notice. With hands steady as a gunfighter's she poured a portion of red

261

crème de noyaux over the back of the spoon into the cordial glass. Next came a layer of a deep red maraschino liqueur, followed by yellow chartreuse. After these set a moment, Di took a fresh egg in her fingers, delicately cracked it against the counter edge, then separated it yolk from white, the white going into a side dish. The yolk she dropped ever so gently on top of the chartreuse.

Meg held her lips between her teeth, scarcely daring to breathe as the egg yolk settled on top of the yellow liqueur and sank about one fourth way into the maraschino, without disturbing the delicate balance of the layers.

Picking up the spoon again, Di deftly added a layer each of green curacao and brandy. Hurrahs greeted her, but she held up her hands to signify she hadn't finished, and with a flourish she struck a sulphur match and ignited the brandy.

Still more voices raised in appreciation. Then Di sprinkled a finger or two of orange peel over the flames, causing them to spew and sputter like sparkles at Christmastime.

At Christmastime, Meg thought, hearing all the laughter, gaiety, and happiness one associated with the season. Hearing, but not feeling.

Georgie returned with word from Chou Ling that supper was served, and Di scurried Meg from the saloon, through the freezing night, and into the comfort of the luxurious railcar.

The first thing she noticed upon entering were the roses, red and fresh, as usual. Grimly, she thought she should start appreciating them.

Supper consisted of beefsteak with potatoes and cabbage. Every time Meg tried to apologize to Di, Di changed the subject. At last, after she had described the fight and her chance meeting with Rube in detail, then answered all Di's questions about feeding the crews, the Christmas Ball, and Hank, Katie, and Mary Sue, Meg objected.

"I've been so terribly unfair to you, Di," she said. "I came back from school thinking I was better than everybody here." She shrugged, trying to control her emotions.

"These last few weeks I've blamed Kalib for causing me to feel this way, but I know that's unfair, too. I had these feelings before I even met the man."

Chou Ling took their plates and served them cheese and fruit. "I am sorry I have no dessert," he told Meg, bowing as usual.

She smiled, started to reassure him, but Di broke in.

"Could we have a couple of hot spiced rums, Chou Ling?"

He smiled, nodded, and bowed at the same time. But instead of leaving, he looked to Meg, still bowing. Finally, Di nudged her.

"He's waiting for your approval of my order, dear."

"Oh," Meg replied. "Yes, Chou Ling, two spiced rums, hot, please."

"Tell me about this handsome, black-bearded stranger who's come into your life," Di encouraged her when Chou Ling left the room.

Meg looked into her sympathetic eyes, then quickly away. Tears fell unexpectedly onto her lap, as from a waterfall. "He isn't in my life anymore," she cried into her oversized linen napkin.

Di sat silently while Meg cried. Chou Ling returned with their hot drinks. Finally, she looked up, patted the last of her tears, and sipped the hot cinnamon-flavored drink. The liquor burned her throat. "How could I have been so stupid?" she asked.

Di sighed. "Falling in love isn't stupid. Sometimes it's painful, but never stupid."

"It wasn't love," Meg said quietly. "Not for both of us, anyway. He was only using me." She drank the spiced rum and felt tears flow down her cheeks again. She dabbed at them half heartedly.

"Are you sure about that?" Di asked. "I saw the look on his face the night he carried you out of the saloon. I've seen a lot of men in my day—in love and out; impostors and the real thing. And the expression on that man's face with you slung over his shoulder—well, it's a look most women will go to their graves without ever seeing."

Di's words sang a strange love song in Meg's heart—a song of hope. But only for a moment. "There were times I saw it, too." She sighed heavily, recalling against her will the sensuously beautiful feeling she got every time she was in Kalib's arms. "But it wasn't real. He's a fake, a mysterious impostor."

"It's the mysterious ones who get us every time," Di told her.

Meg frowned. "He's like two different people—one whose identity he guards from everyone, even from me. The other is a demented man who's determined to fight Rube to the finish." Her anger now grew, meshing with her softer emotions, turning them all to anguish. "He was only using me to get to Rube. And now I'm frightened . . . for Rube."

"Don't worry about Rube, dear. He's fought stagecoach lines, steamship companies, the mighty Wells Fargo Express Company, the Sitka Ice Company. Three Texas treasure hunters aren't likely to stop him."

Meg smiled. "He's had quite a life, hasn't he?" She studied Di, her short curly hair, her still youthful appearance. "And you, too. And me," she added. "I wouldn't trade this life for anything in the world."

Di studied her solemnly. "One of these days you'll have to, Meg. Not because I'm trying to get rid of you, or because Rube is—but for yourself. One day you'll meet your prince. . . ."

"Not me," Meg swore. "If . . . when," she conceded at Di's scowl, "when I meet someone, he'll have to work for the railroad. I can't leave Rube . . . or you, either. You're my family."

"Rube said you talked to him about finding Kalib employment with the railroad."

Meg scoffed. "I spoke in haste. Whatever the man's hiding from will catch up with him sooner or later. It could even be the law. Anyway, the railroad wouldn't have a trouble maker like him. And neither would I."

The next few days passed with agonizing slowness for Meg. Every now and then someone rode in with word of the crews on the other side of the Silver Creek River. From these sketchy reports, she gathered the work was progressing undisturbed, but she knew they were simply rebuilding, not pressing forward.

Her biggest concern became what Kalib would do next, and to whom. She worried continually over Rube. If anything happened to him because of her dim-witted emotional involvement with Kalib, she would never live long enough to forgive herself.

Di spent a lot of time with her, including her in all the holiday preparations going on at the Diamond-Stacker. After she described to Di the decorations the Silver Creek women used for the Christmas Ball, Di insisted on a tree for the Diamond-Stacker. Georgie and Bart cut a large cedar and built a stand, and Meg spent many hours stringing berries and attaching candles to holders the boys made from tin can lids.

Christmas Eve night after dinner, while they waited for Rube and the rest of the crew to come to town for tomorrow's holiday, Di broached another painful subject.

"So we'll have the air cleared when Rube returns," she told Meg. "I've given a lot of hard thinking to what you said about my part in Rube's drinking. I've decided you're right. I don't know why I haven't seen it myself. I promise you, dear, I'm on your side now, and we're both on Rube's side. With the two of us after him, he'll have to stay sober."

Jumping up from the table, Meg hugged Di. "That's the best Christmas present I could ever receive."

As it turned out, it was the best. The worst came the following afternoon—Christmas Day.

They'd eaten—stuffed quail prepared in a wine sauce with all sorts of jellies and breads and a pumpkin pie for dessert. Rube was on his best behavior. Di was obviously on cloud nine with the family reunited in such a loving nature. No one mentioned Kalib.

But he was never far from Meg's mind. Over and over she had to push him out of her thoughts. She had planned to spend this day with him, and in her imagination, she had envisioned a day of endless joy and loving. Now he was no longer a part of her life, and the bittersweet memories of what might have been marred the otherwise lovely day.

Regardless of a person's religious beliefs, Christmas Day was a holiday in a railroad community. Some spent it in private worship, some drinking and celebrating a day of relaxation, others washed clothes, read, or caught up on letter-writing. However it was spent, no one ventured near the work sites.

Except on rare occasions like the present, when trouble brewed imminently along the line. The crew members had drawn straws; the six short straws denoted guard duty on Christmas Day. Everything went along peacefully enough until about midday, when one of these unfortunate six raced up to the Diamond-Stacker with word that the trestles for the bridge across the Silver Creek River had been burned.

"Burned?" Rube raved at the man who had been guided to the *Texas Star*. "How the hell did that happen without someone catching those damned prospectors?"

The answer, it appeared, lay in a misunderstanding— none of the guards had considered the trestles part of their assignment. Instead, they had concentrated their efforts around the newly laid rails on the other side of the ridge of hills.

"Close enough together to engage in a game of poker, I'll wager," Rube hissed.

Fury clouded Meg's already troubled thinking, enraging her so that her voice actually shook when she spoke. "He promised . . . he promised me he wouldn't fire at the bridge monkeys."

"He didn't," Rube retorted. "He fired the damned bridge."

"This is one thing he's going to explain to me. I'm riding out there." She stormed to her bedchamber, where she threw on a riding habit and heavy cloak. "Chou Ling," she called down the hallway. "Send for my sorrel from the livery, please."

"I can't let you do this, sugar," Rube told her when she

266

returned to the salon.

She studied him, quivering with fury and unshed tears. "It's all my fault, Rube. I'm so sorry. I should have let you stop him that very first day. I was blinded . . . but now . . ."

"Meg, you can't go out there. The man's crazy. Likely he and his men are fighting it out with the guards this very minute."

Clutching her bottom lip between her teeth, she shook her head. "This is the last time I'll go against your wishes, I promise. But I must see him . . . this one time." Tears blurred her vision, and she hated them. How could she cry for someone she detested with such vengeance?

Kissing Rube on the cheek, she heard him begin to protest again, but Di stopped him. "Let her go, Rube. She's right. This is something she must do. She'll be all right afterwards."

All the way to the river Di's last words echoed through her brain, and she prayed they would be true. She had to be all right . . . afterwards. She had to go back to feeling, being, living—the way she was before Kalib had come into her life.

She crossed the river in the usual place, raced up the hillside, half her attention trained on the distant work site. Her ears fairly prickled with the expectation of hearing gunshots. So far, all was quiet.

Nudging the sorrel to a faster gait, she pressed him up the hill. Then, just as she topped the crest and looked down onto the camphouse, Tobin and Wash pulled out of the trees and stopped her.

"No further, Maggie," Wash told her.

His voice was quiet, almost apologetic, she thought. And he called her by name. Why? she wondered, frantically searching for some other space, some other time, some place where barriers didn't separate her from . . . from . . . She swallowed, refusing to let herself finish her thoughts.

"I have to see him," she said.

Tobin shook his head. "He said no."

"What do you mean, he said no?" she stormed, attempting to urge her mount past them, "I *must* see him. He went back on his word. He knows good and well he did, and I must . . ."

"No, Maggie," Tobin told her firmly. "Kalib said not to let you come any closer. He . . . he doesn't want to see you."

Her mouth dropped open. She felt as though a hot dry wind blew straight down her throat, strangling her, leaving her mouth dry, hot. . . . "He . . . ?" What words would she use? What could she say? What . . . ?

"It's best this way, Maggie," Wash told her. His voice was soft, kind, infuriating. Her breath came in short bursts, and she began to feel light-headed.

"Go on back to your life," Tobin said. "It'll be . . . easier that way."

"Easier?" she whispered. The word tasted bitter and felt as though it had come from the depths of her broken heart.

"Easier?" she repeated. Raising her head she stared at the camphouse, seeing in her mind the inside . . . the inside where . . . .

"Easier?" she demanded, tugging fiercely at her reins, which Tobin held firmly in his own hand. "Who the hell cares what's easy?" She screamed toward the cabin. "Easy? He lied to me."

"Go ahead now, Maggie," Wash told her. "Take your reins and ride on back to Hell on Wheels. You'll be all right."

She stared at him, unseeing, hearing only his strange, humiliating, damning words. Not understanding . . . seeing only Kalib's eyes . . . feeling his touch . . . hearing the love words he mumbled against her hair . . . calling her Maggie, Maggie, Maggie.

Numbly she took the reins from Tobin and stared each one separately in the face. The shame and humiliation burning her cheeks were not reflected in their faces, but she nevertheless straightened her shoulders, lifted her chin, and held herself precariously erect in the saddle. Turning the sorrel, she nudged him, as if in slow motion, taking great care not to slam her heels into his flanks with all the fury mounting rapidly inside her. "You're damned right, I'll be all right," she whispered.

Kalib watched her through field glasses from a point beyond the cabin. After the fight three days earlier, Tobin and Wash had prevailed upon him to move to a rock shelter hidden among the hills. A precaution, they argued, against a surprise attack. Now, as he sat watching them carry out the other plan they had also prevailed upon him to agree to, to send Maggie away for her own good, he hated himself for giving in.

How could such a simple thing as spending a few weeks looking for a lost silver mine have turned his world upside down? But it had. Or, rather, that beautiful, spirited, wonderful woman he watched through the glasses had.

Maggie had turned his world inside out, and him with it. And now, he had agreed to a plan he could plainly see had hurt her beyond measure.

The pain on her face when she looked toward the cabin brought tears to his eyes, and when he saw her straighten her back so proudly in the saddle and lash out at Wash and Tobin, the tears ran unchecked down his cheeks and into his black beard.

"God, Maggie," he swore aloud, "*I'll make it up to you. If I live long enough, I'll make it up to you.*"

Chapter Fourteen

The next few days passed as in a hazy mist, reminding Meg of the rain forests in South America she had read about in school. She didn't actually cry that much, she realized later. In fact, she hardly cried at all—except at night.

During the daytime, Di kept her busy. The morning after Christmas Day, Di and Meg removed all the salvageable decorations from the tree so Georgie and Bart could dispose of it.

"I can't stand it in here another minute," Di complained. "The smell of cedar makes my nose itch and my eyes water."

Meg agreed. The pungent cedar aroma brought moisture to her eyes, too. It reminded her of the Christmas Ball in the depot—that glorious night!—and of the cedar brake where Kalib had shown her what he said was a landmark in the puzzle of the Lost Bowie Mine. The quicker she could be rid of all reminders of him, the better off she'd be.

Rube spent his days at the work site, but he returned to Hell on Wheels every evening in time for supper in the *Texas Star* with her and Di. As soon as she recovered from the shock of Kalib's final rejection enough to become aware of the goings-on around her, she noticed the chill between Rube and Di.

For her part, Di skillfully played the supportive mother

hen. Concerned, sympathetic, but not overly protective, she seemed to know exactly what Meg needed moment by moment, whether it was involvement in the Diamond-Stacker affairs or to be left alone in her bed chamber in the *Texas Star*.

When Rube returned in the evening, however, Di became agitated and silent, and Rube querulous. Although they never argued in front of her, Meg's suspicions mounted that she was the cause of their discord.

A couple of evenings later, Rube came to supper in a particularly combative mood, and Meg pinned him down.

"That blamed newspaperman came out to the site today," he told them over coffee, his meerschaum clamped firmly between his teeth. "Said his *sources* in Austin confirmed reports that we haven't been following specs. Said the Silver Creek Railroad Committee is considering holding up bond payments until an outside investigation is made."

That night, for the first time since Christmas, Meg worried over Rube more than she did over her own state of affairs. If anything was to drive him back to Demon Rum, this would be it.

True to her worst fears, he came to breakfast the next morning with an ashen cast to his skin and blood shot eyes. The coffee cup wobbled in his hand. When he left the railcar she watched out the window as he returned to the Diamond-Stacker and didn't emerge again. Neither he nor Di came to the railcar at noon.

For the first time in her life, she didn't know how to approach him. In the past she had ranted and raved, dragged him away from the bottle almost forceably. Now . . .

Now she felt responsible in a very real sense. If she hadn't insisted on reasoning with Kalib, things more than likely would have settled down by now, the problems would already have been solved. But for her own stupidity, Rube wouldn't have cause to drink.

Although deep inside she knew her reasoning was unsound, she couldn't restrain her feelings of guilt. No more than she could hold back her irritation at Di for letting him drink.

Di couldn't keep Rube from drinking. Meg knew that. Yet her anger at the woman mounted as the day progressed. After a light noonday repast of oyster soup, fruit, and hot biscuits, she decided she must take some action, lest all be lost. They had both let him down, she and Di.

Dressing hastily, she threw on a brown wool gored skirt and white pongee shirtwaist with lace bertha, tied her hair back carelessly, and flung her merino cloak over her shoulders.

Two steps outside the railcar the wind whipped her cloak over her head, almost tossing her to the ground. When she regained her footing, the sight she saw in front of the saloon took the rest of her breath away. A carriage full of riders pulled up in front of the saloon, all people she recognized instantly.

The Silver Creek Railroad Committee. Libbie Lancaster, Mavis O'Keefe, Woody Woodson, Slim Samples, and yes, even Hank Jefferies, back from South Texas.

Hurrying down the street, she rushed into the saloon behind them. Hank saw her first; his face warned her that Fredericks' prediction had come to pass. He stretched an arm toward her, and she walked to him, returned his hug, and smiled solemnly into his distraught face.

"I'm sorry, Meg. I tried to hold them up, but . . ."

"I know," she answered. She was the sorry one, she the one most to blame. Not for a single minute did she doubt Kalib's involvement in this latest setback, since he had been behind all their other problems on this dratted spur. How could she have let him use her so shamefully? How could she have been so dim-witted?

They took their places around one of the gaming tables in a quiet corner of the near-empty room, and she left Hank's side and sat with Rube and Di. Fortunately, she sighed within, Rube hadn't had time to get drunk. The faint smell of liquor on his breath, however, told her the inevitable wouldn't be long in coming.

Libbie Lancaster spoke for the group. "We're holding up payment of any more bond money until a special investigator gives us a favorable report."

Rube held his meerschaum in his hand and stared at it a moment. "There's no need to waste all that time," he said at length, looking her directly in the eye. "I'll take you on an inspection tour today. My assistant and I can verify every measurement and the quality of all our materials. I keep close rein on such things. I'll guarantee everything on this spur has been and is being done strictly according to the specs."

The Silver Creek Railroad Committee shook their heads as one. Meg glanced at Hank, who shrugged helplessly. "It shouldn't be long, Mr. Britton," he told Rube. "We've already wired Austin for an independent engineer to come out."

"You know what this will mean," Rube replied. "Without money to pay the crews, they'll stop work." He looked around the group. "We'll lose time, time we may not be able to make up. The governor will be disappointed. And all for nothing. There's not a damned . . . pardon me, ladies . . . but there's nothing wrong with my railroad."

"We figure you're right," Woody Woodson told him. He pushed a copy of the *Silver Creek Sun* across the table to Rube. "This says otherwise, though. If we were to side with you, and you turned out wrong . . . well, I think you see our point, Britton. We're not a wealthy community; our money's hard-earned. The committee can't chance throwin' folks' money away."

Meg studied Rube. To all appearances he remained calm, but she knew otherwise. She could see the telltale signs—his white knuckles, the almost imperceptible twitch at the corner of his mouth as he read Fredericks' latest denunciation. "Beats me where such fine folks as you came up with a scoundrel like Fredericks."

Looking around the assembled group, Meg could see many of them agreed with his assessment of their newspaper editor.

Woody Woodson spoke up. "Silver Creek's liable to grow by leaps and bounds once we get this new railroad rolling. We're hopeful another editor'll move in an' give ol' Fredericks some competition. Then he'll have to clean up his act or move out."

"Until then, though," Libbie Lancaster said, "we must check into his allegations. We can't afford to slip up, using the community's money. I'm sure you understand our position, Mr. Britton."

Rube nodded agreement. Then he gave Di an innocent wink Meg knew all too well. "Why don't we offer the folks a round of drinks . . . on the house?"

Di raised her eyebrows and Meg started to protest, but Rube spoke again. He was sly, Meg thought later, too sly for both of them put together, even though they knew him so very well.

"What'll it be folks? Name your poison. I'll stick with a double Scotch whiskey, neat."

"I have an idea," Di suggested. "A round of my new temperance drinks—a Glasgow flip, perhaps, or a Saratoga Cooler?"

"These folks can have apple cider and ginger ale at home," Rube cut in. "Fix 'em up something fancy—some of those concoctions you're putting in that Bartenders' Manual you're writing."

The next couple of hours passed with excruciating slowness for Meg. She could hardly force herself to stay in the room, knowing what was happening to Rube and being unable to stop it. The Silver Creek delegation, apparently relieved at the way Rube accepted their actions in regard to the bond money, took their visiting seriously, as they sampled, questioned, examined, explored.

Woody Woodson expressed a special interest. "I've been thinkin' how I needed a fancier establishment," he confided to Di. "This would suit my purposes to a tee." With a minimum of coaxing the older man prevailed upon Di to lead him on a tour of the premises, exclaiming time and again how he must look into a modular saloon to replace the present Woodcock.

Hank and Meg found a corner where he could tell her about his trip to South Texas.

"I suppose her folks approved of me," he said with a confident wink. "The wedding is set for June."

"Oh, Hank, how marvelous! See, I told you not to worry."

He studied her a moment. "From the looks of you, you need the same advice. Want to talk about it?"

She sighed, tempted. "It's Rube," she said at last, relieved in a painful sort of way to have something truthful to tell Hank, even if it weren't the *whole* truth. "He may not act like it right now, but he's taking this hard. He'll likely stay drunk from now until your engineer makes his report."

"He appears to understand our position. . . ." Hank began.

"Oh, he understands," she admitted. "It's just that . . . well, he doesn't need much excuse to start drinking, and once he starts, it's hard for him to stop."

They sat a while, talked about other things—how Katie had gone back to school, and whether Meg would come to the wedding.

"You're one of my best friends," Hank implored. "You have to be here."

She smiled. "I will, if I possibly can. No telling where we'll be come June."

"Wherever you are, it won't be too far with our new railway." He studied her with a curious grin. "When I left, you said you would have some news by the time I returned. I sort of thought. . . ."

Her throat constricted. She had hoped he'd forgotten. With a shrug, she tried to answer in a lighthearted fashion. "It . . . ah, it didn't work out like I thought."

"I'm sorry. . . ."

She shook her head. "Don't be, Hank. It wasn't important . . . just . . ." Swiping her hair back from her face, she held it in place a moment while her heart steadied. "It wasn't really anything at all."

"Katie thinks . . ."

"Katie's imagination runs rampant sometimes," she laughed.

Hank squeezed her hands, which lay clasped on top of the table. "It'll happen for you one day, Meg. And when it does, I expect to be the first to know."

In the railroad community, as in Silver Creek and in every other small, close-knit society, word traveled fast. By the time the Silver Creek delegation left Hell on Wheels, Rube was well on his way to being drunk, and by that night when members of the grading and tracklaying crews began drifting in by two's and three's, eager to learn whether their new orders were to work or to fight or merely to loaf and drink until payday, he was staggering drunk.

Animosity rose quickly within the saloon and elsewhere in Hell on Wheels as the crews returned to wait out the investigation. No pay, no work had always been the policy. And the fact that this happened to be the day before New Year's Eve made the occasion all the more festive, in a negative fashion, Meg thought.

She had just given up on getting Rube to leave the saloon for supper when the double-action doors swung open, and the figure of one of the two men who had been foremost on everyone's tongue all afternoon stepped from behind the screen.

Ellsworth Fredericks's appearance was greeted by catcalls, curses, and a verbal hostility that sent chills down Meg's back. She wondered what perverse urge for self-destruction brought him inside the enemy's camp.

"There's the little sonofabitch," one rust-eater hollered across the room. Instantly a swarm of men surrounded the newspaperman.

"Let me at 'im," Rube shouted, shouldering his way through the growing throng. Meg followed in his wake. "What do you have to say for yourself, Fredericks?" Rube demanded.

"I only print the truth," Fredericks hissed. Meg studied him through the smoke and haze. His cheeks were flushed, his eyes bright.

"Whose truth?" Rube demanded.

276

"You can't scare me," the newsman bragged, but his sideways glances belied his defiant exterior.

As the curses and catcalls mounted, Rube stared the man down with a surprisingly steady gaze. "We don't aim to scare you, Fredericks. Way we see it, you have a lesson to learn about truth and how to use it."

"Not from some old drunk like you, I don't. . . ." Fredericks started. Rube grabbed his shirt, and Meg knew this fight, once started, would end in much more than a few split lips and bleeding knuckles.

Quickly, she edged around Rube and pushed Ellsworth Fredericks in the direction of the double-action doors.

One of the rust-eaters picked up a chair and slammed it down on top of Fredericks's head. He stumbled, and Meg pulled his arm. "If you want to get out of here alive," she shouted above the clamor, "you'd better hurry. Follow me."

She fairly dragged him to the *Texas Star*, and she knew they made it only because the angry men inside the saloon were liquored-up enough to be momentarily confused at their disappearance.

"Sit down," she ordered, locking the railcar door behind her for the first time ever in Hell on Wheels. The only noise she heard outside was the eerie sound of the howling north wind. No running feet. No shouts or threats. She relaxed.

Fredericks removed his hat and wiped his brow with a striped handkerchief. He eyed her suspiciously. "From the skillet into the fire?"

She sighed. "In this case the fire is a lot safer than the skillet. All I want from you is a few answers. Those men out there won't be satisfied until they get their pound of flesh."

Chou Ling rushed into the salon to see how many for supper.

"Two," she answered, then grinned in spite of herself at the surprised look on Fredericks's face. "We travel in style," she told him. "Now, the price of your escape. . . ."

Chou Ling served the two of them—venison steak in

277

wine sauce with scalloped potatoes and stewed tomatoes, and for dessert, ice cream with strawberries. Ellsworth Fredericks moved like one inside an eggshell, while Meg enjoyed his discomfiture. The man had certainly heaped enough turmoil on everyone else lately, let him stew in his own curiosity for a while.

"Where did you get your report about the specs?" she asked.

"From a reliable source," he told her. His continued defiance rankled her.

She squinted at him through the flickering light of the kerosene lamps. "What source?"

"I can't tell you that, Miss Meg, even if you did just save my life. My sources deserve protection."

She scoffed. "Protection? *You* should be protected from such sources. They're wrong. This railroad is being built according to all the proper specifications. Rube doesn't do anything but the best work."

He challenged her with raised eyebrows.

"It's true. Why didn't you check it out first? Why didn't you spend time in the field with him? He measures everything. He takes endless samples. He's considered one of the hardest men in the country to work for, because he follows the rules to the letter. Rube Britton would not build an inferior railroad, not for any reason."

Fredericks shrugged. "You aren't considered a reliable witness, being his daughter and all."

She glared at him. "You're unfair, Mr. Fredericks. In fact, I don't think I've ever met anyone as biased as you. I'm sure you realize what your actions accomplished—all work has stopped and will remain stopped until the bond money is paid and the rust-eaters get their wages. That, in turn, means the railroad won't be finished on time . . . which means the governor will not . . ."

"My information came straight from the governor's office," he told her. "The office of the governor-elect. I can't say more."

She stared at him, stunned by this news.

"I've answered your questions. Now, how do you plan

to get me away from that mob in the saloon?" he asked.

Her eyes narrowed. "Not so fast. There's another matter I want some answers on, before . . ." She nodded toward the Diamond-Stacker, then continued. ". . . before I help you escape."

He cocked his head at an arrogant angle. "What, exactly?"

"Tell me everything you know about the prospector," she said slowly.

He returned her solemn stare with one of mock surprise. "I'm sure you know more about him than I do."

She shook her head. "I know nothing. Tell me what you've uncovered."

He sank into the horsehair-stuffed sofa, drank a swallow of Chou Ling's *café noir,* and took out a cigar.

Reaching over, she jerked it from his mouth. "If you don't mind. Smoke spoils the aroma of my roses."

His eyes widened. He stuffed the cigar back into his pocket and studied the roses. "Fresh red roses. Way out here."

"Way out here," she repeated. "Every day. Now, about the prospector."

"I'm suspicious by nature," he told her, still eyeing the roses. Then he looked straight at her. "There's something familiar about that prospector. I haven't been able to put my finger on it yet, but he's familiar. Real familiar. And I'm closing in. Tell me what you know."

She sipped the strong coffee and considered what she knew about the prospector. What she knew that would help Ellsworth Fredericks unmask the man.

Inside, deep inside, something bitter stirred, telling her she didn't want Kalib unmasked. "His name is Kalib," she said.

Fredericks crossed an ankle over the opposite knee. "Kalib's a common name."

Meg nodded. "So common it might not even be his," she admitted. "I don't actually *know* one single thing about him, not for certain."

"I take it you've been inside his camphouse."

She stared at the bottom of her coffee cup. An uneasiness crept into her veins, cautioning her. What did she owe Kalib? she demanded of herself. She deserved to know the truth, and if Ellsworth Fredericks could help her, why not?

She shrugged. "It's an ordinary camphouse. Nothing to set it apart. He appears to be exactly what he claims. A prospector." Curiously, her voice seemed to be following a different master than her mind. Why was she lying to the only man who could help her understand Kalib? Why did she feel this insane need to protect him, even yet, after . . .

"I sent those photographs to Austin," he told her.

She tensed. "The ones you took at the fight?"

He nodded, his lips curling in a perverse sort of smirk. Later, she knew she sensed it coming before he uttered another word. Later, she knew she had opened herself up to his filthy mind by broaching the subject of Kalib in the first place.

"I caught you in some of the action, too."

"Me?"

He smiled, again a smirk. "You should see yourself, cheering him on to victory. What's really confusing, is why you were so concerned about someone you profess not to know at all. Someone in a fight against . . . you might say, in a fight against your own father."

Meg jumped to her feet, as angry at herself for bringing him here as she was at him for his uncomfortably accurate assessment of her relationship with Kalib. "Mr. Fredericks, it's safe for you to go, now." She called down the hallway, "Chou Ling, would you send for Mr. Fredericks's horse from the livery, please?"

Fredericks rose, grinning. "I'm sure you recognized his companions," he added. "The same men who came to me with that story about the governor . . . the night of the ball when you . . . so conveniently disappeared."

She stiffened against the realization that she had actually invited his recriminations by her own questions, by her own desperate attempt to learn something about Kalib. She chastised herself soundly. She had certainly underestimated Ellsworth Fredericks.

280

"Your insinuations are shocking, Mr. Fredericks. I've done nothing to earn your . . . your brazen denouncement."

"I'm not denouncing you, Miss Meg. Not in the least. I merely find it amusing—you carrying on with the man who may ultimately be responsible for costing your father his job."

Meg felt as though he had slapped her in the face, because, in fact, every word he spoke was true . . . too true. "If Rube loses his job, it will be *your* doing, Mr. Fredericks. Not that of . . . of some dastardly old treasure hunter." Her hand rose in midair to strike his face, but she caught herself, recalling the day she struck Kalib. Her fury at Ellsworth Fredericks fizzled beneath her own private anguish. Would she never be free of the multitude of memories Kalib had left her with?

The next day was all she had dreaded it would be. Rube slept until midmorning, and by noon not only he, but the whole teeming town was, if not drunk, on the verge of becoming so.

The supply train came, and Di selected provisions she hoped would last the week. "If you'll help, me," she told Meg, "we'll set up a punch table and shut down the bar for the remainder of the day. I think we can get away with champagne punch, since it's New Year's Eve."

Bart shaved ice for a few special drinks, then washed several chunks for the punch and stored all in the ice box. As instructed, Meg placed Di's cut-glass punch bowl inside a large tin wash tub she found in the storeroom. Then she packed the space between the two with ice, sprinkled a little rock salt over the ice, and wrapped towels around the outside of the tub.

Georgie set a special table along one wall of the saloon and covered it with an immaculate white linen cloth. When Di gave the word, Meg unwrapped the chilled punch bowl, and they placed the first of many chunks of ice inside it. Di prepared the punch—a mixture of lemon juice, raspberry syrup, and seltzer water, to which she added a couple of quarts of champagne. Meg topped it off with a few sprigs of mint leaves and slices of orange and lemon.

"When it gets low," Di told Georgie, "add seltzer and more ice. We'll keep just enough champagne in it to be honest. I don't want to go broke before the year ends at midnight."

Rube, of course, was not restricted to champagne punch, nor did he stay in the saloon proper.

For days Meg had said nothing, hoping he would take charge himself. Finally, however, she could stand it no longer. The throng of men, all out of work, all drinking, played on her nerves like a bad dream. The streets were aswarm with disgruntled railroaders. Inside the saloon the constant noise of off-key singing, off-color jokes, and generally discontented voices combined with her own tumbled-up state to set her mind reeling.

Late New Year's Eve afternoon, she found Rube in Di's parlor and lit into him as she hadn't done in weeks. "Why don't you do something about all this?" she demanded.

He shrugged. "What's to do, sugar? I have to wait until the inspector clears the money."

"No, you don't," she insisted. "I know the men don't usually work without getting paid, but this is different. If you'll sober up, you can convince them. You know perfectly well the inspector will find everything all right. Kalib's behind this . . . I know he is. And you're letting him win. . . ."

"Now, sugar, just because that man didn't do right by you, I can't . . ."

"If you don't finish this railroad in time, you're letting him win, Rube. He doesn't deserve to win. You know that. All you have to do is stop drinking."

"The boys won't . . ."

"Those rust-eaters will do anything you tell them to. All you have to do is sober up."

Di stepped into the parlor from her bedchamber, dressed for the evening's festivities. "Meg, dear, we'll have word soon. Grady sent a wire down to Austin. We should hear . . ."

"You're both disgusting!" Meg cried. "All you think about is this damned saloon . . . and drinking like fish. Why can't you straighten up and live like normal people? Why do you do this to me?" Tears burned in her eyes, and she couldn't keep them from rolling down her cheeks. Di put an arm about her, but she pulled away.

"Come here, sugar, an' sit by ol' Rube. I know this has been rough on you, but . . ."

Meg stormed across the room and jerked the bottle of Scotch whiskey from his hand. "Look at you! Just take a look! Both of you. You don't even know how . . . how badly you're ruining your lives. You're the best railroader in the whole country, Rube, and here you sit, drinking your future away."

She turned to Di. Somewhere inside she knew she was being unreasonably cruel; somewhere deep inside she tried to let go; but deeper within her being, her anguish was so great it felt like a volcano exploding, and she was helpless to control her feelings or her mind or even her voice.

"Look at you, Di. All dressed up to spend your life in a stinking, smelling saloon, feeding men liquor. You said you understood Rube's problem. But you don't. You don't understand at all. Neither of you has the faintest idea what you're doing with your lives . . . and with mine! You're the children, and I . . . I'm the parent. I have to take care of you . . . and . . . and I'm tired of it. So very, very tired of it."

Chapter Fifteen

By the time Meg reached the *Texas Star*, her mind swirled in eddies, as though it were being tossed and torn by the north wind. The bitter cold chilled her flesh through her blowing cloak and skirts, and she wished desperately it would freeze her raging emotions, as well.

When she entered the salon its warm glow enveloped her. Chou Ling had lighted the lamps as usual, and now, through her tear-glazed eyes, everything in the room—the table set for supper and even the roses themselves—took on a golden sheen. Warm, inviting, comfortable. . . .

In a world where she would never be comfortable again, she cried inside. Day by day she had watched herself become a wretched shrew, like a butterfly in reverse, and she hated herself for it.

She hated the way she lashed out at those she loved most. Rube couldn't control his drinking; Di had been right, her own nagging only drove him to drink more.

And Di—dear, dependable Di— Recalling her cruel words to Di tonight only brought more tears.

Drying them quickly, she called down the hallway to Chou Ling. "I'll be the only one for supper, and I'll just have some broth, please. After my bath."

Soaking in the hot water and rose-scented oils provided by Leslie Hayden, Meg forced herself to relax. She knew the problem, and it didn't lie with either Rube or Di.

It was Kalib. She still hadn't recovered from his latest—

and last—rejection. But she would. Lathering her body with suds, she considered washing her hair—scrubbing her hair always soothed her—but tonight was so cold, she'd take a chill for sure.

She stayed in the tub until the water began to cool, then she quickly buffed her body and chose a dressing gown from the wardrobe, her thoughts were on Rube and Di. She'd not soon forget the shocked, hurt looks on their faces at her diatribe.

The dressing gowns Leslie Hayden had provided disturbed her with their elegance and sophistication. She had to admit, however, that such finery gave her spirits a lift, and her mind something to dwell on besides her own stupidity.

Finally she chose a beige cashmere gown, topped by a flowing caftan of *velours frappe*, the beige velvet stamped with an intricate maroon design. The fullness of the wide plush revers massed narrowly above full sleeves at the shoulders and fell in Watteau-like pleats down the back.

Bending from the waist, she brushed her hair one hundred vicious strokes, for atonement, she thought, as with each stroke she swore to return to her former kind, considerate self by morning. She would take a bowl of broth and retire. Tomorrow marked a brand-new year, and she would arise with it, a brand-new woman. She would approach Rube and Di with contriteness, plead for forgiveness, and they would soon learn she had changed, returned to the normal terminus girl they'd sent away to school four years ago . . . before eastern boarding shools . . . before Kalib. . . .

The first thing she noticed when she entered the salon was the table—set for two. Approaching it, she reached to stack the second place setting for Chou Ling, when the roses caught her eye. An unusually large bouquet tonight, they were . . .

Yellow! Not the golden yellow of reflected lamplight, as she had thought upon entering the salon. True yellow.

Yellow roses. Her pulse slowed to a crawl; her breath stopped altogether. As if in slow motion, she reached to withdraw one stem from the cut-glass vase.

With a reverence she didn't dare try to understand, she lifted the fragrant yellow blossom to her lips. Soft, so very soft. Her eyes blurred.

Then she squeezed her fist around the thorny stem. Anger seethed inside her, returning her pulse to its normal pace through her veins. She dashed through the hallway to the galley.

"Chou Ling?" she called. "Chou Ling? Where . . . ? Why . . . ?" Stopping her rush of words, she slowed her voice. "Why are the roses yellow?"

Her mouth was dry, her thoughts raced in angry darts about her brain.

Chou Ling bowed and nodded. "Yellow," he told her. "Why?"

"You do not like yellow?"

I hate yellow, she raged inside. "Why? What happened to the red ones?"

He looked confused a moment, then shrugged and grinned broadly. "The train brought yellow, miss."

She inhaled deeply, tried to steady her now racing heart, and chastised herself for the temporary insanity that took hold of her every time she was confronted by even the smallest reminder of that dastardly man who had stolen her senses away.

Gritting her teeth, she gathered a firm hold on her wits. "Take away the extra place setting, Chou Ling. There'll be only me for supper, and I asked for broth. . . ." As she spoke her eyes riveted on the elaborate preparations he continued to make for the evening's meal.

"Rack of lamb?" she asked incredulously. Sniffing the air, she squinted at the green sauce. "With mint and potatoes in cream? Chou Ling! Whatever has gotten into you?"

He grinned amicably. "It's New Year's Eve, miss."

Furious at him, though she knew unjustly, she stared at the usually cooperative man. "All this food will keep until tomorrow. Tomorrow," she repeated. "We'll share it with Rube and Di tomorrow."

His quizzical look stopped her a moment, but she remained firm. "I'll have broth, Chou Ling. For heaven's sake, tomorrow is New Year's Day. We can save our celebrating until then."

Bowing, he grinned agreeably. "Yes, miss."

"And the other place setting . . ." Suddenly she heard something clatter to the floor. But not here in the kitchen— The sound came from down the hallway, from Rube's room. She jumped, then chastised herself for being so skittish. "Who is that?"

Chou Ling shrugged, unconcerned, and kept right on basting the rack of lamb.

Rube, she thought. She must have truly hurt his feelings for him to leave Di and spend the night in the railcar. The only other time . . .

Her knock was answered by a simple "Come in," and she already had the door open before she recognized the voice—the thunderous voice that had ravaged her senses for such a very long time now.

Standing in the open doorway, she stared, mouth agape. "What in heaven's name are you doing?"

His smile melted her from the inside out. She gripped the door frame for support.

"Now, Maggie, don't tell me after being raised up in the all-male world of terminus towns, you never saw a man shave before."

"I know perfectly well *what* you're doing," she retorted, finding her strength return in dangerously small increments.

"Then what did you mean to ask?" He returned his attention to the looking glass, while she stared in awe. The entire top of the bureau was littered with black hair. His beard . . . his soft, wonderful beard had vanished down to a graceful moustache.

"Why?" Her mouth was so dry she had difficulty speaking.

"Why what?" He slapped his face with a splash of bay rum and turned for her approval. "Why did I shave? Or why am I here."

Suddenly her senses reeled and swayed. He was *here*. And that meant only one thing . . . one sweet, damning thing. Tobin and Wash had been wrong. He *did* want to see her, after all. But not here—not in Hell on Wheels. . . .

"Kalib, you're crazy. You must leave immediately. The Diamond-Stacker is full of men who want to hang you to the nearest tree, and soon they'll be drunk enough to do it." The moment the words left her mouth, she marveled at them. Would she never stop trying to protect this despicable man?

He merely stared at her—all of her—so directly that the once chilly air became stifling with the heat radiating from within . . . from without . . . from him to her . . . from her to him . . . sweet, hot yearnings that came close to erasing her hard-earned anger and fear.

"What do you think?" he asked glibly, struggling into a deep green velvet smoking jacket. "Should I leave the moustache long, or . . ."

"Stop! Stop it this minute!" Turning, she ran to the salon. Chou Ling had not removed the extra place setting. The yellow roses stood in grand defiance of her exploding emotions. "Chou Ling!" she called.

Kalib walked silently to her side. "We're not quite ready to dine, Chou," he told the bobbing chef. "Bring a bottle of champagne, first."

Moving away from him quickly, she wished the tiny salon were twice as large. Her anger rose full and hot and she stared at the retreating form of Chou Ling, thinking how before now the polite little chef had refused to do the bidding of anyone but herself.

"What right do you have, storming in here, taking charge?" she challenged furiously. "This is my home . . . for the time being, anyhow. You have no right to invade my . . ." She stopped, pressing her lips over the words that issued mindlessly from her mouth. He had invaded her life, but she certainly didn't intend to give him the satisfaction of hearing such an admission from her own lips. She must retain her anger and her wits . . . and her distance. Moving a step further away, she seated herself primly in a corner where he could not approach.

Chou Ling brought the champagne, cooling in its stand of ice. "That'll be all for the moment, Chou," Kalib told him quietly. "I'll served this myself."

She watched, her heart beating fiercely, wishing she were more decently clothed so she could dash out the door and into the Diamond-Stacker.

If only she hadn't left Di and Rube in such a rage. How could she run to them for help now, after the way she had just treated them? The champagne cork popped, and she jumped in her seat.

"Easy now," he murmured. His voice trilled down her spine, leaving her quivering with the same desperate desires and yearnings she had felt in his presence from that first day. He was a demon. There could be no other explanation.

"I realize what a shock finding me here . . ."

"A shock! Not a shock, more like a nightmare. Now, will you please put *my* champagne down and leave *my* railcar this instant, before I scream for help."

Without so much as batting an eyelash, he crossed the room and handed her a glass of bubbling champagne. "This one is to soothe ruffled feathers. We'll save the other bottle for celebrating later."

Her eyes flew to his arrogant face. "Don't you understand me? There will be no later. You're trespassing. . . ."

"Not exactly," he replied in an even, though somewhat amused voice. Setting both glasses on the linen-covered table, he knelt before her. When she started to rise, he pulled her back to a sitting position. "I can't very well be trespassing in my own car."

She frowned, wondering at his words, finding it difficult to concentrate on anything but his hands on hers, warm and soft and oh, so . . . so *unwelcome*. "You never make sense," she retorted. "This is one piece of property whose ownership can be vouched for by every person in town."

He ran the tip of his tongue lightly around his lips, and

289

she blanched, knowing he could feel her reaction to him as surely as she did herself.

"I rented it from Hayden," he told her quietly.

"You what?"

"I rented it . . . for you."

Her mouth felt dry and cottony. She looked down at her night clothes, thought of the roses, the food, the chef, the wardrobe full of clothing and the bureau full of delicate undergarments—all a perfect fit, just for her.

"Why?"

He squeezed her hands, and she knew he wanted to kiss her. She wanted it, too . . . so very badly. She leaned back on the horse-hair cushion, farther away from his face.

"I told you why. Several times."

"Why should I believe you?" she demanded.

"Why shouldn't you?" he questioned.

Suddenly she found the opening she had been searching for. Pushing him backwards, she stood and fled to the far side of the room, beyond the dining table. "Because you've done nothing but lie to me the whole time I've known you. I could never believe you again. Never."

He sighed. "Why don't we eat. Chou fixes the best rack of lamb this side of New York, and he's mighty particular about serving dinner on time."

How would you know? she thought angrily, but she held her tongue, realizing he would have a ready answer for anything she might say. "I'd rather you leave," she told him simply. "I'm going to bed." She took a step toward the hallway, but he caught her arm. She froze in her tracks; his fingers burned through her layers of clothing.

"First, we'll eat." Though spoken in the quietest of tones, his words shattered her senses. He led her to a chair and seated her at the elegantly set table. All she could do was stare at the yellow roses and hope she didn't cry . . . from anger, from frustration, or from relief.

Without another word Kalib plucked a rose from the vase, snapped the stem and tucked it through a split in his lapel. With the greatest of care he chose another rose, and, studying her with the most solemn look she'd ever seen

290

him wear, he placed it through the strands of her hair behind her ear. Then he leaned forward and kissed her lips gently, firmly, briefly.

After he seated himself, she still sat erect and deathly calm, her lips burning from the heat of his, her heart vying with her very soul for control of her emotions. To whom would she be loyal? To Rube or to Kalib? And whom would she betray?

Chou Ling served, and they picked at their food in silence. At last, Kalib sighed, wiped his lips with the generous linen napkin, and studied her frankly. "I deserve to burn in hell for hurting you like I have."

Tears burned behind her eyelids. She fought desperately to keep them from rolling down her cheeks. She couldn't cry; she couldn't. If she would stay calm and still he would go away. Soon. Pray God, he would go soon.

"But it's all over now, Maggie," he continued. "I came to tell you the worst is over. We can begin our life all over again."

She felt his eyes on her, but she dared not look at him. She tried to close out his words, as well.

"Actually," he went on, "I came to do three things. First, to show you who I am. That's why I shaved." Reaching across the table, he attempted to take her hand, but she jerked away. "Look at me, Maggie," he insisted. "You can't very well recognize me, if you don't look at me."

Inhaling a deep breath of anger, she pursed her lips and looked at him. She'd been right. She knew that the moment she'd stepped through the doorway and found him shaving. He was indeed the most handsome . . . She swallowed her thoughts. He was *not* going to win, she vowed. Not after all he had done to her and to Rube. Not after he had caused her to turn such angry words on Rube and Di . . . he was not going to win. "You're right," she told him in the coldest voice she could master. "I don't recognize you at all. Especially since you shaved, you're a complete stranger to me." She could see his jaw twitch in barely controlled fury.

Chou Ling removed their plates and brought dessert, a Bavarian cream with maraschino liqueur sauce. Again they picked at their food. Again in silence.

Finally, Kalib threw his napkin into his plate. "My God, Maggie! Give me a chance!"

His anger fueled hers. "A chance!" she stormed. "A chance for what? What else do you want to do to me? Burn me at the stake? Throw me to the lions?"

Their gazes held. The pain she saw in his eyes was so intense that for a moment all she wanted was to hold him and console him. But then she thought of Rube. Of the way Wash and Tobin had so blithely dismissed her from Kalib's life only a few days earlier, and she tore her eyes from his.

His voice, when he spoke, almost ripped her heart from her breast. "One more chance, Maggie, that's what I'm asking. One more chance to prove to you how much I love you."

In her lap, she gripped her hands so tightly together her nails cut into her flesh. Her teeth bit into her bottom lip. Squenching her eyelids together, she succeeded in preventing tears from flowing before his very eyes. And in that success, she found strength . . . and anger.

"Love?" she questioned brutally. "You don't know what the word means. You wouldn't know love if it fell from the sky and hit you on the head!"

"Yes, I would," he insisted, in such a stony voice that she looked at him involuntarily. "Let me tell *you*. Love is when one person is more important to you than anyone else in the world; love is what you feel for someone when you'd rather die than hurt . . . her; love is the feeling that tells you beyond any doubt that you can't live your life without. . . ." He paused and his eyes held hers, loving, begging, demanding. "I can't live my life without you, Maggie. I don't even want to try."

She jumped from the table, knocking her chair over in her haste. "Don't," she cried, desperately clutching her hands over her head as if for protection. "Please, don't. Leave me alone. Are you so cruel, so insensitive, so . . ."

He held her against her earnest struggles to free herself, murmuring all the time into her hair. "Maggie, Maggie, admit it. You love me. We both know it. Why is it so hard? Why can't you let yourself love me?"

Wedging her arms between them, she separated her treacherously aching body from his. "I don't love you," she insisted. "How could I love someone so . . . so ruthless?"

He tried to wrest her head up to face him, but she resisted, working away from him. "And even if I were so stupid," she cried, "so dim-witted that I couldn't help myself, I'd never admit it. Certainly not to you."

Releasing her abruptly, he turned to the table and tossed down the glass of warm champagne. "I brought you something," he said casually. Picking up her glass, he drank it in one swallow, as well.

She studied him doubtfully, trying to steady her trembling flesh. A lot of good her hot bath had done, she thought. She only calmed down from one disaster to face another.

Chou Ling entered silently and cleared the table.

"You want your tea served now, sir?" he asked Kalib.

"No, thank you, Chou. Bring us a fresh bottle of champagne, then you may retire for the night." When he looked back at Maggie, her mouth was ajar. "You didn't want tea tonight, did you, love?" He asked the question so innocently, she merely shook her head.

Abruptly she caught herself. She thought of going to bed, but she knew he would only follow. So instead, she stomped to one of the banquettes and sat primly erect once more, arms crossed protectively over her chest, legs crossed thigh over thigh. She'd sit here all night, if she had to. She watched him twirl the bottle of champagne in the bucket of ice. Then he left it unopen and walked toward her.

"You're the most arrogant bastard I've. . . ."

His eyes sparkled, and she bit her tongue. Why couldn't she keep her mouth shut? she wondered dismally.

"Back to name calling," he grinned. "At least, we're making progress."

"I wouldn't call it progress," she answered determindedly.

He approached her as though she were the most congenial dinner companion in the world. Sitting beside her, he stretched his arm across the back of the banquette, and she moved her shoulder away from him.

"The second reason I came here tonight is to celebrate."

Her mouth flew open. "To celebrate?" She jumped to her feet. If she had something at hand, she'd throw it at him, she thought furiously. The bastard! "You want to celebrate? Go over to the Diamond-Stacker. Celebrate with Rube. He's been celebrating for days . . . and all because of you."

His eyes turned hard. "I didn't cause Rube to drink."

She glared at him. "Oh, no? You're behind the spurious report Ellsworth Fredericks printed in his paper. The report that caused Silver Creek to withhold bond payments, which in turn resulted in the workers walking off, which . . ."

"Maggie!" Grabbing her by the shoulder, he shook her several times. "I'm responsible for the report. I admit it. But that setback didn't cause Rube to drink. He made the choice to drink all by himself. He's never needed me to lead him to the bottle. Or you, either. Nor does he need us to stay sober. For God's sake, let him live his own life."

Her breath came short and fast. Tears, at last, rolled down her face. "How dare you talk to me like that."

He held her, while she sobbed into the soft velvet of his smoking jacket, smoothing her hair, murmuring into her ear, and he knew he would have a hard time leaving her, even for the next few weeks.

At last she sighed deeply against him and moved her arms around his waist, clutching him tightly. One small gesture, he thought. One faltering step along the road they must travel to return to a place of peace, and trust, and love. The price this trip cost Maggie brought tears to his eyes.

Gently, he held her back and kissed her forehead. With the greatest of difficulty, he restrained himself from kissing her further, knowing once it was set free, his passion for her would be hard to leash again.

"Sit down and let me tell you the rest." He led her to the banquette again. Sweeping his hands down her arms, he held both her hands in one of his, while with his other hand he withdrew a black object from the pocket of his trousers.

"I found it," he told her simply. "Today, I found the proof I need."

She turned the rough black rock over in her hand, studying it in the flickering lamplight. She felt weak, unable to resist, unable to fight on. "Where?"

He ran his tongue around his lips, trying to contain his overpowering desire to forego everything else he had planned for this night and take her straight to bed. But things needed to be settled. Tonight. With a deep sigh, he continued. "Remember the shaft we walked down that day?"

She nodded.

"I went back there, as a last resort. When it seemed like nothing else was going to pan out, I went back with a hatchet and hacked away at the walls deep inside the hill. Using a lantern, I finally found a very small vein of this stuff."

"Is it really silver?"

He nodded.

"The Lost Bowie Mine?"

He grinned. "Close enough to fulfill my promise. Actually, I only got away with a couple of pieces. This one's for you. As a . . ." Without finishing his sentence, he shrugged.

A grim smile played on her lips. "As a souvenir? This is one part of my life I'll never be able to forget."

He pulled her to him and held her so close his heart beat against her face. "Nor I, love." Holding her back, he brushed tears from the corner of her eyes. "Tobin has already left for Austin. He'll have word wired to Silver Creek by day after tomorrow, so work can begin again. Rube can finish on time. Nothing has been lost."

She stared at him, wondering at his inability to comprehend the seriousness of what he had done to her . . . to Rube. "You still don't understand, do you?" she asked quietly. "Sure, Rube can finish in time for the governor to make his speech, but . . . all the heartache, all the misery. In this case—" She paused, took a deep, tremulous breath, then continued. "This is one time the end doesn't justify the means. I can't see why . . ."

Ever so softly he placed an index finger across her lips. Instantly she hushed. The intimacy of the gesture flooded her senses with memories . . . sweet, sensual, painful memories. Every pore in her lips reveled in his touch. "I'm about to explain," he whispered.

Suddenly his eyes grew troubled, and he rose. With the most intense concentration, he opened the fresh bottle of champagne and poured two glasses. This time she accepted the one he handed her and sipped from it.

"Do you recall your reaction the first time I told you about the mine?" he asked, seating himself beside her once more.

She thought back, trying to remember the words they had spoken. That was the first time he'd ever kissed her, and afterwards everything else about the day had faded in comparison. It was also the first time he had touched her lips in that particular way—silencing her with his slender, bronzed index finger.

Shrugging, she answered, "I suppose I thought it a . . . a rather crazy idea."

He grinned, and for the first time tonight she saw golden sparks gleam in his eyes. It almost took her breath away. "You called me a lunatic," he told her.

She nodded. "Yes, I suppose I did."

"Do you know why that's important?" he asked.

She frowned.

"Because," he answered himself, "that's what everyone else in the whole state would think about me if they knew what I was doing out here."

Confused, she cocked her head, waiting.

"Well," he said, fidgeting now. "I couldn't risk

everyone in the state thinking I'm a lunatic." Rising, he refilled their glasses, returned the bottle to its nest of ice, then stood stockstill in front of her, wondering how in hell he was going to tell her. What would she think? What would she do? Would it change things . . . ?

Inhaling a deep breath, he touched his glass to hers. "Maggie Britton . . . meet Kalib . . . Chaney."

She stared at him blankly.

After a lengthy pause, he grinned self-consciously. "You don't recognize the name?"

"Well, it does sound familiar . . . Kalib Chaney," she repeated. "I know I've heard it. Kalib Chaney . . . ?" Suddenly it struck her where she had heard that name. "You're not *THE* . . ." She shook her head, willing him to do the same. But he didn't.

Pursing his lips, he nodded.

"No," she whispered, draining her glass. With a cough, she rose from her seat, refilled her glass, turned, and refilled his. She stared at him, incredulous. "You can't be *THE* Kalib Ch . . ."

He shrugged, not sure she understood. If she did, she wasn't very pleased. "Say it," he suggested.

"You say it. . . ." She swallowed half the champagne in her glass. "Say it isn't true."

"It is Maggie. I'm the governor-elect. Now, you know why I couldn't let anyone find out who I was. I'd be the laughing-stock of the state. At the same time, my grandmother is getting along in years, and this may well be the last chance I'll have to fulfill that crazy promise. Don't you see? I had to protect my identity. And that meant . . ."

"Keeping everyone as far away from you as possible."

He sighed deeply. It was over at last. The deception. He felt a heavy weight rise from his shoulders, freeing him to be honest and truthful with Maggie for the rest of his life. Taking her glass, he turned to set them both aside, and when he turned back to her, tears were streaming down her face.

"Now what's wrong?" he asked confused.

"That ruins everything," she sobbed.

Holding her desperately, he kissed her hair, then smoothed it with his hands and looked deep into her misty green eyes. "It's only a job, Maggie."

She didn't answer, but the look of absolute despair on her face confused him further. "It'll only last a couple of years," he told her. "I don't have to run again. Two years, that's all."

"Then what?" she cried.

Her reaction bewildered him. Taking her gently by the shoulders, he sat her down again, but this time he held her close and explained quietly. "I own a ranch in South Texas. My family has ranched there since . . . well, since Texas was a part of Mexico. It's a beautiful place. I can't wait to show you. . . ."

As he spoke, tears flowed in earnest down her lovely face, and his heart lurched. "What is it, love? Tell me what's troubling you."

Lifting her hand she stroked his face, feeling his soft skin for the first time without his beard. His eyes bored into her, questioning, begging, loving . . . all she had ever wished for, yet at the same time, nothing had turned out as she had hoped . . . dreamed. How could she tell him her plans for him to work for the railroad? How could she bear to tell him she could never leave Rube?

Gradually, her tears stopped and her heart filled with resolve . . . resolve to replace the horrid memories of the last few days with dreams they would treasure the rest of their lives.

She smiled and watched his eyes light up. "Imagine me . . . a girl from a terminus town . . . loving the governor of Texas."

"The governor-elect," he corrected, as his lips descended to hers, devouring her lips, her face, delving into her champagne-flavored sweetness, delighting in her wondrous touch. Her hair flowed generously around her shoulders and face, and his hands tangled in its silky strands.

Groping beneath her caftan, he crumpled the soft

298

cashmere of her nightdress in his quest for her even softer skin. His hands spanned her slender waist, ungirted, then, moved slowly upwards, at last closing over her breasts, separated from his skin by a bothersome layer of fabric.

Her fingers twined in his hair. Moving her hands to his face, she stroked the clean-shaven skin on his cheeks, his jaw. "You do feel like a stranger," she whispered against his lips.

His eyes pierced hers with longing. "I'll grow it back," he mumbled, nibbling at her lips, her nose, kissing her eyes. "If you like it. . . ."

"No." She kissed the smooth, fresh skin. "A beard is mysterious, and the governor shouldn't be mysterious."

Lifting his face, he studied her with a smile. "I can see you'll be an asset . . . every place."

Quickly she pulled his face to hers and kissed his lips, passionately, anxiously, as though she never wanted to stop.

With a deep groan, he scooped her in his arms and carried her to the blue and gold bedchamber. "We'll return later to toast the New Year," he whispered, as he gently placed her in the middle of the bed. After shucking his smoking jacket, he joined her, propping his elbows on either side of her face, studying her loveliness in earnest. "Do you know what really frightens me?" He shifted to catch a strand of her chestnut hair between his fingers.

She shook her head, reaching to pull him close.

"Our meeting was such an accident. . . ." he began in awe. "What if . . . ?" His suddenly troubled eyes searched hers. "God Maggie, what if I'd never found you?"

"You didn't find me," she told him playfully. "I found you." One lamp glowed from the bureau, and a small flame flickered from the oil-burning heater in the corner of the room. In this dusky light she studied his face, memorizing every line, every angle, the warm glow of love in his dark eyes. "You're very handsome," she whispered, running a finger down his jaw, sending tremors the length of his body.

Finally, he grinned and pulled her on top of him, "I'd

better be. If not, you'll be the laughing-stock of the state. Everyone will twitter when we go out. 'How could such a beautiful woman have taken so ugly a husband?'"

She laughed in spite of the anguish such words brought her. Nothing was going to ruin this night. Now that she knew the truth, every remaining moment they had together must be a time of the purest joy.

Her laughter sent additional trills through his tormented body, and he stood up abruptly, pulling her along. Silently he edged her caftan off her shoulders, and she felt it flutter to the floor. Breathlessly she waited while his fingers, like tiny flames, unfastened the mother-of-pearl buttons on the yoke of her nightdress, then tugged the garment over her head and cast it aside.

Still she stood, scarcely breathing, while he gazed at her, his hands following his eyes up her slender form, past her waist, lingering, then past her aching breasts, at last capturing her quivering chin in his palms. Gently, he guided her lips to his, where he kissed her passionately, desperately.

His shirt and trousers felt crisp and rough against her bare skin as he crushed her in his arms. His hand massaged her hair, her head, her neck.

Finally, she drew back, and, their foreheads touching, together they watched her fingers work against the buttons on his shirt, the waist of his trousers.

"Maggie, Maggie," he murmured in a tremulous voice from deep inside. Stripping his clothing now quickly, he lifted her again and lowered them to the bed once more.

His lips fired her skin. His fingers ignited her senses, and when he stretched beside her and their two bodies pressed together, she thought she would surely soar with the wildly blowing wind.

His lips moved against her own in gentle, tormenting urging, and when she opened them beneath his sensual demands, she delighted in the heightened cravings he created within her. Shamelessly, she snuggled her body against his, tempting, urging, begging.

Moving her lips back from his, she smiled. "Is this the

third thing you came to do tonight?"

He groaned. "Maggie, my love, my dear, sweet love. The third thing I must do tonight is to prove my love to you and to—" his breath came short, his need for her growing quickly out of all bounds. His hands traveled her love-heated flesh. ". . . to never stop proving it."

Shifting, his lips kissed her neck. "Like this. . . ." he mumbled, moving down, kissing her chest, claiming at last one aching breast. ". . . and this." His lips closed over her nipple, his teeth teased, tormented, and she writhed joyously in his arms.

Winding her bare arms about him, she reveled in the feel of his skin, in the ripple of his muscles beneath her as he moved first his hands, then his lips over her body, loving and tantalizing, until every inch of her, inside and out, ached for him.

Her supple, shifting body drove him wild with need, with desire. His senses reeled with the sweet smell of roses, the heady tast of champagne, the wondrous knowledge that Maggie was his, in body and spirit, to love and cherish forevermore. When he trailed his fingers in fiery paths up and down her stomach, around her firm buttocks, into the silky mass of chestnut hair at the base of her abdomen, she writhed against his own aching body with such ardent movements that he shifted to enter her body, then stopped.

Not so fast, his brain objected. Love her slow. Like a rare wine, enjoy her heady passion to the last drop and make sure she enjoys it, too. Dipping his hand lower, his fingers entered her heated, silken lining, and again she moved ardently against him, this time calling his name in passion-wracked whispers.

Tugging his lips from her breast, he retraced the trail to her lips, where he hovered above her, watching the smoldering emerald light in her eyes burn more brightly with each probe of his hand.

"Kalib, please," she begged against his lips. Her hips moved, struggling to find his and the relief she knew awaited her beneath them. At last, she could bear it no longer. Her hands left his back, traced through the mass of hair covering his chest, to his waist, and lower. Capturing at last the instrument of release, she guided him to her, and together they traveled the last short distance to the summit of their passion.

Afterwards they lay clasped firmly, each in the other's embrace, he thankful for the new beginning they shared tonight, she, grateful for the memories to carry away with her.

At last their breathing slowed, and conscious of the chilly air, he pulled back the layers of quilts and covered their bare bodies.

Her thoughts drifted to earlier when he had told her who he was, and she laughed softly into his chest. "Did it bother you when I didn't recognize you?"

He stared down at her in amusement. "Guess it put me in my place," he said. "Actually, I figured since you'd lived in Austin, you would have heard. . . ."

"I didn't live in Austin," she objected. "I was only there a couple of weeks after I returned from school, and . . ." Raising quickly, her head hit him on the chin.

He drew back, studying her through the flickering light. "Where did you go to school?"

She sighed. "No place special," she answered, then she recalled her conversation with Katie and Mary Sue. "I did meet one of your Texas friends there, though."

He raised his eyebrows, waiting.

"Sara Ann Chrystal," she said slowly, watching his reaction. "She lived across the hall from me for four years."

He frowned, then grinned. "Smith College, huh? Why did you keep it such a deep secret?"

She shrugged, studying him closely, not sure how she would reply until the words actually came out of her mouth. "At first . . . well, you *did* look down on me . . . on where I came from, and I . . . I didn't want to see the shock on your face when you learned I've had a *proper* upbringing, after all."

His arms tightened protectively around her. "I *never* looked down on you, Maggie."

"You thought . . ."

"Damnit, am I to pay for every stupid thing I ever thought? If so, you'd best get out a long pad of paper, because the list will take all night."

"Kalib, don't. Let's not argue. Please, not tonight."

Reaching, he kissed her lips. "We *have* done our share of arguing, haven't we, love. It's important to me, though, for you to understand how very much I respect you—and love you."

She kissed him back, silencing him. Later, she grinned through the flickering light into his eyes. The golden glow set her blood to boiling all over again. "Sara Ann Chrystal?" she asked.

He looked at her amused eyes a moment, then shrugged.

"According to my sources, she came back to Texas with a mission."

He frowned. "What sort of mission?"

She tightened her arms around him and playfully kissed his nose. Reaching, she kissed his eyes, each in turn as he so often did hers, then she leaned back and grinned at him. "She's set her cap for the . . . uh, for the governor-elect."

For a moment he just stared at her, then her words took hold, and he laughed out loud. Hugging her fiercely to him, his chest bounced against hers. "I hope she won't be too disappointed," he whispered, staring lovingly into her face. "He's already spoken for."

After they loved a second time, her mind suddenly buzzed with questions. She knew so little about him—and she had so little time to learn. Fiercely, she shoved aside the despair welling inside her. This night was for happiness, she demanded of herself. This night was for joy. This night was to create memories enough to last a lifetime.

"So, I've been a kept woman all this time, and not even by the gentleman I thought," she quipped lightly, kissing his chest.

"You don't think I would have been so tolerant of all this, if some other man were responsible, do you?"

"But you said . . ."

He laughed and squeezed her to him. "It was easier to

303

say what I said, under the circumstances," he admitted. "The lodging, itself, would have been all right, I suppose. But not the . . . roses. . . ."

"You must have had a big laugh at my expense," she told him, "when I threw those roses out the door, vase and all."

He kissed her nose. "To tell the truth, it comforted me," he said. "Expensive comfort. But comfort, nonetheless. Now, the clothes. . . ." As he spoke he ran his hand enticingly up and down her satiny skin. "I wouldn't have stood for him giving you clothing, not for one minute."

She laughed. "How did you know my sizes? I mean . . ." She felt herself blush in the darkened room, so she snuggled closer to him. ". . . *all* my sizes."

His hands roamed freely beneath the covers, over all her more sensitive places, tantalizing, exciting, reminding himself that she was his, forever. "The story isn't as sensational as the question," he admitted. "My sister, one of my sisters, is just about your size, so when I sent Tobin to Austin to arrange for this car, I sent a special message to Delores. She demanded a king's ransom in return for secrecy, but . . ." Pulling her back, he studied her again, as if to reaffirm his conviction. ". . . you're worth it, love."

They lay in silence then, basking in the warmth of their love. After a while, she resumed her desperate search for answers to the multitude of questions she had about this man. "I realize you have no brothers," she said, recalling the very reason he was destined to carry out his grandmother's wishes. "How many sisters do you have?"

"Five," he answered, then quickly reassured her. "You'll love them . . . every one of them, I think. I know they'll love you, Maggie. And my mother . . . you can't possibly understand what this will mean to her. She's been after me for. . . ." he sighed. "She considers me her biggest failure—elected governor, and still no wife!"

After a while Kalib dozed, and Meg lay in his arms, desperate to control the impending sense of doom she found overwhelming her even before he left. At length, she turned in his arms, awakened him with kisses, and they

304

loved again.

"When will it be safe to talk to Rube?" he asked, when once more they lay damp and exhausted in each other's arms.

"Talk to Rube?" she questioned.

He chuckled. "I know I haven't made a very good impression so far. In fact, I wouldn't be surprised if he refused my request for your hand. But he's your father, love. I have to pay him the courtesy of asking."

She tensed in his arms, and while he spoke, her mind raced. She didn't want another fight, not tonight. And she knew he would never understand. Kissing his chest, she tried to draw his mind away . . . to other matters.

"I know you ladies like fancy affairs," he told her, holding her back. "But I have . . . well, I have an urgent request. I want us to be married right away."

She stirred, and he tightened his hold. "Hear me out, Maggie. The inauguration is January twenty-first, not more than three weeks off. It doesn't give you much time, but . . ." He grasped her head in his hands and kissed her mouth, her eyes, her nose. When he looked into her eyes, she saw more golden highlights than she had ever seen there before. Her sudden, impulsive thought was that love certainly agreed with Kalib Chaney.

"I want us to be married before the inauguration," he said at last. "I want you to stand beside me that day as my wife, Maggie. I want you to hold the Bible when I take the oath of office . . . beside me, the way we'll stand beside each other through the rest of eternity."

Without the slightest bit of warning tears poured from her eyes. She sprang from his arms and sat naked and trembling on the edge of the bed.

Quickly he knelt before her and took her in his arms. "What's wrong? If it's such a terrible idea, we'll change . . ."

"It's a wonderful idea," she sobbed.

"Then what. . . ?" His words broke off and he stared at her, his mouth aslack. "Maggie, look at me." Gently, he tipped her chin upwards, but the tears continued to gush from her eyes. "Are you . . . ? I mean, are *we* . . . ? I mean . . . I've never seen you cry so much. Look at me, love. Are we going to have a baby?"

Her breath caught in her throat, and her tears dried instantly. "No!" she told him, then recanted, thinking of tonight. "I mean . . . ah, no, we're not. What made you think that?"

He stroked her hair and held her wet face against his chest. "With five sisters, a man learns about such things. But if it isn't that, what is it? What did I do . . . ?"

Inhaling a deep, quivering breath, she drew back and ran her fingers through his hair. Then she clasped his head to her breast, so she wouldn't have to see his face when she told him. "You didn't do anything. It's me. I . . . I can't marry you."

He tried to pull away, but she held his head firmly against her fiercely beating heart. "I can't marry you. That's all there is to it. If I could, it wouldn't matter where the ceremony was held or how plain it was or how simple my dress. You're . . ." She held his face in both hands as he had hers only moments before and stared into his distraught eyes. "You're what would make it special. You're all I need for a perfect wedding. But I can't marry you. I can't leave Rube, and you . . . you have to go be governor of Texas."

Chapter Sixteen

"Like hell I do!" Kalib raged, shaking her shoulders. "I haven't taken oath of office yet, and I don't have to. I won't. . . ."

"Yes, you will," she argued. "You must. You'll make a wonderful governor; you have all the qualities—loyalty and dedication and . . ."

"You aren't listening, Maggie," he shouted at her. "Without you beside me . . ."

"Kalib, please. Don't shout. Not tonight." She slid her arms around his waist and hugged herself close to him. The hair on his chest caressed her bare body, soft and warm. His heart thumped furiously against her face.

"If this night is all we have," she cried, "please, let's not ruin it by arguing."

Angrily, he pried her arms from around him and shoved her back to the bed. She watched, horrified as he stalked to the other side and began putting on his clothes.

"Get dressed before you catch your death," he hissed.

Scooching across the bed, she reached for him. "Don't Kalib. Please."

Pausing, he regarded her with deathly quietness, holding the tips of his trousers loosely in place around his waist. "You beat all I've ever seen," he whispered.

Her hair streamed across her face, and she pushed it back and stared at him still, her trembling lips caught between her teeth. "Kalib, don't walk out like this. Please, don't leave . . . not like this. . . .''

His breath came short. He fastened his trousers, then buckled his belt. "One night may be enough for you, but it isn't for me." He spoke angrily, while he struggled into his wrinkled white shirt. "I need a lifetime, and that might not even be enough. I want to *live*, don't you understand. Not to dream of what was . . . or what might have been. I want . . ." Suddenly his anger caught in his throat, and he fell to his knees beside the bed and crushed her to him, smothering her face against his heaving chest. His husky voice broke with emotion. "I want *you*, Maggie, beside me, forever . . . I want *you, you, you*. . . ."

Then take me and hold me and love me, she thought wildly, welcoming this respite, however brief. His lips found hers, and she kissed him desperately, determined to salvage something wonderful from this night.

When at last he lifted his lips from hers and looked into her eyes, his adoring gaze further weakened her already reeling senses. And when he spoke, his voice reminded her of the time he had shown her the hole in the ground by the cedar brake, animated, as if he were certain beyond a doubt he had the perfect solution to their problem.

"You can visit Rube whenever you like . . . wherever he is. I promise, I'll never keep you from visiting him. Even . . ."—he grinned at her—"even in Hell on Wheels."

Squeezing her arms about his neck fiercely, she pressed her face close to his, cheek to cheek. Her tears returned, but this time silently and without sobs. "You still don't understand. Unless I'm with him all the time, he drinks. I can't simply abandon him."

He stared at her. "Maggie, love, you're the one who doesn't understand. You have your own life; *we* have our lives . . . our life together. That's what growing up is all about . . ." he shrugged and nipped her lips, "falling in love and making your own life. It's perfectly normal. I'm sure Rube expects you to leave him."

Impatiently, she squirmed in his arms. "He's a child, Kalib. He and Di are both like children. They should never have sent me away to school. I worried the entire time I was

308

gone, and with good reason. When I returned, Rube had been drunk so long his reputation with the railroad was almost ruined—one of the best railroaders the country had ever had, drunk and out of work. Since then, he's used every opportunity as an excuse to drink."

"What did he do before he had you?"

She gazed sadly into his eyes. "He's always had me. Just like your grandmother has always been able to rely on you. You were the one appointed to find the mine; I'm the one who has to care for Rube. It's called loyalty."

"Loyalty?" he stormed at her. "This has nothing to do with loyalty." Setting her aside, he found his boots and struggled into them. "Nor with my grandmother, for that matter. I didn't give up my life for her."

"You risked your reputation for her," she retorted. "Along with the lives and reputations of a lot of other people, if I may remind you."

"I did no such thing." Grabbing her arm, he jerked her around to face him. "I fulfilled a promise, and regardless of what you say, nothing harmful came from the method. Something . . ."

His words ground to a halt, and she watched his Adam's apple bob in his throat. "It's almost like it was divined," he said more quietly. "Our two stars coming together at exactly the right time. And you . . . you're hell-bent on destroying it all." Sweeping her body with one brief, distraught glance, he turned and stalked from the room, calling over his shoulder, "Get your goddamned clothes on!"

With trembling fingers she found her caftan and slipped it over her shoulders. Loosening the revers, she buttoned the fancy frog closures across her bare chest. She found him in the salon, staring at the yellow roses.

Crossing the room, she encircled his waist from behind and lay her face against his back. At her touch she felt him stiffen. "You'll make a wonderful governor, Kalib. I'll be so proud of you . . . so very proud."

With a vengeance he tore her hands away, then grabbed the roses in his fist, and stomping to the doorway, he chucked them into the street. When he slid the door open the north wind gushed into the small room, causing the wicks in the lamps to gutter.

"Kalib, please. . . ." She ran forward, and just as she reached him the wind tossed her hair about her face and whiffed open the revers of her velvet caftan, skimming her body with an icy breath.

He turned and stared at her, wishing she hadn't caught her hand to her hair in that particular gesture, knowing he would see it in his mind for days and months . . . forever.

She stretched her hands toward him. The wind blew between them, separating them with its chilling swirls. He stepped backwards through the door, unable to tear himself away from the terrified look in her eyes.

Suddenly she knew he was leaving, and her heart lurched painfully in her chest. He couldn't . . . not yet . . . oh, dear God, he couldn't. . . . "Kalib, please. . . ." The wind tossed her words back in her mouth, and she shouted, desperate for him to hear . . . for him not to leave . . . not before . . .

"Kalib, please. Kiss me . . . kiss me good-bye. . . ."

His face turned to stone. Her words hung as a barrier between them. "Never!" he shouted above the wind. Pivoting abruptly on his heel, he left.

She watched from the window. The sky was by now awash with streaks of light. The new day was upon them. The new year. His last word echoed through her mind like the icy wind calling down an empty canyon—*Never . . . Never . . . Never, my love . . . love . . . love.* He hadn't added the last, of course, but the longer she thought on it, the clearer those words sounded in her tormented mind.

And she suddenly felt very old and very alone, and never was such a very long time.

Returning to bed, she tried to sleep, but all she managed to attain was a quiet state of absolute sorrow. By noontime, she knew Kalib had been right about one thing—one night was not enough. Even if they had spent it without a cross word between them, it wouldn't have been enough. She needed him desperately; she was sure she always would.

Di came at dinnertime and roused her from bed. Feeling especially contrite, Meg arose, dressed quickly, and joined Di for the simple meal she usually enjoyed of oyster soup, fruit, and hot biscuits.

Meg poured out her apology to Di, after which Di told her exactly what she had expected to hear. Her apology was accepted; they understood, she and Rube; and Rube hadn't had a drop to drink since her little lecture. Maybe he would make it this time. If Kalib thought *she* was a dreamer, Meg thought, he should hear Di.

"Now, the real reason I'm here. . . ." Di studied her carefully. "You had company last night."

The statement had come without warning, and Meg blanched. Inhaling a deep, quivering breath, she held her secret safely inside with pursed lips.

"I'm not questioning your behavior, dear," Di continued. "But he was seen leaving."

Meg studied her, horror-struck. "Who saw him?"

"Georgie," Di said. "He'd gone out to get fresh eggs from my pen of hens, and he saw a . . . a tall, dark-headed man'" she quoted, "leaving the *Texas Star* in haste."

"Who else knows?"

"No one," Di assured her. "I just . . . well, I wanted to be sure you're all right."

Meg slid her chair back from the table and sat, hands clasped in her lap, limp, and at the same time desperate to cry her heart out to Di. But it wouldn't help. Besides, she still needed, now more than ever, actually, to protect Kalib's identity. "He's finished out at the mine shaft," she said at last. "Word will arrive in Silver Creek by tomorrow; they'll pay the bond money. Then it'll all be . . ." She inhaled again and tensed against the tremors wracking her body. "It'll all be over."

Di studied her until she began to squirm. "Will it, dear?" she asked. "Will it *all* be over?"

"He . . . uh, he won't be working for the railroad. He has another . . . an important job. . . ."

Reaching over, Di patted her hands where they lay in

her lap. "He didn't ask . . . ? You decided not to go with him?"

Not trusting her voice, Meg nodded.

They sat silently a while, then Di rose to leave. She stroked Meg's hair sympathetically. "The hurt won't last forever, dear. One of these days someone else will come along. . . ."

Never, Meg cried inside. *Never . . . Never . . . Never. . . .*

"You know what they say about love, Meg—there are two in every woman's life—the one she gives up, and the one she keeps forever."

Forever, forever, forever. The words echoed alongside their negative counterpart through Meg's brain. Wherever she went, whatever she did the rest of the day and into the evening, these tormenting words ricocheted through her senses.

The next morning she awakened feeling leaden and listless. She wondered whether this were the way Rube felt after a lengthy drinking spell. Thinking of Rube, she knew she must see him today and make amends. Before she even finished dressing, however, the Silver Creek delegation, true to Kalib's word, drew up in front of the Diamond-Stacker.

Fetching her cloak, she joined them in time to hear Libby Lancaster's apology. "We received a wire today from the office of Governor-elect Chaney," she told Rube. "The earlier report was a mistake, there is nothing whatsoever the matter with your procedures." She handed Rube a copy of the telegram along with the bond payment. "A message was included for you from the land office— something about the right of way over the Silver Creek River being settled in your favor."

Thumping the paper with his index finger, Rube looked around the room. Meg quickly ducked her eyes, for she knew he intended to exchange a knowing glance with her. And she had no intention of letting him see anything but a glow of accomplishment on her face.

Again the Silver Creek entourage lingered at the Diamond-Stacker. Woody Woodson once more perused every nook and cranny of the saloon. He even enticed Di away from the bar, where this time she served her new temperance drinks to everyone, including Rube, and they spent a good hour in her office, going over the details of purchasing and erecting such a building.

Meg didn't have as much success keeping her melancholy a secret from Hank as she had from Rube. He finally pinned her down with the threat of an examination.

"Well, I am a doctor, Meg. And you look like you're about to come down with a case of . . ." He scrunched his face around, thinking, then finished his sentence. "Actually, it doesn't appear to be anything we studied in school." He felt her hands. "You aren't cold and clammy, but you definitely don't have the warm feel of someone who's among the living."

He laid the back of his hand against her forehead. "Nope, no fever, either. If it continues much longer, I'm afraid we'll have a terminal case of . . ." Pausing, he cocked his head and studied her in a teasing manner. Distress showed clearly in his eyes, however.

"I'm all right," she protested. "You brought the only medicine I need with you today—the bond payment. Now, maybe we can finish this dratted railroad, and . . ."

Hank cleared his throat. "Ellsworth Fredericks has been asking about the prospector who's behind all this trouble," he told her carefully. "He even asked me what I know about your visits to the man."

She stared at him, feeling weak and sick inside. Was everyone to be dragged into her personal life? "When did you start believing *anything* Ellsworth Fredericks says?" she demanded.

He shrugged. "I know he isn't the most reliable source of information. His accusations didn't go unchallenged, either. I didn't flatten him on the boardwalk, like I wanted to, but I jerked him by the collar and threatened him with reprisals if he ever mentioned your name in such a manner again." He studied her closely, then continued. "But, Meg, dear girl, something *is* wrong with you, and . . ."

"Hank, you're treating me just like you would Katie!"

313

As soon as the words left her mouth, she laughed, for the first time in two days, she thought suddenly. "And I love you for it. I've always needed a brother, but now that I have one, I'm not sure I want him meddling in my affairs."

Reaching over, he hugged her around the shoulders. "If I see someone doing you wrong, you'd better believe I'll meddle in your affairs, and fast. In the meantime, my prescription is to get this whole railroad business off your mind. I've written Mary Sue and Katie. You're to take your prettiest party clothes when you go down to Austin with Rube for the stockholder's meeting. It's the same weekend as the inauguration of the new governor. I'll be going down too, you know, along with a dozen or so other folks from Silver Creek. We'll show you how to forget your troubles."

In his good-natured, big-brotherly fashion, Hank Jefferies had sent her already muddled world spinning precariously on its axle. When he returned to Silver Creek, he left her with a painful new fear—going to Austin. How could she *possibly* go to Austin?

She couldn't. She'd have to persuade Di to go in her place.

The next few days passed in a blur of activity. Spurred by the complete vindication the telegram communicated the crews worked against time and freezing weather—bedding the ties, slapping iron down with feverish speed, erecting falsework for the bridge with abandonment. Instead of rebuilding the burned trestles, Rube set out the newly arrived diagonal truss preconstructed set, patented by a man named Post—a construction method he was fond of using when the span was short enough.

Hand-spiking the rails remained time-consuming, as usual, especially around the curves, where he insisted on using hardwood ties. But even then, she heard only jubilation. The track would be completed, with time to spare.

Almost every day someone from Silver Creek rode out to bring word of the progress at their end. The turnaround was completed, the pens and loading chutes were in place, and the only major project remaining was to finish the water and fuel stations.

Rube stayed sober and on the job, and Meg survived each day, one by one. Most of the time she successfully closed out thoughts of Kalib during the daytime, since he hadn't been a part of her life here in Hell on Wheels, except—except for that one painful night in the *Texas Star*.

And she became especially inventive at finding things to keep her away from the railcar . . . everything from helping Di to riding out to the construction train to visit with Uncle Grady.

When she returned at night to the *Texas Star*, memories of Kalib assailed her senses, beginning always with the sweet aroma of the ever-present now yellow roses, followed by Chou Ling's gourmet cooking, the clothing Delores had purchased for her, the empty room where he shaved, the rose-scented oils for her bath, the bed where they had loved and argued and loved some more.

Night by night it became more difficult for her to return to the railcar, while at the same time, she longed to relive the beautiful memories of him. Gradually her new routine became set—Di and Rube came to the *Texas Star* for supper, then she accompanied them back to the saloon for a while.

One evening when she returned to the railcar alone, bundled snugly in her cloak, she chanced to look up at the heavens. The sky was midnight blue, and the stars shone in brillant array from their patterns.

She had always delighted in studying the patterns, in watching them change with the seasons. But tonight her gaze was drawn to a solitary star. One star, apart from all the rest. Alone in the sky.

And she wondered suddenly, quite without intent, whether Kalib could see it, too. Sitting on the back steps of the railcar, she hugged her skirts about her legs and gazed at the star until her teeth began to chatter from the cold night air. As she watched, anguish more devastating than she had ever known filled her mind and weighed heavily

315

upon her heart. For she knew, wherever he was, he could see the same stars. No matter how many hundreds of miles separated them, he would always see the same sunrise, smell the same flowers, feel the same cold winters, the same hot summer days, be drenched by the same raindrops, whipped by the same wind. They would forever be united by the very world that separated them.

Heedless of the freezing wind, she sobbed into her folded arms until at last the heat of despair cooled within her, and her thoughts came back to earth.

The camphouse. Was he still there? With the inauguration not much more than a week away, he must have returned to Austin by now. But the camphouse was a part of him—a tangible part of their time together—and she might not feel so lonely there. She would ride out to the camphouse. First thing tomorrow, she would go to the camphouse.

Not until she reached the river, however, did her true purpose for returning there become clear in her mind. All along the way she had passed furiously working men— happy men—men who hailed her as she rode along the right of way. Deep inside her spirits tried to escape, but her despair was too heavy.

Painfully she recalled the excitement she always felt during the inevitable feverish rush to complete a railroad project. Kalib's shenanigans hadn't wrought this frenetic activity—it was the same during the last weeks of every job Rube ever had. The charge to the finish line was always the same. Exuberance fairly burst from the pores of each and every rust-eater, as he drove himself and his equipment beyond human limits. And Meg herself had never failed to catch the fever of the high-spirited railroaders. Until now.

Now, she found herself hard-pressed to return their greeting with a smile. How could a scant two months have turned her entire life so topsy-turvy? And how would she ever be able to right it again?

At the river she dismounted to take a drink, then stopped. While the sorrel drank from the cool water, she chastised herself for this trip, knowing now that somewhere inside her anguished soul she had expected Kalib to be here . . . to meet her at the river . . . to ride with her across the valley . . . to carry her into the camphouse . . . to . . .

With gritty determination, she mounted and rode alone across the valley. Sitting her horse atop the rise, she watched the bridge monkeys hard at work. The bridge was almost ready for the rails to be laid, she thought abstractedly.

No sign of life greeted her either outside the camphouse or inside. She pushed through the door and stood holding her hair away from her face, surveying the room where they had shared laughter and tears, truths and lies, but through it all love, always love. Now it was empty.

Not of furnishings. Apparently he had left without packing up anything. For a moment her heart soared with the thought that he would return, that she could wait right here. He would return for his belongings.

Then she reproved herself properly once more and walked through the camphouse, tears flowing freely down her face. The tea kettle still sat atop the stove, and after a while, she built a fire and fixed tea. Sitting in the chair she always took, she drank the hot, bitter liquid alone.

All this time, her mind raced from one event they had shared to another, but on a superficial plane, as though she were shielding her true feelings, protecting herself from the unbearable aloneness that awaited her.

Finally, taking quilts from the other cots, she rolled up in a ball on the cot they had shared. The poem from Burns echoed and re-echoed through her mind as she dozed and aroused time and again.

> Had we never lov'd sae blindly,
> Never met—or never parted—
> We had ne'er been broken-hearted.

Once during the night, she awakened, stoked up the fire, and returned to bed. Briefly, she thought of Rube and Di. When she'd left Hell on Wheels, she'd told Di she was going to Silver Creek. Surely, they wouldn't worry tonight.

She slept again. When the morning sun shone through the canvas top of the camphouse, bringing light and a small measure of warmth, she arose, put out the fire for good, and left, filled with renewed determination and strength.

At the top of the hill she looked back, torn for a moment by an intense desire to stay in the camphouse. But she couldn't, of course. It suddenly reminded her of a tomb. She had brought her sorrow here, and now she would leave it behind, returning only in her dreams.

In that manner, she knew, she could handle her life. Her broken heart would heal—perhaps not mend—but heal enough for her to go on with her life. Always in her dreams she could return to this remote camphouse, to a rendezvous with her mysterious, dark-eyed stranger named Kalib. For she knew beyond a doubt that he would remain an enigma—black-bearded, compassionate, and sensual. . . .

Forever in her dreams.

Chapter Seventeen

Fired by her new resolve, Meg arrived in Silver Creek somewhat revived in spirit. Maintaining this determination took a firm hand and continual supervision, however, as little reminders of Kalib stole into her mind's eye without warning.

Suddenly, for no apparent reason, his face would flash before her eyes, and she would find herself correcting the image: *No, Maggie, he shaved his beard, remember?* And, of course, the most painful of all—the emphatic tone in his voice when he uttered the last word she ever heard him say: *Never. Never. Never, my love.*

Even though his name, Governor-elect Chaney, was on everyone's lips, that name meant little to her, and there were few physical reminders of the Kalib she knew in Silver Creek. For that, she was grateful. Whenever a poignant memory assailed her, she became adept at banishing it instantly: *Tonight, Maggie. Wait until tonight, when you can be with him in your dreams.*

Rob and Jim had fallen into their own routine of cooking for the crews, so she tried not to interfere. Occasionally she baked bread, but they had arranged to buy bread fresh daily from the Widow Evans. Understanding the importance of railroad money to local economies, Meg didn't resume baking for the men.

Preparations for the joining of the rails took priority for just about everyone in town. A contest was being held to select the best original poem to be read at the festivities. The local schoolmaster asked Meg to serve as one of the judges. Hank Jefferies was the other, and they had a good time with the entries—some of which were comical, some ardent, and some . . . hopeless.

Herman Crump was put in charge of getting a band together for the ceremony. They rehearsed endlessly, or so it seemed to the Hotel O'Keefe guests, who were entertained by rehearsals twice daily in the hotel dining room.

Miracle Westfield headed up the food committee, but she had the help of all the women in the county. A barbecue dinner was to be served directly after the joining of the rails with a golden spike. Miracle was worried about the weather.

"If you'd been here in the winter of eighty-six and eighty-seven, you would understand," Davy told Meg. "That winter nearly froze the boots off everybody in Texas. Ruined a bunch of local ranchers, too. But Miracle's worrying needlessly. Weather as bad as that only comes along once in a blue moon."

Woody Woodson had been assigned to the committee to build the speaker's platform, but he spent more time in the Diamond-Stacker Palace in Hell on Wheels than he did in Silver Creek.

"Woody has a serious case of the wants," Mavis told Meg, shaking her head in amazement. "Can't recall ever seeing a grown man take a hankerin' to something, like Woody has for one of those modular saloons."

Mavis herself was in charge of the invitations, and she enlisted Meg and every other woman in town who could write plain enough to read to help her address envelopes. Almost a thousand invitations were eventually mailed, to everyone from Panhandle and South Texas ranchers, to each and every member of Governor-elect Chaney's administration, family, and friends.

"Katie and Mary Sue are coming," Hank told her one day after lunch. "They say practically all the town of Austin is making the trip, including that school chum of yours, Sara Ann Chrystal."

"How nice," Meg mused, knowing she herself would be nowhere around for the festivities. Where she would be, or for that matter, how she would get there, were yet to be determined. But she didn't intend to stay in the same state with the governor-elect any longer than she absolutely had to.

A couple of days later, Hank found Meg in Mavis's office, addressing invitations, as usual. "Put those away for a while, and take a ride with us," he suggested.

She massaged her cramped fingers. "Where to?"

"Miracle wants to ride out to the prospector's camphouse. It's close to where the ceremony will be held, and she figures if the weather turns bad, we can have the barbecue indoors. Fredericks has been out there. He says the place is enormous."

She stared at him. For an instant, aggravation rose inside her that anyone would dare invade her own private domain, the only place she had where she and Kalib could . . . quickly, she gripped her emotions. Then another thought struck her, the idea that Fredericks knew about her and Kalib, that he had told Hank, and that Hank was now baiting her. But Hank was always so open, and he sounded sincere. . . .

With a deep sigh, she gathered her wits. "These invitations really need to be finished this afternoon, Hank. They must go out on the stage tomorrow."

"It'll be a nice ride," he prompted.

Her heart beat so fast in her chest, she was sure her linen waist must flutter. "Not this time," she answered lightly. "Later, maybe. . . ."

They made the trip without her, and she soaked in Mavis's tub and took her supper in her suite and slept alone—alone with her dreams. But they were never satisfying, her dreams. Pray God, she never gave up on them, though, she thought. She'd have a hard time getting through her days without being able to convince herself of the beautiful dreams that awaited her alone in her bed after nightfall.

The next morning at breakfast Hank handed her a meerschaum pipe. "It looks like Rube's," he said. "Miracle found it beside the door of the camphouse the prospector uses. Guess it must have fallen from Rube's pocket one time when he parleyed with the man."

"Rube never met him," Meg said, turning the pipe over in her hand. "I suppose he went out there after . . . after the prospector left." She recalled telling Rube how he would like Kalib. He would have, too, she thought now. They were actually a lot alike, except for the effect liquor had on them. Kalib would have made a great railroader. Inhaling deeply, she turned her attention to her breakfast. He'll make a good governor, too, she thought fiercely. A wonderful governor, and she was so very proud of him.

With the invitations addressed and shipped off on the departing stage, Meg suddenly found herself desperate for something to occupy her hands and her mind. All over town women had turned their attentions to themselves— to their costumes for the joining of the rails, for the inauguration, to whom they would see in Austin, and the gossip they expected to hear. Specifically, reports of Governor-elect Chaney's marriage prospects were on everybody's lips. So she decided to escape to the depot and busy herself baking pies for the crews. Perhaps no one would bother her there for a few hours.

She had just begun to mix the dough, however, when a sudden chill took hold of her. A devastating sense of *déjàvu* swept up her neck, and she swirled to face the back door of the depot.

Even though she knew it wouldn't . . . couldn't . . . be Kalib, her disappointment was physically weakening. "You!" she sighed, leaning against the table. "You startled me."

Ellsworth Fredericks sauntered into the depot, apparently oblivious of the commotion he had caused inside her. She had learned, however, that nothing Fredericks did was either innocent or unintentional.

"I received an important wire from down in Austin," he

322

told her. "One I know you'll be interested in hearing about."

She stared at him with a dislike that was quickly approaching hatred. Anything he came to tell her would be about Kalib, she knew for certain. Just as she also knew she would deny, to the last, any accusation he made about the man.

"My sources down there were mighty interested in the photographs I sent them. Especially the close-up pictures of your black-bearded prospector. They feel sure they can identify him for me."

Shrugging, she returned to her baking, but her fingers trembled on the dough. Slapping it furiously this way and that, she shaped a large wad into a ball and began rolling out the pie crust.

"They didn't tell me who they suspect the culprit to be, but they're sending photographic proof by rail to Summer Valley. The evidence should get to me in time for this week's paper."

"Mr. Fredericks," she hissed. "I'm not interested—not in the least—in your sensationalism. Nothing you print— I repeat, nothing—will ever interest me again. After your slanderous articles about Rube, how could you expect me to even read the *Sun*, much less believe anything you print in it?"

A few mornings later, she awoke with a entirely new mission. She must go to Hell on Wheels today and persuade Di to accompany Rube to Austin tomorrow. She had purposely waited until the last minute, hoping to give them time away from her. If she surprised them with her request, and if she made it appear she was needed in Silver Creek for the next week, perhaps Di would agree.

Braced against the memories this trip held for her, she concentrated on the progress of the railroads and arrived in Hell on Wheels in record time. After stabling the sorrel, she went directly to the *Texas Star* to alert Chou Ling to expect three for supper.

The first thing she saw upon entering the salon were the

323

yellow roses, fresh and lovely, and carrying such poignant memories that she, once again, held one against her lips and wept.

But briefly. Too much was at stake for her to go to pieces now. Her future sanity depended on Di's making the trip to Austin in her place.

"There'll be three for supper, Chou Ling," she told him, "Rube, Di and myself. Could we have some of your oyster soup to begin with? Di especially loves your oyster soup."

"Yes, miss. Perhaps beefsteak with *champignons*, potatoes stewed in cream, and trifle with ice cream for dessert. Is that agreeable?"

"Oh, yes, that's fine," she told him, wondering what he knew about Kalib, how much he would tell her, were she to ask. "While I bathe, would you please send word to them at the Diamond-Stacker?"

"Yes, miss," he bowed.

"Chou Ling?" she asked suddenly. "How long have you been with Kalib?"

He grinned from ear to ear. "Ten years, miss. A fine man, Mr. Kalib."

"Ten years?" she mused, thinking of her own few short months with him. How much more could she grow to love the man if they had ten years together? "You've cooked for him for ten years?"

"Cook and . . ." He frowned, then chopped the air in sharp, vicious swipes.

Her eyes widened. "Body guard?" she asked the frail little man.

He nodded happily and bowed again. "Body guard. For you, too. He send me to protect you from . . ." Flinging his arms wide, he included the entire terminus town.

She laughed. "I'll just bet he did."

Later, as she soaked in the rose-scented oils, her tears returned, but again only briefly, and she was suddenly gripped by the sure knowledge that the rest of her life would be plagued by tears for Kalib . . . for the love they had shared . . . and lost. . . .

Had we never lov'd sae kindly,
Had we never lov'd sae blindly,
Never met—and never parted—
We had ne'er been broken-hearted.

Toweling off, she chose a costume for dinner with a sense of reverence, knowing who had provided them. She wondered how many of the girls from school, girls who, with her, had swooned over Burns's poetry, would discover the same dreadful truth she had learned—that in reality broken hearts are much more devastating than they are romantic.

When Di and Rube arrived for supper, Meg could tell immediately that something was up. They were both so skittish they had trouble sitting still. Rube carried a bottle of ginger ale.

"For a toast," he told her with an unusual twinkle in his eyes. "Do you think you can scare up some champagne glasses?"

"Oh, yes," she answered, recalling instantly the glasses she and Kalib had used. Chou Ling brought three and a bucket filled with ice.

Rube twirled the ginger ale in the bucket, and Meg watched him, wondering if he was trying to impress her with his "temperance" drinks.

"Di and I have a little surprise for you, sugar." He poured three glasses of ginger ale. It was still warm and the foam rose quickly, but he appeared not to notice. Sitting on the banquette between them, he took Di's hand in his, then raised his glass in a toast. "We're going to get married."

Meg's mouth flew open. "Oh, Rube! That's wonderfull!" She hugged him first, then Di.

"Are you sure, Meg?" Di asked.

"Of course, I'm sure. You should have done it a long time ago."

"I've been telling her the same thing all these years," Rube said, "but she wouldn't. Said it wouldn't be right for you, her owning a saloon and all."

"Di . . ." Meg began.

Di sighed. "I can see now how wrong I was, dear. You needed a real family. . . ."

"I've had a family," Meg objected. "The three of us—we're a family."

"Not in the true sense," Di argued. "We weren't . . . well, you didn't learn by example how important it is for a man and woman to . . ." She stopped and gulped a swallow of ginger ale.

Meg refilled all three glasses. She could see a reflection of her own flushed face on both of theirs. "I always knew you loved me," she told Di. "You've been like my very own mother."

Di smiled ruefully. "Thank you, dear. I certainly couldn't have loved a daughter of my own flesh and blood any more than I love you. But that isn't the point at all."

"You appear to be having a bit of a problem getting ahead with your own life," Rube said.

Meg's eyes flew open. Her mouth went suddenly dry. She could talk about their situation all day, but hers . . . hers was over and done with. No amount of talking could straighten it out.

"What I'm getting at . . ." he began.

"I know what you're getting at, Rube." She inhaled deeply and studied the yellow roses. "But it's all over."

"It isn't so easy, sugar. Turning feelings on and off. . . ."

Smiling at first one, then the other, she tried desperately to hold her emotions in tack. "He has his own life. If he didn't, well," shrugging, she continued, "if his situation were different, he could have worked for the railroad, but as things turned out, it . . . it just isn't possible."

"Meg," Di said softly, "that's what we mean. You can't expect to live your whole life on the railroad. Perhaps . . . perhaps you'll find someone who isn't a part of this life. If that happens, you'll have to follow him. You'll have to follow your heart."

Stop! she cried inside, as anguish rose hot and fierce. *Stop!* What would they say if she told them about Kalib?

Would they expect her to run straight from Hell on Wheels to the Governor's Mansion without so much as a curtsy in between?

"That's why we sent you to such a good school," Di said, as if she had been privy to Meg's very thoughts. "We wanted you to be able to take your place in life, wherever that place turns out to be . . . wherever . . ."

Meg knelt quickly before them. "Di . . . Rube, listen to me. You're worrying needlessly. Kalib and I . . . well, there was nothing between us, except *my* own fantasies. I came back from school with a head full of romantic poetry, and . . . well, that's all it was. When the time comes . . ." Pausing, she squeezed the tears back. "We can talk about this when the right person comes along. But now, Chou Ling has prepared a celebration meal, and we have a lot to celebrate."

They ate, and she soon turned them away from her problems to their plans. When Chou Ling served the coffee, she remembered Rube's meerschaum and retrieved it from her bedchamber. "Hank and some of the Silver Creek people went out to the camphouse to look it over before the rail-joining celebration. Look what they found."

Rube stared, round-eyed. Taking the pipe, he turned it over in his hand. "I couldn't figure where I lost it."

"It must have fallen out of your pocket when you investigated the camphouse," she told him, occupying herself with her serving of trifle and ice cream.

"Of course, Rube," Di said gaily. "When you finally got a chance to go out there, after the prospector left, it must have fallen from your pocket."

Rube filled and lighted his meerschaum, and Meg found the courage to discuss the inauguration.

"Since you and Rube are to be married," she began, "you must go in my place, Di. You have shopping to do. And the two of you can enjoy the festivities together."

"Oh, no," Di refused. "This is your trip. You have friends in Austin, and I want you to go and have a good time. You've had enough heartaches—with the railroad and otherwise. You need a change. You can see your friends. Rube and I want you to go."

Meg had trouble swallowing her coffee, thinking on the difficulties she would encounter in Austin. "I really can't go," she pleaded. "The Silver Creek people need me to help finish preparations for our festivities here. The joining of the rails will be only a couple of weeks later."

Di smiled. "They'll get along fine without you, dear. In fact, most of them will be in Austin, too."

"But you and Rube could . . ."

Di and Rube exchanged determined glances. "Looks like we'll have to tell her the rest of our secret," Rube said.

Di nodded. "I have some important business to tend to here."

Meg cocked her head, waiting. Her mind spun with the turmoil a trip to Austin would bring. Why were they being so obstinate?

"I've decided to sell the Diamond-Stacker to Woody Woodson," Di told her. "The paperwork is being drawn up right now. This coming week I must see to packing things up. We want to be able to move the saloon into Silver Creek as soon as the rails are joined. . . ."

Meg stared, aghast. "You're selling . . . ?"

Di nodded, and Rube cleared his throat. "Looks like we'll do just about anything to convince you we mean business, doesn't it, sugar?"

She frowned.

"Without the saloon, I won't be living so near temptation, and you won't have so much to worry about."

"You mean you're doing all this to get rid of me?" Meg cried, looking from one to the other of them. "If it weren't so serious, it'd be funny. You can't sell the saloon, Di. It's your life. . . ."

"Rube is my life, Meg." Di's voice carried a quiet tenderness that set Meg's heart to fluttering. She understood those feelings. She understood them instantly, way down deep inside her aching heart.

"He has been for many years," Di continued. "Now I intend to heed your advice and do everything I can to help him stay away from Demon Rum. I also understand how wrong we were to try to hide our feelings for each other from you, dear."

Meg knew when she was outnumbered. Rube and Di left early, and she began to plan for the trip to Austin. How would she ever make it through these next few days? She couldn't attend the inauguration. She couldn't see Kalib. For to see him would be disaster now.

Despair hung over her like a pall. Wherever she looked, she found reasons *not* to go to Austin. She didn't even have any of her own clothing, since she had returned from Silver Creek determined to convince Di to make the trip in her place.

The only clothing she had was what Kalib had provided. And if she wore those costumes in Austin, how would she return them to him? After this trip, she and Rube were to leave the *Texas Star* in Austin and return to Summer Valley by commercial car, then from there to Hell on Wheels on the service train. How would she . . . ?

What would she do? Suddenly, Kalib's words came to her—the words he had spoken in the camphouse when last they had loved there. Soothing words . . . comforting words. . . .

"It'll work out, Maggie. Trust me."

But it hadn't worked out. Nothing worked out. His resonant, soothing voice faded beneath the reality of the words. Untrue words! False promises! Lies!

Throwing open the door to the wardrobe, she buried her face in the clothing, smoothing the soft silks and cashmeres over her skin. Inside, her body ached to feel the mere touch of him.

Racing across the hallway, she pulled open the door to the wardrobe there and stared abjectly at the green velvet smoking jacket. With trembling fingers, she stroked the sleeve, the collar, finding the slit where he had secured the yellow rose . . . now crisp and withered.

Withered like their love . . . like her life. Soon all these reminders of the fantasy they shared would be gone. Soon she would be free of all tangible memories of the stranger she knew as Kalib.

Going room by room then, she studied every item in the railcar, committing it to memory. In three days' time the *Texas Star* would be but a memory, and she intended to hold every inch of it in her heart forever. In the morning Rube would move his belongings into the spare room—she returned to the doorway, where she stood a moment, then crossed and ran her hand over the smooth, cool wood of the bureau where Kalib's beard had lain the night he shaved. Memories. So many memories.

Chou Ling was still in the galley when she went there, so she requested tea, and sat alone in the salon, drinking it and thinking of Kalib and all the things he had done for her . . . and to her . . . and with her.

Briefly she imagined what her life would be like as his wife. By this time he'd probably already forgotten his interlude with her. Not that he hadn't been sincere at the time. She knew he had, and she loved him for that.

But she also recalled in precise detail the kind of girls she had attended school with. Sara Ann, dear as she was, was a society girl—born and bred to the position, as were all five of Kalib's sisters, she was sure, and his mother and grandmother. To say nothing of all his friends' wives and mothers and sisters and sweethearts.

By now he would be immersed in the inauguration festivities with his own social circle. His sojourn here in the hills of Silver Creek was very likely already a thing of the past.

Well, she would take precautions not to see him, she consoled herself. She couldn't bear to see rejection on his face. Their final parting was painful enough, but that pain would eventually fade beneath her sweet memories. A rejection in Austin would be much harder to erase from her mind.

Returning to the bedchamber, she took out the beige cashmere nightdress and velvet caftan she had worn their last night together. Almost reverently, she disrobed and put these garments on her trembling body.

Somehow she felt the need to indulge in a last bit of—

not self-pity, she thought hastily—it was more like homage, an attempt to honor this thing of immense joy and beauty that had been briefly a part of her life.

Or a futile effort to cling to the past, she admitted, settling herself against the plush blue brocade pillow on her bed. She had just picked up her volume of Burns's collected poetry, when a loud noise sounded at the front of the railcar. Jumping to her feet, she raced to the door of her bedchamber.

Chou Ling hurried down the hallway. "I answer the door, miss."

She smiled, warmed by this lingering evidence of Kalib's concern for her. Before her smile had died on her lips, Chou Ling returned carrying a newspaper.

"For you," he said, and bowing, he exited.

"Good night, Chou Ling." Crossing to the lamp beside her bed, she studied the newspaper, while anxiety began to churn like worms in her stomach. Sinking to the bed, she read the lead story in tomorrow's edition of the *Silver Creek Sun*.

"That damned Ellsworth Fredericks," she swore aloud. The headlines screamed the truth—*Prospector Who Holds Up Railroad Identified As Governor-elect Chaney*.

Beneath the headlines were two photographs. One of the bearded Kalib, heaving, hands on knees, staring straight into the camera—actually, Meg recalled, holding a wisp of hair back from her eyes, he was staring straight at Portis Flannery.

Tears blurred her vision as she lovingly studied the other photograph, a studio portrait of the governor-elect . . . her own dear Kalib, without his magnificent beard.

Chapter Eighteen

Meg awoke the next morning to commotion outside the railcar. Gradually the trip she faced this day came into focus. The very thought of it weighed as heavily upon her as the pile of quilts warming her body. But inside she felt cold as ice, and empty.

And she shouldn't. She should feel a sense of fulfillment, she admonished herself. Thanks to her efforts, the spur was completed in ample time to satisfy Leslie Hayden and his stockholders down in Austin. As a result, Rube's future with the railroad should be secure. Tomorrow, she would stand proudly beside him while he presented evidence of his success to the stockholders, and hopefully, before the day was out, he would be offered a new and better job. Wasn't that what her mission here had been about?

Had been, she sighed, burrowing further beneath the warm covers. Until Kalib. Until Kalib filled her life with love . . . then left her empty and so alone. How one person could have created such intense emotion inside her, she was sure she would never understand. Their entire time together had been like being tossed upon a rough sea—loving and arguing, laughing and crying, scheming for and against each other.

Tears formed behind her eyelids, and she bit her lip, holding back tears, holding inside her deepening gloom. How could one person have changed her life so completely in such a short time? Had Robert Burns felt the pain of unrequited love? she wondered. How else could he have written so stirringly of the changes such a hopeless love would bring?

> Had we never lov'd sae kindly,
> Had we never lov'd sae blindly. . . .

Destroyed was more like it, she thought desperately. More than changed, her life had been destroyed.

Well, perhaps she was being a bit dramatic, she admitted, throwing back the covers and reaching for her caftan. Only her future happiness had been destroyed. Unfortunately, her life would go on.

The feel of the caftan aroused even more indignation within her. Stomping to the wardrobe, she searched for something to put on her cold body . . . something that wouldn't remind her of *him*. Everything here reminded her of *him*.

Tears poured from her eyes then, and she sank back to the bed and held her head in her hands and wept. How was she to bear it? Being in the same town with him, hearing his name on everyone's lips, seeing his likeness on the front page of every newspaper and not being able to see him? To talk to him? To . . . ?

Noise in the salon alerted her, and she quickly dried her eyes. She *would* do it, she assured herself. Her nerves were as taut as violin strings, but she would somehow manage to restrain her tendency to fly apart at the slightest barb. Forewarned, she reminded herself. She knew the journey would be difficult, so she would arrive prepared to handle any possible situation.

"I know it's early, sugar," Rube called down the hallway. "But since we'll have to stop three or four times between here and Austin to take on water and fuel, we should get an early start."

Choosing a simple striped dress of rose, green, and brown silk, with vandykes of white Irish guipure lace at the waist and edging the cuffs, she hurriedly completed

333

her toilette and took a simple breakfast of flapjacks with honey and strawberries, accompanied by Rube and Di.

"I wish you would reconsider, Di," Meg told her. "I'd much prefer packing up the Diamond-Stacker to taking this trip."

Rube shook his head. "Not this time, sugar. You and your ol' pa are going to have a fine time down in Austin. Besides, I'm leaving Di with an extra chore." Reaching over, he squeezed Di's hand in a gesture that caused Meg's heart to flutter. "I want you to have our wedding planned by the time Meg and I return. Why don't we have one final fling in the Old Diamond-Stacker before Woody carries it off to Silver Creek—like a wedding?"

Di gasped. "Why, Rube, what a marvelous idea." She smiled at Meg. "You didn't know he was such a romantic old codger, did you, dear?"

Chou Ling finished the dishes. Then, while he secured everything against possible damage on the trip and the engineer turned the short train about on the turnaround, Meg accompanied Di to the Diamond-Stacker for some belongings Rube had left behind.

"The best medicine for a broken heart, Meg, is a change of scenery. So you go down to Austin and have a good time. You've made some nice friends, and they'll help you forget your troubles."

Uncle Grady waited near the rear platform of the *Texas Star* when she returned. He gave her a bear hug before she climbed on board. "I'm mighty curious to see how you make out with old Hayden." He grinned, sweeping an arm toward the railcar. "After all this, I'm expecting big things of the man. He wouldn't have provided these fancy accommodations if he didn't have something special in store for Rube."

Meg blanched. "You're right," she answered ruefully. How could she have been so dim-witted? She hadn't even thought what it would look like for Rube to go into the stockholders' meeting ignorant of Kalib's role in the *Texas Star*. With a heavy sigh, she kissed Uncle Grady, then Di, and climbed onto platform. She'd have to tell him. Sometime during the next six hours, she would have to tell him the truth.

"Miss Meg! Wait up!"

The high-pitched voice cut through her like the north wind. She squinted at Ellsworth Fredericks from beneath furrowed brows. "I can hardly control the engine from here, Mr. Fredericks."

His wily grin never faltered beneath her scathing remark. Outstretching his arm, he fluttered a copy of his newspaper in her face. "Did you get the copy I sent you last night?"

She glowered at him, then a slow smile creased her mouth. "Yes, thank you."

"Well, what about it?"

She cocked her head, mindful of the crowd gathered to see Rube off. "What about what, Mr. Fredericks?"

His cocky grin broadened. "Don't play simple-minded maiden with me, Miss Meg. You knew who he was all along, didn't you?"

"No," she called above the whistle of the little diamond-stacker engine. "No, I didn't, Mr. Fredericks. And I still don't. You'd have to be dim-witted to think those two photographs bear even the faintest resemblance to each other."

The short train—engine, one luxurious traveling car, and a caboose—pulled away from the siding and chugged eastward on the route toward Summer Valley. Meg waved to Di and Uncle Grady. From the corner of her eye she saw Ellsworth Fredericks distributing copies of his newspaper and babbling to all around, babble concerning the lead story of his sleazy paper, she had no doubt.

Rube squeezed her around the waist. "We'd better go inside, sugar," he suggested, leading her toward the salon. Inside, she noticed he held a copy of the *Silver Creek Sun* in his other hand.

They sat on banquettes facing each other. While Rube read the *Sun*, she peered around in an agitated fashion. Chou Ling had battened down the salon in such a way that she felt she was in a new and strange place. The dining table, stripped of its linen cloth, had its leaves dropped, and now stood latched securely in place against one of the walls. Even the roses—the ever-present red, then yellow roses—were nowhere to be seen.

In a few minutes Chou Ling appeared with two small trays, which he hooked onto one side of each banquette. "Would you care for coffee now, miss?"

Glancing at Rube, she caught him staring at her with such tenderness that tears formed in her eyes. "Yes, Chou, that would be nice. For both of us."

Chou Ling brought their coffee and left them alone, and Meg knew she must find the courage to tell Rube about Kalib. Rube himself broached the subject.

"Is this true, sugar?" He thumped the newspaper with the bowl of his meerschaum. "Or is Fredericks up to more of his shenanigans?"

"It's true," she answered slowly, running her tongue around inside her gums. "I didn't know it until. . . ." Tearing her eyes from his, she looked out the window at the passing landscape. Everything was brown from winter, rocky and barren, like her very soul, she thought desperately.

"He came here . . . to the railcar . . . New Year's Eve night. That's the first I knew."

Rube cleared his throat and studied the newspaper. "He's a right handsome man," he said, as though he could think of nothing else to say.

"Handsome is as handsome does," Meg retorted. "How could you find anything good to say about someone who caused you so much trouble?"

Rube shrugged. "He appears to have caused you more trouble than anyone. Did he satisfy your mind as to why?"

Turning back to the interior of the salon, she sipped the coffee. "Yes," she whispered, then she told Rube the story of Kalib's grandfather, and the promise he had made his grandmother.

"Did he find the lost mine?"

She shrugged. "He said he found proof that something like a silver mine actually existed. That's all he was looking for." Suddenly, her voice became desperate, pleading. "You do understand why he had to take such extraordinary measures not to be found out?"

Rube nodded. "Reckon it wouldn't do for the governor of Texas to be caught treasure hunting. Wouldn't be stately."

The day wore on. She rested for a while on the blue brocade-covered bed, while melancholy overcame her at the thought that soon she would leave this place—the one place left to her where memories of Kalib remained tangible.

For luncheon Chou Ling served sandwiches of roast beef, assorted cheeses, and pound cake. Afterwards, she requested tea, desperate to relive one last time this ritual they had shared.

Over tea she finally found the courage to tell Rube about the *Texas Star*. "There's something else you need to know about Kalib before we arrive in Austin," she said.

Rube looked at her, waiting, and she continued. "He's responsible for . . ." she swept her arms about the room, ". . . for all this. Leslie Hayden didn't send the *Texas Star* for our use, Kalib did."

At Rube's frown, she explained. "I told you he didn't think it was safe for me to stay in the Diamond-Stacker." She shrugged helplessly. "He rented this car from Hayden. Chou Ling is his own personal chef and . . ." Looking at Rube, she smiled in spite of her gloom. "Chou Ling is not only an accomplished chef, he's also my body guard. Can you believe it? After spending twenty-two years in terminus towns, someone comes along and thinks I need a body guard."

Rube puffed on his meerschaum thoughtfully. "I can believe it, sugar. If a man loves a woman enough, he'll do most anything to keep her safe from harm."

Pushing a strand of hair back from her face, Meg turned quickly to the window. Her heart raced, and it was with only the greatest effort that she was able to keep from crying. *If a man loves a woman . . . Would it were so simple.*

"What's a puzzlement, though, is why he worked so

337

hard to win you over, and then walked out on you like he did."

Her eyes flew open. "He didn't walk out on me."

"Then what are your plans?"

"We have no plans, Rube. He's the governor. Or he will be, this time tomorrow." The finality of the statement, of actually placing the facts of their lives in a time frame of less than twenty-four hours, caught her unawares, and a tear rolled unchecked down her cheek.

Then several, and before she knew it she was crying silently. "He'll make a good governor," she whispered, staring intently out the window.

"And you'd make him a good partner," Rube told her.

She didn't reply, and after a few moments he spoke again. "Of course, if you're dead set on having a railroad man, we'll have to get busy and find one for you. I can understand if railroading is in your blood; it's all you've ever known." He paused, tamped his pipe, and drew hard on it. "I imagine building a state would be nearly as exciting as building a railroad, but . . ."

"Oh, Rube, stop it! Just stop it!" she cried. Rising, she went to her bedchamber, where she stayed until Chou Ling came through the hallway announcing their imminent arrival in Austin.

Packing hastily, she again wondered how she could return the clothing she must take along to the hotel to wear tomorrow. Perhaps, she could find a chance to shop for something to wear back to Silver Creek. Then she could return these garments to the railcar before they left Austin.

They arrived in Austin near dusk. Although Leslie Hayden himself didn't meet Rube and Meg at the railway station, he sent a carriage to transport them to the Driskill Hotel on Congress Avenue, just down the street from the Capitol itself.

The evening air was cool and dry as they rode through festive crowds of Texans gathered for the numerous celebrations preceding tomorrow's inauguration. The carriage passed along West Tenth Street and turned onto

Colorado. The pink granite Capitol building rose to their left. Only two years old, the grounds still showed scars here and there from the construction. Looking skyward, Meg glimpsed the Goddess of Liberty standing high above the Capitol dome in all her Grecian splendor, holding aloft the five-pointed star Meg had learned symbolized the state of Texas. Hank had a photograph in his office of the Capitol dedication ceremonies of two years ago. At that time the goddess had yet to be placed atop the dome, and a group of Silver Creek citizens had gathered around her where she stood on the grounds for a photograph.

So this was it. Her stomach churned with a quivering combination of desolation and pride. The driver directed their attention to the platform already festooned with red, white, and blue bunting in front of the building where the governor would take the oath of office tomorrow. She stared long, picturing him there now, for she certainly wouldn't see him in real life tomorrow. Suddenly, she wondered what he would wear to the ceremony. All she'd ever seen him in were his work clothes . . . and that elegant green velvet smoking jacket.

"Over there's the Governor's Mansion," the driver called above her thoughts. Turning in her seat, she glanced to the right, and this time she thought she might actually swoon. Her head swam with unwanted visions as she stared at the enormous white colonial home built in the Greek Revival style.

"Been home to Texas governors since the eighteen fifties," the driver told them, "and Chaney is sure enough making a spectacle of himself over it."

"How's that," Rube asked.

"Won't move in there," the driver responded. "He refuses to move out of his bachelor apartment. Says the Mansion is a family home, and until he has a bride to carry over the threshold, he won't set foot inside. He's causing quite a stir, let me tell you, especially among the mothers of our young ladies. I'll wager he'll have the mother of every eligible girl in Texas camping out on his doorstep, if he doesn't make a choice soon."

Reaching over, Rube squeezed Meg's trembling fingers in his strong hand. "Maybe a few fathers, too," he whispered.

She gripped his hand tightly, knowing all the while the signal she was giving him. Later, she could recant her feelings. Later, when she'd had time to recover from this unexpected and very unwelcome glimpse into Kalib's life.

The Santa Fe had reserved a suite for them, and with less trouble than she expected, she persuaded Rube to have their supper sent up. The hotel was aswarm with politicians and outlanders arriving for the ceremonies and parties. In their suite they found an envelope with four tickets to every event, including a ball being held here in the Driskill this very night, seats with the Santa Fe directors at the inauguration tomorrow, and the inauguration ball, which would be held in the Capitol rotunda tomorrow night.

"Why four tickets to everything?" she wondered absently.

Rube shrugged. "Perhaps they figured we'd bring Grady and Di along."

That night when Meg tumbled into bed, her taut body reminded her of the replica of the statue she had seen downstairs, a miniature Goddess of Liberty. With a tremendous effort, she managed to keep her thoughts on the details of the stockholders' meeting and on plans for Rube's future jobs with the railroad. Next, she thought of Di and Rube, and in her mind she planned their wedding in Diamond-Stacker; she thought of Hank and Mary Sue and their wedding; of the other Silver Creek people she and Rube were suppose to picnic with tomorrow on the Capitol grounds; of Katie Jefferies . . . of Sara Ann Chrystal. And that last thought always led back to Kalib and the Governor's Mansion. She thought of Kalib and herself, and of loneliness. Loneliness.

He wouldn't remain lonely long, she knew. Some Texas mother would have her way; Kalib wouldn't be lonely long. He'll soon get over you, she cried into the crisp pillowcase. If he hasn't already, he'll soon find someone to carry over the threshold of the Governor's Mansion . . . someone to laugh with and argue with and hold and . . . and love.

The following morning found her tumbled up and completely out of sorts. She recalled the previous morning when she had arisen angry with the world. Today was the day she had dreaded, even then. Now it had dawned, clear and cool.

And it would end, she whispered into the looking glass. If she could keep that single thought before her all day long, she would make it. This day would end. This day would end.

Withdrawing the costume she had chosen from the *Texas Star* wardrobe, she dressed carefully, keeping her mind, as much as humanly possible, on what this day meant to Rube's future.

Combining a street costume with a visiting dress, the garment she chose intrigued her even through her gloom. The outer dress was of black silk twill. It buttoned diagonally across her bosom ending with a single black button at the waist. The skirt lay flat across the front, with graceful folds down each side, and was banded with a wide row of self ruching. When indoors, she could unbutton the dress, fold the revers back, and attach them with invisible hooks to reveal a pale old-rose silk gown draped gracefully across the bosom, with black embroidery along the revers and across the bottom. The ruching hooked cleverly to one of the folds at either side of the skirt to provide more glimpses of the rose silk underskirt.

With trembling fingers, she coiffed her hair into a pompadour and topped it with a black silk hat, trimmed with rose-colored feathers.

Rube whistled when she stepped from her bedroom into their parlor. "Now, that's quite a get-up! You'll knock the shareholders' caps off, for sure."

"Thanks, Rube." She pecked him on the cheek and took up her parasol. "Shouldn't we be going?"

The shareholders' meeting was held on the top floor of the Tips Hardware Building only a few blocks from the

341

Driskill, so they walked. The air was cool and crisp, and the sun already shone brightly from the winter sky. A perfect day, she thought somberly. Her perfect day. Rube's.

And Kalib's.

Tight-lipped Leslie Hayden awaited them with a smile in the colonnade, which he told them proudly had been constructed of Civil War shell casings. Taking her arm, he led them to the third floor of the ornate building, to rooms he told them Walter Tips provided for the Austin Library Association's use for concerts, plays, and poetry readings. She'd never seen Hayden so cordial. Pumping Rube's hand, he complimented him on a job well done, then he turned his attention to Meg.

"My, my, Miss Britton, you are certainly a sight for sore eyes. A fetching gown, if I may be so bold. And you were right about your old man, here. Didn't he do us proud? The governor is elated." He ushered them through the wide double doors into a room of overpowering walnut paneling, filled with furniture, and hung with burgundy velvet draperies and carpeting. "But, of course, you already know his feelings. You should have told me of your close personal relationship with . . ."

Her heart suddenly stopped in her breast. She had prepared herself for hearing Kalib's name at every turn today, but she certainly didn't intend to stand by and let Leslie "Rattlesnake" Hayden get away with such unseemly remarks. "My what?" she demanded.

He frowned. "Why, your and Rube's friendship with the governor," he said. "When we were . . . uh, negotiating the spur last summer, I had no idea Governor-elect Chaney was a personal friend of the family."

Quite without warning, she found her pain suppressed by rising fury. "Would it have made a difference, Mr. Hayden?" she questioned.

"Well, the governor certainly carries weight," he admitted. "Besides, since he is as dead set on railroad reform as he is, it would not have been good business to irritate him."

Inhaling a deep breath, she dredged up a bit of reason and smiled blandly. "Rube's work speaks for itself, Mr. Hayden. We don't believe in calling on personal friendships, however elevated in stature."

Hayden held her chair, and she sank into it, while memories of long ago and faraway drifted unbidden through her mind. Kalib's words when they waltzed beneath the pecan trees the night of the Christmas Ball— *"Always remember this night, Maggie,"* he had said. *"No matter what grand ballroom we find ourselves dancing in, no matter how elevated the company or our station in life, always remember where we first danced."*

Her mind buzzed. The words swam before her eyes. Now, she knew what he meant. At last she understood, and in understanding, she found herself on the outside of his world, looking wistfully in. In her mind's eye she envisioned them swirling beneath the giant dome in the great rotunda of the new Capitol—a place she would never even see.

Elevated company, she sighed. The only good his elevated company brought her was a favorable word from Leslie Hayden for Rube.

Sipping from the crystal glass of water set before her, she tried to banish the bitter taste in her mouth. Wasn't that what she had set out to accomplish in the first place—to elevate Rube's standing with Leslie Hayden?

The president of the Santa Fe Railroad took his place at the head of the long walnut table and called the meeting to order. Meg inhaled a deep breath. Rube was nervous, she could tell from the twitch in his jaw. Reaching over she patted his hand as it lay in his lap. They exchanged brief, encouraging glances, and pangs of guilt struck her conscience. Here she was worrying over her own lost cause, while Rube needed her.

His nervousness didn't last long, however, as one by one the directors and stockholders praised his work, beginning with the president himself, then the first vice-president, the second vice-president, the third vice-president, all the way down to the comptroller and the general counsel.

343

"Now, Hayden," the president boomed to the far end of the table. "Why don't you tell Britton what we have in mind?"

Leslie Hayden rose, filled with his own importance. Happily, Meg thought, today it served his purposes to be cordial to Rube. As the man spoke, she reworded her thoughts—more than cordial, Hayden was downright enthusiastic.

"We're offering you your pick of three of the best jobs in railroading today," he told Rube. "There's a couple of years' worth of work on the line from Denver to Los Angeles, California; or you can take one of the lines out of Kansas City; or if you'd rather stay in Texas for a while, we're heading from below Fort Worth through Oklahoma, Arkansas, and on into St. Louis. The choice is yours."

Meg bit her bottom lip between her teeth to keep from shouting for joy. He'd made it! Rube Britton was back on top of the railroad world! Back in charge of his own life!

Rube cleared his throat and took a swallow of water. He looked at Meg, then around the table, as though sizing up the stockholders. Each and every man wore a broad, welcoming smile. "How soon do you need an answer?"

"We're ready to roll on all three projects," Hayden told him.

"I need a little time to consider," Rube said, studying the men individually again. "Fact is, gentlemen, I'm planning on taking me a wife soon as I return to Hell on Wheels, and I'd like the little lady to have a say-so in where she'll be living these next few years."

Congratulations and knowing grunts came from around the table. Hayden still smiled, Meg was relieved to see. "We can spare you a couple of weeks for your decision," Hayden agreed.

"I'll be needing some extra accommodations, with a wife and all," Rube told them. "Nothing as fancy as the *Texas Star*, mind you. But a comfortable railcar we can set up housekeeping in."

Hayden looked toward the president, who nodded. "We'll fix you up, Rube," Hayden answered. "Think

344

you'll have an answer by the joining of the rails?"

"Sure thing," Rube replied.

The meeting adjourned soon after, and Rube was rushed by stockholders complimenting him on his style in completing the Silver Creek project.

"Joining the rails was a damned fine move, Britton," one gentleman told him. "Count on us all being there, along with a goodly portion of the Texas press corps."

"Why, Chaney is so impressed, he's making this speech his first major address on proposed railroad legislation."

Rube beamed and Meg was so proud for him. Her jitters didn't return until they stepped from the building onto Congress Avenue, where the inaugural parade had passed a bare half-hour before. Suddenly she knew if she were to see him she would die.

"I can't go to the picnic, Rube. You go ahead, and I'll . . ."

He pulled her hand through a crook in his elbow. "Now, sugar, it'll be just fine. Your friends are expecting you. . . ."

"Rube," she objected through a stricken throat. "By now they've all seen Fredericks' photographs. Why, Fredericks himself will probably be there, and . . ."

"They've likely read the article and seen the photographs," he agreed. "But they don't know anything beyond what the paper says. Besides, the chances of running into the governor on the Capitol grounds a mere two hours before he gives his inaugural speech—which is what's really troubling you—are slim to none. Why, you know derned well, he's off somewhere dining on caviar and practicing his speech.

Rube was right, she was sure. And even if Kalib did wander about in the crowd, why, there were thousands of people on the grounds by now. The chances of seeing him, as Rube said, were next to nothing. Planting her feet firmly on the boardwalk, she jerked on his arm until he turned around to face her.

"If I agree to go to the picnic," she said, "will you do something for me afterwards?"

345

"What's that, sugar?"

"Yesterday when we arrived, I checked the railway schedules. A train leaves the station for Summer Valley and points north at four o'clock this afternoon. Can we take it?"

He stared at her. "Your friends . . ."

"My friends will be talking of nothing but the inauguration and the ball and . . . and . . . oh, Rube, I couldn't bear it."

He shrugged and patted her fingers. "All right, sugar. We'll leave directly after the picnic, if you're sure. You don't want to hear . . . ?"

"No," she answered sharply. She didn't want to hear the address, because she didn't want to hear his voice. She didn't want to see him take the oath, because . . . she swallowed against unwanted thoughts . . . because he had asked her to stand beside him . . . to hold the Bible . . . and she couldn't bear to see someone stand in her place.

In *her* place! Her stomach writhed inside her, as they climbed the steep hill in front of the Capitol, surrounded on all sides by revelers.

Just when she took hope in the idea they would never be able locate the Silver Creek party and would have to turn back, she spied Hank Jefferies standing on a large slab of granite waving both hands above his head.

The Silver Creek group consisted of twelve adults, and so many children, darting in and around the area with such quickness that Meg wasn't sure how many there were or even whether they all belonged to her friends. The adults were seated around several colorful pieced quilts that were heaped with every kind of picnic fare imaginable. As she had both feared and expected, their topic of conversation was Ellsworth Fredericks' lead story in the *Silver Creek Sun*.

"Did you see it before you left, Meg?" Mavis O'Keefe asked. Meg nodded, busying herself with a boiled chicken sandwich someone handed her, and Mavis continued. "Imagine, the governor disguised as a prospector. . . ."

"And giving you such hell, Rube," the judge, Quint

346

Jarvis, spoke up. "I imagine you're glad all that's behind you."

While they talked, Meg chanced a look at Hank, the only person in the group who suspected she might have met the prospector, but Mary Sue had his ear as well as his undivided attention, and he appeared oblivious of everything else.

"Where is Mr. Fredericks?" Meg asked at last. "I never imagined you would be able to get away without him."

The group laughed, and Miracle Westfield answered the question. "We didn't. He's off somewhere dogging the governor-elect. You don't think he would spend time with hometown folk?"

Meg laughed, too, and felt herself relax a bit. After everyone had eaten more than enough, Rube leaned back against the trunk of one of the smaller oak trees and took out his meerschaum. The other men in the group did the same.

"Tell us how the stockholders' meeting went, Britton," Jed Varner suggested.

The women busied themselves covering food, and those who had them tended to children.

Suddenly Katie jumped to her feet. "Come on, Meg. You too, Hank and Mary Sue. You can lie around when you get to be old folks. Let's go see what we're missing."

Meg's heart leaped to her throat. "No, I . . . uh . . ."

But Katie was already pulling on her arm. "Come on. We'll peek into the rotunda where the ball will be held tonight."

Hank rose and extended a hand each to Meg and Mary Sue. "She's right," he told them, giving the group on the blankets a sly grin. "We should take advantage of our youth."

Meg found herself on her feet with no trouble, but the effort it required to stay there was a different matter. Her legs actually wobbled beneath her. "We shouldn't get in the way," she suggested. "They're probably rehearsing. . . ."

"Nobody's in the rotunda now," Katie told her. "The

governor's schedule has been in the Austin newspaper all week." She glanced at the sun above, then back to Meg. "At this moment, I wager he is dining on turtle soup and roast rack of lamb, which is reported to be his favorite entree, in the west wing of the . . ."

"Stop!" Meg insisted. "I believe you." She wanted to cover her ears with her hands in order to stop the incessant talk about Kalib Chaney. She also wanted, fiercely, to see the inside of the Capitol, where he would preside as governor—the rotunda, where he would waltz tonight with . . .

Inhaling a deep sigh, she caught up Katie's hand, and together they trudged toward the front of the Capitol building. She would make it through this day, because this day would end.

This day would end for her in a few short hours when she boarded the train for Summer Valley. She could make it until then. She *would* make it until then . . . without hurting Katie's feelings. And she might as well take a few memories with her.

Hank and Mary Sue lingered arm in arm behind them, and after Katie had chastised them to hurry three times, Meg reminded her of their engagement. "Let them be, Katie. Hank will leave in the morning, and they have precious little time together."

The sun was hot overhead and the sky clear and blue, reminding Meg of an early spring day. Numerous small oak trees, which had been planted after the Capitol was completed two years earlier, dotted the landscape, obscured today by the large crowds of people. They approached the bunting-draped platform and walked around behind it to the Capitol steps.

"We're using bunting for the joining of the rails too," she told Katie. Not titillating conversation, she knew, but she remained determined to steer the conversation away from the topic that was on everyone else's lips . . . and her mind.

As they climbed the steep granite steps, Katie drew her breath. "Meg, stand still a moment. You look just like a picture."

Meg paused, laughing self-consciously. "What are you talking about, Katie? Don't . . ."

"I mean your gown . . . the dusty rose matches the pink granite. You look like you dressed especially for this day."

Sighing heavily, Meg turned to climb the last steps. If she had purposely chosen a costume for this day it would have been the black crepe of mourning. "Come on, if we're to look at the rotunda before the ceremonies begin, we'll have to hurry."

Several hundred people milled about, making it impossible to get a complete picture of the enormous entryway to the Capitol. Katie pointed to the terrazzo mosaic covering the floor, depicting seals of all the nations Texas had been a part of in the past, dissected in the center by the five-pointed star. Looking up, Meg saw the various floors spiral to the top where the brillant sun streamed through windows in the dome far above them. "It takes your breath away," she sighed, thinking once more of Kalib's words beneath the pecan trees. There could be no grander ballroom than this, no more elevated company, she thought, unless it were simply the two of them, alone beneath the trees and the very moon itself.

Katie clutched her arm. "A lady named Leanora Rives wrote a waltz especially for the dedication a couple of years ago, "The New Texas Capitol Waltz." I know they'll play it tonight. Can you imagine yourself waltzing with the new governor here in the rotunda . . . ?"

Meg gripped her trembling lips between her teeth and nervously stuffed a wisp of hair beneath her elegant black hat. "You'll have to ask him for a dance," she quipped, turning quickly to leave the building.

Katie caught up with her and took her arm again. "Why didn't you tell me you know him?" she cried.

Meg's heels ground to a stop on the slick granite steps. "What do you mean?"

Katie smiled conspiringly. "Sara Ann says you know Governor Chaney."

"I don't know . . . *Governor Chaney*," Meg answered softly. "I can't imagine why Sara Ann thinks . . ."

"She said he told her so himself," Katie informed her.
"He . . . ?"

"Well, he *is* the prospector, and you must have . . ."

Meg inhaled deeply, then exhaled in a heavy sigh.
"Katie, Katie. Yes, I met him, but I didn't know he was the
governor-elect then, and . . ."

Katie giggled. "Tell me all about it! You must! It's so
romantic! He's your handsome, dark-eyed stranger, isn't
he?"

Meg studied her a moment longer, while her racing
heart threatened to break loose from her trussed-up frame.
Then she hugged Katie. "Someday, I'll tell you all about
it." Guiding them out the huge double doorway, she
blinked against the sunlight. "Someday it might even
sound romantic. Right now, it more resembles a nightmare, and I'd rather not talk about it."

Katie's mouth fell open. "Oh, Meg. I'm sorry. I'm . . . I
didn't think."

Meg hugged the girl's shoulder again. "It's all right.
Things generally turn out for the best. We'd better get back
to the others before they begin to worry."

The crowds had increased in the short time since they
entered the rotunda. As they rounded the platform, Meg
noticed the chairs for the honored guests being set in place.
Her heart thumped painfully once more. She picked up
her pace.

"Meg! There you are!" Fear washed over Meg like a
rainshower, one instant before she realized she didn't need
to fear hearing her name called . . . not that name. The
only name Kalib would call her was Maggie, and until she
heard that, she was safe.

"It's Sara Ann," Katie responded, drawing Meg to the
front of the platform.

The two girls hugged, then Sara Ann drew Meg back to
look at her, and Meg felt all queasy again. Sara Ann was so
beautiful—thick blond hair, blue eyes, outrageously
long, thick lashes. And her two friends were so sophisticated. "It's wonderful to see you, too, Sara Ann," she said.
"You look like you're in a rush."

350

Sara Ann sighed in mock weariness. "I'm chairing the inaugural ball," she said. "It's as big a production as running for office, I'll wager. Say, you never mentioned knowing Kalib."

Meg swallowed, beseeching her raging pulse to still. She shrugged. "I don't really know him. Actually, we just . . ."

"Well, he knows you!" Sara Ann enthused, giving her a knowing look. "You're all he talks about. If I'd known I'd be quizzed so, I'd have asked you for a written history of your life. In fact, I've given up my suit . . ." Pausing, she winked at Katie, then continued. "I've set my cap a notch lower on the political ladder." Her eyes twinkled. "Have you met his best friend, Tobin Yanek?"

Meg cleared her throat. "Tobin? Why, Sara Ann, how marvelous." Her spirits actually soared . . . for a moment. In the next, the sky came crashing down around her ears, when, without warning, Sara Ann raised her arms in the air and waved wildly.

"Kalib . . . Governor Chaney," she called. "Over here."

A weakness the likes of which she had never experienced before flooded Meg's senses, and she quickly grasped the corner of the platform for support. At the same time every pore in her body prickled, and she was glad she had opened the revers on her dress, or she would have been in danger of smothering.

Sara Ann's voice lowered, speaking to someone quite close. "Governor Chaney, I believe you know these two friends of mine."

As though they were attached to strings being controlled by a puppeteer, Meg lifted her eyes to him. He stood not three paces away, and she was instantly struck by a number of inconsistencies. First, that she didn't know this man. Clean-shaven, except for the graceful moustache she recalled from New Year's Eve night, he didn't resemble the black-bearded lover in her dreams. And his clothing—gray pinstripes with gray satin vest and black tie, when in her dreams he wore work clothes. But he stared at her from the depths of the same dark eyes, with the same passion-

351

igniting golden sparks.

A voice called to him from behind the platform. "Governor, could you lend us a hand with the seating arrangements?

He moved not a muscle, and she ran her tongue between her lips and gums, trying to loosen her lips from her teeth, should she be required to speak. Actually, she wasn't at all sure she would be able to utter a sound.

He held himself in such a dignified manner, she could hardly believe he was the same warm, virile human being who had held her in his arms and teased her with his eyes. This wasn't the same man she had danced with beneath the pecan trees; this was a stranger who would dance with someone else under the great dome of the Capitol rotunda tonight. Both his carriage and his features were rigid, solemn to the point of being stern. Everything about him exuded the proper, dignified demeanor of a gentleman . . . of a governor. Here was a man far beyond her own simple reach, as his behavior so pointedly demonstrated.

But the mere sight of him still set her blood on fire, just like she knew it would. And if her legs weren't two quivering masses of jelly, she would have turned and run away through the clamoring crowd.

Then he moved, and she blanched. But instead of approaching her, he tilted his head only a fraction of a degree down and to his left. Shifting her own gaze, she saw his companion. A slight, elderly woman regally gowned in black silk, with a small black hat, and the darkest eyes Meg had ever seen outside Kalib's own face. Her carriage, like his, was erect and proper, and when she raised a gloveless hand to straighten her hat, Meg's eyes fastened on the enormous emerald ring on her brittle brown-speckled hand.

Staring innocuously at Meg—as if he had never so much as entertained a passionate notion for her, she thought furiously—he spoke to the woman at his side. "Grandmother, may I present Miss Margaret Britton? We met in Silver Creek where her father was chief engineer for the railroad spur I'll be dedicating in a couple of weeks."

Margaret? He had never called her Margaret before in her life . . . Margaret! From lips that had once called her his wife! Suddenly she wilted, feeling horribly outclassed and out of place. Her own elegant costume hung like a washerwoman's garment on inwardly sagging shoulders, and she hated her wobbly knees. How could such a cold man as this fire her treacherous body with so much heat? Had she no principles? No pride? No self-respect?

The elderly woman smiled vaguely, as though trying to decide why she should be introduced to a railroader's daughter, Meg thought. "Margaret," she repeated with brief nod of her head. "I don't recall you mentioning . . ."

Where before her limbs had been weakened first by passion, then humiliation, Meg now felt the fire of intense fury sweep over her. *Margaret! How dare he call her Margaret! How dare he look at her with that stony expression when . . . when only days before . . .*

Without warning all the constraints of Di's upbringing and her own proper schooling tore loose like the strings of a kite being ripped apart from its body by a powerful wind. Suddenly only one thing mattered to her—showing him up for the artificial politician he really was. For the feeble excuse for a human being he was. Showing him that she knew him heart and soul, even if no other person in the world before or since ever had or ever would have that unfortunate opportunity.

Straightening her trembling spine, she squared her shoulders in a defiant gesture, which came not from courage, but from the search of it. She cocked her head, gave him a spiteful glance, and turned her sweetest expression on his grandmother.

"In truth, ma'am, your grandson, being the politician he is, tends to gloss over details he finds distasteful." Feeling her voice begin to falter, she rushed ahead. "My name is *Maggie* Britton, and I *built* that damned railroad . . . in spite of unimaginable . . ." Furiously she looked back at Kalib. The corners of his lips quivered in an ill-concealed effort to restrain a smile. The bastard! she fumed. His eyes had softened, and . . .

". . . in spite of unbelievable interference," she spat before spinning on her heel and striding down the hillside.

Her mind was in such an uproar that she passed the Silver Creek group by without even knowing it until she heard Rube call her.

"We're over here, sugar."

Halting in the middle of a path, she stared at him blankly. "We'll be late," she called, then continued down the hill. At the bottom she stopped to wait for him and found herself staring despondently at the Governor's Mansion.

Kalib watched her go, wanting nothing more than to follow her and take her in his arms. The very sight of her mesmerized him to such an extent that the entire inauguration ceremony fled from his thoughts. But he was here; he must go through with the day as planned. *And by God*, he swore to himself, *the next time he chased that woman, he intended to catch her.*

Weakly, he looked down at his grandmother and shrugged.

"So that's your Maggie," she chuckled. "What a magnificent girl!"

He grinned. "You don't know how lucky you were. For a moment there I thought she was going to call me a bastard to your face."

"She wouldn't have . . . ?"

"It was on the tip of her tongue, believe me."

The old lady smiled. "A fine, spirited girl, your Maggie! I can see why you were ready to give up the governor's office for her. I'm glad you didn't though."

Kalib shrugged heavily. "Her father convinced me that having both is possible. If he hadn't, I'd be out of this fancy suit and walking beside her this very minute. And she'd be laughing instead of crying inside." He looked down at his grandmother. "I've already hurt her so much,

I can't bear thinking about how the vicious wags in this town will go after her . . . being from a terminus town, and all."

She patted his hand. "Don't worry about Maggie, dear. She's strong, and she'll have you beside her." She looked up at him reassuringly. "And she'll have me . . . and we'll let Sara Ann take care of the young set."

Raising her frail hand to his lips, he kissed her fingers. "I believe you approve of Maggie."

"She's perfect for you Kalib," she told him with a twinkle in her eye. "Perfect. If my judgement is correct, you've finally found a girl who will keep you in line." Studying her, he suddenly saw a tear sparkle in eyes he had never known to shed them.

"Those glorious green eyes!" she sighed. Then, as he watched, she reverently removed the emerald ring from her finger and placed it in his palm, closing his fingers around it. "Put this in your pocket, dear. The next time you meet, I want her to have it."

"But Grandmother, this is your . . ."

Her eyes pierced him with a look he knew all too well, reprimanding him as though he were a child in school. "I know perfectly well what this ring represents, young man. Your grandfather gave it to me on the occasion of our betrothal. Take it and use it as it was intended."

Chapter Nineteen

The morning of the joining of the rails dawned crisp and sunny, reminding Meg of yet another early spring day. Almost two weeks had passed since the inauguration, and though she felt queasy in the pit of her stomach thinking of what lay ahead, she knew she would make it through this day as she had all the others. Especially now, since she had a plan, and an ally to protect her. She didn't have to face this day alone.

She and Rube had arrived back in Hell on Wheels one day ahead of the rest of the Silver Creek delegation, who spent inauguration night in Austin. They had left their carriages in Hell on Wheels where they caught the supply train to Summer Valley. When they arrived back, Rube and Di met them with a request for one member of the group—Judge Quintan Jarvis.

"We'll begin tearing down the Diamond-Stacker tomorrow," Di told him. "Woody and I decided not to wait for the rails to be joined. He'll move the saloon to Silver Creek by wagon, which means Rube, Meg, and I will stay in the hotel in Silver Creek until after the joining of the rails. Rube and I figured it would simplify matters if we went ahead and got married now."

Meg decided later Rube and Di must have planned the entire affair before they left for Austin, for while they were in Austin, Rube had managed to obtain a marriage license. And in their absence, Di had planned the ceremony.

Judge Jarvis read the service in front of the curly birch bar. Meg and Uncle Grady stood up for them. The Silver Creek citizens readily joined in the festivities, which included dinner—though without Chou Ling's expertise, the fare wasn't fancy—and a temperance punch Di called a Cider Fizz, a mixture of apple cider, lemon juice, and fine-grained sugar.

Di wore her red velvet dress, for old times' sake, she said and Meg was relieved to be able to put on a happy face. Before the carriages left for Silver Creek, Hank took her aside.

"Hear you had a run-in with the governor."

Meg grimaced. "I didn't intend to offend his grandmother," she admitted, "but . . . oh, Hank, I suppose I did lose my composure."

They sat in a corner, and before she realized it, she told him portions of the story of her and Kalib's brief acquaintance.

"That's all it was," she insisted. "I was the fool. His being a politician explains it, I suppose. Even when his face was hidden by a heavy beard and when he wore shabby old work clothes, he . . . well, he made my heart stand still. Isn't it dreadful, I mean . . . frightening, really, how some people have that sort of power over others. It means we choose our leaders not by their ability and experience, but by a physical presence which doesn't tell us anything about their character—or their qualifications."

Hank agreed to help her make it through the celebration without having to face Kalib. That made it easy.

Easier, she thought, dressing with care. The dress she chose for the occasion was her favorite of all the costumes she had bought before returning from school. Wearing it today might give her a measure of courage and help keep her spirits up.

That was her reasoning, anyhow, as she donned the heavy green silk printed with a lighter green in a large-branched broché design. A three-piece outfit, the skirt was of the prevailing godet shape, with the front breadths caught with a series of green velvet knots each held by a fancy button. The short coat nipped the waist and cut away on a double-breasted, white silk vest with two rows of buttons. The broad revers of the jacket were overlaid by the white revers of the vest, and a large cravat of white chiffon draped the bosom. The jacket had the largest balloon sleeves she had worn, and she considered for a moment whether she would feel conspicuous. Adjusting the green flat-topped hat on her swept-up do, she decided she needed the extra confidence such a fashionable costume would provide. Perhaps when people spoke to her, it would be about her dress instead of about the handsome new governor and his marriage prospects.

Jabbing a couple more pins into her hat against what she expected to be a long, hectic day, she picked up her parasol and looked about the bedroom one last time.

At the door, she panicked briefly. Her stomach felt queasy, and the door knob cooled her heated palm, reminding her to fetch her tan kid gloves.

Every room in the entire hotel had been taken by noon the day before, and now as she descended the staircase the building was abuzz with chattering voices, laughing children, and the clatter of dinnerware from the adjacent dining room.

Again, she quaked, and her hand trembled on the stair railing. Inhaling deeply, she closed her mind, hoping to quiet her heart, as well.

"Well, well, here she is. The loveliest lady in all Silver Creek."

Quickly, she doused her doldrums and smiled. "Hank Jefferies! What a thing to say. Your fiancée will arrive within the hour, and here you are flirting with another woman."

Taking the stairs two at a time, he offered his elbow and escorted her to breakfast. "If you feel as lovely as you look, every eligible gentleman—and a few who aren't—will be at your feet before nightfall."

"I don't want anyone at my feet." She studied him in earnest, while he seated himself opposite her at the long dining table in the rear of the room. "Nor at my side, nor in my sight. Remember your promise?"

He nodded. "I won't let our . . . uh, honored visitor within shouting distance of you, unless . . ."

"Unless nothing," she demanded, knowing he was teasing her now to raise her spirits, but determined nonetheless that he understand the desperate nature of her request. "I promise not to keep you from Mary Sue. I can manage for myself most of the time, but during the meal, and before the ceremony starts when he might be wandering around . . ."

Reaching over he patted her hand. "I understand, Meg. Trust me."

Her eyes flared, then she laughed. "I'm so nervous," she confessed. "Why do those two words—trust me—always seem to bode disaster?"

By the time they finished breakfast and went out front, the street was filled with carriages loading passengers for the ceremonies.

"A lot of folks are going to want to leave these carriages behind and ride the rails back to town tonight," Hank laughed, helping Meg into his carriage along with Rube and Di.

"You and Mary Sue will be among the few who can," she reminded him. "Be sure to park so I can get this rig out after the ceremonies."

Her plan was simple. She would busy herself with the women preparing food until the ceremonies actually started, then she would view them from a distance, and immediately when they were over, she would return to Silver Creek in Hank's carriage.

"You did bring the golden spike?" Rube asked, leaning forward.

Hank nodded and patted the seat between himself and Meg. "What about the maul?"

"I got one to Jarvis this morning," Rube answered.

As judge, Quintan Jarvis was the most esteemed citizen of Silver Creek, and he had been prevailed upon to serve as master of ceremonies for the day's events. In that capacity, they decided to let him call on whomever he deemed appropriate to actually drive the golden spike into the rails. Naturally, everyone supposed he would select Rube.

The site chosen was a mile or so west of the camphouse, on the first level ground past the river. From a distance they could hear sounds of activity, and approaching, they found a couple of dozen men standing around the barbecue pits they had dug earlier in the week.

Women worked around tables set up in the midst of a grove of oak trees, while on the platform the youngest Jarvis daughter, Jennifer, rehearsed her poem, above the discordant notes of the national anthem played by Woody's band on the ground below.

A gay, exciting day, Meg thought, and thankfully, sunny. The balmy weather meant they wouldn't have to go near the camphouse, and for that reason alone, she felt like smiling.

Ever since returning from Austin, she had been priming herself for this day. Since all the Santa Fe directors would be present, she felt obligated to attend. Relying on her time-honored practice of being forewarned, she prepared herself. This was Rube's day, and she wanted to do him proud.

After he and Di had moved into their own suite at the hotel, the three of them had another long discussion on her future. They hadn't been able to convince her to leave their life behind. But they had set her mind at ease about Rube's drinking.

"I'm not saying I'm off Demon Rum for good," he told her. "I'm just saying I'm sober today. And Di's helping me stay that way. If I do happen to . . ." he shrugged and gave Di a grin, ". . . if I fall off the wagon, together we'll pick up the pieces and heft me back on top."

"I'll be right beside him, dear, every step of the way. You have nothing to worry about. And it's time. . . ."

"You can't make me leave now," Meg insisted. "I'm . . . I'm not ready to leave you."

Rube and Di exchanged glances. "One day you will be, sugar. When that day comes, we want you to be able to recognize it. We have our lives, and you must find yours, too."

Rube had decided to take the job that started below Fort Worth. He planned to tell Leslie Hayden today, and they expected to move to their new location as soon as the Santa Fe provided them with the car Rube had requested.

Arriving at the site of the ceremonies, they had but staked the horses, when the air was pierced by the long, shrill whistle blasts from a diamond-stacker engine. Again, panic rose in Meg's throat, and she turned quickly away from the sight.

Hank squeezed her shoulder. "It's the *Texas Star*," he said. "Your old friend Leslie Hayden and his cohorts."

She nodded, but when she looked up, she saw a longer passenger train following the shorter one. This one, she knew, would be carrying far more dangerous passengers. One, in particular.

The new governor of Texas.

The queasiness she had experienced earlier returned, and she felt a case of uncontrollable trembling coming on. "It's Mary Sue and Katie," she told Hank. "You run meet them, while I help the ladies with the food. I'll be all right."

When he balked, she pushed him forward. "You, too, Rube. You'd better meet Hayden and his associates. This is a perfect time to give him your acceptance."

The women were all atwitter, and their chattering did little to calm Meg's nerves. At first she stood with her back to the trains, listening to the crowd disembark. But as time went by, her neck began to prickle with the thought that he might approach her unawares, so she moved to face the trains, keeping herself from view behind a thicket of various-sized oak trees.

Time, which appeared to move at a snail's pace, in actuality raced forward, and sooner than she would have thought possible, she heard the loud voice of Judge Jarvis calling for folks to take their places on the platform and down front . . . to leave an aisle open to the rails . . . to come forward so they could begin the ceremonies and get on to more important matters of the day—like attacking that mouth-watering barbecue they were all starving for. The women moved out, some motioning Meg to follow, some urging.

Busying herself with a tea cloth, she spoke to Mavis. "I'll be along, directly. Go ahead and find a good seat up front. Tell them I'm coming."

Her body trembled, and she admonished herself sharply. It was almost over now. The dignitaries were to sit on the platform—including Rube and Di and Uncle Grady and, of course, the governor. He couldn't speak to her from there. He couldn't even see her. She was safe. At last. She could even sneak a peek at him, before she left.

Woody's band struck up the *"Star-Spangled Banner,"* and the crowd rose and sang along. Meg was stunned by the way the band stayed on key; she'd never heard them play so well.

Then Jarvis introduced his daughter, and Jennifer began to recite her poem. Meg chanced a look toward the platform from behind the tree where she stood at the rear of the gathering. Jennifer's voice was so soft, she could hardly hear the words. But she knew them practically by heart, first from judging the contest, then from hearing Jennifer rehearse in the hotel the last three days.

The platform, festooned with red, white and blue bunting, for a moment took her breath away, reminding her as it did of the speakers' platform in front of the Capitol. Quickly, as though haste would prevent her own discovery, her gaze traveled over the group seated behind Jennifer.

Uncle Grady, Rube, and Di, Di looking lovely in soft blue, then, next to them . . . her eyes riveted on him. The back of her neck turned hot, and she clasped the tree trunk to steady herself. Black suit, not the pin stripe, thank goodness, she thought. Black moustache, still not the man she held in her mind . . . a man with a heavy black beard.

Fortunately, she was too far away to see his eyes. The eyes she had looked into in Austin. Recalling that ill-fated meeting, her resolve strengthened to avoid him here today at all costs.

Glancing quickly behind her, she searched the trees and at last spied Hank's carriage. As soon as Rube—or whomever Judge Jarvis chose—drove the golden spike into the rails, she was gone!

"And now," Judge Jarvis's voice boomed across the applauding crowd, drawing her attention back to the platform, "now, I'll turn the program over to our esteemed visitor, our newly inaugurated governor, the Honorable Kalib Chaney."

Meg stared transfixed as Kalib stood up—he was as tall as the judge. They shook hands, then Kalib sauntered to the podium. Her heart throbbed painfully in her chest, and she looked away, down the line of colorful bunting that ran from the platform to the rails where the graceful little diamond-stacker engine pulling Leslie Hayden's *Texas Star* stood arrayed in all its red, white and blue finery.

Kalib's voice shattered her senses, and she wished frantically she could leave right then. As soon as they began to tie the rails, when the commotion would cover her movements, she would go. She couldn't stay and listen to that voice. . . .

"First, we'd best get these rails joined," he said, "what with all the trouble their laying caused you folks, we shouldn't tarry any longer than necessary." Smiling, he looked back at Rube.

At Rube, Meg thought. He's actually *smiling* at Rube, the bastard. Then her mouth fell agape, when Rube returned the smile with a broad one of his own.

"Since your judge has graciously accorded me the honor of choosing the citizen to tie these rails . . ." As Kalib continued, his eyes traveled over the gathering. Meg shrank behind the tree. "Dr. Jefferies," he called. "You were instrumental in bringing this railroad to town. Will you do the honors for us today?"

Meg watched from behind the tree, only half aware of the happenings. Vaguely, she saw Hank stand and lift the spike over his head. The other half of her mind struggled for control. She had made it this far. She could make it a few more minutes. She could, and she would!

Again, Kalib's eyes scanned the group, and again she scrunched behind the tree. His words sent fear straight to her heart. Fear followed by fury.

"The other person most responsible," he began "actually, the one person most responsible for the timely completion of this spur is Miss Britton. But I can't seem to locate her." He looked questioningly back toward Rube, then again at Hank Jefferies. "Dr. Jefferies, would you find Maggie Britton for me . . . ?"

His words blurred in her ears. How dare he? In front of all these people! In front of Rube and Leslie Hayden and all the Santa Fe stockholders. If she refused . . .

When Hank found her, he took her arm, and she jerked away.

"It's all right, Meg," he whispered above the din in her head. "I'll lead you to the rails, not to the platform. Don't even look at him if you don't want to."

"Well, I don't want to," she fumed. "How could he . . . ?"

"This won't take long," Hank consoled her leading her through the parting crowd. "You did play a big part in all this. Everyone in Silver Creek thanks you for what you've done. This is an honor you deserve." He patted her hand where she clung fiercely to the crook of his arm. "Don't forget to smile."

Inhaling a deep, quivering breath, she straightened her shoulders and held her head aloft. Smile? "If I didn't know better," she whispered, "I'd think you were on his side."

When at last they reached the rails, she caught another sharp breath. Wash stood solemnly before her, holding a maul toward Hank.

"I'm on your side," Hank was saying. "Don't you ever doubt it." The band began to play *"Texas, Our Texas;"* he took the maul from Wash. "Hold the spike in place, Meg. I promise not to hit your hand."

The hole had already been bored, so driving the spike was only symbolic. She held it, while Hank drove it home, to the boisterous singing of the state anthem. As soon as he finished, she stood up and brushed dirt from her hands.

"I'm leaving *now*," she whispered. "Before the music ends, before he has another chance to infuriate or humiliate me, I'm . . ."

Suddenly the music stopped in midscore, and Kalib's voice froze her in her tracks. "Now, Dr. Jefferies, please escort Miss Britton to the platform so the citizens of Silver Creek can show their appreciation."

"What the devil is he doing?" she hissed.

"Shush," Hank whispered, quickly pulling her hand inside the crook of his arm once more. "Stay calm, Meg. Everything will be all right."

Her eyes flared at him. The heels of her green slippers dug into the rocky ground. "Don't do this to me, Hank," she whispered desperately.

"Trust me," he whispered, leading her up the long, bunting-bedecked isle to the platform.

"Trust! Are all men bastards?" she hissed into his downturned face. "Or just the ones I know?"

Her brain swirled anxiously in her ears, and she could barely hear the hands clapping around her. Inhaling another tremulous breath, she held her lips between her teeth. Again she stiffened her shoulders, but inside she felt like a volcano . . . all hot and in turmoil. How could she have gotten herself into such a fix? She should have stayed at the hotel all day. Even if it were Rube's day of celebration.

"Ladies and gentlemen," Kalib's voice boomed toward her.

Some celebration it had turned out to be. With all the Santa Fe stockholders looking on, she could hardly spit in the face of the governor of Texas, but that was exactly what she wanted to do.

Kalib's voice droned on, drifting in and out of her consciousness. "As you read in your . . . uh, respected newspaper, *The Silver Creek Sun*, I'm scheduled to give my first major address on railroad reform here today. . . ."

Her chin held high, she kept her eyes trained straight

ahead, concentrating on the hazy row of feet of the dignitaries on the platform. Hank led her down the length of the standing crowd, around the front row of seats, and to the steps at the right of the platform. At the foot of the steps Tobin took her other elbow in an effort to assist her. The moment he touched her, she froze.

Mounting the steps at Hank's prodding, she shot Rube a desperate plea. He merely smiled and shrugged his shoulders. The platform wasn't very big. Only two rows of seats, ten or so chairs to each row. Rube and Di sat on her right, and she stopped in front of them, but Hank urged her on toward the podium itself.

To this point, she hadn't looked at Kalib, and she had no intention of doing so now. To avoid offending everyone present by snubbing their governor, however, she turned away from him, toward the audience, and tried to smile. But she quivered so inside, she felt dreadfully like she might swoon instead. Kalib's voice, so near now, reverberated through her senses. His words meshed with other words he had spoken, other times he had teased and tempted . . . and humiliated her.

"I decided to forego a lengthy political speech today, in order to share a special occasion with all of you."

His words meant nothing to her, but his voice . . . his voice crashed in her head like waves on a sandy beach. Through hazy peripheral vision, she saw his legs move, and suddenly she knew he had stepped toward her.

Hank nudged her at the waist. "Go ahead, Meg, look at him."

After a moment's hesitation, she gritted her teeth and obeyed. She was here on this damned platform with him for better or worse, and she must get herself together and make the best of it. The intensity in his eyes as her gaze found his almost sent her stumbling backwards. Her heart lunged in her breast, and quite without intending to, she grasped his outstretched hand, then quickly looked out at the sea of people—away from his eyes . . . anywhere but into his eyes, she thought frantically.

"Ladies and gentlemen, please thank the lady who is

most responsible for getting this railroad spur finished in time for today's festivities." His fingers tightened around hers, and she felt him lift her hand with his above their heads. "Miss Maggie Britton—"

His eyes burned into the side of her face, and she felt his hand grasp her still more tightly. His voice halted the pulse in her veins, and she had the sudden vision of herself as the Goddess of Liberty, arm stretched aloft holding the Texas Star in her hand.

"Miss Maggie Britton," he repeated, "soon to be Mrs. Kalib Chaney . . . the first lady of our great state of Texas."

The crowd surged toward her, or, she realized later, she actually swayed toward the crowd, as every man, woman, and child in the audience jumped up and began cheering wildly. The roar was deafening. Her mind raced, trying to assimilate his words, his meaning.

Her eyes sought his, and the desperate, questioning look in his eyes sent her stumbling again, this time straight to his side. His arms encircled her, he pulled her close, and the crowd went wild around them.

He held her tightly against his side, and she felt his heart pound erratically, like her own, against her. She clasped him around the waist, as if for dear life.

Grinning crazily into her eyes, he reached inside his jacket and withdrew a document. Instead of saying a word to her, he addressed the crowd.

"Since Maggie and I are here today in the midst of friends and family . . ." he looked back at her as if to assure himself she hadn't disappeared, although he hadn't loosened his hold around her shoulders, ". . . and since one of our dignitaries happens to be a duly appointed judge, I brought the marriage license, and . . ." Turning, he handed Judge Jarvis the papers. "Look them over. If they're in order, why don't we get this ceremony over with before dinner?"

She clung to him fiercely, unable to utter a word, while her mind swam with yeses and nos, with questions and answers, with all sorts of crazy, wonderful, dreadful possibilities. A flash in front of her blinded her momentarily, and she stared straight at Ellsworth Fredericks.

Looking at her again, Kalib suddenly tipped her chin up. "Your costume is far from simple, love. It's stunning. And you said you didn't care where the ceremony was held. You did mean it . . . ?"

"But . . . ?" She looked back at Rube and Di. Both were standing on their feet along with the rest of the crowd, clapping happily. Rube wore a proud smile, and Di blotted a tear just as Meg turned to her.

She found Hank Jefferies, who had taken his place beside Mary Sue in the front row. Hank, too, was applauding wildly, all smiles. Turning back to Kalib, her lips trembled in a weak smile. "I think I've been set up."

He laughed softly. "I'm not proud. When I need help, I ask for it."

Suddenly, like moorings on a floundering ship, all her rationalizations and fears broke loose—rationalizations that her life had been too different from his, that she wasn't good enough to be his wife, all her fears that she shouldn't leave Rube, that she was destined to spend her life in loneliness—and her spirits soared with the soft fuzzy clouds above them, lifting the heavy weight of unhappiness from her shoulders, leaving only joy.

She tucked a wisp of hair back beneath her hat with a now steady hand, unable to hold back all traces of a teasing smile. "What if I . . . ?" Glancing at each end of the platform, her eyes found Kalib's again. "What if I decide to run . . . ?" she whispered.

He tightened his hold on her. "I thought of that. Why do you think Tobin and Wash are standing on the steps?"

She stared down the isle in front of them, straight into Ellsworth Fredericks's black-shrouded camera.

"And if you jump off this stage and run down the aisle, I'll follow you."

She cocked her head. "I have no voice in this decision?"

His eyes glistened with golden highlights. "You made your decision a long time ago, Maggie. You just didn't know it. I wasn't positive how you felt myself, until

Austin." She watched the vein in his neck swell. "When you got so mad at me for calling you Margaret."

She bit the corner of her bottom lip. "But you said you'd never . . ."

"I said I'd never kiss you good-bye," he whispered, running the tip of his tongue around his lips in a gesture that almost caused her to swoon against him.

Without giving a second thought to where they were, she stood on tiptoe to reach him. "Then kiss me hello."

Their eyes held for an eternity as the crowd noise swelled around them. In the background, she vaguely heard the band start to play, but the song inside her heart was so poignant she had trouble concentrating on anything else. She was here with him, and as on that first day in the valley, their universe suddenly included only the two of them.

Grasping her forearms in his hands, he lowered his face to hers and kissed her soundly, firmly, convincingly. She felt his lips tremble against hers as he lifted them and stared a moment longer into her sparkling green eyes.

The judge cleared his throat. "These papers seem to be in order, governor. Where do you want the ceremony performed?"

"Here," Kalib told him, then he turned to Meg. "Katie's down front. Do you want her to stand up with you?"

Focusing on the front row again, Meg spied Katie, who looked more ready to swoon than she herself felt. "I don't think she could make it up the stairs," she laughed. "I'll ask Di." As she spoke, Kalib motioned for Rube and Di to join them. But just as Judge Jarvis cleared his throat again, this time to call for the crowd's attention, Kalib held up his hand for him to wait.

"Tobin," he called. "The flowers."

While her mind whirred and her heart fluttered, Tobin raced down the aisle to the *Texas Star* and returned carrying a bouquet of yellow roses. The sight of them brought tears brimming in her eyes. Kalib held the roses toward her, then stopped. "Take off your gloves," he whispered.

After she complied, he handed her the roses, stuffed her gloves into one of his pockets, and the ceremony began.

Rube had to clear his throat twice to be able to answer "I do," when Judge Jarvis asked who gave the bride away. And when he got to the part about the ring, Kalib started fishing around in his pockets.

"Give your flowers to Di," he instructed. She stared transfixed into his beaming face, feeling him take her left hand in his and place a ring on her finger.

"Look at it," he whispered.

Tearing her eyes reluctantly from his, she stared at the enormous emerald and gasped. "It's like your grandmother's!"

His hands trembled as he squeezed hers. "It *was* my grandmother's." His words sent shivers down her spine.

"But . . . ?" Meg objected.

"It was her idea," he said. Seeing her eyes widen, he grinned and added, *"After* she met you, love. For some reason, she thinks you'll be able to keep me in line."

The ceremony ended with a kiss. Her fingers ached to touch his face, his silky moustache, and she smiled into his questioning eyes.

"What is it?"

She caught her breath, then grinned. "Later," she whispered. And he winked.

A glorious surge of joy swept over her. Later. Later. They had so many laters now. So many tomorrows. Forever.

An informal receiving line formed along the platform, and they suddenly found themselves overwhelmed with wellwishers. After hugging her, Rube and Uncle Grady moved away, and Di started to follow, but Meg held her back.

"Stay with me," she pleaded. So Di and Rube stood beside them and between handshakes and congratulations for the groom and hugs and kisses for the bride, she and Di whispered back and forth. "You knew?"

Di shook her head. "Not everything, believe me. I had no idea he was bringing the marriage license."

"How did you know any of it?"

Di smiled at her. "Let Kalib tell you the story, dear."

"But tell me why you went along," Meg insisted.

Di raised her eyebrows. "Why? Doesn't the joy you feel inside right now answer that?"

Meg inhaled a deep, happy breath. "Yes, but I still don't understand how you knew I . . . ."

Di studied her solemnly. "You always were such a responsible little girl, dear. And you were correct in believing that Rube depended on you, he did. Somewhere along the line, though, Rube's dependence on you changed directions, and you became dependent on him . . . on helping him. I'm not sure why it happened, or how, but we decided we should help you break away, especially since it was so obvious this is what you wanted."

Vaguely, she knew Di was right. She didn't understand it, either, but it had come close to wrecking her life. Standing here beside Kalib now, she felt so secure, so protected, so loved . . . at this moment, she couldn't even recall her earlier fears, but they had been real.

Her senses were so finely attuned to him that she shivered at the rub of his sleeve against hers. They had been real, her fears. Real enough to almost ruin her life.

Feeling her tremble beside him, he reached around her waist and drew her to him playfully, comfortingly. . . . Real enough to almost ruin his life, too, she thought, casting him a loving glance, as they received the next of the well-wishers, Ellsworth Fredericks.

"How about the whole story?" Fredericks inquired.

Meg shook her head. "Go write your own story, Mr. Fredericks. No matter what we say, you'll tell it your way in the end, anyhow."

Then Katie Jefferies came along the line, bubbling, her eyes practically rolling around in their sockets at the romantic turn the day had taken.

"Why didn't you tell me?" she demanded of Meg.

Meg shrugged. "I didn't know, Katie. Truly, I was the last to know." Then she laughed and tugged at Kalib's sleeve to draw his attention away from Leslie Hayden for a moment.

"Katie Jefferies, meet my handsome, dark-eyed stranger."

Katie giggled and accepted Kalib's kiss on her cheek. "And you called it a nightmare."

Kalib found Meg's hand and squeezed it, and she gazed into his serious eyes. "That's why I couldn't let her get away," he told Katie quietly, while still studying Meg with thinly veiled passion. "My life would have been a nightmare without her."

Hank and Mary Sue followed, with the end of the line in sight, at last. Mary Sue hugged her dreamily, thinking, Meg knew, of her own wedding, which wasn't far off now. Hank kissed her in a brotherly fashion and grinned sheepishly.

"You were in cahoots with him all the time," Meg accused. "Why did you . . . ?"

Hank shook his head, still grinning broadly. "I watched you mope about, giving me nothing except lame excuses. Then, down in Austin . . ." He turned to Kalib. "When the governor here, who, incidentally, pined away the evening at his own inaugural ball, approached me for help, I felt it was in the best interests of both of you . . . from a physician's standpoint, of course."

Offering his hand to Hank, Kalib squeezed Meg to his side with his other arm. "Thanks for your help, doc. I'll be happy to return the favor, anytime."

Hank fixed them both with a serious expression. "Mary Sue and I expect you to show up for our wedding in June."

"We'll be here," Kalib promised him, to Meg's delight.

Then came Wash, followed by Sara Ann Chrystal and Tobin. Wash cleared his throat, kissed her on the cheek, and mumbled his congratulations to Kalib. "Hope I wasn't too rough on you, Maggie," he said.

She smiled. "You weren't, Wash. I'm looking forward to getting to know you under happier circumstances."

Sara Ann was all smiles and kisses and hugs. "I'm thrilled you'll be so close," she told Meg. "When are you moving into the Mansion?"

Meg's eyes blinked, as a vision of the elegant Governor's Mansion flashed through her mind, accompanied by their driver's remarks that Kalib wouldn't move in until he had a bride to carry over the threshold.

Shrugging, she grinned. "This is all a surprise to me," she admitted with a laugh. "I have no idea where I'll be in five minutes' time."

As if on cue, the diamond-stacker engine, followed by the other locomotive, blew its whistles and began chugging up the joined track toward Silver Creek. She raised questioning eyes to Kalib.

"They'll use the turnaround in Silver Creek," he told her casually. "When the *Texas Star* returns, we'll leave . . . if it's all right with you."

She grinned. "You've made all the plans today, and so far," suddenly, she wished they were alone so she could tell him how lovely she thought his plans were, "so far they've been wonderful."

She felt his body chuckle against her own, and when he looked at her, he waggled his eyebrows suggestively, setting her skin on fire. "Don't worry, I won't let you down. I think you'll approve of the rest of the plans, too."

For the next hour or so they followed the wishes of the Silver Creek ladies and ate barbecue and all the trimmings, while accepting more and more congratulations and good wishes, until Meg thought she would burst the seams in her corset, if they didn't have some time to themselves.

Finally, the welcoming whistle of the little diamond-stacker engine alerted them, and Kalib took her arm. "Time to go," he whispered in such a husky voice that her spine quivered.

But as they approached the rear platform of the railcar, she suddenly had a sinking feeling. Glancing around the gathering, her eyes sought Rube. He and Di hurried forward, and she saw a tear glisten in his eye.

"I hope you'll forgive me, sugar. It seemed like the only way to get you two together. I wouldn't have done it, if I didn't know deep in my bones you'll be happy."

Her answer choked in her throat. Tears brimmed in her

eyes, and she hugged him fiercely. "Thank you, Rube. I'm already happier than I ever dreamed possible."

Turning, she hugged Di, and felt Kalib tug at her arm. When she looked he was shaking Rube's hand. "Thanks Rube. And don't you worry about her. She's the most important part of my life. You can rest assured I'll see she's taken care of." He kissed Di on the cheek.

"You two remember what I told you, now," he insisted. "There's a room in the Governor's Mansion with your name on it, so don't be strangers. We expect you to visit every time you can get away."

Di reached over and blotted a tear on Meg's cheek with her handkerchief. "Be happy, dear," she whispered, just as Kalib pulled Meg onto the back of the train.

Before them stood the entire community of Silver Creek and all the directors and many stockholders of the Santa Fe Railroad. She inhaled a deep breath, feeling Kalib draw her close to his side.

And beside her stood . . . Kalib . . . her beloved husband.

The band broke into *"Texas, Our Texas,"* and people cheered, and Kalib spoke in her ear. "Throw your bouquet, Maggie."

She looked down at the yellow roses, not sure she wanted to part with them.

"There's more yellow roses inside," he told her. "There'll always be more."

And there before her stood Katie Jefferies—lovable, romantic Katie. The train moved away from the gathering slowly, and she tossed the bouquet.

"Katie caught it!" she sighed.

"And look who's standing behind her," Kalib laughed, pointing to Wash. They waved until the train pulled them out of view, then he turned her in his arms and kissed her deeply, passionately. . . .

As she had wanted him to all day . . . as she had dreamed about for weeks.

"I've been straining at the bit to do this all day, love," he whispered. "Let's go inside."

Suddenly her knees wobbled and she felt faint, and she didn't understand it. She could never recall being so happy in her entire life. Not ever. Closing the door behind them, he drew her down on the banquette and smothered her in his arms, holding her close.

She clung to him, wondering what had suddenly come over her, and he gazed lovingly into her eyes. "I know I took you by surprise, Maggie. You probably feel more like you've been kidnapped than married, but it was the only way I could figure to convince you."

"You convinced me," she whispered. "But . . ." She stopped. She had started to ask him to tell her the story everyone except she herself appeared to already know, then she saw the gleam in his eyes, and all else fled.

Raising her hand, she stroked his cheek. "I've wanted to do *this* all day, too," she told him, moving her face to receive his kisses.

His mouth caressed hers, and she opened her lips eagerly to his questing passion. Without dislodging their lips, he unpinned her hat and tossed it aside, then his fingers fumbled through her curls, removing the pins and pulling the silken strands wonderingly through his fingers.

Her hands stroked his back, his hair, his neck, running finally beneath the collar of his jacket and pushing it over his shoulders.

Gripping her head in his hand, he held her face back and studied her seriously. His hands felt warm and sensuous against her face, and her heart pounded feverishly at the sound of his husky voice.

"God, Maggie, I've wanted you so long . . . so desperately. Not just your body, but all of you. We belong together, you and I. Don't you feel it inside you, too? The wonder, the excitement, the almost unbearable joy of knowing we'll be together . . . forever."

Her skin prickled with sparks of passion, and she raised one index finger and placed it softly over his lips. "I feel it, Kalib. In every pore of my body, I feel your love." Moving her finger, she kissed his lips softly, then more desperately.

375

At last, he stood and drew her to her feet. With a wicked grin he perused her body, twirling her by the arm to inspect her dress. "You're a beautiful bride, Mrs. Chaney. Now, let's see if I can please you with the rest of my plans for your wedding day."

Scooping her in his arms, he carried her to the blue and gold bedchamber. Inside, he closed the door with his foot.

Her eyes widened. "We're not alone?"

He grinned. "You mean Chou Ling? He's in his room behind the galley. I loaned him a volumn of your favorite poetry."

She shook her head in amazement. "Is there anything about me you don't know?"

Waggling his eyebrows, he proceeded to remove her clothing with deliberate, infuriatingly slow motions. "If there is, I certainly won't let up until I discover it." Then he recited from memory. "Let's see, it's called 'Ae Fond Kiss,' I believe."

"How did you . . . ?"

"Shush." He tossed aside her green silk cutaway jacket, then her chiffon cravat, and began unbuttoning her white silk vest, all the while reciting in a husky voice:

> "But to see her was to love her,
>   Love but her, and love for ever.
>   Had we never lov'd sae kindly,
>   Had we never. . . ."

Moving quickly, she covered his mouth with her lips, stopping him, but he held her at arm's length and finished removing her vest.

"Where did you learn all that?"

He grinned, running his hands sensuously up her lacy chemise, cupping her breasts as they lay captured in her corset. "Not at Smith College."

"Bastard!" she whispered into his face.

He laughed. "I wondered if I'd escaped your wrath entirely."

Suddenly, her breath caught in her chest, and she was

overcome by the magnitude of her situation. She was married! Married! To the only man in the whole wide world she could ever love!

Clasping her arms about his neck, she drew his head to her breast and held him in a tight vise. "I'm so happy Kalib. So very, very happy. Thank you for not giving up on me."

They fell to the bed together, clutching each other fervently. They kissed intensely, deeply, and long, and her head spun with the thought that time didn't matter anymore. No more worry about tomorrow . . . tomorrow was theirs. They would be together tomorrow, just like today, and the day after, and the day after that. Together . . . forever.

He ran his palm up and down her back, feeling the heat of her flesh even through her layers of clothing. His body ached to feel hers, skin to skin, beside him, but still he lay with her in his arms, unwilling and unable to break apart even to remove their clothing. He kissed her lips, her nose, her eyelids, her forehead, tangled his fingers through her hair.

Sighing, she looked into his loving eyes, and a question popped suddenly into her mind. "When did you meet Rube?"

He studied her with a crooked grin for a moment. Then, sitting up, he pulled her to her feet and untied the ribbon on her corset cover and discarded it. "When I rode away from you New Year's Eve, I saw one of Di's boys out behind the Diamond-Stacker, so I stopped and told him to tell Rube to sober up and meet me before noon the next day at the camphouse. That it concerned you."

Her eyes widened. "Did he come?"

Kalib nodded, scrunching his lips at her clothing. He unfastened her skirt and she stepped out of it. After which, he began unbuttoning her petticoats, which she also stepped out of, one by one.

"What did you talk about?"

He looked at her quizzically, and she felt him tug at the hooks on her corset. "I told him we were in love, but you refused to marry me because of some darned fool notion you had that he couldn't get along without you." Tossing her corset aside, he sat back on the bed and studied her lacy one-piece chemise and bloomers. "What kind of get-up is this?"

"A combination," she answered, feeling a delicious flush sweep across her skin with his gaze. She swallowed and continued. "What did he say?"

Kalib looked up absently, then chuckled. "He told me he had been trying to find some way to get rid of you for years, so he'd be glad to help me out."

"He did not! You demon!" she laughed, then quivered as his fingers tantalized her aching flesh.

He unbuttoned her chemise, drew the straps over her shoulders, and let the entire garment drop to the floor, and she stood naked before him. Flames of desire shot throughout her entire being at his impassioned look.

"Kalib . . ."

"Shush," he murmured, quietening her with his lips. Quickly he disrobed himself with the help of her trembling hands.

Clasping her to him, he kissed her deeply, all the while running his hands up and down the softness of her back, molding himself to her, feeling her breast burrow hot and tender into the mat of hair covering his chest.

Her heart beat fiercely as she clung to him, reveling in the touch of his skin, the wonderful sensual smell of him. Burying her face in the crook of his neck, she kissed the tender skin there and heard him groan with desire . . . for her . . . for her, his wife.

Lowering them to the bed, he gazed into her eyes and ignited her passion to even greater heights with the golden glints she saw reflected there. His voice trembled down her spine, shattering what senses she had left.

"Maggie, Maggie, Maggie. You're mine at last." Nipping her skin with his lips, he continued as he kissed her face, her neck, her chest. "Really mine. Forevermore." He lifted one breast to his lips and devoured her sweetness with the intensity of passion long denied, and she melted dreamily in his arms.

With quivering fingers, she caressed his head, ran her hands through his hair, pressed his face closer, ever closer, to her aching breasts.

His hands caressed her skin, traveled up and down her back, over her hips, between the aching valley of her legs. His lips tormented her breasts, one after the other, then dropped, trailing kisses along her stomach and lower, until she writhed beneath his tempestuous hands and lips, feeling her entire being consumed with desire, intense, unbearable, heavenly desire for this man . . . for Kalib, her husband.

When she could bear the torture no longer, she drew his lips to hers. At her urging, he entered her body, and together they consummated the pledges they had made this day with a fervency that left them damp and limp and clinging to each other.

He gazed deep into her smoldering emerald eyes. "I'm the luckiest man alive," he whispered, wiping a strand of hair away from her love-dampened forehead. "You can't imagine how frightened I was today."

Her eyes widened. "Frightened? Whatever for?"

He tightened his arms around her tender body, held her against him urgently, and swept his hand up and down her satiny back, "That you wouldn't have me."

"I didn't notice I had a choice," she reminded him with a laugh.

He nipped her nose with his lips, then pressed them against her forehead before answering. "If you had really rebelled, I would have probably let you off . . . for today."

"Probably?"

His eyes danced again. "Probably. Where you're concerned, I couldn't promise."

"At your next inauguration. . . ."

"Maggie, I told you there doesn't have to be a next inauguration. I guarantee you an equal voice in every decision for the rest of our lives."

"Oh, yes, Kalib, we must have at least one more inauguration, so I can hold the Bible." She kissed his lips and spoke earnestly against them. "And so we can waltz in the Capitol rotunda."

He squeezed her so tightly that she thought for a minute she might expire in his arms. Then he kissed her soundly, rekindling their tender yearnings. Lifting his lips only inches from hers, he gazed into her eyes with such an intense, loving expression that she trembled in his arms. When he spoke, his rumbling voice was husky with emotion—

> "But to see her was to love her,
> Love but her, and love for ever."

Author's Note

Railroad building in Texas had waned by the time of this story. Back in 1882, a special session of the state legislature repealed the Land Grant Law of 1876, and for good reason: to the embarrassment of all concerned, the state discovered it had given the railroads 8,000,000 more acres than it actually possessed!

Records show that in 1890 only 181.15 miles of railroad were constructed in the entire state of Texas. These miles were not in one line, however, as I have placed them in this story.

Railroad reform was the hot political topic in 1890. However, I purposely set my gubernatorial election in an "off-year," so the characters in this story would not be confused with their historical counterparts.

As Quint Jarvis mentioned in *Hearts Desire*, the Lost Bowie Mine is the "granddaddy" of all the treasure stories in this region of Texas. Therefore, I have saved it for this, the last of my Silver Creek stories. When I was in junior high school, my classmates and I spent many a lunch hour at the "old mission" outside Menard searching for Bowie's lost silver mine. The fact that we never found it bears no relation to whether or not the mine exists. After a few years, we shelved our interest in buried treasure in favor of other conquests—the two-legged variety known the world over as the West Texas Cowboy! Kalib Chaney didn't find the Lost Bowie Mine in this story, because it is still out there somewhere, beckoning grown men and women today to follow in Coronado's footsteps in search of The Seven Cities of Cibolo, and always, in the words of Coronado's scout, the treasure is *"más allá"*—on beyond.

I juggled the dates of Jim Bowie's expedition to fit my story line. Historically, Bowie's ill-fated search for the Lipan silver mine took place in 1831, and the Alamo fell five years later, in 1836. The fight in which Bowie's nine men and two boys held off 150 Indians, known as the Calf Creek fight, occurred along Calf Creek in McCullouch County.

Lest the character of Ellsworth Fredericks be taken too seriously, I would like to thank publicly some of the newspeople who have been both gracious and professional in covering my career: Dorothy Kerns of *The Menard News*, Suzanne Perry of *The San Angelo Standard Times*, Micky Ennis of *The Alvin Sun*, Margaret Ann Zipp of *The Bryan/College Station Eagle*, Debbi Pomeroy of *The Houston Chronicle*, Margaret Mulreany of *The Beaumont Enterprise*, and Charles Alman, freelance journalist.

Again, I bow to Mason County for use of their blue topaz.

To read more about railroad building, lost treasures, and such, here are a few of the books I enjoyed most while researching this story. Happy reading!

The Katy Railroad and the Last Frontier, by V.V. Masterson, University of Oklahoma Press—a fast-paced, exciting account of railroad building during its peak.
Coronado's Children, by J. Frank Dobie, University of Texas Press—treasure stories of the Southwest.
Wild West Bartenders' Bible, by Bryan A. and Sharon P. Johnson, Texas Monthly Press—everything you ever wanted to know about saloons in the Old West.
Adult Children of Alcoholics, by Janet Geringer Woititz, Health Communication, Inc.—a wonderful, positive self-help book.